ONE Summer AT THE VILLA

LYNN RAYE
HARRIS

REBECCA
WINTERS

MAGGIE
COX

ONE
Summer
COLLECTION

June 2016

July 2016

July 2016

August 2016

August 2016

September 2016

ONE *Summer* AT THE VILLA

LYNN RAYE
HARRIS

REBECCA
WINTERS

MAGGIE
COX

MILLS & BOON

First Published in Great Britain 2016
By Mills & Boon, an imprint of HarperCollins*Publishers*
1 London Bridge Street, London, SE1 9GF

ONE SUMMER AT THE VILLA © 2016 Harlequin Books S.A.

The Prince's Royal Concubine © 2010 Lynn Raye Harris
Her Italian Soldier © 2011 Rebecca Winters
A Devilishly Dark Deal © 2012 Maggie Cox

ISBN: 978-0-263-92233-2

09-0816

Our policy is to use papers that are natural, renewable and recyclable products and made from wood grown in sustainable forests.
The logging and manufacturing processes conform to the legal environmental regulations of the country of origin.

Printed and bound in Spain
by CPI, Barcelona

THE PRINCE'S
ROYAL CONCUBINE

LYNN RAYE HARRIS

*To all the editors at Mills & Boon for
holding a competition to find new writers
and for choosing me as their winner.*

*I am truly honoured by your faith in me, and
thankful for the opportunities you have given me.*

*But most especially to my editor,
Sally Williamson, who pushes me to be
the best I can be and encourages me
to stretch my wings with each book.*

USA Today bestselling author **Lynn Raye Harris**
burst onto the scene when she won a writing contest
held by Mills & Boon. The prize was an editor for
a year – but only six months later, Lynn sold her first
novel. A former finalist for the Romance Writers
of America's Golden Heart Award®, Lynn lives
in Alabama with her handsome husband and two
crazy cats. Her stories have been called 'exceptional
and emotional', 'intense', and 'sizzling'. You can
visit her at www.lynnrayeharris.com

CHAPTER ONE

PRINCE CRISTIANO DI SAVARÉ slipped the last stud into his tuxedo shirt and straightened the points of his collar as he gazed at his reflection. The yacht rocked gently beneath his feet, but that was the only indication he was on board a ship and not in a luxury hotel room. He'd flown over two thousand miles to be here tonight and, though he wasn't tired, the expression on his face was grim. So grim that lines bracketed his mouth, furrowed his forehead, and made him look older than his thirty-one years.

He would have to work on that before he hunted his quarry. Though his task tonight gave him no joy, it had to be done. He forced a smile, studied it. Yes, that would work.

Women always melted when he turned on the charm.

He shrugged into his jacket and whisked a spot of lint away with a flick of his fingers. What would Julianne think if she saw him now? He'd give anything for another glimpse of her, for the little pout on her face whenever she concentrated—as she surely would while she straightened his tie and implored him not to look so serious.

Cristiano turned away from the mirror, unwilling to see the expression he now wore at the thought of his dead wife. He'd been married for so short a time—and so long ago now that he sometimes couldn't remember the exact shade of Julianne's hair or the way her laugh sounded. Was that normal?

He knew it was, and yet it both angered and saddened him. She'd paid the ultimate price for marrying him. He would never forgive himself for allowing her to die when he could have prevented it. *Should* have prevented it.

It was four and a half years since he'd let her climb onto a helicopter destined for the volatile border between Monterosso and Monteverde. In spite of the unease churning in his gut, he'd let her go without him.

Julianne had been a medical student, and she'd insisted on accompanying him on an aid mission. When he had to cancel at the last moment, he should have ordered her to stay behind with him.

But she'd convinced him that the new Crown Princess should work toward peace with Monteverde. As an American, she'd felt safe enough visiting both countries. She'd been certain she could make a difference.

And he'd let her certainty convince him.

Cristiano closed his eyes. The news that a Monteverdian bomb had ended Julianne's life, and the lives of three aid workers with her, triggered the kind of rage and despair he'd never experienced before or since.

It was his fault. She would have lived if he'd refused to let her go. Would have lived if he'd never married her. Why had he done so? He'd asked himself that question many times since.

He didn't believe in lightning bolts and love at first sight, but he'd been drawn to her. The attraction between them had been strong, and he'd been certain marrying her was the right decision.

Except that it hadn't been. Not for her.

The truth was that he'd done it for selfish reasons. He'd

needed to marry, and he'd refused to allow his father to dictate who his bride would be. Instead, he'd chosen a bold, beautiful girl he barely knew simply because the sex was great and he liked her very much. He'd swept her off her feet, promised her the world.

And she'd believed him. Far better if she hadn't.

Basta!

He dropped a mental shield into place, slicing off his thoughts. He would be unfit for mingling with Raúl Vega's guests if he did not do so. Those dark days were over. He'd found a purpose in their aftermath, and he would not rest until it was done.

Monteverde.

The princess. The reason he was here.

"It is a beautiful night, is it not?"

Princess Antonella Romanelli spun from her cabin door to find a man leaning against the railing, watching her. Faintly, the ocean lapped the yacht's sides, someone laughed on another ship anchored not too far away, and the smell of jasmine hung in the air.

But her gaze was locked on the dark form of the man. His tuxedo blended into the night, making him nothing more than a silhouette against the backdrop of Canta Paradiso's city lights. Then he stepped forward and the light from the deck illuminated his face.

She recognized him instantly, though they'd never met. That handsome countenance—the jet-dark hair, the sharp cheekbones, the sensual lips—belonged to only one man in the whole world. The absolute last man she should be talking to at this moment.

Or ever.

Antonella drew in a sharp breath, fighting for that famous

detachment for which she was renowned. Dear God, why was he here? What did he want? Did he know how desperate she was?

Of course not—don't be silly!

"Cat got your tongue, I see."

Antonella swallowed, willed her thrumming heart to beat normally. He was more beautiful in person than in the photos she'd seen. And more dangerous. Tension rolled from him, enveloping her in his dark presence. *His unexpected presence.* Warning bells clanged in her mind. "Not at all. You merely surprised me."

His gaze raked over her slowly, leaving her skin prickling in its wake. "We have not been introduced," he said smoothly, his voice as rich and alluring as dark chocolate. "I am Cristiano di Savaré."

"I know who you are," Antonella said—and then cursed herself for saying it so quickly. As if words were weapons and she could use them to push him away.

"Yes, I imagine you do."

He made it sound like an insult. Antonella drew herself up with all the dignity and hauteur a princess could manage. "And why wouldn't I recognize the name of the Crown Prince of Monterosso?"

Her country's bitterest rival. Though the history between the three sister-nations—Monteverde, Montebianco, and Monterosso—was tangled, it was only Monteverde and Monterosso that remained at war to this day. Antonella thought of the Monteverdian soldiers stationed on the volatile border tonight, of the razor wire fences, the landmines and tanks, and a pang of dark emotion ricocheted through her.

They were there for her, for everyone in Monteverde. They kept her nation safe from invasion. She could not fail them— or the rest of her people—in her mission here. *Would* not. Her nation would not disappear off the face of this earth simply because her father was a tyrannical brute who'd bankrupted his country and driven it to the very edge of oblivion.

"I would not expect it otherwise, *Principessa*," he said with cool certainty.

Arrogant man. She lifted her chin. *Never let them see your fear, Ella,* her brother always said. "What are you doing here?"

His grin was not what she expected, a flash of impossibly white teeth in the gloom. And about as friendly as a lion's feral growl. The hair on the back of her neck stood up.

"The same as you, I imagine. Raúl Vega is a very wealthy man, *si*? He could bring many jobs to a country fortunate enough to win his business."

Antonella's blood froze. *She* needed Raúl Vega, not this…this arrogant, too-handsome man who already had all the advantages of his power and position. Monterosso was wealthy beyond compare; Monteverde *needed* Vega Steel to survive. It was life or death for her people. Since her father had been deposed, her brother had been holding the country together through sheer force of will. But it wouldn't last much longer. They needed foreign investment, needed someone with the clout of Vega to come in and show other investors through example that the country was still a good bet.

The astronomical loans her father had taken out were coming due, and they had no money to pay them. Extensions were out of the question. Though Dante and the government had acted in the nation's best interest when they'd deposed her father, creditor nations had viewed the events with trepidation and suspicion. To them, requests for loan extensions would mean Monteverde was seeking ways to have the loans declared void.

A commitment from Vega Steel would change that.

If Cristiano di Savaré knew how close they were to the brink of collapse—

No. He couldn't know. No one could. Not yet, though her country couldn't hide it for much longer. Soon the world would know. And Monteverde would cease to exist. The thought dripped courage into her veins, each dose stronger than the last until she was brimming with it.

"I am surprised Monterosso cares about Vega Steel," she said coolly. "And my interest in Signor Vega has nothing to do with business."

Cristiano smirked, but it was too late to take back the words. She'd meant to deflect him, but she'd opened herself up to ridicule instead. *Careless.*

"Ah, yes, I have heard about this. About you."

Antonella pulled her silk shawl closer over the pale cream designer gown she wore. He made her feel cheap—small and dirty and insignificant—without saying one word of what he truly meant. He didn't need to; the implication was clear.

"If you are finished, Your Highness?" she said frostily. "I believe I am expected at dinner."

He moved closer, so nearly into her personal space that it must be intentional. He was tall and broad, and it took everything she had not to shrink from him. She'd spent years cowering before her father when he was in a rage; when he'd been arrested six months ago, she'd promised herself she would not cower before a man ever again.

She stood rigid, waiting. Trembling, and hating herself for the weakness.

"Allow me to escort you, *Principessa*, for I am headed in the same direction."

He was so close, so real. So intimidating. "I can find my own way."

"Of course." His smile didn't reach his eyes.

Beneath his studied demeanor, she sensed hostility. Darkness. Emptiness.

He continued, "But if you refuse, I might think you afraid of me."

Antonella swallowed, forced her throat to work. *Too close to the mark.* "Why on earth would I be afraid of you?"

"Precisely." He held out his arm, daring her to accept.

She hesitated. But there was no way out and she would not run like a frightened child. It was a betrayal of Monteverde to be seen with him—and yet this was the Caribbean; Monteverde was thousands of miles away. No one would ever know.

"Very well." She laid her hand on his arm—and nearly jerked away at the sizzle skimming through her. Touching Cristiano was like touching lightning. She thought he flinched, but she couldn't be sure.

Was that brimstone she smelled? It wouldn't surprise her—he was the devil incarnate so far as she was concerned.

The enemy.

But, no, it was simply her imagination. He smelled like a sea-swept night, fresh and clean with a hint of spice. When his hand settled over hers, she had to force down a sense of panic. She felt trapped, and yet his grip was light. Impersonal perhaps. It was the touch of a man schooled in protocol, a man escorting a woman to an event.

It was nothing.

And yet—

Yet her heart tripped as if it were on a downhill plunge. There was something about him, something dark and dangerous and altogether different from the type of men she usually met.

"You have been in the Caribbean long?" he asked as they strolled along the outer deck.

"A few days," she replied absently, wondering how to make him pick up the pace. At this rate, it would take several minutes to reach the grand ballroom. Several minutes in which she would be alone in his company. "But I haven't seen much of the island yet."

"No, I don't imagine you would."

Antonella ground to a halt at his tone. *Smug, superior.* "What is that supposed to mean?"

He turned toward her, his eyes slipping down her body, back up again. Evaluating her. Judging her. Oddly enough, she found herself wanting to know what color they were. Blue? Grey like her own? She couldn't tell in the yellowish light from the deck lamps. But they left her shivering and achy all at once.

"It means, *Principessa*, that when you spend much of your time on your back, you can hardly expect to do much sightseeing."

She couldn't stifle a gasp. "How dare you pretend to know me—"

"Who does *not* know you, Antonella Romanelli? In the past six months, you have certainly made yourself known. You parade around Europe dressed in the latest fashions, attending all the *best* parties, and sleeping with whoever catches your fancy at the moment. Like Vega."

If he'd notched an arrow and aimed it straight at her heart, it could have hurt no worse.

What could she possibly say to defend herself? Why did she even want to?

Antonella spun away, but Cristiano caught her wrist and prevented her from escaping. His grip was harder than any she'd imagined. Her heart raced so hard she was afraid she'd grow light-headed. Her father was a strong man. A man with a hair-trigger temper and a quick fist when angered. She'd borne the brunt of that fist more times than she cared to remember.

"Let me go," she bit out, her skin prickling with icy fear.

"Your brother should control you better," he said—but his grip loosened and she jerked free, rubbing her wrist though he had not hurt her.

Anger slid into place, crowded out the fear. "Who do you think you are? Just because you're the heir to the Monterossan throne does not make you special to *me*. And my life is none of your business." Her laugh was bitter. "I know what you think of me, of my people. But know this—you have not beaten us in over one thousand years and you will not do so now."

"Bravo," he said, eyes glittering dangerously. "Very passionate. One wonders how passionate you might be in other circumstances."

"You will have to continue to wonder, *Your Highness*. Because I would throw myself over the side of this yacht before ever entertaining a man such as you in my bed."

Not that she'd ever entertained *any* man in her bed—but he didn't know that. Regardless that she'd never found a man she trusted enough to give herself to, that she was still a virgin, all it took were a few parties, a few rumors, and a few photos to turn the truth into a lie. Most men believed her sophisticated and worldly, and the one she'd actually been brave enough to date once she'd been free of her father's iron grasp had told the lie he'd slept with her after she'd rebuffed him. Others had taken up the rallying cry until it was impossible to separate truth from rumor.

God, men made her sick. And this one was no different.

They could not see beneath the surface, which was why she primped and pampered and wore the careful exterior of a worldly princess. Her beauty was her only asset since she'd never been allowed to pursue any kind of profession.

It was also her shield. When she focused the attention on her physical appearance, she didn't need to share her secrets or fears with anyone. She could hide beneath her exterior, secure in the knowledge that no one could hurt her that way.

The sound of Cristiano's mocking laughter startled her back to the moment. She realized too late that she'd just done the unthinkable. She'd challenged a man with a legendary reputation for bedding women. A man about whom women spoke in tones of rapture and awe. She might not have anything to do with the Monterossans, but she'd heard the gossip about their Crown Prince.

He'd been married once, but his wife was dead. Since then, no woman had held his attention for longer than a few weeks, a couple of months at most. He was a serial dater and a heartbreaker. A smooth operator, as her friend Lily, the Crown Princess of Montebianco, would have said.

"Perhaps nothing so desperate as that," he said, closing the distance between them. Antonella took a step backward, coming into contact with the solid wall of the yacht. Cristiano put a hand on either side of her head, trapping her. He leaned closer without touching her. "Should we test this vow of yours with a kiss?"

"You can't be serious," she gasped.

He loomed over her. Dark. Intense. "Why not?"

"You're Monterossan!"

He laughed again, but there was no humor in it. It confused her—or maybe it was simply his overwhelming nearness bewildering her senses.

His head dipped toward her. "Indeed. But you are a woman, and I'm a man. The night is warm, lush, perfect for passion…"

For a moment, she was paralyzed. Any second his mouth would claim hers, any second she would feel the hot press of his lips, any second her soul would be in danger—because something about him sent her pulse skyrocketing. Her nipples tightened, her skin itched, and the deep, secret recesses of her body felt as if they were softening, melting—

At the last possible moment, when his lips were a hair's breadth away, when his hot breath mingled with hers, she found her strength and ducked beneath an imprisoning arm. He caught himself, shoving away from the side of the yacht.

Swore.

"Very good, Antonella. But then you are quite practiced at this game, aren't you?"

Antonella held herself rigid. Why did her name sound so exotic when he said it? "You're despicable. You seek to take what is not yours, and you resort to force to get it. Exactly what I would expect from a Monterossan."

If she thought to anger him, she was disappointed. He merely smiled that wolfish smile of his. The ice in it made her shudder.

"Excuses, excuses, *Principessa*. That is what your country is good at, *si*? Because you are not as successful or as wealthy as us, you blame us for your ills. And you take innocent lives to justify your hostility."

"I'm not listening to this," she said, turning away from him. She had no time to engage in an argument with him. Nor would it do any good. She would simply be upset, and she couldn't afford the distraction right now.

"Yes, run away to your steel magnate. But let us see what he values most—his mistress or his bank account."

Antonella whirled. He'd dropped all pretense of friendliness; his voice dripped menace. "What do you mean by that?"

Cristiano stalked closer and once again she found herself trapped. Not physically this time, but it felt the same as if he'd grabbed her and refused to let her move. Her feet may as well have been glued to the teak decking.

"It means, *bellissima Principessa,* that I too have a proposition for Vega." His gaze slid over her, and again she felt as if she'd stood too close to a lightning strike. "I am betting that my money trumps your…shall we say…*obvious* charms."

"How dare you—"

"I believe you have said this already, yes? It grows tiring."

Antonella trembled with fury. The man was impossible, aggravating—and having the most incredible effect on her senses. Surely it was anger that made her flush hot and cold, that made her skin tingle. He was threatening to ruin all her hard work, to turn Vega away before she'd managed to hook him. She *had* to get those steel mills for Monteverde. *Had to.*

And in order to do it, she needed to focus. Needed to will her heightened senses to calm. Needed to cloak herself in her ice princess mantle. No matter how this man made her feel, no matter how hot and achy and angry she was, she *had* to play this right.

Antonella dug down deep, found what she was searching for. By degrees, she felt her body loosening from its rigid stance. Felt confidence and calm wash over her. She would not let him intimidate her.

"Perhaps we have started on the wrong foot," she purred. She needed to misdirect him, befuddle him. To do that, she would play the part he'd given her, make him believe there was indeed a chance of sex. It would buy her a little bit of time, at least. She could hold out the promise of a night together, keep him guessing while she worked hard to reel in Vega Steel before he could snatch victory from her.

In spite of her inexperience, it wasn't difficult to act the part. At times like this, she disappeared deep within herself, separated her inner being from the shell and watched everything from outside the scene. It was the only way she could cope—by pretending to be someone else. It was a skill she'd honed over years of living with an abusive father.

Cristiano stood his ground as she reached for him, as her fingertips stroked along his freshly shaven jaw, over the fullness of his hard mouth, his chin.

His eyes were impossible to read. And then something kindled in their depths, something that both frightened her and compelled her. Perhaps she was going too far, making a mistake…

"You play with fire, *Principessa,*" he growled.

She worked hard to ignore the warning bells in her head as she slipped her hand around to the back of his neck, into the soft hair at his nape, bringing herself closer as she did so. Could she really do this?

She could, and she would. Let him see what a Monteverdian was made of. He would not intimidate her. He would not win.

Slowly, she pulled his head down. So slowly. He didn't try to move away, simply followed her bidding. She didn't kid herself she was in control. He was interested, like a cat was interested in a mouse.

But, for now, he let her guide him. And that was all she needed.

When he was only inches away, she stroked her fingers down his jaw again. Over that gorgeous mouth because she couldn't help herself. She couldn't play it too easy, of course, because he would see right through her. But if she got him worked up a bit, made him think about how to storm her defenses, she might buy enough time to get Raúl to commit to Monteverde.

"Know this," she said softly, her voice as sultry as she could make it. "Know that you have been this close to paradise…" She lifted herself onto her tiptoes, leaned in so close that her lips could have ghosted over his with little effort. "…this close, Cristiano," she said, using his name for the first time. "And no further."

Then she took a step back, intending to leave him standing there, puzzling over what had just happened.

A split second later, Cristiano caught her waist in two large hands, yanked her against the full length of his hard body. The wild thought that she should have run while she'd had the chance flashed into her mind. Instead, she'd pushed the thorn deeper into the lion's paw when she should have given him a wide berth.

Cristiano's mouth crushed down on hers with devastating precision. The kiss was masterful, dominating, unlike any she'd ever experienced before. Antonella's head tilted back as he bracketed her face between two broad hands. He slanted his mouth over hers, forced a response. When she opened her lips—to protest? To bite him? To do what?—his tongue slipped inside and tangled with her own.

Heat flooded her like melting wax, dripped into her limbs, made her languid and pliable when she should be anything but. He'd caught her by surprise and she couldn't seem to separate herself from the act. It wasn't the first time she'd been kissed—but it was the first time she'd felt on the verge of losing herself in a kiss.

She wanted to dissolve into him, wanted to see where this hot achy feeling would take her if she let it. It was marvelous, extraordinary—

Reality trickled through her as his hands slipped down her back, over her hips, pulled her against his body. His hard, tense body.

Oh, my, was that—?

No. She couldn't do this. He was the *enemy*, for God's sake! She fought against nature, against him, against *herself* to claw her way back to the surface.

And though it was a cheap thing to do, she bit down on his questing tongue just enough to make him withdraw. It was that or allow him to so completely dominate her senses that she lost the power of her convictions.

He swore. And then he laughed. Actually *laughed*. "You need a spanking, *cara*. I'll be sure to remedy that when we are naked together."

Antonella managed to jerk free from his grip. She was off-balance, her heart pounding and her blood simmering, and she wanted nothing more than to escape. But she had to stand firm.

She jerked her shawl back into place. "If this is how you usually set about your seductions, it's a wonder you have any success at all."

His eyes burned into her. "When I want something, I get it. Always."

Against her will, a hot little flame smoldered deep inside. She had to get away, far away. "I can't say it's been a pleasure meeting you, but if you will excuse me, my *lover* is waiting. Ciao."

"For now, *Principessa*," he said. "But I have a feeling you will take a new lover quite soon."

She'd made a mistake thinking she could manage him. A huge mistake. And yet she desperately wanted to wipe the smirk from his face. She gave him her best ice princess glare. "Yes, well, that man will *not* be you."

"Never make promises you cannot keep. The first lesson of statecraft."

"This isn't a negotiation between nations."

"Isn't it?"

When she couldn't think of a rejoinder, she pivoted and hurried to the dining room. Raúl stood on the opposite side of the room, speaking with a short, bald man. He looked up

when he saw her, smiled. She smiled back. He was a handsome man, tall and rather good-looking in his custom tuxedo.

But he did not make her blood hum. Not the way Cristiano
seemed to do. Angrily, she shoved away thoughts of the prince
and crossed to Raúl's side, letting him kiss her on both cheeks
in greeting.

"There you are, Antonella. I was about to send a search
party."

Antonella laughed. Was she the only one who thought the
sound brittle, false? Other guests clustered together, talking
and sipping cocktails. A few watched her from beneath
lowered lids. One man stared openly.

"I'm afraid I must always be fashionably late, darling," she
said.

Raúl swiped a champagne glass from a passing tray and
handed it to her. She murmured her thanks before lifting it to
her lips. Cristiano di Savaré walked in at the moment she sipped.

Her pulse jumped and she swallowed too much of the
bubbly liquid, coughing as it seared a path down her throat.

Raúl failed to notice as he murmured, "Excuse me a
moment, my dear," and strode over to Cristiano.

Oh, God. She had to keep them apart. She had to convince
Raúl to invest in Monteverde *tonight*. There was no time to lose.
She wasn't about to let that arrogant, rude bastard derail her
plans.

Just as she got the coughing under control and started
toward the two men, someone bumped her elbow.

Antonella held her glass out in time to prevent a spill. An
elderly woman in a garish tropical-print muumuu gasped,
her hand over her heart as if she were having an attack.
"Please excuse me, Your Highness! Oh, how clumsy of me!"

"No, no, it is fine," Antonella said, her voice a little rough
from the coughing. "I didn't spill a drop."

But the woman was unconvinced and insisted on a thorough inspection. Then it took several more minutes for Antonella to disentangle from the ensuing conversation. Once the poor lady seemed soothed, Antonella moved away with a murmured apology and went looking for Raúl.

It didn't take her long to realize the frightening truth, however.

Raúl had left the room. And so had the Crown Prince of Monterosso.

CHAPTER TWO

SHE stood for everything he despised.

Cristiano sat at the polished mahogany table, directly across from Antonella Romanelli, and watched as she directed all her attention on Raúl Vega. Vega basked in her lovely glow like a man showing off a prized possession.

And why not?

She wore an ivory silk gown that clung to her body like a sleeve and displayed her breasts to perfection. With her sooty fall of hair, generous cleavage, and sharp sense of self-awareness, Princess Antonella was the kind of woman who lit up a room simply by entering it. He'd seen photos of her, but nothing had actually prepared him for the impact of her physical beauty. She was, in a word, stunning.

She had a voice that reminded him of a hidden spring, sweet and pure until she poured on the honey, and a sensual way of moving that made a man's mind turn to more elemental matters. When she'd turned to him outside her cabin door, he'd felt as if a weight had settled on his chest and wouldn't lift. He'd come prepared for battle, certain he was more than ready for it, and been felled by a lightning strike to his gut.

Dio.

He had to remember that without the Romanellis, peace

would have come to Monterosso and Monteverde many years ago. Countless people would have lived instead of dying senseless, bloody deaths.

Paolo Romanelli had been an egomaniacal despot. His son, Dante, was certainly no better. He'd deposed his own father, after all. What kind of son did that? What kind of daughter flitted around the world, taking and discarding lovers, seemingly indifferent to her family's excesses?

He'd counted on that indifference to help him gain what he wanted. Antonella was a woman of expensive tastes and a dwindling bank account. He had the means to keep her in designer gowns and expensive spa treatments, yet he'd nearly blown the whole game with his visceral reaction to her on deck. He needed her pliable, not bristling with indignation.

Cristiano's fingers tightened on the stem of the wine glass he held. He had a chance to end it. A chance to crush Monteverde into submission once and for all. Once he gained control of their government and deposed the Romanellis, children from both nations would grow up happy and free instead of living in fear of bombs and bullets.

There was currently a ceasefire, but it was tentative. One random bomb from an extremist group, and even that fragile peace would be in jeopardy.

He intended to make it permanent, no matter the personal cost. No matter who he had to destroy.

Antonella laughed, the sound light and bubbly. So what if she was beautiful, so what if she seemed to possess a hint of vulnerability that intrigued him? Because surely it was an act. A very polished, very accomplished act. He'd known women like her before. Spoiled and shallow, nothing more than beautiful exteriors with empty souls.

Raúl bent toward her. At the last second, she expertly turned her head and his kiss landed on her cheek. Interesting.

Cristiano took a sip of wine. She thought she had Raúl wrapped up and tied with a pretty bow, but she was mistaken. Cristiano had gone to a lot of trouble to sweeten his deal. Though Raúl had yet to commit, he would not refuse Monterosso's offer. He was far too good a businessman to allow a woman, no matter how enticing, to divert him from his company's best interests.

For the first time since they'd sat at the table, Antonella's gaze landed on him. He felt the jolt to his toes, and it irritated him. He refused to look away first. A pale flush crept over her cheeks as their gazes held.

He wouldn't have thought she had it in her to be embarrassed, but perhaps sitting in the company of her current lover while contemplating another man was a bit much even for one so jaded as she.

Raúl's hand came down on Antonella's and she jumped, her head whipping around to look at him. Her flush deepened and Cristiano felt a stab of triumph. She wanted him, no matter what she'd said on the deck. It was a start in the right direction.

She looked guilty as hell as Raúl gazed at her with concern. "Are you feeling well, my dear?" Raúl said. "You look distressed."

"What? Oh—no, I'm fine. It's just a little hot. Don't you find the tropics rather hot?" she asked the gathered diners.

Several people chimed in with opinions and a discussion ensued about the balmy temperatures, the fact it was hurricane season, and whether or not—God help him—a Piña Colada was preferable to a Bahama Mama. Empty chatter that scraped across his raw nerves and made him resent her even more.

When dinner was finally over, the guests adjourned to the deck to watch the fireworks over Canta Paradiso. Antonella, he noticed, clung to Raúl as if she were afraid to let him out of her sight again.

Too late, mia bella.

"Ah, Cristiano," Raúl said as he guided Antonella over to the railing where Cristiano stood, "are you enjoying yourself in this lovely paradise?"

"*Si.* The scenery is quite…extraordinary."

Antonella dropped her gaze as his own slipped over her. Was that another blush?

Raúl failed to notice the exchange. "I still can't believe it's been five years since last we met."

Antonella blinked up at her lover. "You know the Prince?"

"We attended Harvard together," Raúl replied, breaking into a broad smile as he clapped Cristiano on the back.

"Actually, it's only been *four* years since we last met, Raúl."

"Ah, yes," Raúl said, clearing his throat. They both knew that Cristiano hadn't exactly been the best of company in the several months after Julianne's death. He'd been bitter, angry. And he'd pushed his friends and family away with equal measures of wounded contempt.

"We must not allow so much time to pass again, yes?" Cristiano said.

Raúl gave him a solemn smile. "As you say, *mi amigo.*"

Antonella's lush lower lip was fixed between her teeth. A frown drew her sculpted brows together, furrowed her forehead.

An arrow of heat shot to Cristiano's groin. All his senses had gone on high alert the moment he caught a whiff of her luscious scent. Lavender and vanilla? A hint of lemon? He'd wanted to drown in it when he'd kissed her, wanted to breathe her in for as long as he could.

The thought both angered and intrigued him. How could

he react so strongly to this woman? He had not come here with any real intention of seducing her. He'd thought his business could be concluded with a great deal of money, perhaps some flattery. An empty promise or two.

Yet his body was beginning to insist on the idea of a seduction.

It was time to close this deal and move on to the real business at hand before he became any more distracted. "Raúl, if you can spare some time now, I'd like to conclude our discussion. I'm afraid I must return to Monterosso in the morning."

Raúl nodded. "Yes, of course. If you will excuse us, my dear?" he said to Antonella.

"I must speak with you as well," she said, her voice rising. "And I'd rather do it now."

She looked fierce, like an Amazon warrior. Determined.

Raúl seemed puzzled. And perhaps a bit annoyed. Cristiano laughed inwardly. She was making it too easy for him. No man liked petulant demands from his lover, and especially not in front of witnesses. A shrewd woman would have stated her case when they were in bed together later. Her problem, not his.

"Go ahead, Raúl," Cristiano said. "I'll be here when you've finished."

He could afford to be generous. She'd just lost the game.

Antonella wanted to scream. It'd been more than an hour since Raúl and Cristiano di Savaré had disappeared for their talk. What was happening? What if Raúl decided to build his mills in Monterosso?

She'd done her best to convince him, but she didn't have a good feeling about it. What could Monteverde do for Vega Steel? They had vast deposits of raw ore, a necessary ingredient in steel, but they had little else to offer.

Except for a royal title. Yes, she'd put that on the table too when she'd sensed Raúl's reluctance to commit to her country. Why not? She'd been intended since birth to marry for Monteverde's best interests. Her father was no longer King, and she'd had two royal alliances fall through before the weddings could happen, but that didn't mean she didn't owe it to her people to do her part.

Desperate times called for desperate measures. If her choice was marriage to a man she didn't love or the annexation of her country, she'd take marriage.

No matter how angry it made her. No matter how helpless she felt, how useless. *Madonna mia*, couldn't her father have at least let her attend university instead of finishing school? She could pour tea and work a room with the best hostesses out there. And yet what good were those skills?

Raúl had taken the offer in his stride, but was it enough to convince him? In spite of his humble upbringing and his rise from poverty to great wealth, she had a feeling she'd failed miserably. If any man should have been tempted by a royal title, it should have been Raúl Vega.

If she failed, it would be yet another humiliation to add to her long list. Her first fiancé had driven a car off a cliff and her second had married another woman before the handshake had grown cold on the deal her father had made to wed her to him.

She was doomed in love, it would seem. Not that she'd ever been in love, but she'd like a chance to experience it. Like Lily, the woman her second *almost*-fiancé had married instead of her. What was it like to have a man look at you the way Nico Cavelli looked at Lily? To have a man sacrifice everything to be with you?

She would never know. It wasn't her lot in life to find love. Dante had told her she didn't need to marry for

Monteverde now that their father was no longer King, but she'd insisted it was her duty. If it benefited her country, she would do it. No matter how desperate and sad it made her. No matter how much the idea of tying herself to a man terrified her.

Not all men were like her father. Not all men would grow violent when they were angry.

Antonella shook her head to clear it. She didn't know for certain that she had failed this time. There was still a chance she'd won, that her royal title and her ore would be more enticing than anything Cristiano di Savaré had to offer.

She threw the tail of her shawl over her shoulder and continued her pacing on deck. Most of Raúl's guests had returned to shore or to their own yachts, with the exception of those who had cabins aboard. In the harbor, yachts, a cruise ship, and fishing boats lay at anchor for the night, though the sounds of laughter and music drifted across the bay.

She chewed on the edge of a fingernail, then jerked her hand away with a curse when she realized what she was doing. She hadn't chewed her nails since she was twelve and her father made her drink half a bottle of hot sauce to end the habit. It had certainly worked—she'd spent two days so sick she'd thought she would die; afterwards, she could hardly look at her fingernails without retching.

But Cristiano unsettled her in ways she couldn't quite fathom. He was Monterossan, which was a big strike against him. He was the future King of that nation, an even bigger strike. He was tall, incredibly magnetic, and arrogant beyond all imagination.

And yet, a little thrill of excitement insisted on rearing its ugly head whenever she thought about him. *Stop.* She didn't like him, and she damn sure didn't trust him.

A shiver slid over her. What if she'd failed?

"Perhaps you should drink fewer espressos so late at night, *cara*."

Antonella whirled to find Cristiano emerging onto the deck. Her heart thumped, though not from fright. Why did he disconcert her so? "What are you talking about?"

He tipped his chin to her. "Pacing. Less caffeine would help."

Antonella closed her eyes and counted to five. He knew he irritated her. Worse, he seemed to take great pleasure in it. She must not allow him to do so any longer. She could control her reactions. *Would* control them.

"I had one espresso, *grazie*. Your concern is touching."

He came over and leaned against the rail, watching her. His eyes dipped to her chest, back up. Typical. Half the time, men talked exclusively to her breasts. She'd grown quite accustomed to it.

"You are dying to know what we talked about, aren't you?"

Antonella shrugged. "You are mistaken if you think I care. I'm not here for business."

He laughed. "So you have said. But what do they call it now, if not the oldest business in the world?"

She would not react. Would *not.* Had Raúl told him what they'd discussed, that she'd offered herself in exchange for the mills? Or was he simply baiting her?

"Is that what it's called when *you* sleep around, Cristiano?" she said very coolly, her heart throbbing with hurt and anger and the urge to deny she'd ever slept with any man. He'd never believe her, of course. Nor did he deserve an explanation.

Why did men have a double standard when it came to sex? He could bed countless women and it only added to his allure.

"Sensitive, *cara*?"

"Not at all. I simply don't like you. Or your hypocrisy."

"I'm hurt." His teeth flashed in a grin.

She wished he'd jump off the side of the yacht and leave her alone. "Where is Raúl?" she demanded.

"I'm not your social secretary, *Principessa*. If you want him, go find him." The words were said mildly, almost mockingly. And with a hint of steel beneath the velvet. "And what makes you think I'm a hypocrite? I quite like that you've had lovers. It means you know your way around a man's body. It means we will not need to waste time once we are naked."

Perhaps she'd had too much caffeine after all. Her pulse raced like a bullet fired from a gun. "I'm not sleeping with you, Cristiano."

"Don't be too sure," he said, his voice a sensual growl that scraped over her nerve endings and left her shivering.

"I know my own mind, and I know what I *don't* want. I don't want you."

Cristiano reached for her hand, slipped his fingers between hers and brought them to his mouth. She tried to pull away, but he held her firm. "And do you know your *body*, Antonella? Often, our mind and our body are at war. Did you not know that?"

Before she could formulate an answer from her scattered thoughts, he touched the tip of his tongue to the center of her palm.

Antonella sucked in a breath as rivers of sensation spilled down her spine, through her limbs, into her feminine core. Why? *Why?* Men had been trying to get her into bed for as long as she could remember and she'd yet to feel anything remotely as exciting as what she felt when Cristiano touched her.

Too bad he was the wrong man. She needed to pull her hand away forcefully, needed to put distance between them and never allow herself to be alone with him again.

But she couldn't. She was trapped, as trapped as if he'd bound her to him with iron shackles.

"Stop," she forced out, her voice little more than a tortured whisper.

"Are you quite certain?" he murmured. "Your body says otherwise."

"You don't know that."

"*Si,* I do. You are flushed…"

"It's hot."

Cristiano laughed low in his throat, kissed her fingers and settled her hand on his shoulder before he tugged her closer. His broad fingers splayed over her hip. "And it's about to get hotter. Why deny this attraction, hmm? We will be good together."

"I—"

A shadow passed over them and then a voice said, "I beg your pardon."

Antonella jerked out of Cristiano's grip just in time to see Raúl turn around and slip back inside. Oh, God! Furious tears pressed against the back of her eyes but she refused to let them fall. She would have to go after him, would have to try and repair the damage. She'd just offered to marry him, for God's sake. What would he think of her now?

She *could* repair the damage. Surely she could. *She had to.* For Monteverde's future.

But not before she turned and gave the arrogant man who'd caused her so much trouble in such a short time a piece of her mind.

"You did that on purpose!" She should have listened to the voice telling her to get away from him. Because she hadn't, because she'd been riveted by his handsome face and sizzling touch, she'd risked the future of her entire nation. And for what? A kiss? A kiss from a man she despised?

He wasn't insane; *she was.*

"What makes you think so, *Principessa?*" he asked coolly, his expression both smug and devilish at once.

Antonella's hands clenched into impotent fists as her heart-beat thundered in her ears. She was a fool, a hopeless fool, still looking for some spark of feeling with a man. And he was the enemy, plain and simple. He hadn't forgotten it for one moment, even if she had.

"Because you're selfish, that's why. You don't care who you hurt or what you have to destroy to get your way."

One corner of his mouth curled, but it could hardly be called a smile. "It seems as if we are kindred spirits, then."

"No. I *care* about people's feelings. And now I'm going to apologize to Raúl."

"There is no need."

"Of course there is."

"Afraid not, Antonella. You were part of the deal."

"Deal?" She thought her heart would stop as she waited for his answer. How could they make deals that included her? It was impossible. She'd offered herself in marriage, but it had been her choice. Neither of these men owned her, neither could make decisions *for* her.

"Vega Steel will be building in Monterosso. And Monteverde will supply the ore."

"Never," she bit out. It was unthinkable! To sell their ore to Monterosso? So the King could build more tanks and guns in his factories? So the di Savarés could slowly strangle the life from her country? It was the money Monteverde desperately needed, yes, but at what cost?

"You may wish to rethink your position." He sounded mildly friendly, though she knew he was anything but.

Antonella thrust her chin out in answer. "I can't see why we need to."

"One word," he said, his eyes now empty, flat. So cold she hugged herself to ward off a chill. "One very important word: existence."

CHAPTER THREE

"THERE is a storm, Your Highness."

Antonella blinked at the steward as he placed a breakfast tray on a table in her room. She pulled the covers up to her shoulders as she propped herself on an elbow, still groggy after too much worry and too little sleep. "A storm?"

He carefully repositioned the flowers in the small vase on the tray. "Yes, a hurricane. It has swung off track and is coming straight for Canta Paradiso. We are putting to sea very shortly. You may stay aboard if you wish, or you may transfer to the island for a flight out."

"Where is Signor Vega?"

The steward stood at military-like attention. "He was called back to São Paulo on business. He left before day-break."

Her heart sank. She'd known it was futile, and yet she'd hoped to speak with Raúl once more, hoped to convince him to give Monteverde a chance. Too late now.

No. She would not allow Cristiano di Savaré to defeat her so easily. There was still a very little time left before the loans came due, and she'd spent the night thinking about what Monteverde's next move would be if Raúl would not change his mind. She'd come up with only one solution.

What if Dante went to Montebianco and asked for a loan to get them through this crisis? Their father had nearly started another war when he'd arrested the Crown Princess of that nation, but that was months ago. Would Montebianco help them now? Could she convince her brother to try? She knew he wouldn't want to do it, but it was their last chance.

And if Dante wouldn't approach the King, Antonella would go to Lily and beg her to ask her husband, the Crown Prince, for help. Either way, there was still a chance for them—if she acted quickly.

"Thank you," she said to the steward. "I will go to the airport."

He gave her a formal bow before slipping out of her cabin and closing the door. Antonella bolted from the bed and grabbed her mobile phone. She had to reach Dante. She'd tried last night, but the call wouldn't go through. Perhaps the wind had knocked out a tower.

Or, more likely, something was wrong with Monteverde's communications. They often had trouble with the utility companies as the infrastructure crumbled and there was no money left to repair the aging equipment.

An automated voice informed her that her call could not be completed as dialed and suggested she check the number. She snapped her phone shut and hurried to get dressed. The sooner she was on a plane home, the better.

Antonella emerged onto the top deck of the yacht, in search of someone who could arrange for a launch. She nearly stumbled when she caught sight of the man conversing with the yacht's captain.

Cristiano di Savaré in a tuxedo had been magnificent. But Cristiano in Bermuda shorts, a crisp polo shirt, flip-flops, and Ray-Bans was downright sinful. He looked nothing like a prince and everything like some erotic fantasy of a muscled cabana boy who lived to serve the woman lucky enough to hire him.

He turned at her approach, no doubt because the captain ceased paying attention to him and watched her progress. She could see the captain's eyes moving over her appreciatively, but it was Cristiano's gaze she felt most keenly. Though he wore mirrored sunglasses, she was aware of the burning scrutiny behind them.

She'd dressed in a cotton wrap dress and sported a pair of sandals with a sensible heel. Her hair was pulled into a ponytail, and she'd gone minimal with her make-up. She wasn't trying to attract attention, and yet it never seemed to matter. Attention was what she got.

"You have heard about the storm?" Cristiano said, skipping the preliminaries.

Antonella pushed away a tendril of hair that had escaped her ponytail and blew across her lips. "Yes. When is the launch?" she asked, turning to the captain.

"There is a slight delay," Cristiano said before the captain could reply. "Many in the harbor are requesting transportation."

"I see."

"Have you made flight arrangements yet?"

"No. I had hoped to go straight to the airport and take care of it."

"*Bene.* You may fly with me."

Antonella's pulse beat like the wings of a thousand hummingbirds. The man was unbelievable. "Thank you, but no. I will get a flight when I reach the airport."

Cristiano shoved his shades onto his head. The sunlight had disappeared as clouds rolled into the harbor. His eyes, she realized, weren't blue or gray. They were deep, dark brown.

No, green.

Hazel, that was what it was called. Brown ringed the pupil, but most of the iris was green.

Striking.

How had she missed this at dinner last night? She'd sat across from him, but she'd barely looked directly at him with Raúl sitting beside her. The one time she had, she'd been far more mesmerized by the look on his face than the color of his eyes.

"Antonella," he said sharply.

She jerked. "What?"

"Did you hear me?"

"You were talking about your jet."

"Yes. It's ready, and I have room for you. All commercial flights off the island are booked."

"But you just asked me if I'd made arrangements!"

"I meant last night, before the hurricane changed direction."

She shook her head emphatically. "I'll take my chances at the airport."

Was she crazy? She might despise him, but was it worth putting herself in danger to have the satisfaction of refusing him? Wasn't the most important thing to get back to Monteverde and speak to her brother? If only Dante had been the one to come to Canta Paradiso! He'd have gotten Vega Steel and this would all be moot.

Except he had to stay to hold the country together. And his wife was about to give birth. Antonella had been the only choice, and she'd failed. She wanted to climb back into bed and pull the covers over her head until it all went away.

But she couldn't. Cowardice was not an option.

"Don't be childish," Cristiano snapped.

She forced herself to take a long, slow breath before

speaking. "It's not childish to avoid the company of people you despise."

"No, but it is childish to put yourself in danger because of it."

It was disconcerting to hear her thoughts echoed in his words.

Antonella stared at the mountains rising around the harbor. The airport was on the other side of those mountains. It could take hours to reach at this rate. Dark clouds billowed over the green peaks like a thick blanket unrolling. The wind had already picked up speed in the few hours between the time she'd gone to bed and now.

How she got home didn't matter, so long as she did. "I will fly with you if there is no other option. Though when we reach the airport, I will check to see if I can book a flight first."

"As you wish, *Principessa.*"

"But I cannot fly into Monterosso." How would that look? And how would she get home to Monteverde? There were no direct flights, and the border was cut off. A Monteverdian princess could not be ferried across the border by Monterossan soldiers. It was unthinkable.

His expression hardened. "Of course not. We will land in Paris first. You can arrange transport from there."

A dark thought occurred to her. "How do I know you will keep your word? That you won't take me to Monterosso and demand a ransom for my return?"

His voice stroked over her like silk. "If I were to kidnap you, *mia bella,* I could think of far more interesting things to do than demand a ransom."

By the time they were ferried to shore and found a taxi, three hours had passed. Everyone was rushing around the town, trying to batten down the hatches or get off the island. Canta

Paradiso was a private resort island, but there was a town and many residents who lived there full-time. In spite of that, the traffic to the small airport was unbelievable.

Cristiano tucked his cell phone away with a growl. Since the rain had begun, the cell towers had ceased carrying calls for very long. Now, they were dropping altogether. Antonella looked at her signal indicator. No bars.

Cristiano raked a dark-fingered hand through his inky hair. The taxi was small, and his leg lay intimately against hers where they were crowded together in the back seat. At first, she'd tried to move away, but huddling against the door was uncomfortable. She'd struggled for the last hour to pretend that his skin didn't burn into her where they touched.

"Will we make it?" she asked.

He was so close. Close enough that if she simply leaned over a few centimeters, their lips could touch.

And why *would she want to do that?*

"We should. It's just rain thus far. We can still fly out."

"Are you certain?" She watched the rain falling harder outside the steamy window beside him, bit her lip.

His gaze dropped to her mouth. "I am a pilot, *cara*. Rain provides good lift. The wind isn't bad yet, and it also provides lift. There are many hours left before the storm is too dangerous to fly."

"That's good, then."

He leaned back, stretched an arm behind her on the seat. She couldn't escape the contact unless she sat forward. To do so would give him power, so she endured the press of his arm against her shoulders and neck.

The trilling of his phone several minutes later startled her from her reverie. The taxi was warm, and she was so tired that she'd nearly fallen asleep on him. Mortified, she pushed herself as far into her corner of the back seat as she could.

Cristiano answered quickly, before the call dropped again. The swearing that issued from him a few moments later wasn't a good sign.

"What's wrong?" she asked when he finished.

He looked grim. "We're stuck."

"What do you mean, *stuck*?" she asked, trying to tame the note of panic in her voice.

He swore again. "The plane has a hydraulic leak in the brakes. We can't fly without a new cowling, and there isn't one on the island."

Antonella bit back a hysterical laugh. "Is there a chance we can get on a commercial plane?"

"The last flight left twenty minutes ago. There are no more flights in or out today."

"You said it was safe to fly for many hours yet."

"It is. But commercial airlines have different schedules, Antonella. And they've chosen to cancel flights that were coming in later today. Those planes would have been the flights out again."

Antonella stared at him, swallowed the giant lump in her throat. "Now what?"

"We must find a place to stay."

Unbelievable. Could her luck get any worse? "And where do you suggest we look? Do we simply drive up to every hotel on the island and see if they have a vacancy?"

He tapped his phone against his leg. "No, that would take too much time and there are no guarantees. I have another idea."

"And what would that be?"

"I know the man who owns this island. He keeps a villa nearby. We will go there."

She stared at him. "Why didn't you mention this before?"

"I didn't think it would be necessary."

Antonella didn't say anything while he issued instructions to the driver. Maybe she should argue about the practicality of his plan, but what other choice was there? Far better to stay in a private home than be seen together in a hotel. There was always a chance, no matter how remote, that someone from the media would be there and would recognize them. A photo of her with Cristiano di Savaré could do irreparable harm to her country right now.

He put his arm behind her again and she pressed herself farther away from him. He frowned.

"It's no use," he said. "The car is small and there's nowhere to go."

"I realize that, but you don't need to put your arm around me."

"And I thought you liked it when I touched you." His voice contained a hint of sarcasm that irritated her.

"Hardly."

"Then why did you come?"

Antonella blinked. "What choice did I have? You said yourself that all the flights were booked."

"Yes, but to accept help from me of all people…" He tsked.

Antonella saw red. "It wasn't my first choice, no, but I'm not stupid."

His gaze grew sharp, thoughtful. "No, I don't think you are."

"What's that supposed to mean?"

A mocking smile curved his lips. "Whatever you think it means, *Principessa*."

"I think you simply like to irritate me. Why did you offer to help me get off the island if you don't like me so much?"

"I don't have to like you for what I have in mind."

Antonella gasped. "How could you possibly dislike someone and still want to sleep with them?"

The look on his face, something between mildly amused and completely arrogant, sent heat flooding into her cheeks. Had she mistaken his meaning?

"There is a fine line between hate and passion, Antonella," he replied. "One sometimes makes the other more rich."

"That's horrible." She'd always thought, assuming she weren't obligated to marry a man of her father's choosing, she would have to like the man she slept with for the first time. She'd never expected to have that choice, however. Now that it seemed she might, she was more than a little appalled at her physical reaction to Cristiano.

He quirked an eyebrow. "Really? You would expect me to believe a woman of your experience has liked every man she's ever bedded?"

Her jaw clenched. She should have realized where this conversation would go. "I prefer not to discuss this with you."

"Why not? Ashamed?"

"Of course not!"

"So how many has it been, Antonella? How many men have you lured to your bed?" He looked haughty, cruel. It made her furious.

"Lured? *Lured*? You make me sound like I'm running a stall at the market! *Come get your peaches, come get your plums—hurry before they're all gone.*"

His expression seemed in danger of crumpling for a split second. She thought he might laugh, but he turned and looked out the window at the rain, ignoring her. He also didn't move his arm. Fury cycled through her in waves until she decided *the hell with it* and flopped back on the seat, wedging him over where he took too much of her space.

What a hypocrite!

His body was hard, solid, and hot. Antonella folded her arms over her chest and leaned her head back—on his arm since he hadn't moved it. He infuriated her with his accusations. He knew nothing about her, and yet he smugly thought he knew everything.

Arrogant man!

He took up all the air in the taxi. She wanted to roll down the window and stick her head out, but it was raining too hard. She was just so tired. So damn tired. As her temper deflated, her eyes drifted closed in spite of the effort she made to keep them open.

Cristiano's scent wrapped around her senses. He smelled like rain and spice, and a pang of sadness pierced her. Why? It took her a moment to realize that it reminded her of something out of her childhood. Was it when her mother had fixed spiced tea for her when she was sick?

Yes, that was it. Spice equaled comfort back then. She could picture her mother as if it were yesterday—her sad, beautiful mother who'd died far earlier than she should have. Was that when her father had grown violent?

She couldn't remember. She'd always tried to block those memories. Like the time he'd squeezed the life from Dante's gerbil because Dante had forgotten to feed it. Her brother, who'd been ten at the time—far older than her impressionable five years—had taken the incident stoically.

Antonella had cried and cried. It was the first time she'd ever experienced such cruelty. She'd never forgotten it, used to burst into tears at the oddest times when the memory crashed in on her. Even years later.

Her face was suddenly cool, and she realized it was the air against her wet cheeks.

No, not now. Please, not now.

She opened her eyes, blinked against the blur. Then she swiped her hands over her cheeks, trying to stop the flow before Cristiano noticed and mocked her. She hadn't cried over that memory in so long she couldn't even remember the last time.

"Crying won't work," Cristiano said coldly—but his voice sounded oddly thick.

Antonella turned away from him. She didn't want him to be here, didn't want him to become a part of her struggle to be a normal person. It wasn't his business! Nothing in her life was his business. "I'm just tired. Leave me alone."

Would she never be free of this? Would episodes from her past always move her to tears when she least expected it? She felt weak, helpless—and angry. Sometimes, in these moments, she thought she could kill her father if he were in front of her and at her mercy.

And she hated that feeling most of all. The tears came faster now, turned into gulping sobs. She couldn't stop the memories, couldn't stop the guilt. She should have done something, should have—

Cristiano swore, then wrapped his arms around her and pulled her against him.

"No, let me go," she begged, trying to rip his hands away from her body. "Let me *go*."

But he didn't. He turned her toward him, cupped the back of her head and pressed her to his chest. She bucked against him, trying to get away, but he was too strong. Eventually, her shoulders slumped.

And once she gave up, his grip softened, his hand rubbing rhythmically up and down her neck while he spoke to her softly. She strained to hear the words over the roar of the rain and wind outside, over her own crying, and realized it was a song.

A song.

Shock was the least of what she felt at that moment. It was such an oddly tender gesture, and from the last person in the world she would have expected it. It was as if he understood somehow.

Her fisted hands curled into his shirt, held tight as she worked hard to stop the tears. She had every reason to hate him, but in that moment he was her ally. He held her for what seemed like hours. It was the closest she'd felt to anyone in a very long time.

CHAPTER FOUR

THE taxi took them to the villa located on a remote beach. By the time they reached the house, Antonella's tears had dried and she'd pushed away from Cristiano again. Fresh embarrassment buffeted her in waves. How could she have lost control like that? And with him, of all people? His shirt was wrinkled where she'd crumpled it in her fist, and a hint of mascara smudged the white fabric, but Cristiano said nothing.

Madonna mia. If the owner took them in, she was locking herself in a bedroom and not coming out again until the storm was over. The less time she spent in Cristiano's company, the better.

Antonella waited in the car while Cristiano went to the door and checked to see if the island tycoon was home. He wasn't, and yet a few minutes later Cristiano had managed to somehow get a call through to the man in New York.

"The staff is on holiday," he said when he returned to the taxi, "but we are welcome to stay until the storm has passed. There is a caretaker in the cottage we drove by. He will let us in."

"Wouldn't we be better off in town?" Despite her earlier relief at not going to a hotel, she suddenly preferred it to being alone with this man for the foreseeable future. She felt too exposed, too raw. She couldn't keep up the barrier of strength she needed simply to be in his company. It was like living on a battlefield.

Cristiano seemed oblivious to her torment. "If others were turned away at the airport, then the hotels could be full."

Antonella reached for her phone, hoping she had a signal. "We can call and check." At least in a hotel, there'd be other people. And maybe even rooms on different floors. She wouldn't have to see him at all. When the airport reopened, she could be on a flight out without ever talking to him again.

He frowned. "We have a safe place to stay, *cara*. And our driver would probably like to return to his home before the worst hits, yes? There is not a lot of time left for error."

A sinking feeling settled over her like a veil. She hadn't thought of that. The driver glanced at her in the rear-view mirror, his eyes darting away a second later. He was young, perhaps had a wife and small children waiting in a tidy house somewhere. And he'd driven her and Cristiano through the rain-swept streets for two hours now.

"Of course," Antonella said. As much as she wanted to get away from Cristiano, she couldn't endanger anyone to do so. They may be alone here, but she didn't need to spend more than a few moments in his company. It would be fine.

Fifteen minutes later, they'd located the caretaker, gotten a key, and let themselves into the house. The place was big, but not as sprawling and opulent as one would expect. It was furnished island-style, with low sea-grass couches, bamboo floors, simple woven rugs, and bright tropical prints interspersed with monochromatic tones. Antonella walked through to the huge kitchen at the back of the house and gazed out at the landscape. A wall of French windows overlooked a patio and pool that gave way to a long stretch of manicured lawn. The lawn sloped down to a retaining wall several hundred meters away. Below that was an extensive swath of white beach. The sky was pale with rain, and palm trees lashed over double in the wind. The ocean that had been turquoise and lapis only yesterday was now grey and roiling. White caps foamed across the surface.

She stood very still, watching and listening. Slowly, it occurred to her that the muted roar echoing through the house came from the wind cleaving around the structure. The power of it was staggering, and nothing like she'd ever experienced before.

"I put us in the master bedroom."

Antonella bit back a scream of surprise and spun to face Cristiano. She hadn't heard him approach. He looked like a beach bum standing in the shadowy entry to the kitchen. A gorgeous beach bum.

He disconcerted her. Too much.

"*Us*? Are you hard of hearing? I said last night I'm not sleeping with you."

He came into the room like a cat—silent, muscles bunching and flowing with oiled grace. She realized he was wet when the meager light hit him. He stripped off the polo shirt in a smooth motion, wiped it across his face, and then dropped it on the marble-topped island that ran the length of the room.

Antonella's breath caught. She had to force her lungs to work as she blanked her expression. Every inch of him was corded with muscle, as if he were a day laborer instead of a prince. Broad shoulders and defined pecs tapered to a narrow waist and lean hips. His skin was tanned, and yet it grew lighter the lower her eyes went. A dark arrow of hair slipped beneath the loose waistband of his shorts, and she found herself wanting to follow it down, see the rest of him.

Antonella snapped her gaze to his face. He smirked as if he knew exactly what she'd been thinking.

"You know you want to."

Antonella blinked. "Want to what?"

The smirk turned into a grin. "Sleep with me. In the master bedroom."

Oh, dear God—

She shook her head, heat suffusing her face. "No, I don't and I won't. I'm taking one of the other bedrooms—there *are* other bedrooms, yes?"

Cristiano shuffled past her, gazed out the window. She refused to focus on his naked back, the taut muscles of his buttocks beneath the damp material of his shorts—

"There are," he said, turning to face her again. "But I just checked the generator and the fuel is nearly spent. Someone forgot to fill it, or it's been drained recently. If we lose power, there'll be no light."

"Surely there are candles. Have you looked?"

"Not yet, but yes, there must be. And yet we need to preserve those as well. Not to mention there are trees outside the front of the home. The other bedrooms are up there. If a tree fell onto the house, then what? I prefer not to have to dig you out, assuming you survived."

Antonella shuddered, but whether it was over the picture of a tree crushing her or being forced to share a room with this man, she didn't know.

"One of us can stay in the living area. There are couches, the floor—"

"And should we lose power, or should something happen to this house, we would be separated. It is best to stay together, Antonella."

She folded her arms. "How can you possibly know that? We don't have hurricanes or cyclones—or whatever you call them—where we come from."

"Every Monterossan prince since the beginning of time has

served in the army, *Principessa*." His eyes grew hard, bleak. She swallowed. "I assure you I have endured things you cannot imagine. Trust me when I say I know of what I speak."

She did believe him, and yet she was still unnerved by the prospect of spending so much time confined with him. "Very convenient, Cristiano. I am forced to share a room with you, it would seem."

"What is your alternative?"

"I don't suppose I have one, do I?"

"Not if you care to survive."

He spoke so casually it chilled her. Antonella went to the window, touched her fingers to the pane of glass as the water chased down it outside. "How much worse will the storm get?"

He came and stood beside her. She glanced up at his profile as he stared out at the churning sea, his expression troubled. Tried resolutely not to look down at all that naked skin.

"I wish I knew. It will worsen as it spins toward land. Possibly a category four when it comes ashore." His head tilted back as he looked up at the sky. "The wind will reach one hundred and thirty-five knots, perhaps."

"I don't know what that means."

He turned to face her. She kept her gaze straight ahead, though she could see him quite well in her peripheral vision. He was too close, too big. His bare skin gleamed in the pale light, and drops of water fell from his head onto his chest, trickled down, down....

"In excess of two hundred kilometers an hour."

Antonella's stomach dropped. She turned without thinking, took an instinctive step backward to put distance between them. "W-what could happen to us? Are we safe here?"

He perused her body in a leisurely way before answering, as if he knew she was as disconcerted by his nakedness as she was by the storm. "The trees could be a problem, and we will probably lose power. Beyond that, I do not know."

"What about the sea?"

"The drop to the ocean is steep, so a storm surge is not likely."

Antonella hurried to the center island and opened the handbag she'd set there. Her cell phone had no signal. She dropped it into her purse again. "Do you have a signal?"

He sauntered toward her, pulled his phone from his shorts. "No."

Antonella leaned against the counter for support and closed her eyes. "I should have kept trying to call Dante. He will worry."

"Perhaps he will simply think you are too occupied with your lover to inform him of your movements."

She stiffened. "I call my brother every day."

Why did she feel the need to justify herself?

"Do you? How extraordinary."

"You don't speak with your family daily?"

His laugh was unexpected. Disbelieving. "No. I am thirty-one, *cara*. My father doesn't expect a regular report."

"Dante doesn't expect a report either. But we are close, and much has happened recently—" She broke off, unwilling to continue. No one knew what she and Dante had suffered over the years at the hands of their father.

No one would, because neither of them was talking about it. Perhaps Dante had shared his story with his wife, but Antonella did not know and would not ask.

"It is good you are close," Cristiano said after a moment. "Very good."

She wasn't certain how he meant that, but a shiver crept along her nerve endings. He turned and started rummaging through drawers. The rattle of silverware grated on her after a few moments and she knew she had to do something or go insane.

"What can I do?" She could've started searching for candles, but it was best if they didn't duplicate effort. Since he seemed to know what to expect from the storm, she would bow to his experience.

If only he'd put on a shirt! Perhaps she could think then. Perhaps this shivery, achy feeling would go away. She'd seen bare-chested men before, but that had usually been poolside. Cristiano, naked to the waist, in a kitchen—

She closed her eyes. When she opened them again, he was looking at her.

"I need you to fill all the sinks and bath tubs with water," he said after a few moments of silence in which she was utterly convinced he knew the effect he was having and did his utmost to draw it out.

She blinked. "Why?"

"Because if we lose power, we lose water."

It made sense, but she'd have never thought of it until too late.

He continued, "Next, see if you can find any flashlights, batteries, candles and matches. If you run across a radio, get that too. Take everything to the master bedroom and leave it. I'll search in here for a few things, and then I'm going outside to close the shutters. If you could get some towels and leave them on the kitchen island, I'll use this entrance."

She bit her lip as she studied him. He was all business now, and nothing like she'd expected. Dante was the most practical person she knew, and yet this man made him look like a cosseted child in comparison. At the moment, he was more like a military commando than an heir to a throne.

"Do you really think it could get that bad?"

His expression was grave. "Anything is possible, *Principessa*. It's best to be prepared."

* * *

Cristiano was soaked. He'd spent twenty minutes in the pouring rain, closing the shutters and hooking them. The caretaker should have done the job when the storm had first been reported to have swung off track, but the man seemed to do little besides sit in his house and watch television.

Cristiano took no satisfaction in knowing it was unlikely the man was watching anything now. The rain was coming down so hard that the satellite signal had gone out a while ago. He knew because he'd turned on the flat-panel television in the bedroom before he'd gone outside. Now, he stood in the kitchen and stripped out of his shorts. Antonella was nowhere to be seen, but at least she'd brought the towels.

A vision of her face, her eyes red and swollen, came to him. He resolutely shoved it away.

He could *not* feel sorry for her.

She was a Monteverdian *and* a Romanelli. And he had a job to do. A promise to keep.

He'd sworn on Julianne's memory that he would put an end to this war if it were the last thing he did. His people needed peace. Too long they'd lived in the shadow of this conflict.

He owed it to them. To her. He should have been there. If he had, he could have stopped her from dying. Could have kept her out of that convoy. He mourned the loss of all who'd died, but he didn't feel responsible for them the way he did for his wife.

Dio, he should have never married her.

He grabbed a towel, scrubbed it over his body. He tried to picture Julianne, to remember the exact curve of her smile, but his mind insisted on seeing another face.

Antonella's.

He couldn't deny that he wanted her. He knew she was a thoughtless, manipulative *puttana*, yet he couldn't seem to overrule the urges of his body. He *should* be able to do so, but he couldn't.

She got to him on more than a physical level. When she'd cried earlier, he'd felt as if someone had stabbed a serrated knife into him and twisted it. He'd held her close and sung the same song his mother sang when he'd been small and unwilling to go to sleep.

Why?

Because something about Antonella defied explanation. She was shrewd and tough, manipulative—and yet there was pain, the kind of pain that only came with depth of experience. He knew because he'd felt that kind of pain too. He recognized something of himself within her.

And he didn't like it one bit. To feel any sympathy at all for her, any kinship, was a betrayal of his dead wife's memory. Not because she was a woman—he'd had plenty of lovers over the past few years—but because she was a Monteverdian.

Cristiano tossed the soaked towel aside and prepared to grab a fresh one to wrap around his waist when a squeak from the entry hall drew his attention. Antonella stood there, her dark hair pulled away from her face, her jaw hanging loose as she stared at him. His body started to react to her perusal.

He didn't care. Let her see the effect she had on him. Surely she was accustomed to it. Hell, she probably expected it.

Maybe, just maybe, if he got this physical attraction for her out of the way, he could think again. Could push her to agree to his plan and get on with the business of taking over her country.

A second later, she pivoted on her heel and disappeared in a rush. She seemed flustered—and yet it was an act. Had to be. She *wanted* him to feel pity for her, to feel protective. She'd already succeeded once today.

He cinched the towel low over his hips. He'd been insane to consider, even for a moment, that this sultry princess—the woman who'd been draped over Raúl Vega last night—was anything other than what overwhelming evidence indicated she was.

She did *not* defy explanation. She was a beautiful woman who enjoyed her pleasures. Aside from her two royal engagements, she'd been linked with one fashion designer, a German count, three Formula One drivers, and an aging Italian billionaire among others. Raúl Vega was only her latest conquest.

Cristiano had spent a lot of money and effort to confirm the rumors of Monteverde's financial crisis. His father believed that if they waited, Monteverde would fall like a domino into their hands.

But Cristiano was taking no chances; he would allow no eleventh hour rescues. Now that he'd dried up the last source of possible investment, what remained of his plan was simple enough: his money for Antonella's cooperation in gaining the mineral rights to Monteverde's ore deposits. With the ore under Monterossan control, he could enforce peace in the region.

It was their last bankable resource. If he controlled it, he controlled them.

Yet he knew his plan wasn't as straightforward as he'd first thought. She was shrewder than he'd imagined, for one thing. Antonella would never allow herself to be bought so cheaply. No, what she would expect was the crown of Monterosso.

And he would offer it to her on a platter if necessary.

But he would never deliver it. To go through with a marriage, to her of all people, was out of the question. She would be humiliated, perhaps, but it wouldn't last. She'd already survived two royal breakups. A third wouldn't shatter her.

He glanced up at the roof as a gust of wind howled along

the structure. He'd expected trouble, but not this kind. While the storm had worked to his advantage in isolating Antonella, it was bad for every other reason known to man.

Cristiano pulled open a drawer and found a roll of utility tape. The patio doors were the only ones with no exterior shutters. The addition was new, and though there was an overhang, he didn't trust that would be enough to protect the glass. Once he finished taping the windows in long spokes across the glass—if they shattered, at least the tape would help prevent shards from going everywhere—he padded toward the bedroom to face his adversary.

Antonella sat in a chair in one corner, flipping through a magazine. She did not look up as he entered. "Is it any worse?" she asked.

Cristiano unzipped his bag and pulled out some dry clothes. "Not yet, but I think it soon will be. Did you find a radio?"

"Yes, but no extra batteries."

They would have to be careful listening to updates once the power failed. "There isn't much food in the house. Crackers, sausage, a jar of olives, aerosol cheese—"

"What's aerosol cheese?"

She'd looked up, her brows drawing together. A moment later, she seemed to realize what she'd done. Her eyes darted to the towel cinched low on his hips, back up again. When her tongue swept over her lower lip, Cristiano thought his body would turn to stone. As it was, the towel was about to reveal her effect on him.

Dio santo.

He clamped down on his will, forced his body to behave. "It is an American product," he said matter-of-factly. He made a motion with his hand. "You spray it on the crackers."

"Spray?" She looked horrified.

"*Si.*"

A shudder passed over her. "That sounds perfectly vile."

"Depends on how hungry you are and how long until your next meal." Though he'd been born into privilege, he'd done his time with the Monterossan Special Forces. He understood deprivation and hunger quite well. While she flitted around her family palazzo, beautiful and elegant, her countrymen— and women—huddled in bunkers on the border, surrounded by artillery and razor wire, and ate meals out of a package. Just like he and the soldiers he'd served with had done.

"We should have returned to town," she said, pushing up out of the chair and pacing toward the shuttered windows. She spun around again before she reached them. "Then we wouldn't be isolated out here with *spray cheese* and no communications with the outside world."

"Be thankful we are in a safe place, *Principessa*. There are those in the world who are not."

If she noticed the steel in his voice, she didn't show it. She seemed oblivious, on edge. Did the storm frighten her that much?

Her gaze raked over him, almost wild-eyed, then skittered away again. Once more, she spun toward the windows, following the track she'd paced before.

Cristiano recognized someone on the edge of control when he saw it. But what was causing her to feel so skittish? Did she have a thing about closed in spaces? Not that the room was small, but with the shutters closed and only a lamp for light, it felt rather cave-like.

Or was it the fact he was nearly naked? An interesting thought, to be sure.

"It wouldn't have mattered where we were. Phone calls can fix nothing right now. And there was no time to make the trek back to town. This is the best we could do."

She stopped and put her head in her hands. "I cannot believe I am stuck here with you for the foreseeable future. This is a nightmare."

"I can think of a few ways to make the time pass." He said it primarily because he knew it would irritate her.

Her head snapped up again. *Score.* "This isn't something to make jokes about."

"What makes you think I'm joking?"

She turned away from him with something that sounded like a growl. She made the circuit to the window again, stopped. Spun around, hands on hips, breasts thrust out enticingly. "Get this in your head, Cristiano—I am *not* sleeping with you. And I'd appreciate it very much if you'd put something *on*."

Her voice rose at the end. Cristiano absently rubbed a hand over his chest, enjoying himself tremendously. So she *was* rattled by his semi-nakedness. Because she wanted him, no doubt. And because she felt guilty for doing so.

He certainly understood the feeling. "Do I disturb you, *mia bella*?"

She stood so stiffly, like a nun who'd blundered into a strip club. Now, why was that a turn-on? She wasn't a virgin, wasn't naïve, and yet she carried off the act so well. The contrast with her sensual body intrigued him. Made him hard. She couldn't help but know it, clad as he was in a towel.

Her throat moved. "Don't be ridiculous," she rasped. A moment later, she waved a hand airily as she seemed to gather her equilibrium. "You don't affect me one way or the other. So you might as well put on some clothes."

The corners of his mouth curled in a smile that was both evil and triumphant. "I think you are right."

And then he dropped the towel.

CHAPTER FIVE

ANTONELLA fought hard not to shriek and spin away like a frightened virgin. No, she had to play this cool. Collected. He thought she was experienced—so experienced she must act.

But Cristiano di Savaré was the first man she'd ever seen naked in the flesh, and the sight affected her quite oddly. She felt dizzy for one thing. Like she needed to sit before her knees buckled.

And she felt hot. Prickles of heat skittered along her skin like tiny flames, scorching everything in their path. Her mouth dropped, snapped shut again.

He was…was…*big*…all over. And completely unabashed.

The towel lay heaped at his feet, forgotten. His eyes glittered, daring her to react.

Every line of him was beautiful. His skin was smooth and golden, yet lighter from a point above his groin to the tops of his thighs. Inanely, she thought he must spend a lot of time outside without a shirt.

Her eyes skimmed downward, hardly believing what she was seeing and yet unable to look away at the same time. His penis thrust out from his body proudly. She understood enough about male anatomy to know what an erect penis meant. But why? That part she didn't understand. How could he be aroused? They'd been arguing, for pity's sake!

Another, more frightening thought occurred to her: should she be scared of him? They were alone here, just the two of them and a storm outside.

He was bigger than she was, stronger. It was in his blood to hate her, just as it was in hers to hate him. Would he use his size and strength against her, take what he wanted by force? No one would come to her rescue if she screamed.

Her mind cast about frantically for solutions, ways in which she could fight him off if he attacked her.

"Want to help?" he said, his voice a sensual purr as he slowly reached for the clothing he'd tossed onto the bed.

Antonella drew in a shaky breath. No, she did not think he would force himself on her. He'd soothed her in the taxi when he could have ignored her. She kept telling herself that for comfort as she turned away very deliberately, very carefully. She couldn't let him know she was flustered—or frightened. She couldn't give him that kind of power.

Somehow she made her legs work. She returned to the slipper chair, sank down on it and picked up the magazine she'd been thumbing through. Thought better of flipping pages when she realized her hands were shaking. She laid the magazine on her lap and opened it to a random page, pretended to study what was there.

Cristiano hadn't moved to follow her, yet he was still naked. Still aroused. Fear seeped away, replaced by heat and the pain of her own desire. Odd. She'd never realized sexual arousal could hurt.

Her heartbeat pounded in her chest, her neck, her wrists. She wanted to go into the bathroom and sink down into the cold water she'd filled the tub with. Perhaps then the heat would go away.

"I take it that's a no," Cristiano said.

Her cheeks were already on fire, but that didn't stop the heat of a fresh blush. She'd forgotten he'd spoken to her, had asked her a question. She'd been so flustered by his body, by her own thoughts, that she'd blanked.

Did he know? Should she answer him now, or play it cool?

She saw movement in her periphery, but refused to look up. A flash of something pale. Clothing, she hoped. Please God, let him cover that body up before she made a bigger fool of herself. Before he realized she was a stammering virgin seeing her first naked man. Somehow, she knew that would diminish her in his eyes. He would pity her then. She couldn't take his pity again today. Didn't want it.

"Too bad, Antonella," he said. The sound of a zipper going up nearly made her breathe a very audible sigh of relief. "The time would pass so pleasantly. Before you know it, we'd be leaving again."

"Oh yes," she forced out. Without looking up, of course. "We'd be leaving. And you'd waste no time informing everyone you could think of that you'd bedded me."

"I never kiss and tell, *Principessa.*"

"Of course not," she said, letting him know with her tone that she didn't believe a word of it.

"But if I want to claim we've been lovers, what's to stop me?"

Her head snapped back as her eyes met his. He was wearing another pair of khaki shorts and a navy T-shirt that molded the shape of his chest and abdomen. He was clothed, and yet her pulse still zipped along like an express train.

"You wouldn't. Besides, I would deny it."

Cristiano laughed. "Who would believe you, *bellissima*? You have a reputation, shall we say?"

Antonella's cheeks burned. Oh, yes, she had a reputation—

gained when men had *lied* about her, as this one threatened to do. It made her angry. She flipped a page in the magazine, ripping the paper as she did so. *Damn him*.

But maybe she could fight back. She arched an eyebrow, affected as chilly a look as she could manage. "Perhaps they would believe it when I claimed you were not so good as *your* reputation? I could say you were a selfish and *hasty*—" she emphasized the word "—lover."

Cristiano's laugh was louder this time. Then he swept her with hot eyes. "You are welcome to try."

Antonella slapped the magazine closed irritably. "This is ridiculous, Cristiano. We could be in very real danger, and yet you keep insulting me and making jokes."

His expression grew serious. "Do you know what I think?"

"No, but I know you will tell me."

He came over to where she sat, towered above her until he dropped to one knee and reached for her. Her heart stopped, simply stopped, as she tried to imagine what he was about to do. He picked up the magazine, turned it and set it back down.

"I think you want me very much, Antonella."

She forced herself to speak past the giant lump in her throat. "You are deluded," she managed.

"Am I?" He stood and moved away without waiting for a reply.

Antonella watched numbly as he disappeared through the door that connected the bedroom with the rest of the house. Then she looked down. And realized that he'd turned the magazine the correct way.

She'd been staring at it upside down the entire time.

By the time Cristiano returned a short while later, she'd managed to calm her racing heart and jangled nerves. She'd tried reading a book, but the power had blinked a few times and then snapped out, leaving her in the dark. She'd fumbled for the candle she'd placed on the table nearby, cursing softly when it rolled away and fell.

Before she could get down on her hands and knees to find it, Cristiano was there, shining a flashlight into the darkness. He retrieved one of the candles from the stash at the foot of the bed and lit it, then switched off the light. A second later, he was stretched out on the bed, leaning against the headboard with his hands behind his head. The pose molded the shirt to his chest, bulged the muscles in his arms. Made him seem so delicious and sexy.

Antonella crossed her arms over her body protectively and concentrated on the flickering candle where he'd set it on the bedside table. Anything except look at him.

"It will be a very long night if we ignore each other," Cristiano finally said.

She forced herself to gaze at him evenly. "It's already been a long day. Interminable."

"Yes."

Her pride pricked at the idea that he found her company tiresome. Why? Wasn't that what she'd just intimated about him?

"Tell me about Monteverde," he said, and her jaw threatened to fall to the floor.

"Why?" she asked a moment later, suspicion curling around the edges of her awareness.

"Because we are alone, the night is long, and it's a good topic."

"Why not tell me about Monterosso?"

He shrugged. "If you wish."

For the next twenty minutes, he told her about his country—about the green mountains, the black cliffs, and the azure ocean. She found herself listening intently, nodding from time to time as she realized how much Monterosso sounded like Monterverde. When he talked of cool forests and bubbling mountain streams, she could picture them perfectly. When he spoke of the dryness along the coast, the cacti and aloe plants, she felt as if she'd stood beside him and looked upon the same things.

"It's amazing," she said when he finished.

"I think so, yes."

Antonella shook her head. "No, I mean it sounds exactly like Monteverde."

He arched an eyebrow. "You are surprised? We were a single country once."

"And you would wish it so again," she said, inflecting her words with steel.

"Have I said that?"

"You didn't have to. It's what your people have wanted for years."

"Is this your opinion, or what you've been told by your father and brother?" His voice was diamond-edged.

"If it's not what Monterosso wants, why must we defend our border? Why are your tanks and guns there? Your soldiers?"

"Because yours are."

My God, men were insane. Was this the sort of circular logic that had caused so many lives to be lost over the years? While the solution seemed obvious, she knew it wasn't. "Then why don't we both turn around and go home?"

"Because we don't trust each other, Antonella."

She sat up straighter in her chair. "But we could sign treaties, pledge to cooperate—"

His laughter startled her. "Do you not think this has been tried?"

"It hasn't been tried since Dante became King. We have only the ceasefire—"

"How would this change anything? He is a Romanelli."

"What is that supposed to mean? That he is untrustworthy? That *we* are not as good as the di Savarés?"

"It means that your word and your treaties have not been enough thus far. Why should we believe your brother any different from your father?"

She ached to tell him. And yet she couldn't. Because it was unexplainable. And private. No, what she and Dante had endured wouldn't convince this man. And there was every danger it would only reinforce his beliefs. Abuse often turned out abusers. For all Cristiano knew, Dante could be just like his predecessor.

"He simply is," she said firmly.

"Yes," Cristiano sneered, "this is quite enough to convince me of Monteverdian sincerity."

"You have yet to prove you are any better. If you would turn your tanks around, pull back your soldiers—"

"And let you bomb innocent civilians?" Rage suddenly seemed to roll from him in a giant wave. It was so palpable she thought it would crush her. His expression was dark, hard.

Intimidating.

Her voice came out in a whisper in spite of her best effort to make it otherwise. "We don't use bombs against civilians. We only defend ourselves against Monterossan hostility—"

His laughter was so sharp and bitter it sliced her off in mid-sentence. She stared at him, at his jaw that had turned to granite. At the bleakness he failed to hide.

A moment later, he shoved both hands through his hair, blew out a hard breath. "You are quite wrong about that," he said, his voice so utterly controlled it chilled her. He'd gone from hot rage to cold hatred in the space of a breath.

"I-I don't believe you." But her heart pounded in her throat.

Could it be true? Her father had been capable of ordering such cruelty. More than capable. She thought of Dante's pet gerbil, swallowed. *No, don't let me cry again. Not now.*

"It is quite true, I assure you," he said, his demeanor smooth. She had the impression he'd just fought a battle with himself and won. A dark, cold battle that she didn't understand.

"How do you know this? How can you prove it?"

"I don't have to prove it. I carry the results in my heart every day of my life."

"You were…hurt?" She couldn't imagine it. His body, as much as she'd seen of it, was perfect. If he'd been hurt, surely there would be signs of it. Or had he lost someone?

"My wife, *Principessa*. She was killed on an aid mission to the border. A roadside bomb blew up under the truck she was riding in."

Her chest squeezed tight as her lungs refused to work properly. "I'm sorry," she managed. She'd known his wife died shortly after their marriage, but she'd never known how it happened. She'd only had true freedom of information for a few months now. Before that, her father had tightly controlled the news she'd been exposed to.

A bomb. My God, how horrible. The poor woman.

Poor Cristiano.

Could her father have supported such a thing? Known about it? *Ordered* it? The thought made her shiver.

"Of course you are." The words were perfunctory, yet each felt like a physical blow.

"I *am* sorry, Cristiano," she insisted. "I've lost loved ones too."

Her mother, her aunt Maria. Leni, her first dog.

"Have you?" His voice was still so cold. "Yet you always manage to find someone new to replace the old."

Her heart hurt. It simply hurt. He believed her the worst kind of monster. The kind of woman who cared for no one but herself, who was unaffected by the pain of others. Why that bothered her, she wasn't certain. But it did.

The tears she'd been holding back threatened to consume her. *No, she would not cry. She would not give him the satisfaction. His opinion meant nothing.*

She got to her feet, her arms wrapped around her body to ward off the ice that hung in the air despite the tropical heat. He wanted to lash out—she understood that. Understood the need to hurt someone when you were hurting.

Yet how did that make him any different from other men she had known? From her father?

It didn't. Cristiano hit with words instead of fists. And the pain was worse in some ways. Psychological pain had repercussions beyond the physical that stayed with you forever. She'd learned that lesson long ago. Hell, she was still learning it. Dante's gerbil was a prime example.

And she was far too tired of it to suffer a moment's more abuse at his, or anyone's, hands.

"Where are you going?" he demanded as she crossed to the bedroom door.

She turned, her head held high, tears in check for the moment. "It doesn't seem to matter where I stay, does it, Cristiano? There is danger for me in every room of this house. So I think I will take my chances in another room for a while."

Cristiano bowed his head and concentrated on breathing evenly. He should not have spoken of Julianne's death to her. But he'd felt the darkness settling over him when she'd accused Monterosso of prolonging the hostilities, and he'd been unable to keep it at bay. He'd wanted to wound, just like he'd been wounded by the guilt of causing an innocent woman to die. A woman whose only crime had been to marry him.

He had to go after Antonella. He couldn't let her wander through the house with the storm intensifying. A tree could crash down on them. Windows could shatter. He could be wrong about the depth of the ocean and a storm surge could sweep into the house and drag her away.

Death lay over the structure like a coiled serpent, simply waiting for an opportunity to strike.

And he couldn't let that happen. He needed her if he wanted to put an end to the violence.

No.

He tilted his head back on the headboard and sighed. It was more than that. She was a person, and though he might not trust her or like her very much, she didn't deserve anything less than his best care for her safety while they endured this storm.

It had gotten out of control so fast.

He'd only meant to find out a bit more about her, but he should have known the conversation would head down a road he did not want to go. Could a Monteverdian and a Monterossan truly spend time together and not fight about the problems between their countries? If it were possible, perhaps there would be peace already.

Still, he was here to make sure it happened. He had to control his emotions and he had to deal with Antonella like a rational man, not a wounded lion.

He pushed away from the bed, grabbing the flashlight, and headed through the door. Outside, the wind howled and moaned. Tree branches scraped across the terracotta roof with an eerie sound like fingernails against a chalkboard. The walls groaned and creaked.

"Antonella!"

She didn't answer, so he passed through the hall and into the living room. She wasn't there. Next, he went into the kitchen. The temperature in the house was starting to climb now that the power had gone out. He would have to open a window soon, though he did not want to for fear of the wind being so strong. But they would need fresh air. Sweat beaded on his skin as he moved through the structure.

"Antonella!" She couldn't have gone far, but she probably couldn't hear him over the wind. He went into the first bedroom, shone the light. Nothing. The second also yielded nothing.

The third time, as the beam swept across the room, he hit the jackpot. She lay on the bed, curled into a ball, a pillow hugged tight to her body. The sight shafted an arrow of regret straight through his chest.

She looked like a child, vulnerable and helpless, and his protective instincts were kicking into gear. *Dio*, he had to remember who she was. What she was. They'd been here a handful of hours and he was already going soft.

"Antonella," he said over the wind and rain pelting the roof.

"Go away."

"It's not safe in here. We have to return to the master bedroom."

She bolted into an upright position, her hair wild as she shoved it out of her face. Her eyes were red-rimmed. "It's not safe in there either," she shot back. "I'll take my chances here."

"Don't be stupid. We're going back."

He started forward and she scrambled against the headboard, folding her knees against her body as if to ward him off.

"It won't work, *Principessa*," he said, exasperation and

fury surging through him in twin waves. His instincts were sounding an alarm inside his head, telling him to get her and get out, no matter how hard she fought. The skin at the back of his neck prickled as the wind surged against the house, banging the shutters. He'd closed them, but they were old and somewhat loose in places. "I'm bigger and stronger; I *will* win."

Her eyes widened as he reached for her. She looked a little scared at his intensity, but he had no time to play nice. He had to get them back to safety. As if to punctuate the point, there was a loud snap outside. The wind howled even louder.

He grabbed her foot and yanked her toward him. She screamed.

But he ignored her feminine hysterics and dragged her up into his grasp. She twisted like a cat. "No!"

Cristiano gripped her shoulders hard and shook her. "Stop fighting me," he ordered. "We have to go."

But she didn't seem to be listening. She twisted again, fell to the bed as he lost his hold on her. He lunged for her, furious—and more than a little concerned at the crackling sound coming from above their heads.

"We have to go," he repeated. "Now."

Instead of cooperating, she flinched and covered her head as if he were about to strike her. The sight gave him pause. He'd never hit a woman in his life. Never had a woman cower from him as if he were about to do so. Did she really think…?

Why?

Why?

Another sharp crack outside dragged his attention up. A moment later, the roof split open. Terracotta and splintered wood crumbled through the opening, showering down around them.

No time left.

Acting on a surge of adrenaline and pure instinct, Cristiano grabbed Antonella and hauled her from the bed. There was just enough time to roll her beneath him before the wall opened under the weight of the tree like a zipper dragging downward.

CHAPTER SIX

WHEN Antonella came to, the first thing she noticed was the heavy weight pressing down on her. She could barely breathe. The second was the sharp smell of rain and the dark odor of wet wood. Wind whipped in gusts against her body, chilling where her dress was soaked through. She tried to push the weight off, but it shifted. Suddenly, she was looking up into Cristiano's dark face.

Her heart turned over at the sight of blood trickling down his cheek.

"You are not hurt?" he said before she could manage to speak.

"I-I don't think so. But I can't breathe," she rasped.

He shifted to the side and Antonella drew in a deep breath, nearly coughing with the relief of feeling her lungs expand. "What happened?"

Cristiano glanced up. Her gaze followed his and she gasped as she realized what she was seeing. A jagged piece of the roof was gone. And the wall. But that wasn't the most amazing thing. No, it was staring up at the rain-lashed sky through the branches of a tree that caused her insides to liquefy. The bulk of the tree had hit the bed, the branches splaying out crookedly in all directions.

Oh, God.

If he hadn't pulled her off there in time…

Only the mattress prevented the tree from falling to the floor and crushing them beneath the weight of the branches. As it was, they would have to crawl out from under the limbs that spread over them.

Antonella touched his face, flinching at the same time he did—and trying very hard to ignore the sizzle arcing through her at such simple skin on skin contact. "You are bleeding."

He swiped his fingers over his face, then probed upward, stopping just beneath his hairline. "It's not serious, just a scratch."

"It's a lot of blood."

"It's fine."

Antonella bit down on her lip to stop it trembling. Surely he would know if he were badly hurt. He'd said he'd served in the army, so he must have experience with this kind of thing. She had no choice but to trust that he did.

He lifted his shirt and wiped it across his face. "We'll have to crawl out of here. Can you manage it?"

"Yes."

He nodded once. "The going will be rough, but stay close."

Though Cristiano picked his way carefully, Antonella scraped her arms and legs more times than she could count. Shards of wood had splintered off from the main tree, and crumbled terracotta and stucco littered the area, making the process slow and painful.

She suppressed her cries of pain. It would do no good and she was determined to get out from under this tree before the storm did something worse. The wind swirled through the collapsed wall, whipping her wet hair into her face and making it hard to see anything in front of her. Rain pelted her, chilling her heated skin.

Fortunately, it was still light outside, because if it'd been dark, she didn't see how they could have made it. How would they know where to go? She'd stupidly left the master bedroom without a flashlight or a candle. She'd made her way to this bedroom in the meager light coming from the kitchen, the only room without shutters. Cristiano had a flashlight when he'd arrived, but he'd lost it, probably during the struggle with her.

It was all her fault.

They'd nearly died because of her, because of her wild emotions and stupid phobias.

Around her, the wood creaked ominously. Leaves rustled and the branches bit and scratched her tender skin. After what seemed like an hour, Cristiano turned back to look at her and she realized he'd made it through and was now holding the last of the branches up for her.

Antonella slipped beneath them and resisted the urge to collapse on the floor. Cristiano didn't give her the chance anyway. He stood and offered her a hand. When she took it, he pulled her to her feet. Pain shot through muscles cramped from crawling across the hard floor, but still she didn't cry out. She'd learned long ago not to show pain.

Pain equaled vulnerability.

And vulnerability to a man, in her experience, was like blood to a shark.

"Hold onto my shirt," he ordered. She obediently grabbed a handful, and then they were moving again. A few moments later, they reached the master bedroom. Compared to where they'd just been, it was so peaceful. The white sheets on the bed glowed in the candlelight, making the bed seem even larger than it was. Antonella wanted to collapse on it, fall asleep, and pray this was a nightmare and she would wake up in her room at home in Monteverde. Dante and Isabel would laugh when she told them at the breakfast table about her strange dream.

"Come into the bathroom," Cristiano said, grabbing the first aid kit he'd brought into the room earlier, "and we will clean these cuts."

For the first time, she noticed that he too was scraped and bloody. When he turned, she stifled a gasp. "Cristiano, your back!"

She hadn't been able to see him well when they were in the darkened hall, but his T-shirt was torn open over his shoulders and a gash spread across their width.

He glanced at her. "I know. You'll have to tend it for me."

In the bathroom, light from three skylights shafted down and lit the area well enough they didn't need a candle. Cristiano took a towel from a stack on a bamboo shelf and dipped it into the water in the sink. After he'd wrung it out, he handed it to her.

"Wipe away the blood and dirt," he said, then retrieved another towel for himself. He stripped out of his shirt while she worked on her arms and legs.

Several of the cuts welled up again and she spent more time pressing the towel hard against them in succession, trying to stop the bleeding. No cut was very deep, thankfully. She would certainly be bruised, though, where Cristiano had slammed her to the floor.

"When you've finished, spray some of this on," he said, pushing a bottle of antiseptic toward her. "I'm afraid it will sting, however."

"I've cut myself before. I'll survive a few stings."

When she sprayed the first cut, she thought she would scream. Sharp pain lanced through her, diminishing after a few moments. She repeated the process again and again, biting her lip and working quickly.

Cristiano was waiting with bandages. She had three cuts that needed taping up—one on her left arm and one on each knee. "I can do it," she said when he started to rip at the adhesive strip.

He was standing so close, his naked chest gleaming with sweat and fresh blood. His hair was damp with rain, and a smear of dirt crossed beneath his right eye. He'd wiped the blood from his face, but had missed the dirt. Even dirty and somewhat disheveled, he made her heart thud.

He didn't say anything, simply handed her the strip and let her do it herself. She bandaged her arm first, then her knees. When she looked up, Cristiano was watching her, an odd expression on his face.

Or not so odd, in fact. When she'd bent to bandage her knees, he'd been able to see straight down her dress as the wrap gaped open. In spite of the lingering pain of her cuts, heat slipped through her veins, caused a fine sheen of sweat to rise on her skin. Moments ago, she'd been chilled and sober.

Now, she marveled at the languid warmth creeping along her nerve endings and pooling in her deepest recesses.

Cristiano's eyes clouded for a moment. When he reached for her, she thought her heart would stop. Would he kiss her? Would she let him? *Should* she?

His fingers brushed her ear as he tucked a stray lock of hair behind it. A shiver ran down her body.

"Why did you think I would hit you, Antonella?" he said softly.

She stiffened. She knew he couldn't miss it, though she tried to shrug it off. She even forced a "how silly" laugh. But it sounded fake—and he knew it as well as she.

She didn't want him to see how close to the truth he was, how it rattled her to have him know something so deep and personal. How many times would she fall apart in front of this man she was supposed to hate?

"I'm sorry," she finally said. "I'm just a bit stressed. I over-reacted."

But Cristiano would not be stopped. "Did one of your lovers hit you? Is that why you thought I would do so?"

"Of course not!"

It was embarrassing to think of how she'd reacted, starting from the moment he'd told her about the bomb that had killed his wife. She was usually so in control of herself. But she'd let emotion get the better of her this time. She'd been shocked, hurt, and angered by the brutal death of his wife and by his accusation that she didn't love anyone but herself.

And then…

Antonella swallowed. Oh, God, she'd thought when he'd come in so angry and insistent that he was about to get violent with her. He'd been reaching for her, trying to tell her they needed to go, and she'd been so blindly out of control of her emotions that she'd panicked.

"You need to turn around and let me see your back," she said firmly. She couldn't bear the scrutiny of his gaze, the probing that threatened to unveil all her secrets if she were too weak to resist. And she was beginning to tire of always keeping up her guard, beginning to worry she would indeed spill too much if he continued with his sympathetic act.

Because he didn't care about her. She had to remind herself of that. It was most assuredly an act. His wife had died at Monteverdian hands—he had no reason to care one whit for any Monteverdian, no matter the circumstances of their current situation or the fact he'd saved her life when he'd yanked her from the bed and covered her body with his own.

Why had he done it? He could have left her there, could have stayed where he was and not come for her in the first place. But he had. And she hated the feelings of guilt and gratitude swarming through her because of it.

She prayed he wouldn't push her any further, wouldn't demand answers or keep probing. She didn't think she could take much more of it.

Silently, eyes hot in his tanned face, he handed her a fresh towel and turned. Antonella breathed a mental sigh of relief. It was short-lived, however, when she got a better look at his back. Blood dripped from a long, clean gash that went from one shoulder blade to the other. The skin of his back was stained red as blood and sweat mingled, and she hastily wiped it away.

She had to stand on tiptoe to see the cut better. Carefully, she pressed the towel along the edges, cleaning away any dirt and debris. Blood welled up as soon as she moved to the next section.

"I think it will need to be bandaged."

"I suspected that," he said with a sigh.

"Does it hurt?"

"Like hell," he replied, startling her. Not because it hurt, but because he admitted it.

"I'm sorry, Cristiano," she said softly.

"I've had worse, *Principessa*."

She turned the bloody towel and continued cleaning the wound. "No, I mean for causing this."

"It is not your fault a tree fell."

"But if I'd stayed in the room with you—"

"It doesn't matter, Antonella. It happened. Let's deal with right now."

"Are you always so stoic?" She'd meant it as a gentle tease, yet he stiffened. A moment later, he relaxed again.

"I was not always, no."

She didn't ask what he meant. She didn't have to. He'd lost

his wife. It was a wound with the kind of pain that was worse than any other, she imagined. Did such a wound heal? Or did it scar forever? Would he ever love anyone again? Could he?

"I think I've just about got it now," she said, squeezing water over the wound for a final rinse and then mopping it up with a fresh towel. "I need to spray the antiseptic."

"Go ahead."

Antonella picked up the bottle and took a deep breath. "Are you ready?"

"Do it."

She sprayed the liquid over the wound, wincing as she did so. Cristiano didn't make a sound, though his fists clenched at his sides and his skin seemed to ripple from one long shudder.

"I think that'll do," she said, setting the bottle down again.

He dug in the first aid kit, came up with bandages, gauze and tape. "You'll need to wrap it tight."

She took the bandages from him. Another quick dab at the new blood, and then she placed the bandages over the wound and wrapped him with gauze. When it was done, she let out the breath she'd been holding.

He turned to her then. White gauze stretched across his chest, making him seem somehow more human and vulnerable than he had before. Where was the arrogant prince of last night? She had no doubt he was in there. No doubt she had to keep up her guard. Appearances were deceptive, were they not? She certainly knew that better than anyone.

"Are you okay?" he asked.

Antonella folded her arms over her chest. "Why wouldn't I be?"

He shrugged. "It's been a trying afternoon. And I'm fairly certain you are not accustomed to dressing wounds, *Principessa*."

She couldn't stop the bitter snort that escaped her. "You would be mistaken, then."

His brows drew together. "Do you volunteer in hospital?"

Antonella dropped her gaze. She started to tidy the items on the sink. "No. Forget I said it."

Now she felt even more inadequate. She'd never considered volunteering because she couldn't stand the pain and anguish in a hospital. Seeing others hurting made her hurt too. Yet another flaw, she supposed.

His hand closed over her wrist. She stilled, her heart pounding—and not from fear this time. He opened his hand, slid his fingers over hers. Then he trailed them up her arm.

"You are an interesting woman."

"I'm really not."

"But you are. You are a princess, a Romanelli, and though I believe you are quite spoiled, there is another side to you as well. A most puzzling side."

Antonella jerked free from his grip. "There is nothing puzzling about me, Cristiano. I am a spoiled princess, as you say. I've been around quite a bit, as you've repeatedly pointed out. I've seen things."

"In Milan or Rome perhaps? On the catwalk? Or maybe one of your Greek lovers dashed himself against the cliffs of Santorini when you threatened to leave him?"

"It was the Greek lover, of course," she replied, as flippantly as possible.

Before she knew what he was planning, he'd crowded her against the vanity. The granite pressed into her buttocks as she leaned back. Cristiano put a hand on either side of her, trapping her. The hard pressure of his body against hers was enough to make her weak with need.

Crazy.

"I find I have a need to know what it is that could drive a

man so insane," he said, his voice a deep purr in his chest. "Will you give me a taste, Antonella?"

"I-I…don't think…that…" She lost her power to speak as his head lowered. In spite of her inner voice telling her not to allow this under any circumstances, her eyes fluttered closed. His lips brushed hers. The contact jolted her so deeply that she gasped. He took the opening of her mouth as an invitation.

This time when his tongue slid along hers, she was prepared for it. And yet the feeling was every bit as disconcerting as last night on the yacht. She answered him with a stroke of her own.

Thrilled to the growl in his throat as he deepened the kiss.

She wasn't even aware of her arms moving, but suddenly she had them wrapped around his neck. She'd kissed men before, certainly, but never had she wanted *more* the way she wanted more of Cristiano. My God, he smelled delicious, all man and sweat and blood and spice. The combination was strangely arousing.

The kiss slid into the danger zone much faster than she could have ever expected. Cristiano's mouth was ravenous— and, shockingly, so was hers. Was it because they'd just survived death?

She wasn't certain. And she didn't seem to care. Cristiano's mouth was magical, his kiss the absolute center of her gravity at the moment. If she were to let go of him, would she float away into space?

It certainly felt possible.

Her arms tightened around his neck, her head tilting back so he could gain better access. A moan escaped her as his hands slid up her sides, his palms skimming along the outer curves of her breasts. Would he touch her? How would she react? Part of her was begging for him to touch her—and part was telling her that she had to stop this immediately.

She could not lose her virginity to the Monterossan Crown

Prince! It was unthinkable. The humiliation of giving herself to a man who hated her would be devastating.

Cristiano's palms slid back down her body. Then he gripped her hips and lifted her onto the vanity without breaking the kiss. His hands were hot and smooth on her knees as he parted them. Then he pulled her forward, her dress sliding up her thighs as her legs widened around him. When their bodies connected in that most intimate of places, the shudder that went through her was mirrored in him. The only thing separating them was a bit of cloth.

So many sensations careened through her: the hard ridge of his groin pushing against the softness of hers; the sparks of desire zinging into her nerve endings; the delicious pressure building inside her, demanding release.

And more.

The urge to *know* what happened next, to feel that glorious oneness that she'd heard so much about. To feel it with this man in particular.

The kiss hadn't stopped for even a moment. If anything, it intensified—

And then his hands were on her bare skin. His thumbs brushed the insides of her thighs, the elastic edge of her panties. Any second he would be beneath the thin barrier of silk and lace, his fingers touching her where no man had ever touched her before.

It scared her. The alarm bells clanging distantly in her head suddenly got far, far louder. This was going too far, too fast. No way could she have sex with this man.

And on a bathroom vanity? Did people even do that?

Oh, God, of course they did. She suddenly had an image burned into her head of Cristiano's nude body, of her naked and willing, him stepping between her legs like this, pushing into her…

She had to bite back a moan.

It would hurt the first time. She knew that. But after? Would it be as magical as she believed? As incredible as the novels she'd read? As amazing as she'd heard other women say?

She'd never wanted to find out.

Until now.

But it was out of the question. She had to stop him before it was too late.

"Cristiano, no," she gasped as his mouth left hers, as his lips trailed over her jaw and down her neck. His thumb slipped beneath her panties, brushed over the most private part of her.

"Please stop," she gasped again, gripping his wrists. Squeezing to get his attention.

And he stopped. Backed away, confusion clear on his handsome features.

"I can't," she said, knowing how inadequate it sounded but unable to explain. How could she ever say everything she would need to say in order to make him understand? "I can't."

Frustration crossed his face. And, surprisingly, resignation. How many men had tried to convince her, after one kiss, that she should allow them into her bed? None had ever simply given up.

But Cristiano backed away, removing the delicious pressure of his body. She wanted to weep with the loss. And yet she was relieved too. It was wrong to want him. And futile.

"Because I am Monterossan, of course."

Her throat was tight. "No, not because of that."

He raked a hand through his hair. She could still see the firm ridge of his arousal beneath his shorts. "Then why, Antonella? I know when a woman wants me. And you do. As much as I want you, God help me."

God help me.

Her heart ached as she hopped off the vanity and tugged her dress back down. "Maybe that is why, Cristiano."

"Because you want me, you will deny me?" Fury took the place of resignation.

"No, not because of that. Because you despise me—and you despise yourself for wanting me anyway."

His eyes glittered hot. "I am a man. I don't hate myself for wanting a beautiful woman."

She swallowed the lump in her throat. "Maybe not, but you hate *me*. I am Monteverdian—and Monteverde killed your wife."

Monteverde killed your wife.

Cristiano stared after her. As soon as she'd said it, she'd turned and hurried away. Left him standing here, contemplating her words.

The truth in them. Or nearly the truth, anyway. An enemy attack may have been the cause, but *he* had killed his wife. Killed her by marrying her. If he'd been honest with Julianne—about his feelings, his history and duty to the throne, the depth of conflict between Monteverde and Monterosso—would she have taken the risk?

It was a question he would never have the answer to. A question that both tormented him and drove him.

As if his thoughts weren't complicated enough, Antonella was adding to the burden. That she'd seen deeply enough into him to recognize his turmoil was not at all what he'd expected. *She* was not what he expected, if he were honest with himself. In spite of his best efforts to believe otherwise, his view of her was being forced into new parameters.

And he didn't like it.

Dio santo, his back still stung, he was in a constant state of arousal, and he was angry with himself. And with her.

She was getting under his skin in ways he didn't like. It was partly sexual, of course. She was beautiful, sexy, and with an edge of innocence he found absolutely riveting. How did she do it, as worldly as she was? It was no wonder men flocked to her.

He'd replayed the last hour in his head until he could no longer view it objectively. She'd been frightened of him when he'd tried to force her from the room. Frightened in ways he could only attribute to some trauma in her life.

But what? Who had hurt her?

Or was it an act? Was anyone truly capable of that level of deception?

If she was, she'd nearly gotten them both killed for it.

He simply didn't know what the truth was. And what he needed to do was shove all the doubt and thought and even the sexual attraction down deep where it wouldn't affect him. He didn't need to know Antonella, didn't need to understand why she'd looked so terrified, didn't need to know why she'd cried her eyes out in the taxi, or why she spoke to her brother every day and seemed surprised that he did not speak with his family as frequently.

None of that made her good. None of it excused her from the crimes of her family and their despotic grip on their nation. She was too intelligent to be a pawn.

Which meant she had to know what kind of things happened to those who'd dared oppose the Romanellis' rule. Journalists, engineers, scientists, teachers—those who'd spoken out during her father's reign were silenced. Some had fled to Monterosso and Montebianco. Others were thrown into Monteverdian jails, never to be heard from again.

Cristiano had no doubt the same thing was still happening. What incentive did King Dante have to allow his people their freedom? He'd deposed his own father, yet the military dictatorship continued. He'd made no moves to pull back his troops from the border, sent no peace overtures aside from agreeing to the ceasefire.

It would simply be more of the same if Cristiano failed in his mission here. More bombs, more guns, more tanks, more lives lost.

Cristiano threw the towels into a nearby hamper, put the supplies back into the first aid kit, and turned to go. A glimpse in the mirror stopped him. He looked cold, ruthless.

Exactly what he needed to be.

CHAPTER SEVEN

ANTONELLA dug a jersey dress from one of her suitcases. She frowned as she held up the jade-green garment. The fabric was soft and she knew she would be comfortable, but it was a little too fancy for a hurricane.

Unfortunately, it was the most casual thing she had. She went into the adjoining dressing room and locked the door before stripping out of her wet, torn dress. Tiny cuts lay across her pale skin like the tracks of birds' feet, remembrances of getting a little too up close and personal with Mother Nature.

After she slipped into the clean dress, she balled up the torn one and unlocked the door to the bedroom. She tossed the dress into her suitcase and dug out a comb. Her hair was a rat's nest of tangles. She'd had it pulled back in a ponytail, but that hadn't mattered in the gale force winds they'd endured while crawling from beneath that tree.

Oh, God.

Without volition, her hand stilled in the act of lifting the comb; that was when she realized she was shaking. She'd known it was close, but it wasn't until she'd had to clean and bandage Cristiano's back that she'd realized *how* close they'd come to dying.

It was a wonder they hadn't been impaled.

Surely she could be forgiven for losing herself in his kiss in the aftermath of such an event? Just as he could. She had to admit that if he'd been any other man, and she'd felt this kind of exhilaration when he touched her, she'd have thrown caution to the wind and let him do what he'd wanted.

Because there might not be a tomorrow.

Antonella shuddered. There *would* be a tomorrow. There would.

But if there wasn't?

She gave her head a little shake. It didn't matter. He was still Cristiano di Savaré, the Crown Prince of Monterosso. He was not, and never would be, her knight in shining armor. She wouldn't even be so attracted to him if they weren't stuck here together, if he weren't the absolute last man on the planet she should ever desire.

It was her perverse nature at work. The side of her that reveled in attracting trouble. Wasn't it her fault when her father got mad at her?

It's not your fault, Ella, Dante said after their father had sent them away without any food for being late to the dinner table once many years ago. But it had been her fault. She'd dawdled in the bath when she'd known she shouldn't. And she'd brought down her father's rage on them both. They'd been given nothing to eat for twenty-four hours.

Whenever she remembered an episode with her father, always there was something she'd done before he got violent. The last time was on the day he'd arrested the Crown Princess of Montebianco. Antonella had dared to tell him she had no intention of attending his event that night. She hadn't wanted to be humiliated when Nico Cavelli showed up with his new wife. And she hadn't wanted to see Lily Cavelli, to be forced to speak with her, especially not after she'd fallen apart in front of the woman in a Parisian salon only a couple of weeks before. Her father had been furious when Nico broke the engagement with her and married Lily; she'd mistakenly thought he would understand why she wouldn't want to be there.

But he'd backhanded her across the face, told her she would be present at the event and be dressed to kill. And then he'd threatened Bruno if she dared defy him. Bruno, her sweet little dog who loved her so purely.

She'd gone to the party, of course, in spite of the bruising on her cheek and under her eye.

And it had turned out to be one of the best things she'd ever done, because she'd gotten to know Lily. In the months that followed, she had become friends with the other princess. Aside from Dante, Lily Cavelli was her only friend in the world.

What she wouldn't give to speak with Lily right now! She should have talked Dante into going to Montebianco in the first place, and to hell with Vega Steel. But he was proud and stubborn and he wanted them to save their country with their own sweat and blood. He'd truly believed they could, and she'd believed because he'd wanted her to.

She heard the door to the bathroom open, but she didn't look up. Her heart rate bumped up a couple of degrees. She was beginning to get used to it, though she didn't like that she couldn't control her reaction to him.

In her periphery, she saw him cross to the bedroom door. He was still shirtless, the white gauze standing out in the darkened room like a beacon. He pulled the door open. A gust of wind blew into the room, and guttered the candle. Cristiano closed the door again and the candle flared back to life.

"Is it bad?" she asked, and then felt silly for doing so. Of course it was bad. There was a tree in the house, for heaven's sake.

"The storm is blowing a lot of rain our way. I think it will intensify over the next few hours." He retrieved another shirt from his bag, slipped it over his head.

"That door isn't going to hold, is it?" Antonella said.

"No, probably not."

"Shouldn't we go into the bathroom? Or the dressing room? At least it's another door between us and the storm."

He nodded. "*Si*. The dressing room is better. It is an interior room, and there are no skylights that could shatter in the night."

It didn't take long to gather their minimal supplies. Antonella tried not to think about how it would feel to be confined in such a small space with Cristiano for the next few hours. She would get through it, however. She simply had to remind herself it could be worse.

They could be impaled beneath that tree, for instance...

When she thought they had everything, Cristiano left the small room, returning with the blankets and pillows from the bed. Antonella accepted a pillow gratefully, putting it behind her and leaning back against the wall. She tucked her legs under her and bowed her head. Her eyes were heavy, but she couldn't succumb to sleep just yet. She was far too keyed up.

That kiss. It didn't matter how hard she tried to shove away the feelings, the images, she kept feeling his mouth on hers, his tongue stroking hers, his hands hard and smooth against her heated skin. She'd wanted him.

She still wanted him.

It was disconcerting as hell.

If she hadn't stopped him, where would they be now? Would they still be making love? Or would they be tangled together, sleeping?

She wished she'd never seen him naked, because it was simply too easy to imagine his body lying alongside hers. To imagine the smooth, tanned flesh, the ridges and knots of muscle, the flat, hard stomach that begged her to press her mouth against him, to explore him completely.

"What are you thinking, Antonella?"

Her head jerked up, her gaze colliding with his. Seeing her need mirrored there no longer surprised her.

"I was thinking how I wished I were at home in my own bed. With Bruno."

His gaze shuttered. "Bruno? This is one of your lovers?"

Antonella laughed. "Bruno is my dog. He is the light of my life and I miss him."

"You were thinking of your dog," he said, clearly not convinced. "This is not what I would have guessed."

"Then you don't know everything, do you?"

"Not everything, no. But the things I do know, I know quite well."

"And yet you can be mistaken, it seems." Except he hadn't been mistaken at all. But she wasn't about to admit it to him.

"What kind of dog?" he asked.

Antonella nearly breathed a sigh of relief. "Bruno is a Pomeranian. He's very cute."

Cristiano's mouth twisted, but she was relieved to see it was only mock disdain. "A girly dog. I should have known."

"And I suppose you have a great big pony of a dog, yes? The kind you can saddle up and let a child ride?"

Cristiano shifted his pillow and leaned back. "I have a cat, actually."

Antonella felt her jaw drop. She snapped it shut again. "A cat? Seriously?"

"Scarlett is quite probably bigger than your Bruno."

A giggle bubbled in her throat. "You have a cat named Scarlett?"

Now that was completely unexpected.

Cristiano answered her with a grin that made her heart turn over. "Scarlett O'Hara, because she is a self-centered Southern Belle." His smile faded by degrees. "She was my wife's. Julianne was from Georgia, and *Gone with the Wind* was her favorite movie."

"Oh." Antonella busied herself smoothing the fabric of her dress over her thigh. What was she supposed to say in reply? And why had he shared this now when he'd been so angry with her earlier? It forced her to see him as human, and she wasn't sure she liked that.

When she thought of him as a Monterossan, an enemy, she could fight her attraction to him. But when he was a man who'd lost his wife? A sexy man who seemed tender and caring? Who kept a cat named Scarlett O'Hara and knew she'd been named after the main character in his wife's favorite movie?

Madonna mia, it was too much.

"She's getting old now," he continued. "And she's very spoiled. I cannot seem to say no when she wants a treat."

The picture of this hard, ruthless man feeding a cat treats was mind-boggling. "She has you wrapped around her paw," she ventured.

"Yes."

His stoicism in the face of so much pain saddened her. She had to speak, even if he got angry with her. "I did not know about your wife," Antonella said, her heart tripping along faster now. "How she died, I mean. I know you may not believe me, but I wouldn't wish what happened upon anyone. I *am* sorry for your pain."

He closed his eyes. "Perhaps you are."

She waited for him to say something else. When he didn't, she prepared to lie down and try to get some sleep. The day was catching up with her and she just wanted to forget all the pain and trouble for a few hours. Maybe when she awoke, the storm would have abated and they could get out of here. It was a lot to hope, but hope was all she had left at the moment.

Her stomach rumbled loudly and she pressed her hand against her belly to muffle the sound.

Cristiano's eyes snapped open. "Why didn't you say you were hungry?"

"I didn't realize it until now." She truly hadn't. Besides, how was she supposed to be hungry when she'd been riding an emotional roller coaster since this morning? The emotion hadn't slowed, much less stopped. Hunger seemed minor in comparison.

Cristiano glanced at his watch. "It's been hours since breakfast. We need to eat, though we'll have to ration what we have." He handed her a box of crackers. "Open these while I uncork the wine."

"How long do you think we could be here?" she asked, homing in on his comment about rationing food.

"Hopefully not more than a day or two."

Antonella felt her breath catch. A day or two. Here. In this room. With Cristiano.

Heaven help her.

He finished uncorking the wine and poured them each a glass. Then he took a small knife and cut off a few slices of sausage. "Cheese?"

"I'll pass."

She watched Cristiano layer a neat dollop of the spray cheese over a slice of sausage on a cracker and pop it into his mouth. He didn't grimace, so perhaps it wasn't too bad after all.

They ate in silence, if you didn't count the wind and rain hammering the roof. Antonella sipped the wine, thankful that at least the island tycoon had a good supply, even if he had little else in the house. She wasn't much of a drinker, so it didn't take much to make her mellow.

And right now, she needed mellow.

"You never told me about Monteverde," Cristiano said a few minutes later. He sounded mildly interested, conversational—and yet there was an edge to him that hadn't been there a few moments ago. As if he'd made up his mind about something.

"There's not much to say. It sounds almost exactly like Monterosso."

"Yes, but Monterosso isn't on the edge of bankruptcy."

Antonella had to work not to choke on the swallow of wine she'd just taken. "I'm not sure where you hear these things," she replied carefully, "but we're moving forward now that Dante is King. Monteverde is fine."

"And did you support that? Dante deposing your father?"

"Yes," she said simply. What was the use in denying it? "My father was…unbalanced."

"I had heard of this. But what if it was simply an excuse for your brother to take the throne?"

"It wasn't." She picked up a cracker, nibbled a corner. "I was there, and I know what happened."

His eyes narrowed. "Interesting."

Anger began to uncoil itself in her belly at the tone of his voice. "Interesting? You have no idea, Cristiano. Do not presume to judge me or my brother for things you know nothing about."

"Then tell me."

She set the cracker down. She was no longer hungry, though whether it was because she'd had enough to eat or because of the sick feeling settling into the pit of her stomach over this conversation she couldn't say. "Why would I want to do that? It's my business, not yours."

"It could be my business."

She gaped at him. "How is this possible? You aren't Monteverdian, and you mean nothing to me—just as I mean nothing to you."

"I'm hurt," he said. "And after all we've been to each other."

Antonella set down her empty glass and leaned back again. "I don't want to play these games with you, Cristiano. I'm tired, I'm sore, and I just want to go home."

"But you were on a mission here. A mission you failed. Surely you aren't ready to give up so easily?"

Her heart thundered in her ears. Cristiano leaned over and poured more wine into her glass. She picked it up, only half aware of what she was doing. Sipped.

You failed.

"I'm sure you are mistaken. Yes, we wanted Vega Steel to invest in Monteverde." She shrugged. "We have a lot of ore, and it seemed quite natural. It would have been a good partnership. But there will be others."

"I think not," he said, one corner of his mouth curving in a knowing smirk.

Had she really felt sorry for him just a few minutes ago? It seemed impossible, incongruous with the man speaking to her now. This Cristiano elicited no sympathy in her soul.

"I think this was Monteverde's last chance," he continued.

The world threatened to cease spinning. "Last chance? You are deluded, *Your Highness*. This is only Monterossan wishful thinking."

"You can still save Monteverde, *Principessa*."

"You aren't listening to me. Monteverde doesn't need saving."

He leaned forward, eyes intense. "We both know it does. And I will give you a chance to do so."

Antonella ran her finger along the top of the glass to steady herself. Was he fishing for information? Or did he know the truth? She had to know if he was simply making wild guesses, or if he truly had a plan.

"*If* what you say were true—and I am not saying it is— what are you proposing? Will you tell Raúl you've changed your mind? That he should invest in Monteverde instead?"

"Monterosso will buy your ore."

In spite of the heat in the room, a chill washed over her. "We don't need to sell you our ore, Cristiano. We can sell it to anyone we choose."

"Except no one else wants it. Vega Steel will build in Monterosso, and while we have ore deposits of our own, yours are bigger. Between our mines, and the incentives I offered Raúl on behalf of the kingdom, Vega Steel can import materials from Europe or South America just as easily. We do not need your ore, but I am offering to buy it."

"You will build guns and tanks," she said.

He shook his head. "Vega Steel builds ships, Antonella. Ships, girders, and industrial products."

"They will build what you want them to build."

"It does not work that way. Raúl has contracts to fulfill. And Monterosso is not a dictatorship."

"Neither is Monteverde."

He frowned. "You know that is not true."

"My father is no longer King, Cristiano. Monteverde is not a dictatorship."

"Nevertheless." He poured more wine into his own glass. "You can save your country, Antonella. You have only to sell me the ore."

Her pulse was tripping into the danger zone. Her stomach threatened to upend everything she'd just put into it. She was trapped in this tiny room with him, and he was pressing her hard to admit truths she couldn't.

"The ore is not mine to sell, even if I were inclined to do so."

"The veins are on state property. Your brother is the King. It is in your ability to do this."

Was he insane? How did he expect her to talk Dante into such a thing, assuming she would ever agree it was for the best? It would be hard enough to convince him to seek help from Montebianco. But from Monterosso? Unthinkable. "I believe you are mistaken, Cristiano. Monteverde does not need to sell her ore to you."

His sneer was not encouraging. "Stop prevaricating, Antonella. We both know the truth. Monteverde is falling apart, and you have loans due that you cannot repay. Without this deal, you will fall into ruin."

"Then why not simply wait for it to happen? Monterosso can pick up the pieces," she said bitterly. "You will finally achieve all your aims."

"Stability," he said softly. "If Monteverde falls, there will be greater troubles in the region than you can imagine. Our enemies would pick Monteverde apart, and use the fragmentation to destabilize markets across the three nations. The war could spread with the chaos such events would inspire. I will not let this happen."

"If stability is so important, then why not loan us the money to make the payments?"

"What is in this for Monterosso? Nothing, except money we would never see repaid." He shook his head. "The ore, Antonella. It is the only way."

"What you say is impossible. Dante will never agree to it."

His gaze was sharp, as if he were scenting the air for weakness. She was very afraid he'd found it in her reaction. "He would if you convinced him it would work."

"It's impossible," she repeated. "Even if you are correct,

we cannot trust you. If we sold you the ore, we'd have no guarantees you wouldn't turn against us. You seek to claim Monteverde for your own."

His eyes glittered in the candlelight. A smile curled the corners of his mouth. Her breath caught. Why did he have to be so handsome? And so dangerous at the same time?

"You can trust me, Antonella. I would never turn against my own wife."

CHAPTER EIGHT

HER pretty pink mouth dropped open. Cristiano had to force himself not to lean forward and close it for her with a kiss.

"You cannot be serious!"

"Why not? It makes sense, does it not?" He leaned back against the wall and gave her a lazy look. He was so close to achieving his goals now. So close he could taste the triumph.

Her brows drew down as she studied him. It didn't surprise him she was suspicious. She was far stronger in spirit than he'd given her credit for when he'd first met her. Was it only yesterday? It seemed like weeks rather than hours.

Another woman would have fallen apart after nearly being crushed to death by a tree. But she'd endured, and she'd expertly taken care of his wound without a moment's hesitation or squeamishness. He was quickly learning not to be startled by anything she said or did.

"Which part makes sense, Cristiano?" she asked. "The part about selling you our ore, or the part where you think I could ever agree to marry you?"

He resisted the urge to scowl.

"Both. You sell us the ore to guarantee your loans, and I agree to marry you as a show of good faith. You and your brother cannot doubt my sincerity if I pledge to make you a di Savaré."

She snorted. Then she shook her head. "I could never do that to our people. They would see it as selling out to our enemies."

"Selling out? Or saving your country from a worse fate?"

"What is worse than subordination to Monterosso?"

"Ceasing to exist. Becoming a fragmented people owned and controlled by differing factions. Being consumed by civil war as your people turn against each other. No other nation will risk their assets to help you then."

Her grey eyes were huge in her face. A small cut over her cheekbone marred the perfection of her creamy skin. She seemed so young and vulnerable just now. Not at all the sophisticated and self-centered princess he'd counted on meeting when he'd flown to Canta Paradiso.

"You intend to gain control," she said. "I'm not quite sure how, but this is your aim."

"There is nothing in it for me." Guilt pricked him, and he shoved it down deep. He could not afford to feel remorse about this too. Lives would be saved. He had to focus on that fact. Once he paid Monteverde's creditors, it would establish who was in financial control to the world. Cristiano would make sure Monteverde was stripped of its weapons as part of the agreement. Without its ore, or the independent means to repay its loans, Monteverde would never again be sovereign.

Antonella tilted her chin up. Defiant to the end. "We still have options, Cristiano."

"Time is running out, *Principessa*. The loans are due in a week's time."

He could see the calculations taking place in her head. She was trying to decide if the storm would be finished by then, and how much time that would leave her to explore other options.

"Vega was your last hope, and he's gone. If you are thinking of approaching Montebianco, you should realize there is nothing they can do. They have agreed to sell Vega Steel their own mills, which will be run as a subsidiary. The incentive to do so was quite substantial, I understand."

Her expression hardened, but not before he glimpsed her despair. "So you have brought Montebianco along on your journey. I should have guessed as much."

"Perhaps you should have. It benefits both our nations to have Monteverde return to a free market system. There will be no more kidnapping of royal family members or attempts at blackmail."

Her eyes gleamed with unshed tears. "Blackmail," she snorted. "And what do you call this?"

"I will do whatever is necessary for an end to this madness. Monteverde cannot continue the way it has been. It's past time for change."

Antonella tossed her dark mane of hair. "Why are you even asking my opinion? My cooperation? Go to Dante and force him to agree with your scheme. See how far you get then."

Cristiano bit back a growl. "You will agree to do this, Antonella, or when the loans come due, I will make certain that Monteverde is destroyed forever."

Her breath caught. And then her brows drew down. Fury saturated her voice. "I thought you wanted stability. Or do you simply want revenge? Make up your mind, Cristiano."

He refused to acknowledge that she'd scored a hit. Yes, on some level he wanted to punish Monteverde for Julianne's death. Perhaps he would finally be free of this guilt once he had. But in punishing them, he would make the world better for them as well. Ironic. "Stability is preferable. But I will take my chances if you do not cooperate."

He knew she couldn't doubt he was serious; his tone was colder and more brutal than an Arctic winter. Part of him disliked being so remote and cruel. But a lasting peace was more important than her feelings. More important than his.

She remained very still, her grey eyes fixed on him—and then her chest heaved. Once, twice. A third time. He expected tears to flow at any moment. Prepared to deal with a tantrum.

She'd caught him off guard in the taxi. But not again. She would not manipulate him with her tears this time. He would not relent.

She wrenched her gaze away and pinched the bridge of her nose. Her chest continued to heave.

And then she looked at him once more. Speared him with a glare so full of hatred that he felt the icy blast down to his toes. Oddly, his admiration for her increased. And his desire.

"I will speak with Dante, but I cannot guarantee he will agree to any part of your plan. He may prefer annihilation to a devil's bargain with Monterosso."

Satisfaction settled over him like a warm blanket in winter. "I'm glad you see it my way."

"I don't, but you've given me no choice," she bit out. "Why didn't you save us both the trouble and simply tell me what you wanted hours ago?"

It was his turn to laugh in derision. "Would it have made any difference? Perhaps you would have fled into the storm instead of another room. We both know how that worked out." He shook his head. "No, I need you alive, Antonella, not running away like a spoiled child."

Her chin quivered, but still she did not cry. Amazing.

"Not all children who run are spoiled. Have you ever thought of that? Sometimes they run for self-preservation. Not that you would know anything about that, of course."

"I know about self-preservation, *Principessa*. I've sat in a bunker on the border while Monteverde lobbed shells at us. And I've rescued our soldiers from your torture chambers—"

"Stop," she hissed. "You chose to do those things. A child can't choose her parents."

Cristiano blinked. What the hell was she talking about? With a growl, she turned away from him and punched her pillow into a ball. Then she slid down onto her side and curled herself toward the wall.

He wanted to ask what she meant, wanted to probe and question until she spilled all her secrets to him.

But he would not. He'd gotten what he wanted. He was another step closer to victory now. Soon, Monteverde would belong to the di Savarés. It was what he'd wanted for the last four years, what he'd worked for.

So why wasn't he feeling triumphant? And why was he more interested in what she'd just said about children and their parents?

The scream that woke her was long and agonizing. So wrenching it made her throat hurt. Antonella bolted upright, but she couldn't see in the inky blackness surrounding her. It was hot, and darker than any night she'd ever experienced before.

Panic clawed at her, grabbed her around the throat; another scream pierced the blackness.

"Antonella!"

Hands settled on her, dragged her against a large, warm body. She fought, twisting and kicking, until something heavy settled over her legs, clamped her against the body that was so overwhelmingly strong and solid.

"Antonella," he hissed in her ear. "Wake up! You're safe here...you're safe."

Something in the voice pricked the bubble of her panic, deflated it—

And then she was crying, shaking, remembering.

She'd been dreaming. *Oh, God.*

"You're safe," he repeated, one hand stroking up her arm, back down again.

A trail of fire followed in his wake—and she just couldn't take the sensation right now. Not on top of the agony of her nightmare.

Her father, the lifeless gerbil, Bruno taking its place. Begging for her dog's life, her face bruised and bloody...

"It's okay, Cristiano," she forced out. "You can let me go. I'm fine."

She wasn't, but she couldn't let him keep touching her. He might want to soothe her, but he didn't care about her. He needed her as a pawn in his game, nothing more. He needed her alive and whole, but he didn't care if she was happy or sad or depressed or traumatized. Nothing mattered except his revenge.

Had she really agreed to marry him?

She hadn't actually said the words, but it was implicit in the bargain. Cristiano might intend to marry her in order to gain advantage, but she had no illusions about what a union between them would be like. There was no love, no hope. There was only suspicion and hate. It was a worse fate, in some respects, than a marriage to Raúl would have been.

"I'll light another candle," Cristiano said, his voice strangely disembodied as he let her go.

She took the opportunity to scoot away from him. "You don't have to. I'll be fine."

But she heard the flicker of a lighter a split second before she saw the flame. The metallic odor of sulfur and flint was followed by the waxy scent of a candle flaring. Cristiano's face was the first thing she saw.

Light spilled across his cheekbones, his nose, illuminated his eyes. Eyes fixed intently upon her.

"What were you dreaming about?" he asked.

She wrapped her arms around herself. "It's nothing I wish to share with you."

"Sometimes it helps," he said. "I know this from experience."

She shook her head, squeezing her eyes shut. "Stop pretending that you care, Cristiano. You don't, and I won't share the things that haunt me with you. It will only make it more difficult."

"How do you know it won't help to talk about it until you try?"

"If you're so into the idea, tell me about *your* life," she shot back. "Tell me what happened when your wife died."

She didn't miss the bleak look that crossed his face—and though she didn't wish to harm him, she wanted him to understand how it made her feel when he so casually suggested she talk about herself. Just because she hadn't lost someone she loved in so public and tragic a manner didn't mean she had less to grieve for than he did.

The tension in the small room was thick—and then he shrugged, and the tension dissipated.

"I wasn't myself," he said. "Not for a long time. I did things, said things. I hurt people, Antonella. I hurt them because I wouldn't let them help me."

She pictured him alone, raging, lashing out at everyone and everything. In spite of the heat, a shiver crept up her spine, made the hair on the back of her neck stand up.

"You must have loved her very much." She couldn't help but be curious. She wanted to know what it felt like to be loved so devotedly, how amazing it felt. She would never know that feeling, no matter what Lily had once said to her about the right man coming along when she least expected it.

There was no right man for her. She couldn't trust men, didn't believe any of them capable of loving her. She was damaged inside, emotionally, and that made her hard to love. Dante was the only man in the world who loved her, and that wasn't the same at all.

Cristiano flexed the fingers of one hand. That gesture might have made her recoil if he had been anyone else, but oddly enough she felt no sense of danger.

Suddenly, she felt as if she'd crossed a barrier she shouldn't. "I'm sorry, don't answer that. Forget I said anything."

He shrugged. "No, it's fine."

But he didn't say anything else.

Antonella cleared her throat. "How long were you together before…"

He seemed to understand what she meant without her finishing the question.

Once more, he shrugged. The movement was at odds with what he must be feeling, but perhaps it was his coping mechanism. She certainly knew about coping mechanisms.

"It was a whirlwind romance," he said. "We were together six months before we married. My father was not happy, you may imagine. She died a month later." He sighed. The sound was lonelier than she could have ever imagined a sigh could be. "There was nothing left of what had once been a vibrant, beautiful woman. Julianne's DNA was all we had left to identify her with. I buried a nearly empty casket."

She dropped her gaze to her clasped hands. He'd lost so much, had endured such pain. Because a Monteverdian bomb had exploded beneath a truck. It saddened her, pricked her with a guilt that she knew was not justified. She was Monteverdian, but she had not built the bomb. Nor did she believe it was the way to solve differences between nations.

Brutal, senseless violence.

Would he stop the violence? Was that why he'd pushed her

into agreeing to marry him? Did he truly believe a union between them could set an example for their countries?

Another thought occurred to her: why hadn't Dante done something to end the hostilities? She'd never considered it before. And it bothered her that she hadn't. But she'd trusted her brother implicitly, trusted that he knew what he was doing and that he was looking out for the best interests of Monteverde.

She still did.

And yet…

Why hadn't he done something, besides agree to a cease-fire, before now? If he had, would Cristiano be doing this? Would prosperity have followed on the heels of peace? Would she be here now, sheltering from the storm with an enemy prince and learning things about him that made her want to put her arms around him and hold him tight?

"My mother died when I was four," she said into the taut silence. "I know it's not the same thing, but her death left a hole that has never been filled. I empathize, Cristiano, even if I do not share the same experience."

His gaze sharpened. "And you still dream of this all these years later? Or is it something else that disturbs your sleep?"

She twisted her fingers into the blanket on her lap. She was tired and sad and—*Madonna mia*, did it matter if she told him? Would it really help? She wouldn't tell him everything—she could never share that with anyone—but could she at least give him a version of events that would make him understand her better? Was it worth the effort?

She took a deep breath, let it out again in a sigh. He'd just shared something very personal and devastating with her. She could give him something in return.

"My father grew violent after my mother's death. He became a stranger to Dante and me. We did our best to avoid him, but it wasn't always enough."

"He is the one who hit you." It wasn't a question, and she didn't look up. She simply nodded. He swore.

"He was ill," she explained. "I knew this. I should have been a better daughter—"

The swearing increased in volume and intensity, cutting her off mid-sentence. Hot fury crackled in the air between them.

Yet she wasn't afraid. Strangely, she wasn't frightened of his anger. It was…liberating to feel this way. She'd never experienced a man's fury without feeling the urge to flee.

Until now.

"That's ridiculous," he finally said, his voice roughened as if it had been scraped over sandpaper. "Children are not to blame for abuse. Not ever."

"No, but I knew I shouldn't do things to anger him. And I did them anyway sometimes."

"You were a child," he said fiercely. "It's not up to you to bear the responsibility for what happened. Your father is to blame, not you."

She believed him, and yet there was always that niggling doubt. If she'd tried harder, been better—

No. She had to stop thinking like that. Dante had always told her it was wrong. And now Cristiano. Why couldn't she accept that perhaps some things were out of her control? That she couldn't change the outcome simply by acting differently?

She swiped her fingers beneath her eyes, unsurprised to feel moisture. But at least they were controlled tears this time. She didn't feel on the verge of sobbing or falling apart.

"What time is it?" she asked, too emotionally drained to continue this line of conversation. And tired. She was still so tired.

He picked up the watch he'd removed and set aside. "Three in the morning."

No wonder her eyes felt so gritty. She shifted—and her body fought back with aches and pains she hadn't realized she possessed when she'd been struggling with Cristiano in her sleep.

He scraped a hand through his hair, yawned. Then he pushed to his feet. "I need to take the radio into another room to see if I can hear the weather report. The signal will be too degraded in here."

A sharp sense of loneliness stabbed her. Surprised her with its force. She didn't want him to leave her alone, and she didn't want to analyze why in any depth. It was a reaction based on their earlier experience with the tree. Had to be.

"I'm coming with you," she said, climbing to her feet. Pins and needles stabbed into her cramped muscles, made her long to sink back down again until they went away. But she wouldn't. When she made up her mind to do a thing, she did it.

His grin was almost tender. "I'll be back, Antonella. You don't have to come with me."

Her heart thumped. "How do you know? What if another tree falls, or if the roof rips off and you get sucked up by the wind?"

"You think you can stop this? Or do you wish to be sucked up with me?"

She crossed her arms. "Don't be silly. I don't like you that much."

His laughter surprised her.

"What?" she demanded when he didn't tell her what was so funny.

"You just admitted you like me."

"I did not!"

He reached for her hand, lifted it to his mouth and pressed a kiss against her skin. Shivers radiated along her nerve endings, through her bones. Rooted her to the spot and made her want so much more.

"You like me," he said. "You can't help yourself. Now, let's go see if we get swept away or if we can learn what the storm is up to." He handed her the candle. "Try not to let it go out. The wind will likely be strong in the house now."

Antonella followed on his heels, shielding the light with one hand. But her mind was working overtime as she concentrated on her task. The truth was more surprising than she'd have ever believed possible.

She did like him, in spite of everything. But the most frightening part of all? With the exception of her brother, she liked Cristiano di Savaré more than any man she'd ever known.

CHAPTER NINE

THE weather report, what they could hear of it, hadn't been good. The storm had strengthened, and the eye wall wasn't expected for another few hours. The rain and wind were torrential. She didn't need to see it to know. The sound was devastating. Though the master bedroom door hadn't blown open—likely because they'd shoved a dresser against it—she could feel the angry power on the other side.

For the first time, she began to think they might not live through this. She'd believed him thus far, believed his certainty and confidence in the face of danger, but her mind threw scenarios at her that had the two of them crushed beneath walls, washed out to sea, drowned, or even impaled by whirling storm debris.

Antonella shivered in spite of the heat in the dressing room. Across from her, Cristiano appeared to doze as he leaned back against the wall. She'd told him he could snuff the candle, but he'd said they had plenty.

She knew he did it for her. Did it so she wouldn't be scared or have another nightmare.

She couldn't tell him that simply falling asleep could bring another nightmare. It had been months since she'd felt too vulnerable to her wild emotions. Once her father had been put in prison, where he belonged, she'd slept better. Had fewer bad dreams. She'd become more confident in who she was, though she also knew it was merely a façade. Deep down, she was still the scared little girl cowering from her daddy's wrath.

Cristiano's eyes drifted open. She could tell the instant that he remembered where he was and who he was with. Awareness snapped into his gaze like a spark from tinder.

"You are not sleeping."

She shook her head. Her eyes felt as if someone had propped them open with toothpicks, yet she couldn't relax enough to sleep. Were they really about to die? There were so many things she'd never done, so many things she'd never said that she should have. Why had she never appreciated how precious each moment was? She'd spent so much time hiding, cowering, burying her feelings deep.

Even now. Shouldn't she be focused on living instead of worrying about dying?

"I can see the wheels turning, Antonella. What are you thinking?" His voice was deep and rough with sleep. Sexy. It stroked over her nerves like the lightest touch of a feather.

"Nothing important," she said. "I think quite a lot, actually. Sorry to say I'm not as empty-headed as you might have hoped."

His brows drew down as he studied her. "I never said you were empty-headed, *Principessa*. What's brought this on?"

How could he see past her veneer of scorn so quickly? How could he know in so few words there was something bothering her? It was simply another thing that made her feel more drawn to him than she should.

And more resentful.

"I'm just tired, Cristiano," she said on a sigh. "And I can't sleep."

"Did you lie down?"

"No."

"Maybe you should try that."

"It doesn't matter. It won't work." She chewed on her bottom lip. Cristiano's gaze dropped to her mouth.

Heat rolled in her stomach. Intense, overpowering. "Don't look at me like that," she managed.

"Like what?"

He was so incredibly male, so sexual. He aroused her senses simply by being in the same room. Looking like a bronze-muscled god.

"Like you want to kiss me."

His laughter was soft, but it sent a shiver through her nonetheless. "I want to do more than kiss you, Antonella. Much more."

She held up a hand. "I don't want to know. Please don't tell me."

"It seems like the perfect opportunity to pass some time. Don't we need to know if we suit?"

She blinked. "Suit?"

"Sexually."

The word sizzled into her brain. "I didn't realize I had to pass a test. Is this how you usually get women into bed? By asking them to take your test?"

She couldn't help the indignation that crept into her tone.

He grinned, disarming her once more. "I don't usually have to ask. And it's not a test; it's simply an experiment to see if we want more."

"More," she repeated.

"Of each other."

Her breath caught. Oh, yes, she could see wanting more. Wanting more of *him*. Never getting enough.

"That's ridiculous."

One eyebrow lifted. "Is it? Haven't you ever slept with a man who did nothing for you? Who didn't know his way around the territory, so to speak?"

Her breath strangled in her chest. "No."

"That's it? Just 'no'? How fortunate you have been, *cara*."

"I don't know what else you expect me to say." There was no way she could explain without also explaining she'd never slept with anyone in her life.

Something crashed against the wall outside. Antonella jumped, her heart in her throat as the aftershocks reverberated through the small dressing room. A second later, a gust of air blew under the door and the candle guttered. Cristiano grabbed a blanket and wedged it against the bottom edge, swearing. The candle flared to life again.

"The bedroom door has blown open, hasn't it?" she asked. The dresser must have sailed into the opposite wall. She could only spare a momentary pang for the Colonial French chest of drawers that had surely been smashed to a thousand bits by now.

"*Si*."

But maybe it was worse. Maybe the wall had blown down. The grave look on his face made her heart pound. "Will we make it, Cristiano?"

His gaze swung toward her. He looked troubled. But his answer wasn't what she expected. "I believe we will, yes."

She'd thought he would try to prepare her for the worst—or tell her how silly she was, and of course it would be okay. She respected that he did neither, though she still thought the outlook was more critical than he let on. The storm was sweeping closer every moment. The power of it was staggering. Her hope was minimal.

"I wish I'd spoken with Dante," she said. Poor Dante. He would have to face the crisis alone now.

Cristiano reached for her, pulled her over and tucked her against his side. She did not resist. In this moment, it was nice to have companionship. To feel that someone cared. She knew he didn't, but at least he made her believe it for a moment.

"We'll make it, Antonella," he said, his breath hot against her ear. Did his lips touch her hair? She wasn't certain, and yet her body flamed at the thought.

Madonna mia, not now!

"You can't be sure," she said, drawing in a shaky breath. "But I won't break down, Cristiano. I know how to be strong in the face of danger. You can count on that."

"*Dio santo*," he breathed. "I'm sorry I ever thought you were shallow."

She tilted her head back to look up at him. In spite of everything that had happened between them, in spite of the anger and pain of being on opposite sides of a bloody war and the prospect of dying here together tonight, she smiled at him. Genuinely. He was more than she'd thought he was as well. Better. If they could come to this kind of understanding under these circumstances, what was possible for their people?

"No one is truly shallow, Cristiano. I believe everyone has a story. You only have to look deeply enough."

He slipped a hand into her hair, cupped her jaw, his thumb stroking her cheek. "What is your story, Antonella?"

"I've already told you more than I've told anyone else."

"I believe you have," he said. "But there's more, I'm certain."

She dropped her lashes, too startled by the intensity in his eyes to keep looking at him. He wanted her, she knew that. And she wanted him. But how could she when he wanted to steal her country?

She was weak, far too weak.

"A girl has to have *some* secrets."

His head dipped down and his lips touched hers. Softly, gently. There was no pressure, no urgency, just a sweet kiss that slayed her heart and left it wide open to him. Once more, she was aware of the fact she'd never felt this way with any other man. She'd never wanted one the way she wanted him.

Had never wanted to slip out of her clothes and feel her skin naked against his.

Had never wanted to open herself to him and feel the stunning beauty of his possession.

She wanted all this and more with Cristiano. What did it matter anymore? They would very probably not come out of this storm alive. He simply didn't want to tell her the truth of it.

This was her last chance to experience physical love between a man and a woman. It couldn't be wrong, not under these circumstances. She opened her mouth beneath his, touched her tongue to his bottom lip very delicately.

He responded with a groan. And then he kissed her again, more urgently this time. His mouth slanted over hers, his tongue demanding access. She willingly gave it to him.

So many feelings crashed through her.

Desire, of course.

Fear. Regret. Anticipation.

Of their own volition, her hands threaded into his hair, pulled him harder against her. His kiss shot up another notch, deepening, devouring.

She met him with equal intensity, shifting until she was practically on his lap, until the only thing supporting her was the strength of his arms around her. The kiss was spiraling out of control, but she didn't care. She only wanted more of this intoxicating feeling, this heat and fire that sizzled beneath her skin and made her think of things she'd never imagined.

Naked bodies entwined. Sweat and pleasure. Bliss.

But when he pressed her back against the carpet, panic assailed her. Part of her wanted to shove him away and run as fast as she could. She tried to withdraw into her shell, tried to view the events dispassionately from that deep, disconnected place within her—

And found she couldn't do it. Her usual refuge was denied. Anxiety spiked.

Something of her struggle must have communicated itself to Cristiano because he stopped kissing her, lifted his head to look down at her.

"What's wrong, Antonella?"

He sounded so tender, so concerned, and her heart careened wildly, skipping into her mental roadblocks, leaping against the constraints she placed. Her heart wanted to be free—and yet she knew it would never be free. Never free to love or be loved. Never free of the pain and anger of her past. Even if by some miracle they lived through this night, she would never be free.

Suddenly, it was very important to her that he understood she was innocent, that she'd never done this before. Because if they did move forward, if this was her first and last time, she wanted to know that the man she gave herself to believed in her.

"I—I don't know what to do."

He frowned. "You don't know whether or not to make love with me? It will be glorious, Antonella. Let yourself go—feel what we do to each other."

She closed her eyes, shook her head. "It's not that."

His fingers spread over her stomach, slid up to cup her breast. "Then what is it, *bellissima*?"

She dragged in a breath as his thumb brushed her nipple through the fabric. "I've never done this before," she blurted.

His thumb stilled its torturous track across her sensitive flesh. "Never done what?"

His voice was like a whip and she flinched away from it. He would never believe her. Never.

She pushed his hand away, struggled to move out from under the weight of his body where he half lay across her. "Forget it, Cristiano. It's just a bad idea. I'll sleep now."

He refused to let her go. His body pressed down on her, pinned her in place. And every wiggle of her hips against him only communicated to her the state of his interest in completing what she'd so foolishly begun.

"I don't want to forget it, Antonella. Explain to me why you do this. Why you are hot one minute and cold the next. Are you trying to punish me for wanting you? Do you enjoy these games? Because I grow weary of them."

She grew very still beneath him. Her eyes filled with angry tears as she looked up into his handsome, cold face. "I'm still a virgin," she forced out. "And I know you don't believe it, so please let me go."

"A virgin?" he repeated. "This is not possible."

There was a hint of self-doubt in his voice, but it did not cheer her.

She pushed at his chest. "Why not? Because you've *heard* about me, Cristiano? You know what they say about gossip, don't you?"

Cristiano watched the pink stain creep over her delicate features. Was she telling him the truth? Or was she so skilled at manipulation that she could stammer and call up a blush at will?

Dio santo.

He thought back to her reaction when he'd been naked, the way she'd seemed uncomfortable. The way she'd grown frightened earlier when he'd kissed her. She hadn't truly panicked until he'd hiked her dress up her thighs.

Looking into her expressive eyes now, seeing the hurt and anger and uncertainty there, he wanted to kick himself. They'd shared too much tonight to fall back on entrenched beliefs. He could no longer think of her as the shallow, greedy woman he had only yesterday.

She was innocent. In spite of everything, she was innocent.

She had every reason in the world to fear him, yet she'd trusted him enough to let him get close to her this way. She'd been trying to tell him she didn't know what she was supposed to do, not that she was uncertain of her decision.

The fact she'd chosen him, of all the men who had no doubt tried to bed her, staggered him. Humbled him. He did not deserve her trust.

"Antonella," he said. "I'm sorry."

Her eyes widened briefly. But then the cool princess was back. She was so good at hiding her feelings. Had she always been this way? The thought troubled him. She'd been abused and she'd learned to shield emotion as a way to cope. No one should ever experience what she had.

She looked away. "It's nothing. I am over it already. And I'm sorry to inconvenience you."

"Inconvenience me?" He laughed, a dry raspy sound. The irony of what he was about to do hurt more than he would have thought possible, given the circumstances. But he couldn't do this. He couldn't, in good conscience, accept the gift of her innocence when he never intended to marry her. When everything he did was for the sole purpose of gaining control of her nation and bending it to his will.

She deserved better. He threaded his fingers through hers, pressed a kiss to the back of her hand. Closed his eyes as her intoxicating scent stole to his nose. *Dio*, he should be nominated for sainthood after this.

"I cannot make love to you, Antonella."

* * *

Her heart was pounding so hard she thought she'd misheard him. But she hadn't. His face said it all. He had refused to make love to her.

Another man who'd rejected her, who'd seen that she was a damaged soul and refused to have anything more to do with her. Yes, he was the first man she'd ever wanted to make love with, but it was no different than her first fiancé driving off a cliff or her second rejecting her to marry another woman.

Men didn't want her. Not really. They wanted the idea of her, of her beauty and poise, but not *her*.

She closed her eyes, turned her head and pressed her cheek to the floor.

"Antonella," he said, his voice still raspy. Full of…regret? "You deserve better your first time. Better than a floor, better than a heated coupling brought on by desperation and the belief that our lives are in mortal danger. You deserve silk and roses, a man who cares for you—"

She snapped back to spear him with a glare. "You're forcing me to marry you. If not you, who? Who will make love to me the first time? You will allow me to choose a man, and then you will marry me regardless? I think not."

His brows drew together. He looked fierce. Possessive. Conflicted.

A little thrill shot through her.

"No. Of course I will be your first. But not here, not now."

Her breath caught. She'd heard the words, but this was the first time she truly registered them. "You really believe me?"

"I believe you."

In spite of her confusion and hurt, contentment washed over her. *He believed her*. "Thank you."

His index finger rubbed across her lower lip. Soft, sensual. Her body flamed in response.

"We will wait. We will do this right when it is time." He looked troubled, as if he knew there would not be another time. As if he knew they would die.

She refused to accept his decision. He believed her and he wanted her first time to be special. It was enough.

She caught his wrist, nipped his finger. Then she licked it. It was a far bolder move than she'd have ever imagined possible.

Desire flared in his eyes, scorching her. "Antonella," he grated.

"I want to do this. I want you."

His voice was strangled. "You are making a decision you would not otherwise make if not for the storm."

That he saw deeply enough into her to recognize that the hurricane affected her only made her desire him more. No man had ever known her so well. Not even Dante. How ironic that it was a Monterossan who seemed to understand her best.

"I know. But I don't want to die tonight without experiencing this."

"We aren't going to die, Antonella."

"You don't know that."

"I do. I promise you."

As if in defiance, a roar sounded outside the dressing room. Something exploded with a bang. A tattoo of rain beat harder on the roof, plinking the terracotta with a deafening staccato rhythm.

"Please, Cristiano. If tomorrow comes, we'll deal with it then."

"Antonella," he groaned, tilting his head back, eyes squeezed shut as if he were fighting himself. "You would regret it tomorrow, and you would hate me for it."

"You've forgotten that I already hate you," she said primly.

A smile curved one corner of his mouth. "*Dio*, yes. How could I have forgotten this?"

She lifted a shaky hand, threaded her fingers through his hair. His eyes glittered with heat and need. God, she loved the feel of his hair. Soft, silky. Black as a starless night.

"Kiss me, Cristiano. Pretend we're lying on silk sheets. Pretend that you care about me…"

CHAPTER TEN

SHE didn't think he would do it. He looked doubtful, even a bit bewildered at first. And then he lowered his head, brushed his lips across hers. Back and forth, so feather-light and sensual. She wanted to moan, wanted to clasp him to her and force him to kiss her the way he had earlier.

But she didn't. She waited, let him explore, let him do what he wanted.

"God help me," he said, "I cannot deny you. I should, but I cannot."

"I don't want you to."

"If you become scared," he whispered against her mouth, "or change your mind, tell me. Do not be afraid I will be angry. This is for you, Antonella. It should be everything you want. And if you don't want it, I will stop."

Her heart flooded with a warmth she hadn't felt before. A feeling of rightness and belonging. No matter what happened, this was the right moment with the right man.

"Thank you, Cristiano. Thank you for understanding."

His answer was another kiss, this time deeper and more powerful. Her nerves crackled beneath the sensual onslaught. Her body grew hot and damp. The soft spot between her thighs ached—absolutely ached with the anticipation and fear of what came next.

One hand trailed down her leg, slipped beneath her dress. His palm slid along her thigh, pulling her dress higher.

"Wait," she gasped.

When he pulled back and looked down at her, there was no anger in his expression. The relief she felt was tangible.

"Shouldn't we blow out the candle?"

His hand continued its path up her thigh. "Why would we want to do that, *cara mia*? I wish to see you."

She swallowed. "I…um…well…"

He kissed her softly. "Shh. You are beautiful, Antonella. Believe me, you are quite beautiful. My body aches, just looking at you like this."

He pushed himself upright, and she had a second of fear that he meant to stop, that she'd chased him away with her silliness about being nude with the lights on.

"I will strip for you, yes? If I am naked, perhaps you will have no objections about joining me."

Her pulse shot into a reckless rhythm. She could only watch as Cristiano smiled and pulled his shirt over his head. The white gauze contrasted with his dark skin, and she was shocked to realize that she wanted to press her mouth there, right there on that ridge of muscle below the bandage. She wanted to run her tongue over him as if he were an ice cream cone.

"I like the way you look at me, *cara*," he purred. And then he unsnapped his shorts and pushed them down his hips, along with his briefs. Only her second look at a man's penis up close and personal—and, oh, dear God, was she truly prepared for what was about to happen?

"Don't be frightened, Antonella," he said, dropping to the floor beside her again. He stretched out, propped himself on one elbow, and gently lifted her hand to his chest. "Touch me. Explore me if you wish. Or I will explore you if you are too shy."

She was shy—and yet she wanted to touch him. Her

fingers shook as she traced the hard ridges of his abdomen. His breath hissed inward when she dropped lower. Tentatively, she touched his erect penis.

"*Dio,*" he breathed.

"Does it hurt?"

"Most definitely."

She jerked her hand away from the hot, velvety length of him. "I'm sorry."

"You can touch me again, *cara*. It hurts in the best way possible, believe me."

She tried again, growing bolder when he closed his eyes and didn't watch. His skin was soft, hot, and yet this part of him was so rigid. She wrapped her fingers around him. What had she expected it to feel like?

She wasn't certain. The intake of his breath brought her attention upward. He hadn't opened his eyes, and he didn't appear to be in pain—

She squeezed him. Was rewarded with a groan. A moment later, he'd pushed her back again, fused his mouth to hers and kissed her until she lost her mind. Then he lifted away again and started to pull her dress up.

"This needs to come off, Antonella."

She didn't protest. Instead, she sat up and helped him pull the jade material over her head. Her hair fell in long waves around her, helped to cover the lacy aqua bra she'd chosen this morning. Her panties, while not especially sexy in any way, at least matched the bra in style and color.

Cristiano's gaze devoured her. Oddly enough, she didn't feel shy about it. The way he looked at her made her feel sexy, beautiful. Special.

Had he looked at his wife this way?

No. She couldn't think like that, couldn't allow herself to go there. He'd loved his wife. This was just sex. She knew it, she'd chosen it, and she could deal with it.

He reached up and gently swept her hair back, revealing her breasts. When she would have covered herself, he gave her that sinfully sexy smile of his. "You are everything a man could want, *cara*. Never doubt that."

She wanted to weep at the tenderness of his comment, but he gave her no chance as he eased her back on the carpet once more.

"And now I wish to show you how beautiful this can be," he said, his mouth tracing kisses along her shoulder, up her neck, until he captured her lips once more.

Her body was hot and cold all at once, her nerves singing and snapping with every stroke of his tongue against hers. And then he broke the kiss, slid his gorgeous mouth down her body. When he pushed one of the lacy cups aside to bare her breast, her breath squeezed tight in her chest.

"So lovely," he murmured before his mouth closed over her nipple.

Antonella's back arched as her breath left her in a shocked gasp. An unbelievably pleasurable gasp. She'd never known it could feel so good. She clutched his shoulders, her hands kneading his skin as his tongue teased first one nipple and then the other. Before she realized what he was doing, he unsnapped her bra and shoved it up and out of the way.

Pressing her breasts together, he spent what seemed like hours—but was in reality only minutes—sucking each nipple into a hard peak. Again and again until she thought she would explode from the exquisite pleasure.

"Cristiano," she gasped. "Please!"

And then he was pressing kisses to her belly, sliding down her body until—

Once more, she couldn't breathe. Was he really about to do what she imagined? She wasn't stupid; she knew the kinds of things people did when making love, but she hadn't considered this would happen to her.

He traced his tongue along her panty line. When he pressed a kiss over the silk, she couldn't stop the groan that escaped her.

"You like this?" he asked, his voice rough around the edges.

"I feel so strange," she replied. "Like I'm about to dissolve into a million pieces."

His chuckle was completely masculine. Supremely satisfied.

"Let's fix that, *cara mia*."

When he slipped her panties down her thighs, she didn't protest. He pulled them from her legs and tossed them aside. And then he was pushing her thighs apart, kneeling between them…

The first touch of his tongue against her slick flesh made her cry out. But he didn't stop there. He continued the sweet torture, his lips and tongue doing things she'd never imagined. Vaguely, she recognized she was panting.

Recognized that some feeling was gathering inside her, pressing into a tight, hard knot, compressing again into something so concentrated—

When the knot exploded, she was shocked. Stunned. Gasping. Her back arched as waves of sensation rolled through her limbs, sizzling hot. After it was over, she felt drained of all energy. Exhausted. Ready to sleep for a million years.

Until Cristiano began the sweet torture again.

Twice more she gasped his name into the candlelit air, her body shivering and melting and reforming in the aftermath of stunning climaxes.

"Do you still wish to go forward?" he asked a few moments later.

She opened her eyes to look at him. At his handsome face, his concerned expression. She had the feeling that if she said no, he would stop right now.

And he'd be in agony, she was certain. Because she would have been, had she not reached her peak three times already.

"Show me more, Cristiano."

"Grazie a Dio," he said. "With pleasure."

He stretched out beside her, used his fingers to stoke her passions again. She was no longer surprised at how quickly he was able to push her toward completion.

Just when she was ready to come for a fourth time, he stopped and retrieved a condom from a pocket in his suitcase. She tried not to imagine why he carried condoms with him. And yet he *was* irresistible to women, as she'd heard more than once. No doubt it was wise to always be prepared. But it took a little of the joy out of it for her, knowing this wasn't his first time and wasn't in any way special to him.

It was just sex.

And isn't that what you wanted?

It was. She had no right to get upset because this was a casual encounter to him.

"Antonella," he said, the sexy timbre of his voice stroking into her razor-sharp senses. "You are thinking too hard again."

She blinked up at him. How did he always know? "It's nothing."

"Do you want to stop?"

"No," she replied honestly. She really didn't. Her body, while satisfied, was still keyed up in a very elemental way that she knew would never be fully appeased until he was inside her.

He leaned forward and kissed her again. "I was hoping you would say that. But if you change your mind…"

"I won't," she said, winding her arms around his neck to kiss him back.

Very quickly, the heat and need fanned higher until all she wanted was him. The past didn't matter. The future wasn't a guarantee. Now, right now, was all they had.

"Cristiano, please..." Her body was achy, ready. She reached between them, grasped that hot, hard part of him she wanted.

He gasped. "*Cara*, you will undo me before we begin—"

"Then we need to begin."

Cristiano swore, but he rolled the condom into place in a quick, smooth motion. And then he settled between her thighs. The weight of him, the hot press of his skin against hers, the blunt tip of his manhood sliding into her wet heat—

It was so much to process, and yet she didn't want to miss a single moment of it in her rush to fulfillment. She closed her eyes, tried to feel everything at once.

"This will probably hurt."

"I know," she breathed. "It's okay."

"Look at me."

She did. Cristiano smiled at her, and she felt as if she'd suddenly swallowed the sun whole. It was both a frightening and exhilarating feeling.

"Thank you for trusting me," he said. "I hope you will not regret this moment."

"Kiss me..."

He did, so gently her heart turned inside out. A second later, he pushed forward, sliding into her so far that she knew she was no longer a virgin. The pain was less than she'd expected, but startling enough that she cried out. He drank in her cry, then lifted himself on his elbows and gazed down at her.

"You are okay?"

She tilted her hips, getting used to the size and feel of him. Sensation blazed through her with each small movement.

"I—" She swallowed, tried again. "It's amazing, Cristiano. I had no idea."

His laugh was rusty. "*Dio santo*, it is a crime. And yet I am thankful I am the first."

Slowly, he retreated—and then he slid forward again, filling her more fully than before. Her scalp tingled. Her toes. Everywhere, there was heat. Heat and awareness that she'd never known existed.

Yet he was so careful she wanted to scream. Innately, she knew she could take more. Wanted more. Antonella tilted her hips up to meet him and Cristiano growled low in his throat. The sound thrilled her.

He began to move faster, though he took his time to do so. She knew he was being careful with her, trying to make sure he didn't hurt her, and her heart soared with the knowledge.

Soon, he anchored an arm behind her back, tilted her hips even higher—and Antonella gasped. How could it possibly get any better?

"Yes, Antonella," Cristiano purred, his voice like a sizzling brand in her psyche, "like that. Move like that. *Dio*, yes."

"Kiss me again," she pleaded, surprised at how badly she wanted him to, and at how fast she was spiraling toward a culmination that she sensed would be bigger than the last.

Cristiano's lips fused with hers, his tongue mingling with hers. He tasted of sweat and of her—earthy, sensual, and so overwhelmingly male she wondered how she'd ever thought she'd been kissed before he'd first kissed her.

Her climax hit her with a force that stole her breath away. She wrenched her mouth from Cristiano's, shocked at the speed and intensity with which her release hit her. She'd had warning the last time, a gathering of tension into a tighter and tighter knot—yet this time, the tension imploded in a flash, rocketing outward again in a blinding burst of sensation that had her crying his name in wonder and surprise.

"Antonella, *mia bellisima Principessa*," he said between

wet kisses to her throat, her jaw, her lips. "You amaze me. So beautiful, so sensual."

She couldn't speak. It took too much effort just to breathe, to recover.

Cristiano's hips moved, and she realized he was still hard. Still ready. They weren't finished yet. The thought made her shiver in anticipation.

"Please," she whispered when she had the power of speech again. "Please…"

His gaze was raw—tormented?—but his eyes were suddenly hooded, as if he realized he'd shown too much emotion.

"Anything you desire, *cara mia*," he said. And then he began to move.

It didn't take long before she was gasping at the top of another peak. Cristiano's climax followed hard on the heels of her own as he gripped her hips and ground his body into her one last time.

Her name on his lips at the moment of his release was the sweetest thing she'd ever heard.

She'd thoroughly destroyed him. Cristiano lifted his head, once he had the energy, and gazed down at her. Her eyes were closed, and though a tear leaked from one corner, slipping down her silky skin into her hair, her half-smile of contentment told him she was not in pain.

He was still inside her, and more than anything he wanted to repeat what had just happened. But he couldn't. She *would* be sore, even if she was not at the moment.

Dio, a virgin. If his body didn't know the truth, his mind would insist it wasn't possible. She was hot and tight, and so naturally sensual it amazed him she'd not been with a man before.

Guilt snapped against the surface of his conscience. He'd had no right to take her like this. No matter she'd given herself willingly, she'd done so under false pretenses. Not only because she believed their lives in mortal danger, but also because she believed he truly meant to marry her.

It was wrong…

And yet nothing had ever felt so right—

No.

Guilt of a different kind speared him. Since the moment he'd awakened and looked into Antonella's frightened eyes earlier, he'd not thought of his dead wife once. He'd spent seven months with Julianne, married her, thought she was the woman he would fall in love with. How could he possibly forget her? She'd *died* because of him, because of who he was. Because he'd failed to protect her.

How could he lose himself so completely in the body of a Monteverdian princess?

He let his gaze slip down Antonella's form, over the perfect rounds of her breasts, the pink nipples so stiff and straight, the tiny waist, the apex of her thighs where he still joined his body to hers. A pleasurable shudder went through him.

He was just a man. How could any man look at this woman and not do as he'd done?

No excuse. He was a bad, bad man.

She must have felt him shudder because her eyes opened. She smiled and arched her back beneath him like a cat. One hand drifted up, smoothed over his jaw, tickled his ear before threading into his hair. "Thank you," she said.

Another pang of guilt stabbed into him. "For what, *cara mia*? The pleasure was all mine."

She yawned. "I could get very used to this."

"Yes, I imagine you could."

Her brows drew down at his tone, but she seemed to shrug it off easily enough. He cursed himself inwardly. What was wrong with him? She was a virgin—*was*—not a wanton woman with a whole platoon of lovers. She didn't deserve his sarcasm. She deserved far better. It wasn't fair to take his disgust with himself out on her.

"You deserved a bed," he told her. "Silk sheets, a bubble bath, champagne. You deserved to be treated like a princess."

She frowned. "In my experience, being a princess doesn't mean much when it comes to how I have been treated. I'm glad it happened this way."

Because he didn't want to think too deeply about her meaning, he focused on a red mark that marred her creamy skin where her neck and shoulder joined. And realized it hadn't been there earlier. "I have hurt you."

"What? No."

"Your skin. I'm sorry if I was too rough."

She touched the area in question. "It was nothing like that, Cristiano. Nothing at all." She yawned again, finished with a smile. "You were very patient with me."

Patient wasn't quite how he would have described it, but he was glad she thought so.

He rolled to the side, withdrawing from her body and gathering her against him. For tonight, he would hold her close. If they survived—and he expected they would—he would deal with his tangled feelings about this in the morning. He pulled the blanket over them, yawning.

"Can you sleep now?" he asked once he'd tucked it around her.

The only answer was a soft ladylike snore.

Antonella came awake slowly. Something was different. For one thing, her bed was hard. For another, there was someone else in it with her. Someone large and warm. A man.

Her eyes popped open. And then she remembered.

The dressing room was pitch-black, the candle having died

out presumably hours ago. She was lying on the carpeted floor, wedged up against Cristiano.

They were both naked.

Oh, God.

Images from a few hours ago played in her mind: Cristiano's body tangled with hers, his magnificence, his utter lack of shame in allowing her to explore him. His skill at knowing just what her body wanted and in delivering it so expertly.

The sound of his voice when he came.

She couldn't quite believe her own boldness at asking him to make love to her. She'd thought they would die, yet they were still alive. What was the storm doing now? She could hear the wind, but it didn't seem to be a deafening roar any longer.

She tried to ease away from Cristiano. Perhaps she could open the door a crack and peer out.

Muscles she hadn't known she possessed protested against the movement. Beside her, Cristiano stirred.

"Where are you going, Antonella?"

How did he wake so instantly? "I think the storm has lessened," she said.

He was silent for a long moment. "I believe you are right."

A second later, he was sliding away from her. The flick of a lighter, and then a candle flamed. Instinctively, she clutched the blanket to her breasts.

Cristiano's expression flooded her with heat. Sexy, sensual. Knowing. "I've seen it all, Antonella. It's too late."

"I know." But her cheeks heated anyway.

Cristiano pushed to his feet. His bronze body gleamed in the candlelight. He reminded her of a carved marble statue, he was so beautiful. He stepped to the door, then carefully slipped it open.

The candle flickered in the breeze coming from outside it.

"The wind seems to have lessened a bit, but I'll need to see if I can hear anything on the radio," he said as he closed the door and turned.

She dropped her gaze, afraid of what he might see in it if she kept looking at him. What was this hot, needy feeling uncoiling inside her? Desire, yes. But there was another emotion in the mix.

Companionship. She felt closer to this man than to any other person alive. It was a frightening feeling. Because he was still the enemy. In the cold light of day, he still wanted Monteverde's ore. And the fact she would give him anything, including her soul, if only he would make love to her again, terrified her.

How could she be so greedy? So self-centered?

"Antonella."

She looked up—because if she didn't, he would surely demand to know why. His eyes glittered diamond-hot.

"You are feeling regret?" he asked.

"No."

"Then what is wrong?"

How did he always, always know? It was unnerving.

She tossed her hair over her shoulder, tilted her chin up. "There is nothing wrong. I was simply hoping you would make love to me again."

He didn't say anything for a long moment. Her heart lodged in her throat. Perhaps she should have kept quiet, not been so bold—

"You will be the death of me," he said softly. "And I find I can think of no better way to die."

For the next two days they ate crackers, sausage and cheese from their meager stores, talked, made love, and listened to the weather. Antonella learned so many things about him in those two days—and she shared more of herself than she'd ever thought possible.

It was dangerous, and yet it felt right. They were isolated here, in their own little world, and each moment she kept wondering if it were their last, if the storm would finally claim them.

After their latest bout of lovemaking, her body ached—but in a pleasurable way. The soreness between her legs was simply a delicious reminder of all they'd done. She had no idea how many times he'd brought her to climax, but she was as worn out as if she'd run a marathon.

"I need to turn on the radio again," he murmured.

"Yes," she said as she collapsed against him.

He didn't move, however, and she was almost asleep in his arms when a noise buzzed in her ears. A different noise from the storm. A voice?

It sounded as if someone was shouting…

"Your Royal Highness! Prince Cristiano!"

Cristiano bolted upright. And then light flooded the dark dressing room, blinding her so that she had to throw an arm over her face.

"Your Royal Highness, praise God we've found you."

CHAPTER ELEVEN

EVERYTHING was different. From the moment when Cristiano's countryman had found them, her lover had been cool and businesslike. He'd ordered the man to wait for them outside, then assisted her from the dressing room after they'd thrown on their clothes and shoes. She'd wanted to go into the bathroom and freshen up, but he'd said it was too dangerous—in spite of the fact she'd been in there only hours ago.

Once they left the master bedroom area, Antonella realized the house was a worse disaster than she'd thought, with downed walls, a precariously teetering roof, and debris everywhere she looked. For the first time, she understood how much of a miracle it was that the room they'd sheltered in hadn't been destroyed as well.

Cristiano ushered her into the waiting Mercedes. One man stood at attention, holding the back door stiffly, while the one who'd come in to find them stowed their luggage in the trunk.

The wind blew her hair into her face. She brushed it back impatiently, her heart feeling heavier with each moment that passed. A light rain was falling now, nothing like the thunderous downpour of a couple of days ago. She turned back to look at the house again, but Cristiano's hand was firm at her back.

"Per piacere, Principessa."

She climbed into the car, he joined her, and then they were moving down the drive, away from the house where she'd given herself to this man.

Where she'd fallen for him.

Her heart tumbled into her stomach and she turned her head away, fixed her gaze on the passing landscape. *Madonna mia*, how had it come to this? How had she fallen for the Crown Prince of Monterosso?

It had happened so quickly—too quickly. What would Lily say? She would love to talk to her friend right now. She felt like such a fool in some ways. She'd lost her virginity and fallen in love with the man she'd given it to. How clichéd and naïve was that?

She had no idea when it had happened, but somewhere along the journey from hostile enemies to unabashed lovers, she'd lost her heart. Cristiano was a man of deep feelings and strong convictions. He'd shown her that a man could be a partner rather than someone to be viewed with suspicion and fear. Everything about the last few days had been a revelation to her.

And what about him? What were his feelings?

She had no idea; it disturbed her that she couldn't get a feel for what Cristiano was thinking. She knew he didn't love her, but she thought that after everything they'd gone through he must care at least a little.

Yet he'd been so detached from the moment the man he called Marco had arrived. As if he hadn't been buried inside her only minutes before that, as if he hadn't groaned her name and told her she was beautiful to him.

As if they hadn't shared a thing.

The car whisked them across the storm-torn island to the airport. Cristiano spoke to Marco about the damage. It saddened her to hear that eight people had lost their lives, and yet it was a miracle that more had not. Canta Paradiso was beaten but not defeated. Fortunately, the island would recover. Cristiano instructed his man to call and pledge money for its repair when communications were back up. She wished she could do the same, but it was quite impossible.

Bitterness lay like acid in her stomach as she thought of why she'd originally come here, of all she'd failed to do. Cristiano had promised to rescue Monteverde, but at what price? She still didn't know, though she very much feared the possibilities.

When they reached the airport, the plane was fueled and ready, the cowling having been flown in and replaced just this morning while Marco had searched the island for his prince. Cristiano guided her up the gangway. His touch in the small of her back was light, impersonal. She tried not to dwell on how sad that made her feel.

A flight attendant welcomed them aboard, her smile never wavering though Antonella knew she must look as if she'd just climbed out of bed. She tilted her chin up and found her inner princess. She would need all her strength to get through the next few hours.

The next few days.

Cristiano ushered her to a plush burgundy club chair. "You must be starved. I will order something to eat for us."

"I'd like to clean up first."

"We will be airborne in a moment. You can do so then."

He turned away and went over to speak with the attendant, then returned and buckled himself into the seat beside her. She watched his strong, lean hands, hoping he would reach out and clasp her hand when he finished.

But he did not. He simply folded them on his abdomen and closed his eyes.

Dismissing her.

Antonella bit down on her lip. What the hell was wrong with her? She knew how to do this, knew how to withdraw and pretend not to feel.

Yet she couldn't do it. Not with him.

He'd broken something inside her, made it too hard to hide from him. She loved him, and she felt like an exposed nerve around him. Every feeling assailing her now was agony.

Why had she let him into her heart? Why hadn't she been stronger? When it mattered the most, she'd failed miserably.

As soon as they were airborne, the food arrived. The meal was simple, though far less simple than what they'd eaten over the last few days. She started to rise without taking a bite, but Cristiano touched her wrist.

"Eat first. It will help."

Nothing would help, but she didn't say it. Instead, she sat back down and picked at the plate of salad, the fresh crusty rolls, and the grilled chicken breast.

"Why aren't you eating?" Cristiano asked a few minutes later. His plate was already clean.

Antonella shrugged. "I'm not that hungry."

He put a finger under her chin, tilted her face up to look at him.

Ridiculous how her heart thundered. How her body ached for him, though they'd been intimate only that morning. Ridiculous.

His eyes were hooded, unreadable. Did he feel it too? Or had he already relegated the last few days to memory?

"You would prefer to shower, yes?"

"Yes."

Cristiano waved over one of the flight attendants. "Please show Her Highness to the washroom."

As she stood, he picked up a newspaper and opened it,

dismissing her from his thoughts as easily as he'd polished off the meal.

Once she was alone in the bedroom, she stripped out of her clothing and rummaged through her luggage until she found something suitable. The dress was badly wrinkled, so she rang for the flight attendant and asked if it could be pressed.

"But of course, *Principessa*," the woman said. Her expression was blank, her smile pasted on. Her voice contained a hint of ice that did not surprise Antonella. She was a Monteverdian amongst them, and though their prince didn't seem concerned, the rest of them were no doubt wondering what she was doing here.

In the bathroom, her reflection in the mirror brought her up short. *Oh, dear God.*

She looked like a woman who'd spent the better part of the last three days making love to a man. Her lips were red and swollen from his kisses. Her eyes were still slumberous. Her hair was wild and spilled down her back and over her shoulders in tangled waves. There were marks on her skin where Cristiano's growing beard had scraped her while they were entwined, and of course there were scrapes and scratches from the tree.

The tree's damage faded in comparison, however, to the overt sensuality of the woman staring back at her. Everyone who had seen her since the rescue knew what she'd been doing. What *they* had been doing.

She swallowed a hysterical laugh. Finally, her slutty reputation was true. How ironic.

The hot water on her naked skin felt unbelievably good. She stood under the spray for a long time, hoping her tension would drain away. It did not. Her emotions were winding tighter and tighter the more she thought about the last few days with Cristiano, and about what the future held once she reached Monteverde. How would she ever explain herself to Dante?

When the answer didn't come, she turned off the water and dried herself. The dress was hanging on a hook, the peach silk as smooth and shiny as a glassy lake. She slipped into her underwear, then took the garment from the hanger.

As soon as she put it on, she knew something was wrong. Instead of hugging her curves, the fabric fell away with the slightest pressure. Great gaps appeared along the seams as the dress dissolved into a tissue of scraps.

Whoever had ironed the dress had also sliced all the seams.

Cristiano looked up as she approached. The frown he gave her told her that she wasn't doing a very good job of hiding her emotions.

"Is something wrong, *Principessa*?"

"Not at all," she said smoothly. "Why do you ask?"

In her initial anger, she'd thought about showing him the dress, demanding to know who had destroyed the garment, but she'd realized it would do no good. Cristiano would not take her side against his people. And none of the flight crew would confess to the crime, she was certain.

It was a sign. A sign she didn't belong. And she would never belong here, even if Cristiano married her.

She just wanted it behind her. She wanted to get to Paris and get on the first flight back to Monteverde. The thought of being parted from Cristiano made her ache, but it was the only way she would ever gain any perspective. Perhaps it wasn't really love she felt. Perhaps it was gratitude…or even Stockholm syndrome, though Cristiano had hardly been her captor.

They'd sheltered together during a storm, and barriers that should have never been crossed had been obliterated.

She would pay for the breach. Was already paying for it. She smoothed the cotton of her sundress, the least wrinkled one she could find in her luggage, and sank into the chair across from Cristiano.

"How long before we reach Paris?" she asked.

Cristiano's gaze dropped to her knee, slid down her bare calf, back up to her face. So much heat in that look. So much promise. Her body couldn't help but respond. She uncrossed and recrossed her legs the other way.

Cristiano eyes smoldered. "Uncomfortable?"

"Not at all."

A flight attendant interrupted them, setting an espresso in front of Cristiano. "*Principessa?*" she asked, indicating the cup.

Antonella smiled so wide her cheeks hurt. "*Grazie*, but no." And give someone a chance to spit in it?

When she'd gone, Cristiano lifted the cup and took a sip. "Ah, *Dio*, I missed this."

"You haven't answered me," Antonella said. "Do you know how long it will take to reach Paris?"

"I do know, yes. But we aren't going to Paris. We're going to Monterosso."

If she hadn't already been sitting, she would have collapsed. "Monterosso? But you promised to take me to Paris."

"That was before."

"Before what, Cristiano? Before the storm? Before you blackmailed me into marrying you? Or before you spent the last three days having sex with me on the floor?"

He finished the coffee, the only hint of strain the tic over his cheekbone. "Before I decided it would be better not to allow you out of my sight. You might think, because of what has happened between us, that our bargain no longer applies. I assure you this is not true. I still expect you to work to deliver the mineral rights into my control."

"Work to deliver…?" Pain ricocheted through her. He didn't care about her at all. He only cared about the mines, and about defeating Monteverde. It was a business deal to him. Had always been a business deal. She knew it, and yet she'd allowed herself to begin to believe it might mean more. That *she* might mean more.

Stupid, stupid, stupid. Would she never learn? Had a lifetime of craving her father's love and approval not taught her anything?

Cristiano's gaze was as hard and cold as it had been the first night she'd met him. "You might be tempted to think sentimentality will deter me, now that we have been…close."

"Close?" She stifled a bitter laugh. Oh, my, the joke was on her, was it not? "Yes, very close. But not close enough, apparently."

"Did you expect you could change my mind by giving me your virginity, Antonella? I admit this did not cross my mind in the heat of the moment, but I see now it is a possibility."

"Go to hell," she spat. How could he possibly look back on that first time and think she'd been manipulating him? It was mind-boggling. Hurtful.

And yet she should have anticipated it. How had she ever thought they could put the difference of who they were behind them?

Something flared in his expression, but before she could read it he turned to look out the window. Silence lay between them for several moments. Then he turned back. "I apologize for that," he said. "But it changes nothing. You will convince your brother this is best for Monteverde. Because it *is* best, Antonella. It's the only way to survive."

She crossed her arms and looked away from him. Her throat ached with unshed tears. Oddly enough, his apology hurt worse than the accusation had. Without it, she could convince herself he was evil, rotten, and undeserving of her love. But he'd dashed that hope by reverting to the objective and fair Cristiano she knew lay beneath the cold exterior.

"It wasn't the only way we could survive," she said softly. "But it's the only way we have left, thanks to you."

Cristiano refused to feel remorse. Yes, he'd spent several pleasurable days in her company, but that was over now. He had a goal, and it was within his reach. He would not lose the war simply because he'd thrown a battle or two. He had to focus on the bigger picture.

He'd known, the minute Marco had found them in the villa, it was over; he could not, in good conscience, continue to be her lover.

He hated to hurt her, but she would get over it in time. He would keep her close until he was certain he had the mines, and Monteverde, and then he would send her home. He couldn't drag her through the pretence of an engagement for a moment longer than necessary. Not now.

Sending her away as soon as possible was the best he could do for her.

Even if she hadn't been Monteverdian, he could never marry her. She made him feel things that confused and angered him. Protectiveness, pleasure, companionship. Dangerous things.

Julianne's face loomed in the back of his mind, her soft voice asking why he'd let her go without him. He didn't have an answer. He'd never had one. All he had was the certainty he would end the violence and let her rest in peace.

He heard the click of the office door and looked up. He'd sent Antonella to call her brother. He had no need to be there, no need to listen in. He was certain of his position. Hovering over her would only add insult to injury.

She stood with her back to him, her head bent. His gaze slipped over the curve of her buttocks. Need was a hot current in his veins.

Dio santo, it had been a long few days. A pleasurable few days.

He pushed the insistent memories aside. They made him hard, made him long to take her into the bedroom and make love to her on the silk sheets he'd told her she deserved. She was so responsive to him, so eager and sensual. She may have been inexperienced only a few days ago, but she'd made up for it. When she'd kissed her way down his body and taken him in her mouth only this morning—

Antonella turned from the door and moved resolutely toward him. Her cool princess act was firmly in place, he noted.

She sank down opposite him and crossed her legs. This time, he worked very hard not to let his gaze fall to her bare skin, not to trace it up to where her skirt fell mid-thigh. Not to imagine what lay beneath that skirt.

Heaven. Paradise. Shangri-la.

"Your brother was glad to hear you were safe, yes?"

"He was very relieved." She studied a fingernail. Her hand trembled the slightest bit. Exhaustion, perhaps. Or nerves.

Cristiano frowned. He didn't like that she was tired or nervous. She deserved happiness. Her life, he knew now, had mostly been one of guilt and fear. And it bothered him a great deal that he'd added to her stress.

Yet he had no choice.

She blew out a breath and met his gaze. "Dante wishes to meet with you before he will agree to sell you the ore."

Cristiano masked his annoyance; it wasn't her fault. He'd expected reluctance, naturally, but he hadn't anticipated that the Monteverdian King would be quite so stubborn with time nearly spent. "What is the point? You have no options left.

Unless, perhaps, Dante doesn't mind losing his country to foreign control."

"Isn't that what you are offering us?" she snapped, her eyes flashing.

He ignored the accusation. "We are sister nations, Antonella. We understand each other more than a foreign power ever could."

There was something in her expression he couldn't read. Sorrow? Was she hiding something from him? But then it was gone, replaced by weary resignation.

"I don't believe we understand each other at all, Cristiano. If we did, then we wouldn't be at war."

"I'm going to end the war, *cara*."

Her expression said she pitied him. *Pitied him?*

She shook her head. "It will take more than one determined prince. I wonder if you understand your own people as well as you think you do."

Momentary shock rooted him in place. "What is that supposed to mean?"

"It means that old dislikes go deep. You can't change minds overnight. It's impossible."

He arched a brow. "We changed our minds about each other fairly quickly, did we not?"

She looked so distant in that moment. So fragile and beautiful. He wanted to drag her into his arms and kiss her until she blushed and moaned.

Dio. He was losing his perspective. And he didn't like it one bit.

"We are only two people," she said. "And no, essentially I don't think anything has changed between us. We have been lovers, yes. But you do not care for me, do you, Cristiano?"

"I care," he said, surprised at the vehemence in his voice. He did care, the same as he cared for anyone he considered a friend. It was a huge admission for him, considering how he'd felt about her only a few days ago.

She wouldn't look at him. "Not enough, I am afraid. Not enough."

He grabbed her hand, squeezed. Her head snapped up. "Everything we shared was honest and real, Antonella. Never doubt that."

She seemed to hesitate, as if she were thinking about something. What she said next was not what he expected.

"I want more," she said softly. "Much more. I want love, Cristiano. I want you to feel what I feel."

He let her go, reared back against the seat.

Love. She loved him.

Why had he not anticipated this? She'd been a virgin, an innocent. She had a deep mistrust of men, and yet she'd given herself to *him*. He should have foreseen this complication. Should have been more ruthless with himself and refused to make her his lover.

Fire and ice mingled in his veins, warring with each other. Her words were seductive. He wanted to give in to the heat, wanted to feel that sense of connection with another human being.

But he couldn't do it. How could he possibly ever allow himself to fall in love with this woman? It would be a betrayal of Julianne, a betrayal of her memory and her sacrifice. If he couldn't love his wife the way she'd deserved, how could he ever love anyone?

Anger began to win the battle. Ice crystallized the flame. Shattered it. He'd made his decision years ago. He would not change his course now.

It was too late for him. Too late to ever go back.

"I can't give you more," he said coolly. "I lost the ability to do so when a Monteverdian bomb took my wife's life."

CHAPTER TWELVE

ANTONELLA didn't wake until the plane began its descent into the capital city of Sant'Angelo del Capitano. Sitting up in the recliner, she smoothed her hair. Cristiano sat a few feet away, studying a computer screen.

Her heart ached with love and pain. He didn't love her. Would never love her. He loved a dead woman.

Anxiety spiked in her empty stomach with each meter they dropped. She'd never been to Monterosso. So far as she could recall, she would be the first Romanelli in four generations to set foot on Monterossan soil.

The thought did not give her comfort. Nor did the hooded gazes sliced her way from the flight attendants. They did not want her here. Nor did she want to be here.

Cristiano tapped some keys, shut the computer. He'd showered and changed into a fresh suit, she noted. He seemed so remote, so handsome and regal. She tugged at her skirt, feeling like such a frump in her cotton dress. The silk would have been so much better, but she hadn't wanted to take the chance that another dress would be ruined if she'd asked for it to be pressed. She was so broke she couldn't afford to replace anything.

"You seem nervous," Cristiano said, glancing over at her as if he'd just realized she was there.

"Do I? How odd."

He smiled—and she wished he wouldn't. It only made her heart hurt worse.

"You have no need to fear, Antonella. You are under my protection. And Monterosso is quite civilized."

She wished she shared his confidence. But the remnants of peach silk stuffed into her suitcase were, to her, a symbol of the challenges between their nations. He might intend to end the war permanently, but she thought he would find resistance on both sides. Not because people wanted to fight, but because they didn't trust the other side to hold to their end of the bargain. She'd been naïve when they'd talked of this only a few days ago. But now?

Now she understood how deep the resentment could lie. It was disheartening.

The greeting awaiting Cristiano on the tarmac was nothing short of spectacular. An honor guard stood at attention on both sides of the red carpet as they descended the stairs. Antonella stayed behind him, hoping not to draw attention to herself. It was dark, but the floodlights at the airport lit the area like it was day. She slipped on her oversized sunglasses and kept her head down.

She wished she had Bruno in his leather Gucci bag. If he were here, she'd at least feel as if she had a friend in this hostile place.

As they passed the bank of journalists, flashes snapped and popped and reporters shouted questions. Cristiano turned and looped her arm into his. Then he waved to the reporters and kept walking. The flashes snapped more quickly than before as a collective murmur went through the crowd.

Seconds later, they'd reached the waiting Rolls-Royce and slipped inside. A uniformed chauffeur shut the door and climbed behind the wheel.

"You did that on purpose," she said as the car glided between throngs of well-wishers. Where had they found so many people to come to the airport this late in the evening? It was nearly ten, an hour when Monteverde had usually rolled up the sidewalks for the night. Not that her father hadn't been above staging scenes like the one just now. It made good front-page material for the paper.

Cristiano seemed puzzled. "Did what?"

"Drew attention to me." She knew she was a pawn in his game, but it hurt that he would treat her as such after all they'd shared. *Get used to it.*

He arched a brow. "I have returned with a Monteverdian princess. This is news. Far better to be seen on my arm than trailing behind me like a supplicant, yes?"

"They wouldn't have known, had you not told them."

His laugh was disbelieving. "Trust me, *cara mia,* you are very recognizable. It was only a matter of moments before they realized you were there. And I told no one you would be with me, though I cannot guarantee my staff did not."

Yes, she could well imagine the frenzy her presence on board his jet had created, even if she hadn't experienced the hostility first-hand. A Monteverdian princess was definitely news.

Antonella turned to look at the city. There was activity everywhere. Bars, cafés, and clubs lined the streets. People sat outdoors, sipping coffee or wine, while the streets were packed with cars and motorcycles. Horns occasionally sounded, as motorists got impatient with each other. Shouts and laughter and music mingled together as the Rolls slid past crowded sidewalks.

Sant'Angelo del Capitano was like Paris or Rome or Monte Carlo—always alive and vibrant. By contrast, Monteverde's capital was on its deathbed. Could Cristiano really save her country? Was his plan the key to returning her nation to vitality and prosperity?

She'd thought they *were* prosperous, but her father's downfall had revealed his excesses and how he'd really paid for his luxuries. Monteverde was broke and broken.

Fresh tears pricked the backs of her eyes, but she would not let them fall. She needed to focus, prepare for whatever happened next. "What is your intention now we are here?" she asked.

"As much as I can get away with, Antonella."

Her pulse skipped several beats. *Focus.* He wasn't talking about sex. Disappointment gnawed at her. How could that be?

She cleared her throat. "When will you meet with Dante?"

"As soon as it can be arranged."

"Will you take me with you?"

"Is it necessary?"

"No," she said honestly. "But I want to see him. We nearly died on Canta Paradiso. I want to see my family."

He inclined his head. "Very well."

She hadn't expected him to agree so easily, but she was thankful he had.

A few moments later, the Rolls pulled into a circular drive in front of a tall building. A doorman opened the car and Cristiano stepped out, turning and offering her his hand. This time, there were no photographers and she breathed a sigh of relief.

"Where are we?"

"Home," he said. And then he led her through the double doors and toward a bank of lifts. Another man in uniform greeted them warmly, then slid a card into the reader beside the lift. The doors glided open and Cristiano directed her inside.

"You do not live in the palace?" she said, blinking at her reflection in the spotless mirrored interior. Brass bars lined the lift, and there were no numbers displayed on the panel. It simply said, "Penthouse."

"I have rooms there, yes. But I prefer my privacy."

"It must be easier to bring women home too. Parents can be so style-cramping." She said it jokingly, but the look he gave her was serious.

"I have never brought a woman here, Antonella. I bought this place after."

After his wife died.

The lift came to a stop and the doors opened. She followed Cristiano into a spacious apartment decorated in masculine lines—sleek leather couches, modern artwork, glass and steel, cherry wood floors.

No, this definitely wasn't a woman's home. There wasn't a floral print or a soft line anywhere.

"Our luggage will arrive soon, but the staff won't be here until morning." He kept walking, shrugging out of his jacket and throwing it on a couch. Then he rolled one shoulder as if he were working out a kink.

A high-pitched meow came from one corner of the living area. Cristiano bent down as a fat grey cat lumbered over. A lump rose in Antonella's throat as he stroked the cat, talking to the animal softly while she purred and rubbed against him. This was a cat, not a child—and yet she could see how tender he would be with a baby.

As if he'd just remembered Antonella was there, he picked up the cat and stood. "This is Scarlett O'Hara, mistress of the manor."

"She's quite…large."

Cristiano scratched the cat's chin. "*Si.* I did tell you she was bigger than your Bruno."

For some reason, the fact he remembered about Bruno made her desperate to escape. She needed time, space. When Cristiano was near, he filled her senses. "Which is my room? I think I'd like to turn in."

"Your room? You do not wish to share with me?" He set the cat down again and she flicked her tail before turning and waddling into the kitchen.

"What is the point, Cristiano? You have said you cannot give me what I want."

He stalked over, looming into her personal space. His scent stole to her. If she closed her eyes and dozens of men paraded before her, she could still pick out Cristiano from his scent alone. His nearness set her on edge, made her body sing.

Made her body *want*. Oh, how she ached to slip his trousers open and take him in her hand before pushing him back and straddling him. She ached to do so, but she would not.

"You want me, Antonella. Just as I want you. And yet you are right." He ghosted a hand over her hair, backed away. "I cannot give you what you want, therefore it would be unfair of me to ask you for what *I* want."

Her throat ached. "Yes, quite unfair."

He stood so close, yet he made no move to touch her. His eyes were dark, troubled. And then he turned away.

"Come, I will show you to the guest room."

Cristiano took a sip of the whiskey he'd poured and watched the city lights. He sat on the couch in the living room, in the dark, Scarlett curled up beside him. He had no idea what time it was, though it was well after midnight. He'd tried to sleep, but couldn't. His bed felt too empty.

Antonella Romanelli loved him. *Dio santo*.

Many women had said those words to him over the years, and he'd had no trouble dismissing the sentiment. Typically, the women who'd said them hadn't meant the words so much as they'd wanted to be a princess and future queen. His mistresses soon learned he would not be persuaded by false sentiment.

I love you. Three simple words that hurt so much.

Julianne had meant them. And he knew without a doubt that Antonella meant them too. Or she thought she did anyway. Perhaps that was all it required to be true.

Each time he'd been inside her, his skin zinging with pleasure and a lust so strong it took everything he had not to come immediately, he'd begun to believe he *should* marry her. The physical side was amazing. Sex with Antonella was far more exciting than he'd thought possible. They could build a life on that sexual connection. There were certainly far less appealing things to base marriages on.

But each time it was over, he was torn. Guilt ate at him.

He should have known she would fall in love. She was innocent and sexy, so vibrant she made him crazy with need. He'd shown her physical pleasure, but he'd refused to consider that she might read more into it.

She deserved a man who could love her in return, not a man like him. He should have loved Julianne, and yet he hadn't. He'd cared for her very deeply, but if he'd loved her, he would have never let her go to the border without him.

He'd doomed her. He would not do that to another woman.

Beside him, Scarlett launched into a purr. He scratched behind her ears. She was the only real link he had left to Julianne. His wife's parents had died before they'd met, and her various other relatives hadn't been close to her. There was only this cat.

It was crazy to think it, but when the cat was gone, he would be alone. Shouldn't a man—a prince and future king— have a better outlook on life than this?

"Cristiano?"

He turned at the sound of her voice. It was scratchy with sleep, and she seemed to wobble where she stood, as if she was still so very tired.

"Why aren't you sleeping, Antonella?"

She shuffled over to the couch. "I can't sleep."

He held up his glass. "Do you want a drink?"

"No."

Scarlett stood and stretched, then clambered up onto the back of the couch and meowed at Antonella. She reached out and petted the cat's head. Scarlett began to purr again.

"She likes you," he said softly. "She usually ignores most people."

Antonella shrugged. "You said you've never brought a woman home, so…"

"I have a staff, *cara*. Some of them are women."

Scarlett meowed again. Antonella scooped her up and hugged her close, rubbing her face against the grey fur. The sight brought a lump to his throat. Julianne had done the same thing. The cat purred louder than before as Antonella came around and sat on the couch.

"I wanted to tell you something, Cristiano," she said, still hugging the cat. "It's important you know."

"Antonella, if this is about what you said—"

"It's not."

He could see her chin drop in the pale light coming from the city. She took a breath, then looked at him. She was in shadow, but he could feel her determination even if he could not see it in her expression.

"When we were on the plane, I asked for a dress to be pressed. Whoever did so split all the seams. The dress fell apart when I put it on." Before he could say a word, she rushed on, "Please understand that I'm not trying to place blame, and I don't want to hear you defend your crew against me. I just want you to know because I think it's important to understand where our peoples are coming from in relation to one another. I was under your protection, and yet someone hated me enough to do this. And before you try to say anything, I know the garment wasn't damaged when I asked for it to be pressed."

Anger spread through his veins like fire at the thought that someone had done this to her. Someone in his employ. He would find the culprit and force them to apologize—

Except he couldn't. What good what it do? It would only make them resent her more. Resent Monteverdians more. He wasn't the only person with deep and lingering resentments toward Monteverde.

Dio, and he believed he would end this war?

Yes. He *would* end it.

"I'm sorry that happened, Antonella. I will replace the dress."

"It's not about the dress," she said. "It's about you. About what you plan to do."

"If you are trying to talk me out of moving forward, you are wasting your time."

"It's not that at all, Cristiano. I know you won't stop until you've won. And while I understand your desire to end the war and bring peace, I hope you won't allow your need to punish us for Julianne's death to dictate what you do. Because hatred and resentment go deep on both sides, don't they? Many people have lost loved ones in the fighting. And destroying us, while it might help you feel better for a short time, won't really bring anyone back, will it?"

He couldn't speak for a long minute. Anger and despair boiled together in his gut. "I am not a child, Antonella. I know I can't bring anyone back from the dead. But perhaps I can make sure the dead rest better, yes?"

She set the cat on the couch beside her. Scarlett climbed up into Antonella's lap and curled into a ball. Her purr was still as loud as ever. Cristiano tried to ignore it. Crazily, he felt rejected all of a sudden. By a cat.

He was losing his mind.

"I need to know something," she said. "Is it your intention to destroy us? Or do you truly wish to end the war and help us find our footing again?"

He was on the edge of something, some feeling that threatened to swell inside him and make him burst. He could lie to her, but suddenly he had no wish to do so. She couldn't stop the inevitable, no matter what he told her at this point.

"I will do whatever it takes, Antonella. And I think Monteverde would be better served without the Romanellis in power. Dante may remain as a figurehead, but he will have no practical say in the day-to-day governing. That will be up to Monterosso."

Her breath rattled from her chest. "Yes, I thought as much. You never did intend to help; you only want to rule us." She bowed her head as if she were thinking of something. When she looked up, he could feel her anguish, even if he could not see it in the darkness. "And you never intended to marry me, did you?"

Pain arrowed into his heart, but he shoved it aside. He would not hide the truth from her now that he'd gone this far. It made no difference anyway. "No."

Gently, she picked Scarlett up and set her on the couch before standing. Her voice was soft, sad. "I feel sorry for you, Cristiano. You lost the woman you loved, yes—but would she want you to sacrifice your happiness to make up for what happened to her?"

"I did not love her, not the way she deserved," he lashed out. "Any sacrifice I have to make is my just penance. Julianne died because of me, because of who I am. I will not rest until there is peace between our nations."

She hugged herself, seemingly stunned into silence.

"Go to bed, Antonella. Save your love for someone who deserves it."

"I didn't know your wife," she said, "and I'm sorry she died, but you did not cause her death. Just as I didn't force my father to hit me."

"This is different," he growled.

"It's not." Her voice was tightly controlled, firm. "How can you not see that? You told me I was wrong to believe I could have changed my father's actions, that my behavior had nothing to do with his. And yet you think you somehow forced Julianne into that convoy? That you set the bomb and waited until she was on top of it?"

"Antonella—"

"No. You're wrong, Cristiano. I don't care what you think, but you're wrong. It's not your fault." She sucked in a ragged breath and he realized how close to tears she was.

He also knew she would not give in to them.

"I could have stopped her from going." Should have stopped her.

"You aren't omniscient. None of us are. I should have stayed home instead of going to Canta Paradiso. I would have missed the storm. And I could still call my heart my own."

He didn't say anything as she whirled and strode away. What good would it do? Scarlett jumped off the couch and followed her at a trot. A door snapped shut, then opened again when the cat meowed.

When it shut again, he was truly alone. Even the cat had forsaken him.

CHAPTER THIRTEEN

IN THE morning when Antonella awoke, with the cat curled up beside her, she felt more lonely and angry than she ever had in her life. She was in love with a man who was enslaved to a memory.

A man who'd lied to her. Knowing he'd never intended to marry her hurt more than it should, considering she'd been so angry when he'd forced her into the agreement in the first place. He'd only done so as a method of ensuring she would believe he intended to help Monteverde.

And she supposed he would help, in a way, though he also intended to destroy Monteverde's independence. Was it wrong of her to think that maybe blending the two nations might indeed work toward eroding hostility and misunderstanding? Cristiano was not so stupid as to depose Dante outright, which meant he was actually thinking about more than revenge.

Yet it did not give her comfort.

It was up to Dante now, though she believed he would not fight. It was too late. Without an eleventh hour rescue from a generous benefactor, Cristiano's money was their last resort. It was either that or allow Monteverde to be carved up by squabbling creditors, which could prolong her country's suffering. She did not believe Dante wanted that any more than she did.

After she dressed, she emerged from the room to find Cristiano waiting at the breakfast table. A uniformed woman served coffee and pastries to him while he read the morning paper. Antonella joined him, though her stomach refused to hold a bite of food.

"We will fly to Montebianco in two hours," he said without preamble. "Your brother will meet us there."

He didn't speak to her again. And though she ached for him, ached to reach out and simply ghost her fingers along his skin, as if the touch could last her a lifetime, she did nothing of the sort.

It was a long, lonely ride back to the airport, sitting beside him and not speaking. Feeling his presence in every nerve and cell of her body and being unable to act on it.

Far better to go home and try to build her life without him than be so close to him and unable to reach him.

But, if that was true, why did it make her ache so much?

Men. They were as cruel and untrustworthy as she'd always believed, though not just in the ways she'd always thought. No, some of them were cruel in what they withheld, untrustworthy in what they refused to feel. If only there was a way to know this at the beginning, a way to see inside a person and realize they could never be what you needed. That if they couldn't be honest with themselves, they could never be so with you.

He blamed himself for his wife's death, and he was angry and bitter because of it. She ached for him, but she could never change him. He had to change himself.

The only bright spot about going to Montebianco, aside from being reunited with Dante, was seeing Lily again. She was not on the helipad when they landed, but when they were shown into the palace, a very pregnant Lily rushed—if it could indeed be called rushing—to clasp Antonella in an embrace.

When she stepped back, her gaze widened. "Ella, you've changed!"

Antonella glanced over at Cristiano. He was deep in conversation with Nico Cavelli, the Crown Prince of Montebianco.

"It's nothing, I assure you. It's been a trying few days sheltering from the storm, that is all."

"I heard about that. My goodness, how frightening that must have been. Just you and Cristiano, hmm?" Her eyes gleamed. "Perhaps this explains why you look different to me. What did you and the handsome prince do all alone, Ella?"

Antonella rolled her eyes as if the question was beyond silly. Because, though she'd desperately wanted to talk to her friend just yesterday, she couldn't speak about it right now. She felt too raw, too exposed. "We did nothing except try to stay alive. Your imagination has run away with you. No doubt because you are pregnant."

Lily sighed, resting her hands over her belly. "Another month to go, yet I feel like I could pop at any moment."

Nico must have had some sixth sense about his wife because the moment the words left her lips, he was there, ushering her to a seat, helping her down into it, and offering to bring her a cool drink. Antonella looked away. She couldn't stand to watch a couple in love right at this moment, couldn't bear to see how Nico looked at his wife, or the way her face glowed with unconditional love as he pressed a kiss to her lips.

She didn't mean to do it, but she glanced at Cristiano. He was watching her, his gaze locking with hers for a long moment as her heart thundered in her ears. But then he turned and left her feeling bereft at the loss of contact. She'd hoped he would see why he was wrong, but she knew he would not.

There would be no unconditional love for her. She had always known she wasn't meant to find happiness, so why start crying over it now?

Soon, her brother arrived. Antonella ran into his out-stretched arms and hugged him tight. He held her for a long moment, squeezing her to him. Ridiculously, she started to cry.

"What is wrong, Ella?" he said. "You are safe, and I am very happy to have you so."

"I failed us, Dante," she whispered. "I failed."

"No," he said firmly. "It is I who have failed. Whatever happens now, you will not blame yourself."

"I should have tried harder—"

"Ella," he said, kissing her brow, "sweet little Ella. Always you blame yourself, and always you are wrong. Let it go, *la mia sorellina.*"

He gave her another squeeze, then set her gently away from him. Cristiano stood nearby, his expression blank. Antonella couldn't bear to look at him a moment longer. She turned and walked out onto the nearest terrazzo. She needed a moment to breathe, to get her head on straight again.

But when she'd collected her thoughts and returned to the room, the three men had gone.

Lily frowned at her, determination set in her expression like a sculpture carved from marble. "I think we need to talk, Antonella."

Antonella let out a long sigh. "*Si*, I believe you are right."

The men were closeted together for several hours. Antonella chafed at not knowing what was going on. Anger had begun as a little teasing dance in her heart, then swirled up into a lashing storm that brewed inside her with the force of the hurricane she'd just survived.

Anger at her father for so many things: bankrupting Monteverde, causing this crisis, hurting her and Dante, refusing to see her as anything other than a beautiful object to be bartered in the service of her country.

When this was over, no matter what happened, she was doing a few things differently.

For one thing, she was going to look into taking a university course to learn something useful. Let someone else pour tea and smile delightedly while engaging in idle chit-chat with the spouses of foreign dignitaries. She was capable of so much more, and she longed to prove it.

She was angry with her brother for not acting more decisively sooner, for not making overtures to Monterosso, and for refusing to listen to her advice when she'd given it.

She was also angry with Cristiano. His inability to let go of his wife's death, his need for revenge, and his refusal to accept her love for the gift it was infuriated her. Because, yes, her love *was* worthwhile. *She* was worthwhile.

And she refused to let anyone make her feel inferior ever again. Talking with Lily helped to clarify her feelings. Lily didn't tell her what to do, didn't judge her or offer suggestions— she merely asked questions about what had happened and how those events made Antonella feel.

When she had to consider, *really consider,* what her feelings were about everything, she'd grown angry.

How *dare* he dismiss her so easily? How dare he accept her innocence, ask for her trust, and dig into her personal life, her deep pain and anguish, without ever intending to care for her or to follow through on his declaration they would marry?

She was blazing angry the more she thought about it. He'd

used her, in more ways than one. Yes, he'd saved her life, and she was grateful, but it didn't excuse his deception—a deception that had begun long before they'd sheltered from the storm.

When Lily excused herself, saying she had to speak with the cook about dinner, Antonella remained on the small terrace off Lily's sitting room, sipping a glass of sweet iced tea—a delicacy from Lily's native southern United States—and thinking.

"Antonella."

Her heart leapt into her throat at the deep, sexy timbre of his voice. She set the tea down and gazed up at him as coolly as she could muster. Lily must have told him where to find her. Bless her meddling friend, but the last thing Antonella needed was to talk to him right now.

"How did it go, Cristiano? Are you the conquering hero now? Should I bow and call you master?"

His expression was unreadable. Blank and impersonal. Her fury whipped higher.

"That is hardly necessary," he said. "Dante has agreed to sell me the ore, and I have agreed to guarantee your loans in exchange. It is the best possible scenario for us all."

"Oh, yes, quite the best. How did he take it when you informed him he would only be a figurehead?"

"Monterosso will send government advisors to assist with the recovery. Dante is still King."

"For how long, I wonder?" she said softly. It meant nothing, and she refused to read more into it. The advisors would run the country. Surely Dante knew it as well.

Cristiano scraped a hand through his hair as he threw himself into the chair Lily had vacated. "I don't want it to end like this between us, Antonella."

She crossed her arms to keep from wrapping her hands

around his throat. Her entire body trembled with emotion. Anger, pain, betrayal.

Love.

"End like what, Cristiano? End with you triumphant? Riding off into the sunset with your shiny new toy and your freedom from messy entanglements?"

"You are angry."

She snorted. "What gave it away, I wonder?"

A flash of answering rage crossed his handsome face. "We shared too much to be enemies now, don't you think?"

"I think we were always enemies, Your Royal Highness. I made the mistake of forgetting for a while. I won't do so again, I assure you."

His smile was weary, resigned. "It wouldn't have worked out between us, *cara*. Even if we were to marry, and our people accepted it, you would hate me before the end. I have told you I cannot give you what you desire. As much as I do care for you, and as much as I want you in my bed, it is unfair of me to claim you. You deserve to be loved, Antonella. Loved in a way I can never give you."

A tear spilled down her cheek and she dashed it away. "I'm angry, so please don't think I cry because you have broken my heart," she bit out. "And please stop making excuses for your behavior by telling me what I deserve. I *know* what I deserve, Cristiano."

"I'm not making excuses. I am simply informing you of the facts."

"Yes, well, I am aware of the facts. And I am also aware that if you begged me to marry you right this moment, I would refuse. Because what I deserve is a man who believes in me. Anyone can claim to love another person. Believing in them no matter what, trusting yourself to them—that's the hard part, isn't it?"

"I believe you are capable of anything you set your mind to, Antonella. You will have a good life without me in it. And you will find that man you seek."

She turned her head. She didn't want him to see the despair, the hole his absence would leave. Because no matter what she said, no matter how brave she was or how right her convictions, *he* was the man she loved.

And it would take a very long time to get over him.

"You may leave now, Cristiano. I don't think we have anything left to say to one another."

He didn't move for a long minute. She prayed he would not reach out and touch her, wouldn't try to give her a farewell kiss or shake her hand or something equally devastating.

Because she would crumble into a million bits and blow away in the breeze if he did so. She felt that fragile at the moment. Fragile as spun glass.

It wasn't a good feeling. It was, in fact, quite possibly the lowest feeling she'd ever had. And that was pretty amazing, considering the things that had happened to her during her life.

He didn't reach for her. He stood and strode away without a word. She sat there, quite numb, listening to the wind bringing her snippets of laughter and chatter from somewhere below the terrace long after his footsteps had faded away.

Cristiano was in a foul mood when he boarded the helicopter that would take him home.

Home.

He had no wish to return to his apartment. It had been his refuge after Julianne died, the place he retreated to where he wasn't haunted by memories of her in bed with him or laughing at him over the breakfast table.

It had been safe—until he'd brought Antonella into it. She

had only spent one night there. One morning at the table. Add in one late night talk with Julianne's fickle cat curled up on Antonella's lap as if she were the new mistress of the manor, and his peace was ruined.

Or had it been ruined before that?

The moment she'd given herself to him? The moment he'd dragged her from the bed and rolled her beneath him to prevent the tree from crushing her? The moment she'd sobbed in the taxi as if her heart were shattering? Or was it the moment she'd turned from her door on the deck of the yacht?

He pressed his fingers on either side of his temples, hoping to rub out the headache that was fast settling in. It was strain, nothing more. The strain of the last week—all the planning, the travel, the storm, the talk just now with Dante Romanelli.

Surprisingly, he liked the Monteverdian King. He sensed no deceit in the other man, no sinister intention. King Dante was younger than he was by a couple of years, and yet the other man seemed much older and more worn out. The stress of governing under the circumstances he had for the last six months had taken a toll.

Cristiano found himself thinking, while talking with the King, that this man could be the right person to guide Monteverde forward after all. But he'd already put his plan in motion; it was too late to modify it, nor would he do so based on a first impression. Once Dante had signed the agreements Cristiano had his lawyers draw up more than a week ago, he'd instructed his business manager to contact Monteverde's creditors with guarantees.

Monteverde was effectively under Monterossan control.

Yet the victory felt hollow. He'd thought he would feel triumph, satisfaction. He'd thought he would feel Julianne's approval somehow. But all he felt was empty. As if he'd lost instead of won.

Antonella.

He didn't want to think about her, and yet he could think of nothing else. As the helicopter lifted off the pad and slid across the azure sky toward Monterosso, he thought he glimpsed her still sitting all alone on the terrace where he'd left her. Something twisted inside him, but he refused to examine it.

She was a beautiful, sensual, fascinating woman who was far more than he'd ever given her credit for. She was at turns stronger than anyone he knew, and more vulnerable than a child. She was both innocent and worldly. She set him on fire with a longing look, and tore him apart with her wounded indignation.

She loved him. And while he wanted to accept that love, wanted to turn around and take her with him back to Monterosso—where he wouldn't let her out of bed for a week at least—he couldn't do it. He'd accepted a woman's love once before, and it had ruined her.

Letting Antonella go was the hardest, kindest, most unselfish thing he'd ever done. He would not turn back now.

It was over.

CHAPTER FOURTEEN

THE summer was waning, the days growing shorter and the light growing longer as the sun tracked toward its winter home in the sky. Everything took on a golden hue in the late August afternoon. Antonella smiled at the little girl who jumped rope in the courtyard, her pigtails limned in warm light as they bounced with her movements.

"She is doing well," Signora Foretti, the director of the women's and children's shelter, said. "Her nightmares are less frequent now, and her therapist says she is making strides."

"I am very glad," Antonella replied. The little girl reminded her of herself in some ways. Shy, small, frightened of everyone and everything. She had been that way too, when she was that age.

"She looks forward to your visits, *Principessa*. She is always happy when you come to see her. As are all the souls who reside here."

Antonella swallowed a lump in her throat. "*Grazie, Signora.* I am honored to be here. If my experience helps just one woman to leave an abusive husband, or one child to know the abuse is not her fault, then I am pleased."

In the two months since she had returned home to

Monteverde, she had indeed done a few things differently. She still wished to attend university some day, but she'd been so busy since coming home that she'd had little time to do so. Instead, her days were spent at the shelter and in running her foundation.

She'd wanted to do something useful, and she'd found her purpose when she'd determined to visit the shelter. Dante supported her efforts, for which she was grateful. If he hadn't agreed to her sharing her experiences with others, or to her heading up an effort to help abused women and children, she wouldn't be able to do this. Because in sharing her experience, she also shared his. Not that she would dare to voice his story, but the fact she'd been abused by their father implied he had as well.

Rather than remaining a source of shame and anguish, her secret pain had become her strength. She couldn't save every woman and child, but she could work to save a good many of them.

Her foundation was growing in leaps and bounds; just this morning, her accountant had called and told her they'd had a very large foreign donation. She'd recently begun to think about taking the foundation's work international, and the money had come at exactly the right time. Surely it was a sign that she was meant to do this.

She said goodbye to Signora Foretti and her staff, then climbed into the waiting limo that would take her back to the palace. She would have rather driven her own car, but Signora Foretti had convinced her it was important for the occupants of the shelter to see her as the princess she was. It helped them to know that no one was exempt from abuse, not even the wealthy and privileged.

As always when she was alone, her thoughts turned to Cristiano. She'd heard nothing from him since the afternoon he'd left her on Lily's terrazzo and flown back to Monterosso. If Dante spoke with him at all, he did not mention it to her. Not that she'd told Dante of her affair with Cristiano, but perhaps her brother sensed that her emotions were tangled where it concerned the Monterossan Crown Prince.

Madonna mia, how long would it take to get over these feelings? Each day was as painful as the last, as long and lonely as the endless days since he'd left.

At least Monteverde was recovering, even if she wasn't. The ore was moving into the market at a good pace, and money was trickling into the economy from outside their borders. There had been a few setbacks, not the least of which was a bomb that had exploded in a crowded market two weeks ago. The market was less than a kilometer from the palace. Never before had they experienced the violence so close at hand.

Ten people had died in the attack. A Monterossan group claimed responsibility, though Cristiano's father was swift to issue a condemnation and to state the group had not acted with the approval or authority of the state.

Though there were Monteverdians who did not believe the King's statement, Antonella did. She believed because of Cristiano. He would be horrified by this turn of events, and he would have communicated that horror to his father. The blast would bring painful memories to the surface for him—memories he would not wish upon anyone. The bomb had been the work of extremists, not of mainstream Monterosso.

When they were almost at the palace, the car drew to a halt in a knot of traffic.

"What's going on?" Antonella asked the driver.

"I do not know, *Principessa*," he replied. "Could be a protest."

Antonella took her mobile phone from her purse and dialed

Dante's private number. When he didn't answer, she called her sister-in-law.

"He didn't want to tell you," Isabel said. "But Prince Cristiano is here."

Antonella's heart felt like a lead weight in her chest. How long had Dante known that Cristiano would be here today? "Why would he not tell me, Isabel? Cristiano di Savaré is nothing to me. I have not spoken to him in months. It would be nice to say hello," she lied.

Isabel was silent. "Dante thinks mention of the prince causes you pain," she finally said. "He would have sent you away, but we had no notice of this visit until this morning."

This morning? *Madonna mia.* The bombing must have bothered Cristiano a great deal, until he could stay away no longer. Did he blame himself?

He must. It saddened her. How could he take so much onto himself? And how would she deal with seeing him again? What would she say? Did he miss her? Or was this simply a state visit?

So many possibilities swirled in her mind that she didn't know what to think or how to respond.

"I am stuck in traffic, so perhaps he will be gone again by the time I arrive," she said lightly.

Isabel sighed. "I think not, my dear. He is staying for dinner, and Dante has called several of his ministers to join us. Perhaps you should stay in a hotel for the night."

"Stay in a hotel?" As if she often checked into hotels while driving through town. As if she carried a suitcase with her for just such a purpose. "No, I'm coming home."

"Ella," Isabel said, "there is a woman."

"A woman?" she repeated dumbly.

A heavy sigh came through the phone. "Prince Cristiano is traveling with a companion."

* * *

Antonella looked at her reflection in the mirror with satisfaction. She wore an ice-blue gown that hugged her from breast to hip before falling in soft waves to the floor. The gown set off the grey of her eyes, which she'd taken care to line in dark kohl before smudging the color to replicate a just-got-out-of-bed look. A raspberry stain gave her lips that freshly kissed color she remembered so well.

Sad that it was only a memory, but she'd found no other man she wished to kiss.

She arranged her hair in a loose tumble of pinned curls that trailed down her back in a thick shiny mass. Once she slipped on her jewelry—an understated diamond pendant, teardrop earrings, and a small tiara—she took a deep breath for courage. She would get through this evening, and she would show Cristiano that she was over him completely.

She wasn't, of course, but he didn't have to know that. Obviously, he'd had no trouble moving on to another lover. The thought that he would bring the woman here, knowing he would most likely see her, his former lover, infuriated her.

She'd meant less than nothing to him. He was easily over her while she kept dwelling on every moment they'd spent together.

No more.

Antonella was purposely late to the cocktail hour. She'd considered skipping it altogether, but she wouldn't let Cristiano know he still had that kind of power over her. No, she decided that if she had to be there, she would make a grand entrance.

When she swept into the room, head held high, conversation ceased. All eyes turned to her. She was accustomed to such a reaction, had cultivated it in the past to her advantage, but now it made her feel self-conscious. She wanted to melt into the Persian carpet.

She knew where Cristiano stood the moment she walked

in, but she did not look at him. In her peripheral vision, she could make out a woman standing beside him. A lovely pale woman in glittering jewels and a mint silk dress.

"*Principessa*," a waiter said, stopping before her with a tray of champagne. She took a glass, more to have something to hold than because she wanted to drink it. The waiter moved away again, and conversation restarted. Isabel hurried over.

"You didn't have to come," she said.

"Don't be silly. Of course I had to."

"Oh, dear." Isabel bit her lip as she gazed over Antonella's shoulder.

"What's wrong?"

"Antonella."

She closed her eyes briefly as the deep, sexy voice reverberated through her. *Dear God, please give me strength.*

"Prince Cristiano," she replied, turning and smiling politely. "How lovely to see you again."

His eyes were as hot as ever. They scorched her as his gaze took her in from head to toe. "I wish to speak with you privately," he said, catching her off guard.

No small talk? No polite chit-chat?

He seemed so serious—and yet her inner voice sounded a warning. She could not be alone with this man ever again. Not if she wanted to maintain her dignity. "I'm sorry, Your Highness, but that is quite impossible. Dinner is about to be served."

He looked as if he would argue, but then he inclined his head in agreement. "After dinner, then."

"Yes, of course." She kept her smile in place and hoped he would go away. After dinner, she would find a reason to absent herself.

"May I escort you to the table?" he asked, reaching for her hand before giving her a chance to reply.

Heat blazed through her at the first touch of his skin against hers. She swallowed against the sudden dryness in her throat. "Certainly."

Thankfully, once she was seated, he moved away and took the seat that had been assigned to him.

Dinner was an interminable affair. Antonella didn't notice anything about what was served, or how it tasted. Cristiano sat a few places away, and though he spoke pleasantries with the people around him, she was aware of every move he made, as if he did it solely for her. Each time his fork touched his lips, she remembered his mouth on hers. Each time he sipped his wine, she pictured him in the dressing room, sipping wine with her and talking about his life.

His companion was a beautiful woman who smiled and laughed a lot. And no wonder. She was sharing the bed of a man who knew how to make a woman happy, at least physically. Antonella hated her—and she hated herself for feeling this way. It wasn't the woman's fault she'd captured Cristiano's attention, or that she was the current object of his desire.

As soon as the final course was served, Antonella placed her napkin on the table and excused herself, pleading a sudden headache. She just couldn't take another moment of pretending to be fine while the man she still loved—God help her— sat nearby with a new lover.

Cristiano's gaze bored into her as she stood. She forced herself to turn from those hot, seeking eyes and walk from the room.

The fastest way back to her rooms was across the courtyard. She hurried outside and down the broad stone steps, cursing as one spiked heel slipped between the cobblestones of the path that took her through the gardens.

"You should wear more sensible shoes."

Antonella wrenched her heel free and spun to find

Cristiano on the path behind her. Her breath caught. He was still as dark and devilish in his custom tuxedo as the first time she'd turned to find him standing outside her room on the yacht.

"What do you want?" she demanded. Anger was her only refuge. Anything less and she would crumple into an emotional mess. Perhaps when she was older, more jaded with her affairs, she would not feel everything so keenly. The thought did not give her comfort; it left her feeling hollow.

"I want to talk to you," he said.

"They make telephones for this purpose. You could have talked to me at any point in the past two months."

He took another step forward. His hands were shoved in his pockets. His expression, she noted, was less controlled than she'd thought. He seemed…uncertain.

"I missed you."

She wrapped her arms around herself. "Do not say such things," she bit out. "I don't want to hear it, Cristiano. I'm not falling into bed with you ever again, so please, *please* just go away and leave me alone."

He swore softly, raked a hand through his hair. "I can't go away. Not without you."

She put her hands over her ears, her heart thundering so hard that the movement was probably unnecessary. She could hear nothing but the pounding of her blood through her veins.

Cristiano gently grasped her wrists and pulled her hands away. "Listen to me."

"Let me go! You have no right—" She sucked in a breath to halt the sob that wanted to break free from the tightness in her chest. "You have no right, Cristiano. What would your girlfriend think?"

He blinked. "My girlfriend? What are you talking about?"

"The woman with you tonight," she practically shouted.

"You did not listen to a thing we talked about at the table, did you?" he said, looking suddenly amused. But he let her go.

She took a step back. "I have a headache," she lied. "I was preoccupied."

"Rosina is my third cousin on my mother's side. She is a doctor, and head of a surgical program that works with traumatic injuries. Bomb blasts, *tesoro mio*. I have brought her to Monteverde so she can offer her expertise."

His cousin? A doctor? Heat crept across her skin. She'd heard nothing of the conversation, it was true. Her mind had been racing with thoughts of him. She'd withdrawn into herself in order to insulate her heart. She couldn't even remember what she'd talked about with the matron seated beside her.

"That is good of you," she heard herself say. Inane response.

"The bombing is my fault. It is the least I can do."

She stifled a defeated sigh. *Oh, Cristiano.* "How is it your fault? You would never sanction such a thing."

He shook his head. "No, of course not. But you warned me I had not considered how deep resentments went, that I could not single-handedly end this war of ideology between our nations. You were right."

"Monteverde is recovering, thanks to you. You saved us from ruin. And you can't prevent a few extremists from trying to take us all backwards. The bombing is not your fault."

His gaze dropped for a moment. "Perhaps you are right. Perhaps I take too much upon myself." When he lifted his head, what she saw in his eyes made her blood beat. "I dragged you beneath our control without regard to what was best for Monteverdians. I have come to change that."

"I don't understand."

"We can only move forward if we work together, not if one nation dictates terms to another. Dante is a good man. He is a good King, and he is the right person to guide this nation. Our governments will work side by side to end the mistrust and hostility."

She gazed at him in wonder. "You have returned the mineral rights?"

"*Si*. We are guarantors of your debt, not your overlords."

"But Dante could sell the ore to someone other than Vega." And they could use the money to do what they wished, not what Monterosso wanted them to do. It was a huge concession on his part—and it was contrary to everything he'd ever wanted.

Cristiano shrugged, though she knew he did not do so lightly. "Then Raúl must either pay a good price or see the ore go to his competitors. I assure you he will not allow that to happen."

"Why are you doing this?"

His expression was haggard for a moment. "I mistakenly thought that Monterossans were superior, that it was simply Monteverdian greed and recalcitrance that was prolonging the hostility between us. I thought if I could control Monteverde, I could end it. I was wrong."

"I'm so sorry, Cristiano."

"What do you have to be sorry for? You tried to tell me."

She swallowed. "I'm just sorry that it hasn't given you the peace you wanted. The personal peace, I mean."

"Ah, yes. Julianne's ghost." He tilted his head back for a moment, then speared her with an intense look. "I have made many mistakes she would not have wanted me to make. But she is gone now and I am finally ready to move on with my life. She knew what she was doing when she went on that aid mission. It was what she was trained to do. If I'd stopped her then, I wouldn't have been able to stop her the next time"

She gave him a watery smile. He'd finally accepted that it wasn't his fault. He was ready to live again. It was what she wanted for him, all she'd ever wanted. "I'm happy for you, Cristiano. And I hope you will be happy, that you will find someone—"

"I have found someone," he said softly. "I have found you."

Her knees were so weak she had to put her hand against the stone balustrade to steady herself. "Please don't torment me, Cristiano. I can't bear to watch you walk away again."

He crossed the distance between them, lifted his hand to her cheek. His fingers shook. But for that, she would have turned away. That one movement, that single vulnerability, made her think he might feel something for her after all.

"It is hard for me," he said. "Hard to let go, to feel love when it terrifies me that I could lose you too. But I do. I love you, Antonella."

She couldn't stop the tear that spilled down her cheek. "I want to believe you. But I am afraid."

He pulled her into his embrace, spanning the back of her head with one broad hand and cradling her to his chest as if she were precious to him. "No, you are the bravest person I know. Braver than I."

"No—"

"Yes. I thought bravery was found in things like saving princesses from falling trees, but it goes far deeper. True bravery comes from facing the demons of your past, from refusing to back down from the hard truths. You taught me that. It has taken me too long to realize the truth, but I wish to spend my days making it up to you."

She couldn't stop her arms from going around him, from holding him tight. Because if this weren't true, if it were all a dream, she still wanted to remember the hard feel of him against her body one last time.

Before she could speak, he tilted her head back and kissed her. The kiss was everything she remembered—and more.

"Tell me you still love me, Antonella," he whispered against her cheek. His mouth trailed over her jaw, down her neck. "Tell me I haven't ruined your feelings for me."

Every nerve ending in her body zinged with heat and need. And yet she was still afraid.

"I—I need time," she said.

He lifted his head, disappointment evident in his expression. "Of course. This is too much, too soon. But I have never been good at patience when I know what I want. For you, I will try."

"What *do* you want, Cristiano?"

He seemed surprised. "You. I want you. I thought I said this."

She lowered her lashes, studied the crisp white pleats of his shirt. Her pulse was out of control, and yet she needed to be certain of his meaning. "But I don't know what that means, exactly. You might wish to carry on a grand affair or—"

"Antonella, *amore mio*," he interrupted, cupping her face in his hands and tilting her head back. "Yes, I want a grand affair. I want one that lasts a lifetime. I want you by my side every day. I want you to be my princess, my queen, and the mother of my children."

Her breath caught. "You are certain of this? It will not be easy for you. I am Monteverdian, and—"

"I love you, Antonella. I won't make excuses for it, and I won't compromise. If I had to renounce my place in the succession for you, I would do so."

"I would never ask that of you," she vowed.

He kissed her forehead. "You would have no choice. To be with you, I would give up far more than a throne."

"But I don't want you to give up anything."

He smiled, and the hint of vulnerability in it twisted her heart. "Then tell me you will marry me and put me out of my misery. Because I've given up sleep for the last two months. I've also given up happiness. If you marry me, I will get these things back."

Her heart was swelling, daring to believe—

"I hope you are certain of this."

"More certain than I've ever been."

She closed her eyes, breathing in the scent of him. He was home to her. Home, life, love—everything she'd ever wanted. "I believe in you, Cristiano. I trust you with my soul. I have almost from the first moment I met you."

"Does this mean you love me? That you will marry me?"

Leap, Antonella. Let him catch you. "I do. And I will."

"*Grazie a Dio,*" he breathed. "*Non posso vivere senza voi.*"

"I can't live without you either, Cristiano. *Ti amo.*"

EPILOGUE

ANTONELLA DI SAVARÉ, Her Royal Highness the Crown Princess of Monterosso, lounged in a chair by the pool, her eyes closed as the warm sun beat down on her skin. It felt so good, especially since she'd gotten little sleep the night before.

She could hear the high-pitched laughter, the splashing, but she knew Signora Giovanni had everything under control.

A shadow fell over her. She didn't need to open her eyes to know who it was. She would know his scent anywhere. And even if she couldn't smell a thing, she would still know it was him. Her husband gave off an electric vibe that crackled through her body each time he was near.

She kept her eyes closed, but she couldn't stop the smile that tugged at the corners of her lips.

"I know you are awake," he said, dropping to her side. A kiss landed on her forehead.

Antonella pouted. "Kiss me properly, Cristiano."

"Look at me."

She obeyed and he kissed her so thoroughly that she was panting when he pulled away.

"I want you," he growled. "Now."

Antonella stretched like a cat. "You did not have enough of me last night?"

"You know I did not. Antonio needed you when things were just getting interesting."

She yawned. "He is a demanding baby."

Cristiano's fingers ghosted over her skin, over the smoothness of her belly. She'd worked hard to get her shape back again, though Cristiano had insisted she was beautiful to him whether she carried an extra few pounds or not.

"You are tired," he said. "Go inside and sleep. I will tell Signora Giovanni where you have gone."

"I promised Cristiana I would take her to get *gelato* later."

"We have ice cream here," he said in disbelief.

"I know, but your daughter likes to go to the shop and order for herself."

"She is two. How is this possible?"

Antonella shrugged. "It just is. I believe her Uncle Dante taught her."

Cristiano shook his head. "Very well, but I will take her. You must rest. Between the children and your work with the foundation, I am worried you stretch yourself thin."

"I am fine, Cristiano." She ran her fingers along his arm. She loved touching him. And the more she touched him, the less she wanted to sleep. "How did your meeting go today?"

"Very well. Dante and Isabel send their love, by the way. They wish us to join them tomorrow for dinner."

Antonella smiled. In the three years since she'd married Cristiano, life had been very good. They had two beautiful children, their nations were at peace, and prosperity had once again returned to Monteverde. There were still checkpoints on the border, and factions that required surveillance, but there'd been no violence of any kind in more than a year now. They'd even had an increase in the number of marriage license applications between the two nations.

"I look forward to it," she said. "But I look forward to something else even more."

His eyes blazed. "You need sleep, *amore mio*. Do not tempt me."

She let her hand settle on the bulge of his erection. "You want me."

"Oh, yes, I want you."

"I will sleep better if you make love to me first."

He scooped her into his arms, then called out to Signora Giovanni. Antonella laughed as he carried her toward their bedroom. "You are so easy to seduce."

He kicked the bedroom door shut behind him, locked it. "I seem to remember that I tried to refuse you the first time we made love, but you would not let me."

"Believe me," Antonella said as he set her down and stripped her out of her bathing suit, "I am profoundly grateful you were not so strong-willed as you pretended."

He looked at her with mock offense. "Not strong-willed? I am about to show you how determined I can be."

"And what are you determined to do, my love?"

"I am determined to prove to you that you complete me. Without you, I would still be lost."

Her eyes filled with tears. "I love you, Cristiano."

He took her in his arms and kissed her. "And *that* is what I am profoundly grateful for."

HER ITALIAN
SOLDIER

REBECCA WINTERS

Rebecca Winters, whose family of four children has now swelled to include five beautiful grandchildren, lives in Salt Lake City, Utah, in the land of the Rocky Mountains. With canyons and high alpine meadows full of wildflowers, she never runs out of places to explore. They, plus her favourite vacation spots in Europe, often end up as backgrounds for her romance novels, because writing is her passion, along with her family and church.

Rebecca loves to hear from readers. If you wish to e-mail her, please visit her website: www.cleanromances.com

CHAPTER ONE

ANNABELLE Marsh stood at the bathroom sink while she began removing her makeup. She didn't recognize the blond woman in the mirror staring back at her. There was an unnatural gleam to her shoulder-length hair she could never have achieved on her own. Her eyes really weren't that violet. Nor were her brows and lashes quite as dark.

Artificially flawless skin highlighted by a subtle bloom brought out her high cheekbones. The makeup artist had defined her mouth to make it look more voluptuous. Her fingernails and toenails possessed their own polished sheen.

She'd had a bevy of fairy godmothers doing what they did best as they'd transformed her. Marcella of Marcella's Italian haute couture salon in Rome chose all the designer clothes that Annabelle would wear throughout her photo shoots in Italy. She'd added jewels as the final touch for the shoot that had started four days ago at an air force base outside Rome in front of an MB-Viper fighter jet.

It had been a lark so far—loads of fun.

"Three weeks of being the Amalfi Girl," Guilio told her. "My wife and I will see to your every comfort.

Then—since you insist—you can go back to being Ms. Marsh."

"You mean the forgettable Ms. Marsh." She'd had long enough to stop grieving over a failed marriage and divorce two years earlier, and had taken back her maiden name. But a lack of self confidence, remained as one of its by-products.

His brown brows lifted. "If you were forgettable, I wouldn't have picked you for the most important project of my life."

Annabelle shook her head in disbelief. "I still don't know what you see in me."

"My brothers and I, the whole Cavezzali family, have been in the business of designing cars since World War Two. But I was the one who dreamed up the Amalfi sports car. It's been my life's work. I saw the lines of it in my sleep years ago and *lines,* Annabelle, are like the bones of a beautiful woman. What lies beneath determines what will eventually become a masterpiece."

She flashed him a teasing smile. "You saw my bones?"

"Right away. They spoke to me. They said, 'Guilio? At last you have found what you've been looking for.'" The charm and exuberance of the attractive sixtysomething Italian couldn't be denied. "I am going to form a marriage that will show a whole new face of the elegant world of the Italian sports car."

Annabelle would never forget that day two months ago when the dynamic car designer had come to the Amalfi dealership in Los Angeles, California. He and her boss, Mel Jardine, the owner of the complex who sold the most Amalfi cars in the States, had business to talk over. Guilio was launching a spectacular new sports car.

Being Mel's personal assistant, Annabelle had taken care of all the arrangements to make Guilio comfortable, including catering their meals. He'd insisted she remain for the day-long meetings and he was so attentive, she feared the married man might be interested in her in a nonprofessional way. But he soon dispelled that worry by bringing on another one. He told her in front of Mel he wanted Annabelle to be the model to advertise his new car.

She laughed at the absurd notion, but he kept right on talking while Mel shot her a glance that said she should listen to this Italian genius.

"I'm perfectly serious. For the last year I've been searching for the right woman. I had no exact face or figure in mind. I only knew one day she would come along and I would know her." He stared at her. "And here you are. You have that Amalfi Girl look. You're unique, just like the car. Mel will tell you I've never used a female model before."

Annabelle knew he spoke the truth. She was familiar with the brochures around the shop. They only featured prosperous Italian men in ads with his cars, like a businessman from Milan, or a socialite from Florence.

"I'm so flattered I don't know what to say, Mr. Cavezzali."

"Guilio. Please."

"Guilio, then. But why bring in a woman now?" She was filled with curiosity. "Out of the whole car industry, your ads are the most appealing just as they are," she assured him and meant it.

He tapped his fingertips together. "That's gratifying

to hear, but I want this campaign to be sensational. It's in honor of my brilliant boy." The hushed quality in his tone told Annabelle how very deeply he loved his son.

"Lucca went to military school at eighteen and has distinguished himself as a fighter pilot with many decorations to his credit." His eyes moistened. "He's my pride and joy. I've named my latest creation the Amalfi MB-Viper to let him know how much I admire what he has accomplished."

Ah… Now she understood. He'd named his new sports car after the fighter jet his son flew.

He gazed at her for a long time. "I want your picture to adorn the brochures, the media ads, the video and the calendar I'm having made up to commemorate the launch. Every Amalfi dealership around the world will be sent posters and calendars ahead of shipment to create excitement about a whole new market of future Amalfi sports-car owners. Be assured I'll have security with you at every shoot for your safety."

When Annabelle got over being speechless, she said, "I'd be *honored* to play a part in its launch."

Someone else, like her ex-husband Ryan, would be speechless, too, when he saw her picture on the calendar. He'd dreamed about owning a flashy sports car when he'd finished his medical residency. One look at the new Amalfi MB-Viper and he would covet it. That is until he saw his boring, predictable ex-wife draped over it, swathed in silk and diamonds.

After their marriage, his affair with another nurse at the hospital where Annabelle had been finishing up her nursing degree had left her feeling like her soul had been murdered.

A chance meeting with Mel, who'd been one of the heart patients on her floor at the time, had resulted in her going to work for him. His job offer had spirited her away from a world of pain she'd wanted to put behind her and hopefully forget.

Now Guilio's faith in her being attractive enough to grace his ads gave her another shot of confidence her damaged self-esteem had been needing.

"You will stay at my home with my wife, Maria, and me. I'm eager to introduce you to my brothers and my two married stepsons, who work for me. They and their families live nearby."

"I'd love to meet all of them, but I couldn't impose on you and your wife that way."

"Hmm. I can see you're stubborn like my son. All right. I'll put you up in Ravello's finest hotel."

"No hotel. If I'm going to be in Italy, I want to stay in some quaint, modest bed-and-breakfast where it's quiet, away from people and I can soak in the atmosphere. Here in Los Angeles we're constantly hemmed in by each other."

He turned to Mel. "You won't mind loaning her to me? This is business."

Mel smiled. "Not if you send her back soon. I couldn't get along without her. She's the reason I haven't had another heart attack."

Guilio smacked his own head. "*Cielo!* We don't want that."

All three of them had laughed.

Eight weeks ago she'd agreed to model for him and now, having completed her first four days of work in Rome, she found herself transported to Ravello, home to the Cavezzali family and the Amalfi car, a design as spectacular as the Amalfi coast itself.

Perched high above the water, Ravello was more like a giant garden than a town. Guilio, who had his own villas here, called it the crown jewel of the Sorrentine Peninsula. Princes, movies stars and sheikhs, among others, were drawn to the cluster of colorful cliff side villages and sparkling harbors dotting the world-famous stretch of Italian coastline.

This was her first vacation since her honeymoon to Mexico four years ago. After telling Guilio she wanted to stay in one of those charming little Italian farm-houses like she'd seen in films and on television, the kind that made you dream about the countryside, he'd installed her here.

She'd learned this house sat on the little farm his first wife had left to his son Lucca. It had stood vacant for fifteen years. She was welcome to stay here.

The exterior was orangy-pink with jade shutters. The only door to the house was on the side and led into the kitchen. Pure enchantment. Since leaving the bustle of Rome earlier in the day, nothing could have delighted her more.

While its terrace overlooked the brilliant blue Tyrrhenian Sea, an explosion of white daisies reached for the sky and pushed their way through the bars of the railing. It was as if the house had been planted inside a basket of blossoms. She couldn't wait to go exploring the area in the morning, before her driver came by for her at eleven.

After taking off her clothes, she stepped in the shower. It felt good to wash her hair and emerge later feeling fresh and clean after traveling most of the day.

She threw on her well-worn navy robe and plugged in the adaptor before turning on the blow dryer. When the strands weren't quite as damp, she pinned them to the top of her head. Tomorrow the hairdresser would decide what he wanted to do with her shoulder-length hair for the photo shoot.

Another glance in the mirror proved that the Amalfi Girl was gone for the night.

Was twenty-six still young enough for her to be called a girl? Did her daily makeover at the hands of experts hide the traces of the betrayed widow? The camera would tell the truth, but Guilio believed in what he was doing. He believed in her. She already cared for him so much, she wanted this campaign to be a huge success and was determined to cooperate every way she could.

When Lucca learned what his father had done in his honor, he'd be touched beyond belief. It was very sweet really. Guilio was about as excited as a father who'd put his child's most wanted gift under the Christmas tree and couldn't wait for him to open it.

Unfortunately it was only June. Annabelle wondered how he was going to be able to wait until August when the car was finally out in the showrooms. The timing would coincide with his son's next leave and the grand unveiling would take place in Milan.

Guilio intended to fly her back over for the special event, which would be covered by Italian television and other media sources. "We'll do a blitz!" Guilio proclaimed with excitement. "Nothing's too good for my Lucca."

Annabelle imagined his bachelor son had the same Cavezzali drive and charm. She admitted to a growing curiosity about him. Guilio had told her the den at his villa was full of pictures showing his son at every stage of his life. The latest ones showed Lucca receiving commendations and ribbons. She was eager to see them along with everything else.

After stretching her arms, she smiled wryly to herself, still unable to believe that she was in the most glorious place on earth, enjoying a free vacation while she modeled, and having the time of her life. In a few weeks she would have to go home, but she refused to think about that right now.

Once she'd brushed her teeth, she turned out the light and padded down the beamed hall to the larger of the two bedrooms made ready for her. The cozy feel of the old house, which was filled with old family pictures and furnishings, enveloped her. So many stories these fieldstone walls would tell if they could speak.

Annabelle climbed under the covers of the double bed. With a sigh she sank back against the pillow and closed her eyes, more tired than she realized. On such a beautiful June night, she wished she could leave the windows open, but Guilio had warned her against it.

"You can't ever be too careful."

Annabelle knew he was right.

"Tomorrow after the shoot, I'll give you a car so you can come and go as you please."

"Thank you for everything, Guilio. I guess you know you've brought me to heaven."

"Ravello is the closest thing to it. Call me if you need anything. Sleep well, Annabelle. *Ciao*."

"*Ciao*."

She didn't know why, but as she nestled into a more comfortable position, she had a feeling that love and laughter had filled this house years ago. Some marriages lasted. Her eyes misted. How nice for those lucky people…

At the base of the tiny farm bordering the serpentine road, Lucca Cavezzali got an urge to go on foot from here and told the driver he'd hired to stop the car. After paying the man, he got out of the backseat with some difficulty and reached for his duffel bag.

There was a full moon overhead. Anyone up at two in the morning would see him and wonder who was trespassing on private property. He took a long look around. In the next instant the perfumed breeze brought back memories from the past. The scent of orange blossoms hung heavily in the air, recalling his childhood, which had been idyllic when his mother had been alive.

After her death, everything changed. Lucca had watched his father turn into a different man, who soon after her death married a widow with two sons. At fourteen years of age Lucca couldn't forgive him for that and pretty well closed up on him.

Uninterested in going into the family car business like his stepbrothers and cousins, he'd left to join the military at eighteen. His grandfather Lorenzo had served in the Second World War. Lucca had made the old farmer out to be a hero and had romanticized about going off to war himself.

That decision had caused a serious rift between him and Guilio, who raged that Lucca might not be as lucky as his grandfather and not make it back at all. Still, nothing had dissuaded Lucca from leaving. But as he grew into a man and had firsthand knowledge of what war was really like, understanding of a lot of things caught up to him, like his father's fears for his only son's safety, and Guilio's need for love and companionship after losing Lucca's mother.

Lucca had long since let go of his teenage hang-ups. Over the years he'd mended the breech between them and had come to like his stepmother. She'd been good for his father, who was married to his work building up the Amalfi car industry.

If there was anything left over from the past, it was his guilt for not having been around the last fifteen years for his father. But the hospital psychiatrist had worked through those issues with him as well as his survivor's guilt. The doctor had told him most career servicemen and women suffered the same problems. Guilt went with the territory.

The only issue that Lucca didn't want to see turn into a problem had arisen on his last leave. He'd found out his father was considering selling off the two remaining farm properties from his mother's side of the family that were in sore need of care. Lucca had immediately made an offer for them.

His father looked at him as if he were crazy. If Lucca wanted to build up some investments, it would be a better use of his money to buy a prime piece of business real estate in town. Guilio was a shrewd businessman and considered his opinion to be the final word on the subject.

Rather than get into a full-blown argument as they'd done too often in those early years, Lucca decided to leave it alone for the time being. All he asked was that his father not do anything about the properties until he came home on his next leave in August, when they had more time for a business discussion.

But since their last meeting, he'd undergone a life-changing experience that had altered his timetable.

Four months ago Lucca had been shot down and it had ended his military career. Guilio didn't know about the crash that had left Lucca permanently injured, or that he'd been in the hospital all this time.

Aware how his father would have suffered for him had he known about the operation on his leg and the long rehabilitation, not to mention his post-traumatic stress disorder, Lucca made certain no news had leaked out from his superiors or doctors. It was a time he preferred to forget.

Tomorrow he would show up at his father's house after a good night's sleep. That's when he had less pain. He wanted to feel rested when he told Guilio about his future plans to be a full-time farmer. It was possible he'd meet with the same negative reaction of years ago, but Lucca had to try.

Before turning eighteen, Lucca had talked to his father and told him that he wanted to be a farmer, but Guilio had thrown up his hands. "For your mother's family, farming was fine. But no son of mine is going to do that kind of work! You're a Cavezzali with a superior brain!

"Our family has been designing and manufacturing cars since World War Two. There's no distinction in being a farmer who's always subject to the elements and works all hours of the day and night with little to show for it. No, Lucca. You listen to your father!"

After Guilio's tirade, Lucca kept the dream to himself. Instead of joining the Amalfi car business after graduation, he went into the military. Not to spite his father, but because he had plans to be a farmer one day and that ambition meant he would have to make some real money at a job that appealed to him first. Being a fighter pilot satisfied that need.

Now that he was out of the service, he planned to work with the soil and revive the farm. Since he intended to be successful and make a substantial profit, he needed more parcels of land. Along with this farm and those two properties to which he'd always been sentimentally attached, he could make a good start and go from there.

He'd had a lot of time to think in the hospital and hoped that when he talked to his father, Guilio's opinions would have softened enough to really listen to Lucca. But he doubted his father would ever approve of what he intended to do. Already Lucca was bracing for the same kind of lecture his father had given him all that time ago.

However, this time Lucca wouldn't be dissuaded and he wasn't going away. And if his father chose not to sell the properties, then Lucca was prepared to buy others. After his inactivity these last four months, he ached to get busy using his hands.

Once he'd checked his watch, he started for the house, struggling to reach it with every step. Before the injury that could have taken off his leg, he would have ambled up the steep incline between the orange and lemon trees faster than any goat.

As he made his way over uneven ground, he noted with disgust that everything growing required attention and pruning. The whole place needed an overhaul. Weeds fought to displace the flowers growing in wild profusion around the base of the deserted house, particularly in front of the terrace, where the railing was almost invisible. So much work needed to be done.

If his mother were alive, she would weep to see the neglect. Maybe it was just as well he'd lost her in his early teens. That way she wasn't here to see him come home a wreck of a man. Thirty-three years old and he wasn't a pretty sight. Neither was the farm, but he was about to change all that, with or without his father's blessing.

Working his way around the side to the only door leading into the house, he pulled out a set of keys and let himself in. Usually when he had a furlough, he met his father in Rome or Milan, where Guilio often did business at the major showrooms. But those days were over.

He was back on the farm, his own small piece of heaven, and he planned to work it.

From what Lucca could tell, there didn't appear to be any dust. He'd been paying a local woman to make sure the place was cleaned on a periodic basis and was pleased to see she'd followed through. He put the duffel bag down on the tiles in the kitchen with relief. It weighed a ton.

No longer encumbered, he limped past the small table and chairs to the hallway, taking in the living room on the other side. He didn't need lights turned on to find his old bedroom. Everything was still in place, like a time capsule that had just been opened.

He moved over to the window and undid the shutters, letting in the sound of the cicadas. Moonlight poured in, illuminating the double bed minus any bedding. Unlatching the glass, he pushed it all the way open to allow the scented breeze to dance on through. There was no other air like it anywhere on earth. He knew, because he'd been everywhere.

While he stood there filling his lungs with the sweet essence of the fruits and flowers, the pain in his leg grew worse. The plate the surgeon had put in his thigh to support the broken bone caused it to ache when he was tired. He needed another painkiller followed by sleep. A long one.

Diavolo! It meant going back to the kitchen, but he didn't know if he could make it without help. Walking the distance from the car had exhausted him.

Somewhere in his closet among his favorite treasures he remembered his grandfather's cane. His mother's father had lost the lower half of his leg in the war and had eventually been fitted with a prosthesis.

He rummaged around inside until he spotted it, never dreaming the day would come when he would find use for it. *Grazie a Dio* Lucca hadn't lost a limb.

Armed with the precious heirloom, he left the bedroom and headed for the kitchen, where he'd put the duffel bag. He'd packed the pill bottle in his shaving kit on top. Once he'd swallowed painkillers, he ran the tap water, then lowered his head and drank his fill. It tasted good.

He eventually shut off the tap. One more stop to the bathroom before sinking into oblivion.

By now he was leaning heavily on the cane. The short climb to the house had done its damage. Only a few more feet... *Come on. You can do it!* But even as he said the words, the cane slid on the tiles from his weight and he went crashing.

A loud thump resounded in the hallway followed by a yelp and a volley of unintelligible cursing in Italian. Annabelle shot up in bed. Someone—a man—was in the house, thrashing about after some kind of fall. It couldn't be Guilio. He would have phoned if he'd intended to come over for some reason. Maybe it was the caretaker Guilio had forgotten to tell her about.

With her heart in her throat, she slid out of bed. After throwing on her robe, she hurried over to the door. When she opened it, enough moonlight spilled from the doorway of the other bedroom to outline a figure crawling on his hands and knees.

Knowing the intruder was hurt in some way, she felt braver as she found the switch in the hall and turned on the light. His dark head reared back in complete surprise, revealing a striking face riddled with lines of pain. She grabbed for the cane she could see lying a few feet from him and lifted it in the air.

"I don't know who you are," she said through clenched teeth. "You probably don't speak English, but I'm warning you I'll use this if you make another move." With a threatening gesture, she took a step toward him.

"You have me at a disadvantage, *signorina*."

His deep voice spoke beautiful English with the kind of Italian accent that resonated to her insides. He was probably in his mid-thirties. The dangerous-looking male didn't have the decency to flinch. Even on the floor twisting in agony, he exuded an air of authority. She doubted he was anyone's caretaker. This kindled her fear of his lean, hard-muscled body on a level she didn't wish to examine.

"You're trespassing on private property, *signore*."

He strained to brace his back against the wall. A black T-shirt covered his well-defined chest. With his legs stretched out full length in jeans molding powerful thighs, she could see he would be six-two or six-three if he were standing. He put her in mind of someone, but she couldn't think who.

"You took the words out of my mouth, *signorina*. A man has the right to come home to his own house and be alone."

She drew in a fortifying breath. "I happen to know that no one has lived in this house for years."

His lids drooped over his eyes. He was exhausted. Perspiration beaded his forehead and upper lip. She saw the signs of his pain and felt unwanted sympathy for his distress, but it only lasted until he said, "Nevertheless it's mine, so what are you doing here?"

"*You're* the intruder," she snapped. "I'll ask the questions if you don't mind. First of all, I want to see your ID."

"I don't have it on me."

"Of course you don't."

"It's in the kitchen."

"Of course it is," she mocked again. "And if I ask for your name, you'll lie to me, so there's no point. We'll let the police get the truth out of you."

That made him open his eyes enough to gaze up at her through inky black lashes. "How sad your cynicism is already showing."

Heat made its way into her cheeks. "Already?"

"Well, for one thing you're not married." He stared at her ringless fingers. "Disillusionment doesn't usually happen to a woman until she's approaching forty. At least that's been my assessment."

He'd pressed the wrong button. "It would take a broken-down, forty-year-old cynic of a man to know, wouldn't it? Your vast knowledge on the subject doesn't seem to have done you a whole lot of good. No wedding ring on your finger, either. Not even the paler ring of skin to give proof you'd once worn one. What you need is a walker that won't slip, *signore*, not a cane."

The lines around his mouth tightened. She didn't know if she'd hit her target, or if he was reacting to his pain.

He slanted her an impatient glance. "Why don't you admit you're a down-and-out tourist who doesn't have enough money for a hotel room, so you cased the area and settled on this empty house."

Smarting from the accusation she said, "What if I were? You've done the same thing by waiting until the middle of the night to find a vacant spot to lick your wounds."

"Like a stray dog, you mean?"

Behind his snarl-like question she heard a bleakness that matched the whitish color around his lips. They'd traded insults long enough. His pain caused her to relent. "I'm a guest here for a time. My name is Annabelle Marsh. What's yours?"

He rested his head of unruly black hair against the wall. "None of your business" was the off-putting response.

His eyes had closed, giving her enough time to hurry into the bedroom and grab her cell phone off the side table. When she returned seconds later, his lids fluttered open. "What do you think you're doing?" he demanded curtly.

"I'm calling Guilio Cavezzali, my employer. He'll know how to deal with you."

"No, don't—" He lunged forward and pulled her down, cradling her between his legs with great strength.

The gesture sent the cane flying down the hall. His hands tore the cell phone from her other hand. It slid even farther away. She felt his warm breath on her nape. "I can't let you call him at this hour."

Did he know Guilio? The name seemed to mean something to him. Annabelle had been a fool to feel any pity for him. Now she was at his mercy. She schooled her voice to remain steady. "What is it you want?"

"Invisibility for the rest of the night. One word from you could ruin everything."

"I guess if you were being hunted by the police you wouldn't tell me, or maybe you would and don't care."

He made a strange sound in his throat. "I'm not on anyone's suspect list. More to the point, how long have you been staying here?"

She could feel the pounding of his heart against her back. It was too fast. His pain would have spiked from the sudden exertion. "I only arrived in Ravello this evening." In her own way, she'd wanted invisibility after a full day.

"How soon will you be seeing him again?"

"He'll be sending a car for me tomorrow at eleven. I'll probably see him later in the day."

"What exactly do you do?"

This man who'd broken into the house seemed to know more than she'd given him credit for, but she wasn't about to reveal information about Guilio. Seeing as this stranger had her locked in his grip, he had the upper hand. What choice was there except to answer with as much truth as she dared and still protect Guilio. His name was synonymous with Amalfi and prominent throughout Italy. "I'm working for him temporarily."

"Why aren't you living in a *pensione* or an apartment?" The man was full of questions.

"I asked him to find me a farmhouse that rented out rooms. That's when he told me I could stay here. There's no place more beautiful than the Italian countryside. Living here is like walking right into the picture on a calendar of Italy and never wanting to come back out."

"That's very interesting." He'd said the words, but he didn't sound as if he believed her.

She breathed in sharply. "Now that that I've answered all of your questions, it's only fair you answer one for me. Who *are* you?"

"Lucca Cavezzali," he groaned.

"Oh, no—" she cried. This was Guilio's only son, the adored child he'd had with his first wife, the eighteen-year-old who'd gone into the military and had trained to be a fighter pilot for the Italian air force—his father's pride and joy!

If she told him the specific nature of her job, it would ruin the surprise his father had been planning for over a year.

Now that she thought about it, the two men had similar builds, though Guilio was shorter. She saw a vague resemblance in some of their facial features, but Lucca must have inherited his black hair from his mother. Guilio hadn't mentioned anything about his son being injured.

She tried to get away from him, but he held her firmly against him. "Because of you, *signorina*, my best laid plans have been shot to hell for tonight, as you Americans like to say."

"You're right! We *do* like to say," she spluttered back. "Allow me to thank you very much, *signore*. Your unexpected, unforetold nocturnal invasion has changed *my* plans, too. If you'll let me go, I'll phone for a taxi and be gone from here inside of a half hour."

To her dismay she would have to explain to Guilio why she'd suddenly decided to go to a hotel after all. She would have to think up a good excuse for leaving, but she'd worry about that later.

"Now who's licking wounds," he muttered with uncanny perception.

"That's none of *your* business."

"I'm afraid it is. But uprooting you tonight won't be necessary, provided you're willing to cooperate with me and keep my presence here a secret until tomorrow."

Cooperate? For the second time that night she was suffering fresh shock after learning his identity. "You ask a lot of your prisoners." She'd been trying to wiggle free from his viselike grip, but it was no use. He might be injured, but he was incredibly strong and fit.

"I'm a desperate man."

Annabelle moaned. "So I've noticed. Why don't you want your father to know you're back?"

"Back from where, *signorina?*"

His condescending tone told her that no matter what she said, he wasn't going to like it. "He mentioned that you're in the military." She moistened her lips nervously. "Did you arrange for a special leave or something?"

"That's not your affair, either."

She supposed it wasn't. "You're right, but I can tell you're in pain. You should be in bed."

"I was on my way there." He'd come from the other part of the house, probably the kitchen. His speech had slowed, leading her to believe he'd drugged himself with something strong.

"Your bed isn't made up. You'll have to use mine."

"As long as you don't leave my sight. For the rest of the night we'll lie on the same bed to ensure you don't play the informer before morning."

Annabelle had no illusions. That was a command, not an invitation. She refused to react. "Fine. If you'll let me stand, I'll help you get up, then you can lean on me. My bedroom isn't far."

He let her go with one hand, using it to brace himself against the wall while he clung to her arm with the other. She sensed he would have cried out if he'd been alone. Together they moved to her bedroom with him leaning on her. Undoubtedly she would have collapsed from his weight if they'd had to go much farther.

By some miracle they made it to the bed. He fell on his side, taking her with him. She ended up on her back and felt his hand curl around her wrist, making certain she wouldn't get away. As he settled against the pillows, his sigh of relief echoed off the walls of the room.

When she'd helped him up moments ago, the dark stubble on his jaw had brushed against her cheek by accident, reminding her of his undeniable masculinity. No doubt he'd been traveling a long time without stopping to freshen up. Between fatigue and the medication he'd taken for his pain, she assumed he'd be asleep before long.

She, on the other hand, lay next to him, wide-awake. There'd been no man since she'd divorced Ryan. With Guilio's son facing her inches away, her senses were in chaos. The situation was so surreal she wondered if she were dreaming.

"Don't be afraid," Lucca murmured, thinking he'd read her mind. "I couldn't take advantage of you if I wanted to, which I don't."

His words might have pricked her if she hadn't already been through a hell she never wanted to repeat. "Then we're both in luck because I can assure you that a rude, brooding, unshaven male slithering home under cover of darkness is no woman's idea of joy beyond measure." His earlier remarks still smarted.

He made a sound that bordered on angry laughter, but none of it mattered. In another few minutes he'd be dead to the world. Once his hand released her, she would find some clean bedding in the hall closet and make up the other bed.

"Your pillow smells of strawberries."

The observation came as a surprise. In fact everything he said and did had knocked her off balance. "It's probably still damp, too. I'll get you another one."

His hand restrained her from moving. "After the places I've been, I like it." The words came out in a slur.

"You can let go of me. I'm not going to reveal your secret."

"Why not?" came the unexpected question "It's the kind of thing a woman can't wait to do."

If he could still try to rile her, then he wasn't as close to sleep as she'd supposed. Probably because of his pain. She fought an unwanted rush of sympathy for him. "That kind of assumption comes from knowing too many females on a superficial basis."

"You're an authority on my love life now?" he growled.

"Italian men have a certain reputation, *signore*. As we American women understand it, the Italian male is a jack of all trades, but master of none. I think it's one of the personal casualties in your particular line of work."

To his credit he let her baiting go before he said in a raspy voice, "You still haven't answered my question."

For the most important of reasons. She happened to know that Lucca's next furlough wasn't scheduled until August when he visited with his father in Milan. The big surprise Guilio was planning for him would take place at the largest Amalfi showroom in Italy. From there the cars were manufactured and exported around the world.

Annabelle remembered the look in Guilio's eyes as he'd talked about wanting to honor Lucca when they met at the end of the summer. She would never spoil that reunion by revealing ahead of time what she knew he had in store for his son.

Exhausted over the stunning events of the last hour, her eyelids closed. "If I haven't responded, it's because anyone who has gone to your lengths to sneak back under the radar in the dead of night must have the kind of baggage he wouldn't want anyone to know about."

She felt his body stiffen.

"What do you say we both try to get some sleep, *signore*? I don't know about you, but I have a big day tomorrow."

"You've got me intrigued about the nature of the work you do for my father. It must be beyond classified, otherwise he wouldn't be treating you like a princess. Nor would he have installed you in a house that is sacrosanct to me." His voice suddenly sounded as if it had come from a deep cavern.

The blood started pounding in her ears. "Sacrosanct?" she whispered.

"You mean he didn't tell you I was born here? Would it surprise you to know my mother died in this house?"

Oh, no.

To think she'd called *him* the intruder. "Your father only told me your mother willed this farm to you. I didn't realize about the house."

"Let's just say he has kept an eye on it for me."

CHAPTER TWO

A DULL throbbing ache woke Lucca. It radiated up his thigh to his groin. His medication had worn off. He needed some more quick before the pain flared out of control, as it had done last night.

Last night…

He rubbed a hand over his prickly jaws, groaning in self-disgust.

Sunlight filled the room, forcing him to squint. He checked his watch. Twenty to eleven. He found himself alone, still dressed in the same clothes minus his shoes, which she'd removed. The bed was in total disarray, evidence he'd had one of his nightmares. The quilt and pillows lay on the floor.

Naturally she was long gone. By now the American would have alerted his father, who had her allegiance. Lucca was sure he could expect a visitor shortly.

A spate of Italian invective poured out of him.

He turned slowly to roll off the mattress and gave a start to see his near-empty bottle of pills on the bedside table. It hadn't been there last night. She'd even supplied a glass of water. On the other side of the lamp lay the cane. He decided the nurses at the hospital had nothing on her. His father required efficiency. She had that trait down pat.

Lucca had planned on total privacy for one night, but he had to admit that being this close to his pills meant he didn't need to suffer another accident on the way to the kitchen.

After swallowing three, his stomach growled, reminding him he hadn't eaten since yesterday afternoon on the last leg of his flight to Naples. During the long wait for the train to Salerno, sleep had been impossible. The lack of it always increased the pain. By the time he'd hired a car to drive him to Ravello, he'd been ready to collapse.

A quick scan of the room revealed none of her belongings. He heard no noise and imagined the car she'd mentioned had already come for her. Alone at last, he got up from the bed and tested his weight with the cane. Last night's accident had been an aberration. As long as he didn't lean on it too heavily, the cane would do fine until he'd recovered.

The trip from the bathroom to the kitchen wasn't too bad. His duffel bag was still on the floor where he'd left it. It looked untouched.

He opened the fridge and found it stocked. This house had belonged to his mother's family. She and his father had lived in it until she'd died. In the will, she'd left the house and property to Lucca. At the time he'd joined the military, he and his father weren't speaking, but he knew Guilio would keep an eye on it.

How strange he'd decided to install his new American employee here. Even though she'd claimed she wanted to stay at a farmhouse, his father wouldn't have gone to the trouble to open up the house where he'd started out his married life for just any person working for him. This woman had to occupy a unique place in the scheme of things.

That's why she hadn't opened up to him last night. She and his father had something private going on. He had to admit she'd recovered fast from her fright last night. His interrogation of her proved she was a quick study.

Naturally Guilio would have sent down one of the maids from the villa to make sure things were ready for her. He reached for a handful of fat grapes from a bowl and popped them in his mouth. Their juice squirted pure sugar.

The microwave was new. His father had set her up with the necessities. A jar of freeze-dried coffee stood next to it. He preferred *cappuccino chiaro*, but in the military he'd learned to drink it black and made himself a cup.

In his line of vision to the terrace he noticed several branches from one of the lemon trees had grown and formed an overhang. While he leaned against the sink to sip the hot brew, he saw movement beneath them. Beyond the French doors he watched the back of a woman of medium height picking daisies near the half-hidden railing.

Her hair was caught beneath a large, broad-rimmed straw hat. The rest of her was dressed in a sleeveless white top trimmed with a small white eyelet ruffle. Equally immaculate white pants skimmed womanly hips down to the bone-colored sandals on her feet, where he glimpsed frosted pink toenails.

He waited until she turned enough for him to see the classic profile of *Signorina* Marsh. So she hadn't gone off early… Last night her bathrobe had covered up her slender curves.

The whiteness of her fresh-looking outfit combined with the profusion of white petals drew his gaze. With that face partially hidden beneath the hat rim and set against a backdrop of blue sky melding into cobalt waters far below, it was like beholding one of those picture-perfect postcards in dazzling Technicolor.

As she came in through the unlocked doors bringing the sunshine with her, her eyes lit on him, but she kept going and put the flowers in a ceramic pitcher on the counter. After filling it with water, she placed it in the center of the rectangular kitchen table, which was inlaid with hand-painted tiles of lemons.

His mother used to bring in fresh flowers in the early morning. He experienced a moment's resentment to be reminded of happier times that would never come again.

"I've always wanted to be able to decorate with flowers from my own garden. These are for me, but enjoy them if you want to. They're glorious." Dusting off her hands, she reached for a large straw handbag lying on one of the chairs and walked over to the side door.

With a parting glance from eyes a rare shade of periwinkle she added, "My ride will be arriving any minute. I'm going to walk out to the drive so you can remain invisible." She started to open the door, then paused.

"Please wipe that morose expression off your face. You're probably not that bad-looking when you aren't carrying the world around on your shoulders like Atlas. Surely you realize I didn't mean the things I said last night."

"Only half," he muttered in an acerbic tone after finishing the rest of his coffee.

"Hmm, maybe three quarters. When you make yourself another cup of coffee, there's sugar in the cupboard. I'd say you needed a little sweetening. Before I leave, tell me the truth. How recently were you released from the hospital?"

His lips twisted unpleasantly. "What hospital would that be?" He opened the fridge and found a plum to bite into.

"The one where you had surgery on your right thigh. You're favoring your other leg and can't get into any one comfortable position for long."

He munched until there was nothing left but the pit, which he removed and tossed in the wastebasket in the corner. "You're mistaken, *signorina*."

"No." Annabelle remained firm. "The medication you're taking tells me otherwise."

On cue his dark brows furrowed with menace. "What makes you such an authority?"

"I'm a nurse with experience taking care of patients recovering from heart and thoracic surgery, gunshot wounds, broken bones."

Stillness surrounded him before she saw a look of alarm break out on his face. "What's wrong with my father?"

She blinked, trying to make sense of his hyperspeed leap from the subject at hand to Guilio. Once the light dawned, she cried, "No, no— I'm not working for your father in that capacity. I'm helping do some advertising for him. As far as I know, he's fine!" she assured him, noting that his first reaction had been one of a son who loved his father. That cleared up one question haunting her.

His eyes looked disbelieving.

"*You're* the person I'm worried about, *signore*. I've a feeling you left the hospital before it was wise. Combined with the fall you had last night, you need to nurse that leg as much as possible. Even if the pain has subsided for now, you're wiped out."

"*Grazie* for your concern."

She decided the ice between them was thawing a few degrees. His sarcasm didn't come off sounding quite as bitter as before. "*Prego.*" It was one of few words she knew in Italian for *you're welcome*.

"*One* more thing, *signore*. I told Guilio I didn't want any maids or housekeepers around while I'm here, so you should have no worries in that department. After work I'll be back to pack and go to a hotel. I don't know the exact time of my arrival, but rest assured I'll be alone," she promised with a pleasant expression.

He watched her disappear out the side door. If she could be believed, then he had little to worry about for the rest of the day. But it caused him to wonder that she'd be willing to keep his secret that long.

Why would she do it? For how long? She wanted something in return, evidently enough to be willing to cooperate.

Breaking in on a defenseless woman in the dead of night should have scared her senseless. Instead, she'd turned the tables on him and had made threatening gestures with the cane. He felt a grudging admiration for her resourcefulness. But he couldn't help but question what she expected to gain by her compliance with Lucca's wishes. Did she think getting on his good side would earn her a promotion with his father down the road? More perks?

What was his father playing at? To let his alleged

employee have her own way and install her in Lucca's house meant she'd twisted him around her finger. What kind of advertising was she doing for his father?

It was a little late for him to be having a midlife crisis. Surely his second wife—Maria was enough for him. She'd managed to marry him only six months after Lucca's mother had been buried. For years Lucca had blamed her for changing his father. Until one day when Lucca grew up and realized no force could make Guilio marry the attractive widow who had two sons of her own if he hadn't wanted to.

Now this American woman—a nurse, no less—had come into Guilio's life, so different in every way that Lucca was baffled.

He frowned. Nine months ago when he'd flown to Milan on furlough for a brief visit to see his father, *Signorina* Marsh hadn't been on the payroll. That meant she was a fairly recent addition to the company, but because she was in his father's confidence, she had Lucca at a disadvantage.

He didn't like the idea that she would know more about him than he wanted anyone to know, yet for the time being he had no choice but to live with it. It didn't escape him that he bore some responsibility for arriving in the dead of night.

After locking the door, he turned to the fridge. While he rummaged for items to fix himself a sandwich, he heard a car turn into the gravel drive. The voices were too faint for him to make out conversation. Before long it drove off.

In a minute he sank down on one of the hand-carved wooden chairs. He extended his long legs, trying to get into a more comfortable position, which was virtually impossible, just like she'd said. As he bit into some locally grown ham and his favorite *provolone dolce* cheese, he found himself glowering at the daisies she'd put in the old family pitcher and hardly noticed the taste.

He'd wanted complete solitude and sleep for one night. That way he could appear at his father's door today looking rested enough that Guilio's first reaction wouldn't be one of heartache over his son. There'd been enough of that in the early days.

Soon enough his father would learn about the flashbacks, but they usually happened after he fell asleep.

Starting to get that drugged feeling, he headed for the bedroom. Whether *Signorina* Marsh exposed him or not, he was no longer alone in his own home and wouldn't be able to totally relax.

He should phone his father right now, but the pain since his fall last night was more than he could bear right now. Once the pills took effect, he would pass out again for a few hours. When he awakened, he had to pray the throbbing would have died down enough that he could make the call.

Annabelle stepped out of the van where they'd done her hair and makeup. "*Perfetto, signorina.* That's the look I want. Like a *margheritina!*"

"What is that?"

"A flower." Giovanni, the photographer, put one of his hands on top of the other and made spokes.

"Ah. A wheel. You mean like, he loves me, he loves me not?"

He grinned. "*Sì, Sì.*"

Annabelle didn't mind being compared to a daisy. Not at all. The beautiful ones she'd picked earlier that morning had called to her. She'd experienced a euphoric moment until she'd gone back in the kitchen and found the dark Italian owner scrutinizing her with all the intensity of his brooding soul. She wished she still didn't quake when she thought about it.

Meeting him in the flesh in the middle of the night had, to some extent, altered her vision of the picture his father had portrayed of a strong, powerful man. But obviously that was her fault for endowing his hero son with certain admirable virtues. Maybe his good qualities were there, but they were disguised by pain and his participation in a war where no one ever came home the same as before they left.

She admitted to being worried about his insistence on not letting his father know he was back yet. Though it wasn't any of her business, as Lucca had said, she *did* care. More than she should. It made her impatient with herself.

"Annabelle?"

Her head jerked up. "Yes?"

The shorter, overweight man Basilio—one of Guilio's assistants, who'd driven her this morning—provided the interpretation for the pose he had in mind. "We want you to get in the driver's seat now and lean to the passenger side, putting your right arm here. Remember you're out beneath a midafternoon sun, driving for the sheer thrill of it. Then you see the water below and you have to pull over to get a better view. React the way you would naturally. Forget the camera."

Easy for *him* to say. But this was an adventure she wouldn't have missed.

Without needing more urging, Annabelle climbed in the black Amalfi convertible. She could almost believe this was Mrs. James Bond's car. The rich black-leather interior provided the ideal foil for the white outfit she'd put on before leaving the farmhouse. So far she couldn't fault Marcella's superb fashion taste.

Annabelle couldn't decide which sports car she liked better. The other one in Rome parked in front of the fighter jet had been white with light pearl-grey leather. Lucca would look sensational speeding around in either of them, but the thrill probably wouldn't be the same after the years he'd flown above the clouds at super-sonic speeds.

Once she'd gotten into her role, Giovanni put the straw hat back on her head, studying the angle for a minute and doing a rearrangement of her hair before he started taking one picture after another.

The car had been parked next to the wall of the steep highway below Positano. When she looked down, she gasped at the sheer drop to the water, forgetting every-thing else. Such gorgeous scenery—reputed to be the most fantastic in this part of the world—defied verbal description and became a spiritual experience with na-ture. This kind of beauty actually hurt.

With the help of the police, hundreds of cars going both ways had to pass single file where the photo shoot was taking place. Though there were a few angry shouts and horn honks, by far more tourists whistled and shouted "*squisitas*" and "*bellissimas*", throwing her kisses as they passed by.

Yet the view was too mesmerizing and she was barely cognizant of anything else going on around her. If the truth be told, her mind was preoccupied with an image of the wounded Italian pilot who'd finally fallen asleep last night, relaxing his hold so she could escape. Talk about a beautiful man...

When Giovanni announced he had all the shots he needed, she hurried back to the van to remove her makeup. She'd brought her own change of clothes in the straw bag and quickly slipped on her jeans and a blouse. Once she was dressed, she left everything else in the van and stepped outside clutching her own purse.

Besides the sports car and the van, there was the third car Basilio had driven when he'd picked her up at the farm. It was an older model blue Amalfi sedan. He gave her the key, telling her it was now hers to use while she was in Italy.

The police directing traffic indicated they needed to get rid of the roadblock as fast as possible. With the agreement that she'd meet the film crew tomorrow at noon in the town of Amalfi for another photo shoot, she got in the car and followed the policeman riding a motorcycle out into the stream of cars. He helped her get her place in line with the other vehicles headed back toward Ravello.

Through the rearview mirror she saw him blow her a kiss. Annabelle smiled. Italian men. Always open in their enjoyment of women. They were hilarious. Except for one Lucca Cavezzali. She frowned, needing to arm herself ahead of time for a dour reception from him once she returned.

She'd seen his bottle of pills. He was almost out of them. They were the strongest painkillers one could take after surgery without going back to the hospital for a morphine cocktail. His fall in the hallway last night had been doubly unfortunate for him. It came from returning home the hard way, but it *was* his call after all, and his house. The injured man had every right to expect it would be empty.

Before she arrived at the farmhouse, she made two stops on the outskirts of Ravello. One to a pizzeria for a light meal. The other to a *gelateria* that was a few doors down from a charming-looking bed-and-breakfast. She checked it out and found out there was a vacancy. With easy access to the main road, she couldn't find anything better and held the room with a credit card for two weeks occupancy.

Now that Lucca was back home, she couldn't stay at the farmhouse and would check in after she'd gone back to pack. While she ate a delicious lemon ice, she returned her parents' phone call, letting them know she'd left Rome and was now settled in Ravello.

Considering the time difference between Italy and California, they'd already gone to work some time ago, so she left her message on their answering machine. Being the last of three children, she knew they worried about her and wanted her to be happy. The prerogative of parents.

A familiar ache passed through Annabelle because the experience of having a baby had been denied her. But then she quickly brightened, refusing to dwell on it, and assured her folks she was having a wonderful time. How could she not after the sights she'd seen today.

She left out mention of the owner of the farmhouse, who'd come close to giving her a heart attack last night when he'd decided to come home without telling his father. Guilio worshipped his son, but clearly there was some history between them that caused Lucca to hold back.

Annabelle didn't pretend to understand the family

dynamics known only to the two of them, but she respected them. Nothing could be worse for her than to be caught smack-dab in the middle of father-and-son issues.

Whatever Lucca decided to do or not do, tomorrow she would tell Guilio that the farmhouse was too isolated after all and she'd found a place with eating establishments next door that suited her. She wanted out of this precarious situation. It was up to Lucca to contact his father. He'd had a day to think about it.

A minute later she pulled into the drive at the side of the farmhouse and parked the car.

Twilight was fast fading into darkness. Combined with the soft, fragrant air, it was a magical time of night. But when she opened the door to the kitchen, reality intruded because she was met by a man holding on to the kitchen counter. His facial features were taut with pain. Even his knuckles were white.

Without thinking she said, "You need to go to an emergency room."

"What I need are more pills," he corrected in a gravelly voice.

"Why in heaven's name didn't you phone your father?"

"My original plan had been to show up at his house this morning, but the fall put me out of commission. I'd prefer to see him when I'm not writhing in pain."

It would be counterproductive to ask him why he hadn't phoned someone else then. Unless he didn't have a phone, but she didn't believe it. The problem between him and his father was more grave than she'd supposed. "I've been given a car to use and will fill your prescription if you'll tell me where to get it."

"I have to pick it up in person."

"Since you're in no shape to get behind a wheel, I'll drive you." She saw the cane on the table and handed it to him. "After you."

She followed him out, locking the door behind her, then she ran ahead of him and opened the back door of the car. When he'd climbed in with difficulty and more or less lay against the seat, she shut his door and got in the driver's seat.

"Are you hiding, or is that position more comfortable?"

"Both. Follow the road to Salerno." His words sounded like they came through gritted teeth. "There's a *farmacia* in the Piazza Municipio seven miles from here that will be open."

When she'd found the main road she said, "What would you have done if I hadn't come when I did?"

"I was on the verge of calling for a taxi when I heard the car in the drive." He sat up, obviously not worried about being recognized now that they were on the road. Annabelle heeded his precise instructions to get them to the other town. Traffic was heavy. She knew he was suffering, but he'd chosen to be stubborn by hiding out in his own house unannounced and she refused to feel sorry for him.

What was it Guilio had said about her being stubborn like his son? It had frustrated him when she'd told him she refused to intrude on him and his wife while she was in Ravello.

Eventually she slowed to a stop in front of the store. "We've arrived." There were no drive-thru pharmacies here.

"Don't move from this spot. With luck I won't run in to anyone I know."

Maybe not, she mused, but he'd certainly be noticed. Lucca's tall male physique would do wonders for anything he wore including the tan chinos and raspberry-colored polo shirt she hadn't noticed until now. In uniform, he'd really be something.

Knowing he was about to get the relief he craved, she noticed he managed to move quickly with that cane. While she waited for him, her cell phone rang. When she saw Cavezzali on the ID, guilt swamped her. If she didn't answer, he might get worried.

She clicked on. "Hello? Guilio? How are you?"

"*Molto bene*, Annabelle. Basilio told me Giovanni is ecstatic about the pictures he took today."

Thank goodness. "That's wonderful."

"I will come to Amalfi tomorrow. I have some new ideas for the shoot."

"I'll look forward to seeing you."

"Are you comfortable at the farmhouse? Do you need anything?"

Now was the time to tell him. "The farmhouse is a dream, but I've discovered modeling makes me tired and I don't want to do any cooking. So I've made arrangements to stay at the Casa Claudia for the rest of my time here. There are the most fabulous food places all around it."

"That's a good little family establishment. I was afraid the farmhouse might be too isolated."

"You were right after all. I'm sorry you went to that trouble for me. Please don't send any maids. I've cleaned everything including the fridge and will give you back the key later."

"I'm glad you changed your mind."

Only because of Lucca's entry into her life. She'd loved being by herself at the farm, where she could do exactly as she pleased, but a certain unexpected event had changed the situation.

"In truth, I love all the little places to eat. Italian cuisine is the best! I could eat my head off here, but I know I've got to be careful or I won't be able to fit in to the clothes Marcella has chosen for me."

In the midst of Guilio's laughter, Lucca got back in the car. She decided to put the phone on speaker. The last thing she wanted was for him to think she was talking behind his back with his father. Maybe hearing his father's voice would influence Lucca to contact him.

"I'm not worried, Annabelle. Don't forget the party I'm giving a week from Saturday. You'll be meeting our top Italian dealers. I've decided to give everyone a preview to whet their appetites before the big launch." The excitement in his voice was palpable. She was ready to disconnect them if he started to say anything that would give away the surprise.

"I know how much this means to you." So far the man in the backseat had no idea this was all in tribute to him. "I'll give you my very best."

"You always do. Did I tell you Mel Jardine will be coming next week? He's missing you terribly."

"I miss him, too," she said, warmed by his words, "but I have to admit I love it here."

"That's what I like to hear. Does that mean you're reconsidering my offer?" he asked hopefully.

"No. It just means I'm a typical woman who's having more fun than I deserve."

"After what you've been through, no one deserves it

more than you. Now get to bed and I'll see you tomorrow."

"Thank you for everything, Guilio. *Ciao*."

Once Annabelle had clicked off, she turned in the seat and was taken back by Lucca's inscrutable stare. The light from the store illuminated his irises, which were flecked with green among the grey. What a beautiful surprise they were. This was the first time she'd seen their color.

The silence deepened, making her uneasy. "Are you waiting for your prescription to be filled?"

"No. I've taken my medicine and am ready to go home whenever you are."

The knowledge that he would be feeling relief shortly seemed to have revived him enough to be civil to her. He might hate it that she existed as an unwanted encumbrance, but he'd needed someone to help him. Would it be out of the question to hope he might thank her at some point? She started the car and headed back to Ravello without saying anything.

"My father sounded more excited than I've heard him in years."

You have no idea, Lucca. "After meeting him, I had the impression he's always like that."

"You've heard of the immovable object and the irresistible force. My father's the embodiment of both of them," he said in a tone of exasperation.

Her thoughts flew to Guilio, who came across as a dynamo and was infinitely likable. But she hadn't been his child who'd lived with him from birth. That child might have a different perspective altogether.

About to ask him if he needed anything else as long as they were out, she decided against it because it was quiet back there. Annabelle would normally be turned off by such moody behavior, but she knew too much about him already and cared about him in spite of herself. The man had served his country and was used to making instantaneous decisions to take out the enemy and still stay alive.

That kind of sacrifice put him in a special category of human being, particularly since he'd suffered a recent leg injury that had brought him home on unexpected leave. She imagined it wasn't in his nature to show his need of anyone. Proud to a fault, perhaps? Especially around his father? It had to be a man thing.

Being a survivor, he would shun anyone hovering over him. Annabelle could understand that and wished she hadn't been in his house last night. The wounded warrior had the right to come home and deal with his demons out of sight.

It was a case of her being in the wrong place at the wrong time. Guilio couldn't have known that. He'd only been trying to accommodate her.

A shudder wracked her body when she thought of the cruel things she'd said to Lucca. Once she'd realized who he was and had overcome her fear, anger hadn't been far behind. She knew most—if not all—of her comments last night had more to do with lashing out at Ryan. He often came home in the middle of the night after being on rounds at the hospital. Or so she'd thought.

Instead he'd been with the woman who was now his wife. They had a baby, the one that should have been Annabelle's. The one Ryan had said they couldn't have until he'd become a fully fledged doctor and had set up a practice.

No...those salvos she'd enjoyed hurling last night had been aimed at the wrong target. If Lucca ever gave her a chance to explain, she would apologize.

By the time they reached the house, she thought he must have fallen asleep. In fact she was sure of it when she opened the rear door and called to him several times without obtaining a response. The position he was half lying in couldn't possibly have been comfortable. If it were, she'd let him spend the night there.

She reached for the cane and propped it against the side of the car. "Lucca?" She nudged his shoulder gently. "Wake up! You're home now. Let me help you in the house. Come on. You can't stay here."

Something she'd said, maybe just the sound of her voice, must have gotten through to him. Suddenly his body turned rigid and jerked upright. Streams of words poured from his mouth in rapid succession. They hadn't been said in anger or swearing. Though she understood very little Italian, she thought he must be giving orders or delivering instructions.

In the semidark, a look of horror spread across his face. The hand closest to her squeezed her upper arm in a death grip. He was unaware of his strength. His cries rang in the night air. She thought he said a name before low sobs of anguish shook his frame and found their way to her soul.

Whatever he was reliving in his mind had to have been unspeakable. The man battled post-traumatic stress disorder. Annabelle had worked around vets at the hospital and understood even more his natural instinct to hide away from family until he was able to cope.

Still standing, she leaned farther in and put her other

arm around his shoulders. Without conscious thought she rocked him against her, pained for him. "You're all right, Lucca. It's just a dream. You're home and safe," she murmured over and over in soothing tones, wanting to comfort him.

The freshly shaven male cheek pressed against hers was damp with tears. Whether his or hers at this juncture, she didn't know. "It's all right," she whispered against his temple. "I'm with you. Wake up," she cried softly.

After a long moment his hold on her arm loosened enough for her to embrace him fully. In the next breath she felt his body relax, as if he were with her now, mentally as well as physically. No longer seized by what had to have been some kind of flashback, he drew in a labored breath.

His hands roamed her waist and back experimentally. She felt their warmth before they moved around to slide up her arms and cup her face. He gazed at her, still disoriented.

"Hi," she whispered, struggling to keep a steady voice while her body was still reacting to his touch. "Remember me?"

After a silence he said, "*Signorina* Marsh."

"Yes. You had a bad dream on the way home from the pharmacy, but it's over now."

Their lips were close enough she could feel his breath on them. "Did I have one last night?" The man was suffering. Her heart went out to him.

"To be honest, I don't know. As soon as you fell asleep, I moved to the other bedroom. Tell me what happened to you in the war, Lucca. Talk to me! I take it your jet crashed."

Suddenly his hands gripped her upper arms. Even in the semidark, his face darkened. "How much did you hear?"

"Enough to understand what's bottled up inside you."

"You really want to know?" he muttered fiercely.

"Yes! I don't care how terrible."

His fingers tightened, but she knew he had no idea of his strength. "Our squadron was under enemy fire." She heard his labored breathing. "I watched my best friend get blown out of the sky. Why did it have to be him and not me?" His anguish devastated her. "He had a wife and a baby on the way. I couldn't understand why I was alive and he wasn't."

She rubbed his cheek. "After any kind of disaster, the person who survives always feels guilt. It's a normal human reaction. In time, it'll go away. I promise."

"I want to believe you."

"Tell me what happened after that."

"My jet took a hit." The cords in his neck stood out. "I ejected before the next round of fire finished it off. When I came to, I realized I'd ended up a junk heap on a pile of rocks. It took three days before a helicopter found me in that war zone and flew me out of there."

"It must have felt like three years." His pain had to have been excruciating.

"I drifted in and out of consciousness." But she heard the pain in his voice. "After I was picked up, I was transported to a field hospital for immediate treatment. From there I was flown to Germany."

"How long were you in the hospital?"

"Once I was transported there, four months. My thigh bone was broken across the shaft. They had to insert a metal plate."

Annabelle swallowed hard. "That was a bad break, but you didn't lose your leg, thank heaven." She sounded breathless even to her own ears. "The screw-and-plate treatment does help you heal faster."

She heard his sharp intake of breath. "Provided you don't try to climb a steep hill and then crash on the tiles in the dead of night."

Without conscious thought she rested her forehead against his. "What else can you expect from a crack Italian jet pilot so used to protecting others, he forgot about his own safety."

An odd sound came from his throat. He smoothed his thumbs over her moist skin. "I'm not fit to be around, but you seem to have survived listening to me. That was your first mistake." Once more he was on the defensive. "Now you're stuck with me for a while longer."

He'd just given her the answer to the question plaguing her earlier. He hadn't contacted his father yet.

As he removed his palms from her cheeks, she backed away so he could get out of the car. "I believe this is yours." She gave him the cane.

After he emerged, she shut the door. With the feel of his hands still on her making her feel all trembly, she hurried ahead and opened the door to the kitchen. Once they were both inside, she locked it before turning on the light. He moved to the sink and took another drink from the tap, then turned to her.

The latest dose of medication taken in the pharmacy had removed some of the grimace lines. His eyes reflected more green than grey at the moment. Like his father, he had a strong nose and chin. Lucca's features had a more chiseled cast.

She was struck by the warmth of his olive complexion,

the vibrant black of medium-cropped hair and winged brows. Without pain tightening his lips, the mouth that had come close to touching hers moments ago appeared wider than she'd realized. Sensuous even. He was a gorgeous-looking male specimen uniquely Italian, but that wasn't the important thing here.

"When you're ready to go to bed, call me."

"I thought you were going to pack and leave."

"I'll do it tomorrow after work. But any vet leaving the hospital having PTSD should have someone nearby. At least for tonight."

Her comment appeared to have taken him back. "So you're willing to put yourself in jeopardy a second time?"

"Like you said last night, you couldn't if you wanted to, and you don't want to. Did I get that right?"

"*Perfetto.*" Were those little green sparks shooting from the slits of his eyes?

"Good. Then we understand each other. After you get into a comfortable position, I'll put pillows between your legs to relieve the strain. You should feel less pain by morning. Maybe then you'll tell me when you plan to let your father know you're home."

"I'll tell you now." He cocked his head. "If I hadn't fallen, I would have called him this morning to come to the farmhouse so we could talk. But I was in too much pain. I wanted to be in the best shape possible when I told him my plans for the future, knowing he won't like them."

"Why? What *are* your plans?" Annabelle was dying to know.

"I think I was born wanting to farm, but by the time

I turned eighteen, my father wouldn't hear of it. He said a Cavezzali wasn't meant to farm."

Annabelle listened as he told her all the things his father had said to shut him down. It was a side of Guilio's nature she wouldn't have known about unless Lucca had decided to confide in her.

"My mother's family made their living that way and they were the happiest people you ever saw." His eyes lit up. "I liked learning how to grow things and watch the fruit trees change in different seasons. I learned everything from my mother and grandparents. When Papa set off for work, I went off early with Mama before school. We either did pruning, or we picked fruit. Whatever needed doing."

Lucca sounded so happy just talking about it, that happiness infected her. "I have no doubts it would be a wonderful life," she murmured.

"I doubt my father's opinion has changed over the years, but it's the life I want and he'll have to get used to it. If I'm feeling fit enough tomorrow, I'll phone him."

She nodded. "I'll be back in a minute with those pillows."

CHAPTER THREE

LUCCA found it easy to talk to Annabelle, but he realized he *was* wiped out. She'd been right about the PTSD and several other things. Before help had arrived, he'd been fighting pain and felt utterly drained. Though he'd lain around most of the day needing relief from the jabbing pain and finding none, bed had never sounded better.

Ten minutes later he'd brushed his teeth and had pulled on grey sweats and a white T-shirt. If he were alone in the house, he wouldn't have bothered with clothes. No sooner had the thought entered his mind than she appeared in the same robe she'd worn last night, holding two pillows and a glass of water. She'd fastened her hair at the nape.

"How did you know I was ready for you to come in?"

"I didn't. I'm working on *my* time schedule. When you didn't call out, I came anyway."

"Then—"

"Then I could have caught seeing you in the alto-gether," she said, coming around to the right side of the bed. She put the glass next to his bottle of pills. Something about her smelled like fresh lemons.

"I hate to tell you this, but I haven't been living for it. I'm afraid you don't want to know how many men—thin, fat, old, young and in between—I've helped change out of their inadequate hospital gowns, let alone shower. It wouldn't be a new sight, except for the face, of course," she said with a smile.

Lucca couldn't help chuckling. It had been ages since he'd done that.

"He laughs, ladies and gentlemen—and his face didn't crack," she teased. "Okay. Find your favorite way to sleep, then I'll fix you up."

Without thinking about it, he turned on his right side and carefully crossed his left leg over. His body felt like a dead weight. When he was settled, she fit the two pillows in between them. "This helps distribute the weight of your top leg over the whole length. That way there's less strain on the injured bone."

Lucca exhaled a heavy sigh. "Unfortunately when I'm asleep, who knows what I'll do."

"Who knows?" She flashed him a mysterious smile. "You might find your quilt on the floor in the morning. Or, you might actually enjoy a sound sleep in this position for a change." She put the covers over him before turning out the light, cloaking them in semidarkness, due to the moon.

When she left the bedroom, he felt an odd twinge of disappointment. Though she gave as good as she got under fire, she was one of the least unobtrusive women he'd ever met.

If his father didn't require nursing services, then what kind of job in advertising was she doing for him? He had to admit that when he'd heard the two of them talking on the phone earlier, his father hadn't sounded loverlike with her. His tone conveyed that he treated her more like a cherished friend.

What was the other offer Guilio had referred to on the phone, the one she'd turned down so blithely?

Lucca decided that whatever reason she had for not giving him away to Guilio, it couldn't be because she'd decided to come on to his son. That wasn't the kind of embrace she'd given Lucca. Hers had been full of compassion, the furthest thing from a plan of seduction. He'd been moved by it.

Over the years he'd enjoyed his share of women and knew the difference. But something else *was* motivating her.

There were many parts to *Signorina* Marsh still hidden. *Secrets.* While he lay there drifting in and out of sleep, he found himself wanting to expose them. His thoughts wandered all over the place until morning, when once again sunlight streamed through the window. The angle told him it was probably eight-thirty, nine o'clock.

He blinked. During the night he'd turned on his other side. Though his covers lay at the bottom of the bed and one pillow had fallen to the floor, the other one was still in place between his thighs.

Two things surprised him. His first instinct hadn't been to reach for his pills. The pillow trick must have worked because he hadn't awakened in pain. In fact it had subsided enough to give him a good night's sleep. The pills he'd taken last night were still working. He got to his feet actually feeling rested for a change. This morning he would make *café au lait* with sugar, the second best thing to *cappuccino*.

After freshening up in the bathroom, he wandered into the kitchen. Not until he reached it did he realize he hadn't grabbed for the cane lying on the bedside table.

His gaze darted to the terrace. *Signorina* Marsh, still in her robe, had placed one of the patio chairs near the railing. She sat there gazing over the view deep in thought while she sipped her coffee. He quickly heated up milk and fixed his own concoction before walking out to stand next to her.

She must have felt his presence and lifted her eyes. They were more blue than violet this morning. What woman could look so good without makeup? Her hair, caught loosely at the back of her head, hadn't been touched since last night. She was in bare feet.

"I don't need to ask how you slept," she murmured. "It's there on your face. I'm glad."

"Thanks to your expertise." He took a long swallow of his hot drink.

"It's good to see you feeling better, *signore.*"

"You called me Lucca when you woke me out of my nightmare last evening. Since we've already slept together, let's drop the formality, shall we?" He watched heat spiral into her cheeks as he'd intended.

Their first night together had been an interesting one since he'd fallen asleep almost immediately. Looking at her right now, he found that incredible. What in the hell had been wrong with her husband?

She nodded. "I've been hoping you'd say that. Why don't you pull up the other chair and tell me what else is going on inside you."

In an instant his good mood vanished. "What are you? A psychiatrist now?"

"Maybe you need one."

"The hell I do—" Her mild-toned comment had pressed his hot button.

She didn't flinch. "During your nightmare you were

in combat mode and called out a name in agony. Last night you opened up to me, but you've only scratched the surface. Now that you're awake, you need to keep on talking."

"No thanks."

In an unexpected move, she got to her feet. "One of the doctors I trained under at the vet hospital explained that a man who has seen combat needs to validate his existence to another warm body. It's vital that what he did in the war did matter to at least one other human being besides himself.

"If you don't choose to use me for a sounding board, don't wait too long to find someone, Lucca. For your sake it's vital you pick out a person who wants to listen, and do it soon, even if it's a therapist. Is it that impossible to consider talking to your father?"

He darted her a piercing gaze. "You really do go where angels fear to tread."

"If our positions were reversed, wouldn't you want to help me?"

She had him there. During his time in the hospital, part of his therapy had been with a psychiatrist who'd told him everyone's war experience was a singular one. Those in combat lived, died or survived, yet humanity was scarcely aware of it. The worst thing he could do was remain mute.

Lucca closed his eyes and threw his head back. "How's this for starters? My father forbade me to go to the military academy in Bari. I went anyway against his wishes because I wanted to be like my grandfather, who'd fought in the previous war."

A stillness came over her. "I had no idea. Guilio never told me."

"No. He wouldn't. That's because his father-in-law came home minus his lower leg. It's not something my father likes to think about."

"The cane..." she cried softly "Was it his?"

"Yes. If you think my father wants to hear about my injury and relive that horror, then you're very much mistaken. But I realize he has to be told. Despite what I've been through and am still going through, you're not a man and don't understand how much I want to look substantial to him when he first sees me. Is that honest enough for you?"

Her eyes glazed over as she nodded. "I'm so sorry, Lucca," she whispered.

It had been a long time since anyone had responded that way out of concern for him. *It's been too long since you allowed anyone to see into that part of your soul, Cavezzali.* Her reaction surprised and touched him, stirring feelings inside him he hadn't had any idea were there.

"So am I."

"I feel very honored you would share that much with me. Maybe later you'll share more."

"There *is* no more."

"Oh, yes there is." Before he could countenance it, she raised up on tiptoe and pressed a brief kiss to his cheek. Then she quietly moved the chair over to the table and walked back in the house with her empty cup.

He stood at the railing for a long time, realizing he needed to call the doctor. The hospital had arranged for him to see one in Solerno for a checkup and more medication.

Maybe fifteen minutes passed before he heard her car pull out of the driveway. A new sense of emptiness stole through him. He disliked the fact that she was the cause of it. Why *this* woman? *She's getting to you, Cavezzali.*

Diavolo!

You fool, Annabelle.

As he'd said, this morning she'd had to go to a place even the *angels* knew to avoid! Now she'd forced Lucca to open up in ways he might resent her for later. Oh she hoped not! But even if he did, this had been a major step for him to start the healing process.

How would Guilio respond when Lucca faced him? His son's injury would pain him. The fact that Lucca hadn't told him he was back yet would pain him. She knew that. It pained *her*. She was in pain for Lucca.

He hadn't told her everything. The vision of what he'd held back sent a shudder through her body because she'd seen and heard part of it already during his flashback. She marveled that he'd survived and she was absolutely in awe of his instinct for self-preservation.

That was the problem. At this point she felt an affection for *both* men that ran deep. She wanted to help, but it wasn't her place.

She would love to blame this whole situation on Guilio. He'd related so many happy memories of his first wife and their endearing, handsome son, she'd been curious about Lucca long before meeting him.

Her guilt deepened because she hadn't told him the exact nature of her work for his father. He was too intelligent a man not to know she'd been less than forthcoming. Yet unlike her, he hadn't forced the situation out in the open yet, but it was probably only a matter of time.

Fortunately she had a new place to stay and would move there after work. If she ever got there… The traffic in Amalfi was horrendous. She needed all her powers of concentration.

Thanks to the map and specific directions Guilio had provided after settling her at the farmhouse, she found the Hotel Europa overlooking the Piazza Sant'Andrea. Their parking garage had never been more welcome. If her employer hadn't set everything up ahead of time for this special photo shoot, it couldn't have happened, not here in this crowded tourist mecca.

"Ah, you've arrived—" Guilio met her in the foyer and swept her up the stairs to a suite on the next floor.

"I'm not late, am I?"

"No, but Marcella needs more time."

"Why?"

"When I saw the proofs taken in Rome, I was so elated with the outcome, I decided we would substitute a wedding dress for the businesswoman's suit layout planned for today's shoot. She brought several of her own bridal creations. We need to see you in all of them before a final decision is made."

Annabelle didn't mind trying on the various signature outfits meant for someone else. Her own wedding was past history. She'd been there and done that, except her bride's dress hadn't been a gown like one of these $50,000 selections.

The whole crew gathered round to give input. Each rendition was breathtaking in its own way. "Ah," they all cried when she donned the last one of filmy silk and lace.

"That's it!" Guilio declared, voicing his approval above the others.

Giovanni squinted at her before turning to the hairdresser. "Let her hair flow like a maiden's. It will make the most of the mantilla. I'll arrange it after we're outside."

With those words everyone went to work on her. Marcella told one of the assistants to carry the matching high heels out to the piazza, where Annabelle would put them on. For the final touch she wore a dazzling diamond choker and matching diamond earrings. When all was ready and her makeup perfect, she left the room in her sandals and they went down the stairs with the assistants, who carried the long lace train.

People in the packed hotel foyer started clapping. It grew louder as she moved out the doors into the piazza, where she was met with more oohs and aahs. Police had cordoned off the area where a gleaming, flame-red Amalfi convertible sports car stood parked at the base of the ancient staircase. The famed fourteenth century cathedral of Saint Andrew awaited at the top.

Guilio must have seen her expression. "We won't ask you to climb all sixty-two steps."

She laughed to cover her gulp.

Once Giovanni had arranged the floor-length lace mantilla to his liking and she'd stepped into the high heels, he announced he was ready. Leaning close he whispered, "When his son sees this picture, he'll run off with the *bellissima* Amalfi Girl. Every woman on the coast will mourn the loss of the sought-after Cavezzali bachelor."

Her heart raced for no reason. "Right." But she covered her sarcasm with a wink.

Annabelle had news for the photographer. Lucca had already seen her in the flesh. The last thing he wanted to do was run off with the woman who was an intruder in his home. Giovanni, artistic to his core, didn't have a clue about the pilot who'd come back from the war agonizing physically and emotionally.

But the photographer's comment, meant to flatter her, only hit her harder for keeping quiet about Lucca in front of Guilio. As heat poured guilty color up her neck into her face, Marcella unwittingly saved her from having to talk by handing her flowers. Annabelle lifted the bridal bouquet and inhaled the fragrance of the white stephanotis interspersed with tiny flame-red tea roses.

"We want you to try several poses." Basilio took over. He opened the passenger door, revealing the ultraposh tan leather interior, where a long-stemmed rose of flame-red lay on the seat. "First, walk up the steps until your whole train is exposed. Look back toward the car as if waiting for your bridegroom."

Thanks to Giovanni's comment, an image of Lucca rather than Ryan passed through her mind. In a tuxedo, he'd be spectacular. When she realized where her thoughts had wandered, she took a sharp breath and tried harder to follow instructions.

A few more touches here and there and the shoot began. Basilio wanted different looks. So did Guilio. Between the two men, who got into animated conversations and gesticulated with their hands, the day wore on and on. Giovanni had endless energy and continued in his upbeat way to encourage her, but finally even he declared they had enough film.

Relieved it was over, Annabelle hurried inside the hotel. After being dejeweled and disrobed, she freshened up. Once she'd removed her makeup, she changed into her sleeveless orange linen shirtwaist and sandals.

Guilio was waiting for her and invited her to eat dinner with him and his wife at their villa.

Not wanting to offend him, she asked if she could take a rain check because she was nursing a slight headache. It wasn't far from the truth. "This modeling business is much harder than I thought."

He patted her arm. "The sun was warm today. By all means go back to the hotel and have an early night."

"That and a cold drink are all I need, Guilio." Once she knew if Lucca was all right, she'd be able to relax. "Thanks for understanding. Will you be at the shoot tomorrow in Furore?"

"No. I have to fly to Milan for an important meeting, but I'll be back the day after. You can always call me if anything comes up."

"I know. Thank you."

"I told Marcella to save that wedding dress for you with my compliments."

"Guilio—you're generous to a fault, but there's no wedding in my future. I'm done." He knew she was divorced though she'd never told him the details.

A frown appeared. "Only the young say that without knowing what's around the next corner."

"I think you're mixing me up with the Amalfi Girl who still has stars in her eyes. She hasn't been where I've been and doesn't know those stars blaze hot, then run out of hydrogen and fade." From the doorway she blew him a kiss, then hurried down to the parking garage.

The evening traffic was even worse than the morning commute. By the time she pulled in the driveway, her worry over an untenable situation combined with fatigue had caused her temples to throb.

After parking the car, she hurried inside, moving past Lucca, who was cooking something at the stove. The duffel bag was nowhere in sight. A delicious aroma filled the house, even to the bathroom.

Annabelle had to admit she was glad their earlier conversation hadn't driven him away or put him off his food. On the way home from Amalfi, her anxiety level had gone off the charts. She'd feared she might find him in a more troubled state than the night he'd come home.

She reached for the bottle of ibuprofen she'd put in the cabinet. Two pills ought to do it. Cupping her hands, she trapped the water from the faucet and swallowed. In the process, her hair fell forward and some of it got wet. She reached in her purse for the tortoiseshell clip she carried and fastened the ends behind her head.

When she walked back to the kitchen, she couldn't help but notice how good he looked in another black shirt, a polo this time, and jeans. When she'd asked Marcella what it was about Italian men and their clothes, she said it was because the Italian mother considered her son to be so important, she pushed him to turn out gorgeous no matter what. She would actually starve herself to save the money to keep him stylish.

Annabelle smiled, not knowing if that was totally true, but in Italy she'd been surrounded by men who dressed with uncommon flare. Lucca was no exception. Even in the sweats and T-shirt he'd worn to bed last night, he'd looked classy, yet he seemed unconscious of it.

"Something smells delicious."

He was pouring a white sauce over the baked pasta

in a tomato base that was arranged in a large oval dish. "It does to me, too. I've made my favorite meal."

"What is it?"

"Veal cannelloni."

"Did your mama teach you?" Her mind was still on her conversation with Marcella.

"She taught me many things." The affection in his voice was palpable. He'd been his mama's boy all right. Italian men were known for putting their mothers on a pedestal. "Are you hungry?"

The change in his spirits from this morning came as a big shock. "Yes." All of a sudden she was famished.

"Then join me on the terrace and help me eat this."

He was feeling better and wanted to show her. She couldn't turn him down. "Would you like me t—"

"No," he interrupted. "I've managed pretty well on my own today."

He certainly had. "I can see that." So would his father when the time came.

Something dramatic had caused this alteration in his mood. She knew that getting him to open up was partially responsible.

While he carried the hot dish outside, she followed and sat down in one of the chairs. A lighted candle flickered over the table already set for two. On top of the floral cloth he'd placed bread and salad. Between the scent of flowers in the air and the wonderful smell of the cannelloni, it was all too romantic for words.

She watched him sit. He was still careful, but she was confident his pain was diminishing. He served her a sample of everything. "I made tea with lemons from the fruit on that overhang, but if you'd prefer wine, there's some in the cupboard. I won't be drinking any until I'm off my painkillers."

"Tea sounds perfect to me. What a good patient you are!"

"Actually I was the hospital's worst," he corrected her after starting in on his food. "By the time the doctors told me I'd healed enough to leave, they were ready to throw me out, but my psychiatrist said I wasn't ready. He was right. So were *you*."

Annabelle almost choked on the bread she was in the middle of swallowing. "About this morning—"

"We both know I have post-traumatic stress," he blurted before she could finish her thought. "The doctor told me I don't suffer from it as badly as some of the other guys he's treated, but I've been living in denial that it was my problem. You dashed water in my face and woke me up. It's what I needed, so don't apologize."

"If this meal is your way of thanking me, then I'm very humbled." She wiped the corner of her mouth with the napkin. "Thank you for not staying angry with me." The man had a lethal charm she couldn't deny.

"Since it serves both our purposes to live under the same roof, I decided we might as well enjoy our partnership in crime together."

"Lucca…you can't tease about something this serious. After we eat, I really am going to leave. I've already registered at the Casa Claudia."

His facial muscles tautened. "Why would you do that? This morning you offered me your services. Did I misunderstand?"

"No. That offer is still open, but not here in your home. Whether you realize it or not, I care for your father and can't bear the guilt I feel still pretending I don't know you're back in Ravello." She bit her lip. "Yes, I'm worried about my standing in his eyes, but aren't you afraid he'll somehow find out? He loves you. What if it's too much of a shock for him?"

Any parent would be hurt, especially Guilio, with all his plans. She dreaded what his reaction would be to know his son had been staying at the farmhouse with Annabelle and she'd said nothing.

His eyes narrowed on her features. "I'll call him tomorrow and explain everything. I swear it."

Annabelle believed him. "You have no idea how relieved I am to hear it."

"He'll understand I placed you in a terrible position and won't give it another thought. But since we're discussing your sins of omission, how about the one against me."

She was ready to tell him the truth. "Your father met me in California while he was over there on business. He came right out and asked me if I would fly to Italy for three weeks to be a model in a new campaign ad he was working on."

Lucca blinked. "You're a model?"

"Don't flatter me too much," she teased after hearing the surprise in his question.

"You know very well you're easy on the eyes," he drawled. "Go on. This conversation is getting more fascinating by the second."

"I told you I'm a nurse, but he said I had the look he wanted."

"He's never used a female model before."

"I found that out. The other day on one of the shoots I asked him again, 'Why me?' He said I have that all American look and smile that appeals to men who buy his cars. Apparently he's made a study of it or some-thing."

Laughter escaped his throat, surprising her because she so rarely heard it from him and because he was so attractive when he did laugh.

"What's so funny?"

"My father. He's good. In fact he's so good at what he does, even I stand in awe of him. What he really means in the American vernacular is that you're drop-dead gorgeous to every male in sight."

"I think you must be your father's son. You're good at what you do, too. No one's ever told me that before. You've made my heart pound out of rhythm."

When she realized she was actually flirting with him, she couldn't believe it. Not after the winter she'd been living in since the divorce.

He lounged back in the chair. "Where were you when I was recuperating in hospital?"

"Probably changing some old man's dressing at an-other hospital. Back then who would have dreamed that one day you'd be relaxing on your own terrace, let alone feeding your home-crasher divine cannelloni you learned to make at your mother's feet?"

He angled his dark head toward her. "You liked it?"

"Trust me, you could open up your own restaurant on your farming property."

"Now there's an idea! In that case I'll come up with something else to satisfy your taste buds for tomorrow night's menu."

Tomorrow night. The thought of it filled her with a fluttery sensation. "You mean you're going to feed me in return for my listening to you."

Lucca examined her with a speculative glance. "It

makes perfect sense to me. By the way, I need some things from the store. How would you like to drive me to the *farmacia* in Solerno for more shaving cream and blades. Unless you're too tired."

"Not at all." She'd taken something for her headache earlier, but it was the transformation in Lucca that had given her a second wind. She was pleased he was feeling this much better.

What alarmed her was how thrilled she was to be able to spend more time with him this evening. This shouldn't be happening. "We'd better hurry before it closes. I'll get my purse. After we get back, I'll do the dishes."

He got to his feet. "There's a rule in this house. Whoever does the cooking, does the cleaning up." He blew out the candle and followed her inside.

A half hour later they'd made the trip and she came out of the *farmacia* with the desired toiletries. When she would have gotten back in the car he said, "You see that *trattoria* across the piazza?"

"Yes?"

"It's been here for years. They serve a dessert to go called *torta caprese*. I think you'll like it."

"I could go for a *torta*," she said, mimicking his accent.

"*Bene.*" When he smiled like that, she had difficulty catching her breath. "Use the money I gave you to buy some for us. I've decided you were right about something else you said earlier. I need a little sweetening up."

Following that thought she felt another dart of awareness at being alone with him like this. "I'll be right back."

Annabelle wouldn't have said anything else, not when he was coming out of that dark place where he'd been thrust months ago. His appetite was returning and he'd unburdened himself to an extent. It had to mean he was on the emotional mend, but she needed to be careful that she didn't read more into this than the situation warranted.

Lucca was Guilio's son, just home from war, and she'd happened to be on the premises to offer some support. But in less than two weeks she'd be going home. To construe any more out of this would be absurd. If she'd taken it slower with Ryan after they'd first met, she might have picked up on a clue and not have married him. She needed to remember that.

The errand didn't take her long. When she returned, Lucca told her where to drive. Five minutes later he'd guided them to a private place where the view of lights along the coastline filled her vision.

"If the whole world could see what I'm seeing," she murmured.

"Climb in back and we'll look together while we eat."

His suggestion made sense because he'd done enough standing and moving for one day. Yet she couldn't help feeling like she was a teenager getting in the backseat of a guy's car, ostensibly to watch an outdoor movie.

The trouble was, she took too long before she acted. When she joined him, he leaned closer and whispered, "I still couldn't if I wanted to, *Annabellissima*."

CHAPTER FOUR

STEADY, Annabelle.

During the conversation with Marcella about the well-dressed Italian male, the designer had also given her tips about the Italian male himself. "They're born flirts. It's in their genes. They love women, all kinds, sizes and shapes.

"When they flatter you, they mean it, but don't assume it is a serious affair of the heart. A foreign woman does not understand this. She thinks she has his exclusive interest, which, of course, she does at the time, but it's not forever. He loves life, he loves love. The Italian woman understands this."

Annabelle decided Marcella gave out good advice. The change in Lucca from that first night in the hall was like night and day and had thrown her off her guard. As long as she knew to stay on guard, she'd be all right.

"I like your nickname for me, Lucca. No one else I've met has thought of it. It's very clever in fact, if you don't mind my saying." She felt him give her an odd glance while she pulled their cartons out of the sack and opened them. "Here you go. And a spoon."

"This is a local specialty," he informed her. "I've been salivating for one of these for ages."

"How long has it been since you were here last?"

"Maybe eight years."

"That's too long a time to be away from *this*." She'd almost said *home*, but caught herself in time.

He was too busy eating to comment.

"Umm," she moaned with pleasure after eating several mouthfuls. "It's like an undercooked brownie, but much better with that almond flavor. I can't stop with just one. I should have bought seconds."

He lounged back when he'd finished, looking amused. "When I stumbled up the hill between the fruit trees a few nights ago, I couldn't imagine being alive by morning. Now here I am stuffing myself with sweets in the backseat of a car with my new nurse."

No doubt he'd beguiled a ton of willing Italian female nurses, but he didn't know who he was dealing with. She put their empty cartons back in the sack. It was time for this American female nurse to go into action. He'd confided part of his soul to her. Now it was her turn so he wouldn't get the wrong idea that she was blindly attracted to him.

"I, too, can remember one night in the past believing that I wouldn't live through it."

She saw his expression quicken with curiosity.

"One of the nurses working on my shift at the hospital told me my husband had been having a full-blown affair with another nurse, whom I thought had been my friend."

Lucca eyed her for a lengthy moment. "When did it happen?"

"Two years ago. But evidently I did survive, and now here I am having eaten a decadent dessert with an Italian war hero. Who would have thought?" Before this went on any longer, she reached for the handle and got out of the car.

He continued to stare at her. "I hope you realize your ex-husband didn't deserve you. But if you're still so in love with him you can't sit still, then *you* need to talk about it."

She let out a measured breath. "My love for Ryan was burned out of me when I learned their relationship had been going almost from the beginning of our marriage."

After a period of quiet he asked, "How long were you married?"

"A year and a half." She stopped herself before she said anything more. Lucca didn't want to hear it, not when it sounded so trivial after what he'd lived through. She shut the door and opened the driver's door to get in.

"A very wise nurse I met the other night explained that a man who has seen combat needs to validate his existence to another warm body," Lucca continued as if she hadn't left the backseat. "It's vital that what he did in the war did matter to at least one other human being besides himself. *You've* been in combat of a different kind, Annabelle. Isn't that what my father meant about you deserving a break?"

She started up the car. "Yes."

"Why didn't you get help for it?"

Touché.

She waited until they were out on the main road before answering him. "I did. I divorced him and transferred to another hospital in Los Angeles."

"And now you're involved with this Mel Jardine?"

Lucca didn't miss much. "I met him after I moved to L.A."

"Where were you living before you moved?"

"In Fullerton. It's near L.A., where my family lives. My husband was finishing his residency at the same hospital where I'd been getting my nursing degree."

She heard him grind out something in Italian that needed no translation.

"You know what they say about a change being as good as a vacation, Lucca. At my lowest ebb, Mel offered me a job with his company. I took it and never looked back."

As she rounded a curve, another car started passing her. She had to brake so there wouldn't be an accident. That was all they would need, especially Lucca, whose surgery needed more time to really heal.

"Speaking of looking back, keep your head down. We're coming into Ravello. One of your family members or friends might be driving around and see you."

"In the backseat no less."

"And *alone*," she quipped. "No sign of lipstick on your mouth. Just chocolate." Giovanni wouldn't believe it.

A scoffing sound reached her ears and Annabelle grinned.

"So where do you go for these photo shoots?"

He was full of questions. "Besides Rome, where I've already been, they've been scheduled around the most beautiful spots along the Amalfi Coast. Basilio has been the one working with me the most, but your father's in charge of everything."

A brief silence prevailed before he asked her another question. "How did you meet my father exactly?"

"At Mel Jardine's dealership in L.A. He sells more Amalfis than any other in the States. Two months ago your father flew there to talk business with him."

Through the rearview mirror she saw Lucca's head lift. "You work for *that* dealership?"

"Yes."

"After being a nurse?" He sounded incredulous.

At last they were home safe and hopefully still undiscovered, but it didn't matter now that Lucca had promised to call his father. After she'd pulled in the drive, he climbed out of the back with the sacks. In the darkness he made an imposing figure. "What do you do for him. Don't tell me you sell cars."

"I won't. I'm Mel's private secretary."

"There *is* no such animal with the Cavezzali dealers." He stood there looking perplexed with his hands outstretched, Italian to the core. She wished she didn't find him so…appealing.

"That's true, but he created the job after his heart attack." She hurried ahead of him and let them in the house.

When she would have gone straight to the terrace to start cleaning up, he caught her hand. "Not yet. I want to hear the rest to the part where my father comes into this."

He wasn't about to let it go. Naturally he was curious. In fact he'd shown amazing restraint up to now. "I have to be to work early in the morning, but I'll make a deal with you. If you'll let me help you with the dishes, I'll tell you. We can get them done faster so you can get off that leg."

With seeming reluctance Lucca let her hand slip out

of his, but it left warmth curling up her arm to envelop her whole body. "The house doesn't have a dishwasher."

"It does now." She smiled at him. "I'll clear the table while you fill the sink."

He returned her smile. Another one without shadows. *Mama mia,* as they said back in old Napoli.

"You made quite a mess in the kitchen," Annabelle commented a few minutes later, "but it was worth it."

Lucca's arms were up to his elbows in suds. He scooped a few and blew them softly in her face. "Compliments won't get you out of telling me what I want to know."

She rinsed in the other sink and started wiping bowls and pans. "To make a long story short, Mel was one of my patients. He'd had a heart attack and needed special nursing after he left the hospital. The man is superenergetic and very persuasive. He arranged with my supervisor for me to go home with him for a few weeks."

He glanced at her. "I take it you wouldn't have consented unless you'd wanted to."

"No. He's very kind and treats me like a daughter really. Mel's a widower and his grown children don't live nearby. Though he has a housekeeper, he needed a nurse. We formed a friendship.

"When he got well enough to go back to work, the doctor cautioned him to cut down on his load and find an assistant to help handle his hectic schedule. Mel claimed I took such good care of him during his illness, he said he'd pay me triple what I made at the hospital if I'd come to work for him. So I did."

"From nursing to cars. Quite a jump from one arena to another that's vastly different."

"I know. My job description was to keep him sorted

out. I don't know about cars, but I can work with people."

"It's clear to me you'd be a natural at whatever you chose to do." She knew enough about Lucca to realize he never said what he didn't mean. His compliment meant more to her than it should have. She was starting to care too much. "What was the defining factor that made you accept his offer?"

She finished wiping the utensils and put them in the drawer. He'd been honest with her. Why not tell him the truth? What could it hurt?

"When I confronted my ex, he intimated our lives had been boring for a long time. Ryan wanted out of his mundane existence. He said that once we were married, the excitement went out of our relationship."

"Had you been intimate before the wedding?"

Annabelle had been in Italy long enough to notice that Italian men weren't afraid to talk about personal things. They got in your space. In that way they different from the American male.

She shook her head. Even if she'd thought the question audacious, they'd already gone way past desultory conversation to talk from those painful private places. "No. I was raised that you waited until you took your vows."

"So in order to win the prize, he had to marry you first."

"I never thought about it that way, but now that you mention it, I'm sure you're right."

"Some men are like that, Annabelle. Always needing another conquest to validate their existence. I've known rootless types like him."

"Rootless?"

"*Sì*," he said in his inimitable Italian way. "It's my theory they're not centered and therefore destined to be distracted by anything new that comes along, often discarding something or someone who's a pearl beyond price," he added in his deep voice.

A quiver ran through her body. Talking to Lucca was like inhaling a fresh, invigorating breeze. "I appreciate what you're saying, but I'm hardly a pearl. In all fairness, we both had periods where we did twenty-four-hour rounds, often at the wrong times. It wasn't a recipe for togetherness. There's a high ratio of divorce in that field. We ended up one of the statistics."

"You and half the world." She felt his intense gaze. "Your ex—Ryan, is it?—couldn't hold a candle to you."

His words were unexpected. The kind of words you wanted to hear when you weren't so sure of yourself anymore. Not even her husband had said things like that to her before they were married. "That's a lovely compliment, Lucca."

"It's only the truth."

She tossed her head back. "When I got married, I was so certain my marriage wouldn't fail. At the time of the divorce, Mel caught me at the moment when my pain was at its peak. In my vulnerability, I felt that some time away from medicine might be the best thing for me. I guess I thought it was time I stepped out of my predictable life and did something unpredictable. No reminders of the past.

"Mel and I already got along well. The transition to become his assistant didn't sound too difficult. Best of all, the kind of work I would do for him wouldn't tread on anyone else's toes. No one lost a job because of me. All those reasons fed into my decision, but in truth, I didn't want to be around the medical world, where the past would haunt me."

"That makes sense," he murmured. "Now we pan away to my father's arrival on the scene."

"Yes." Her pulse quickened. "The three of us spent several days together. He was gathering ideas for a new ad campaign and wanted my input from an American woman's perspective. I was amazed at his request, but it tickled me that he'd picked me over dozens of beautiful women who were professional models. As you can imagine, it was a boost to my sagging ego. Mel was willing to let me go if I promised to return by the end of June."

While she spoke, Lucca had been staring at her through veiled eyes, preventing her from knowing what he was thinking. "How much longer before you have to fly away?"

"Two weeks." Minus a day. She was dreading the day she had to go back and leave all this…leave Lucca. She carried the dishtowel and cloth to the utility area near the door of the kitchen and put it in the washer with some other things. After turning on the machine, she closed the door and turned to him. "In case you were wondering, Guilio did offer me a good sum of money to come, probably the going rate of a top model."

"I don't doubt it."

"I felt a fraud. What if the camera didn't like me? Out of that fear I told him I couldn't work for him unless I was paid the same salary Mel was paying me. After all, your father was virtually giving me a three-week holiday in Italy, all expenses paid plus the air fare over and back. To me that was a dream come true. In the end, he agreed."

He cocked his dark head. "My father is always in the driver's seat when it comes to establishing terms. For you to have the final say meant he wanted you here any way he could have you. So tell me—has it been a dream come true so far?"

She reeled from his question. Since Guilio had first approached her, she felt like she was in a dream, deathly afraid to wake up and find she was back in that dark place where she'd been existing. Annabelle couldn't bear the thought of ever being there again.

"So far it has been a thrill," she answered honestly, and Lucca was the major reason why. "Ask me again in two weeks. Good night." She started for the bedroom. He followed her down the hall.

"Don't go," he said in a husky tone. "I don't relish being left alone yet."

She turned to face him, alert to a nuance in his voice that sounded like he really meant it. "If you need to talk, just tell me."

"No. I'm too tired for that and know you must be, too." After a pause he said, "In a short period of time it seems I've got used to your company. I like the idea that you're just down the hall from me. You're easy to be around, do you know that? No woman of my acquaintance has ever had that particular quality."

"It's funny you'd say that. During the divorce Ryan accused me of having the opposite effect on him. He claimed he'd started walking on eggshells around me."

"But of course." His Italian shrug fascinated her. *Everything fascinated her.* "That was his guilt talking. In my country, there's a name for a man like that."

Something about the way he said that name caused her to smile. "In my country, too."

He reciprocated with a smile of his own. "As I was saying, you have a soothing effect that draws people to you. No wonder Mel Jardine didn't want to lose you after he left the hospital."

"Thank you," she whispered. This man knew to say all the right things. She was starting to get frightened by the strength of her feelings for him. "*Buona notte*, Lucca."

Lucca *had* got used to having her around. In just a few days he no longer felt like he was falling apart. He had Annabellissima to thank for this much of a sense of well being.

She was *bellissima*, from the inside out. Lucca wasn't about to let her go. He hadn't begun to plumb her depths.

It was time to talk to his father. Lucca decided to make good on his promise to her and call him now. Guilio would probably be in bed, but not asleep yet. Most likely he was enthralled in a good biography, his favorite kind of reading material.

After getting ready for bed, he stretched out in the most comfortable position for his leg and reached for the phone.

"*Lucca*?" his father cried after the second ring. From the sound of his voice, Lucca could tell he was wide-awake. That was good. "What a surprise to hear from you tonight! How are you, *figlio mio*?"

Much better than he'd expected to be when he'd first stumbled through the orchard to reach the farmhouse. "*Molto bene, Papa*. More to the point, how are you?"

"I couldn't be better now that I can hear your voice.

You're not still upset with me about not selling you those properties are you?"

Lucca gripped his phone tighter. "No matter how run-down they are, I still want to buy them, *Papa*, but that's not why I'm calling you now. I know it's late. If you want, I'll phone you back in the morning."

"Are you *demente*?" he boomed. "You call me, then you say I'll speak to you in the morning?"

His father would never change. "I just wanted to be sure you weren't too tired."

"If I were taking my last breath of life, I wouldn't be too tired to talk to you."

He felt his father's love and a bolt of guilt zapped him for not having called him sooner, but he hadn't gotten his pain under control until now. "I have a confession to make."

"What's another one in the long list of my son's antics?" his father teased.

"This is a big one."

"You got married and are bringing her home?" The hope in his father's voice never ceased to amaze him. To Guilio, marriage was everything. Certainly for his father, being married had kept his life stable and fulfilling.

"Not exactly. I've left the military for good."

After a pause Guilio said, "I don't believe it." His voice trembled for joy. "What will you do now that you're coming home?" he demanded.

"I'm going to be a farmer like I always wanted to be."

Rather than an outburst, for once all he heard was silence on the other end. Lucca knew it wasn't the answer his father was waiting to hear, but it had to be said. "*Papa*? Are you still there?"

"Of course I'm still here. There had to be a reason why you suddenly left the service. What was it?"

That brilliant business brain of his never stopped thinking. "I got an injury to my leg that makes me ineligible to be a pilot."

"How bad is it?" Guilio asked in a thick tone.

"I walked up the steep incline to the farmhouse on my own two legs. That's how bad I am." It was the truth. He was thankful to be able to say it.

"You mean you're in Ravello?" he bellowed.

"I was able to catch a military flight with some others guys and got here in the middle of the night. It was too late to disturb you and Maria. Unfortunately I fell by accident after letting myself in the farmhouse. So I loaded up on pain pills and have mostly slept. Would you believe I found an American woman named Annabelle sleeping in my bed?"

He'd managed to take his father's breath away. "You must have frightened her out of her skin!"

"Such beautiful skin, *Papa*. Actually she frightened the devil out of me when she started to call the police. I understand she's doing some modeling for a new ad campaign for you. To be honest, I can see why you picked her."

In spite of all the shocking news, his father managed to chuckle. "She's not as helpless as she looks."

"It's the nurse in her. When she found out I was your son and why I'd come home, she couldn't do enough to make me comfortable in my own home. I have to admit I like all the attention she's giving me. That's because she's crazy about you and upset that I took until tonight to call you. She's so loyal to you, I've been in the dog-house."

"That's gratifying to hear, but you have to understand something, Lucca. She's not like the other women who've come in and out of your life. This one is different."

"I know. As soon as she found out I'd come home, she registered at the Casa Claudia."

"You mean she has already moved out?"

"Not yet. She was planning to go in the morning, but I told her I hoped she would stay on. You know. Finders, keepers."

"Lucca—"

"Seriously, I like having her around and she loves this place. Since you installed her here first, I'd like her to stay. You can trust me to treat her like a princess."

"That's exactly what she is," his father grumbled. Shades of a lecture were in his voice. "Annabelle is a lady, just like your mother."

He blinked. Rare praise coming from his father. "I've already found that out, *Papa*. For one thing she wears her divorce like a shroud."

"She's been hurt."

"It's time she got over it. He didn't deserve her."

"Amen."

"Since the rooming arrangements have worked out for her so far, I've asked her to stay on, *Papa*, but that's up to her."

"If she's still with you, then it sounds like she's agreeable."

"I guess I'll find out tomorrow, but I'll be asleep most

of the day. The medication I'm on for pain puts me out for hours at a time. She makes sure I take it."

"It sounds like a nurse is exactly what you need. Under the circumstances I'm going to fly to Milan tomorrow and get some business out of the way." Lucca was surprised, but relieved, too, since it gave him another day to recuperate from his fall. "When I get back Monday morning, we'll spend the day together."

"Good. I want to buy those properties and settle down to work."

Again there was no outburst.

"*Papa,* remember that I'm not going anywhere."

More silence. "Do you have any idea how many years I've been waiting to hear those words?"

The lump in Lucca's throat grew a little larger. "Forgive me for waiting until I got home to call you?"

"What do you think?" he blurted in a voice gruff with emotion.

Tears smarted Lucca's eyes. "*Ti voglio bene, Papa.*"

"I love you, too. *Grazie a Dio* you're home in one piece."

Lucca seconded the motion. "The minute you're back in Ravello, come to the farmhouse. I'm going to make you a true Cavezzali breakfast."

"I'll be there, Lucca. In fact I'm already salivating."

"*Ciao,* Papa."

With his father's question about Annabelle going around in his head, he hung up and turned on the side he favored because of his leg to go to sleep. He had no doubts she wanted to stay. She *did* love the farm. What he'd told his father was the truth. It was very clear in the way she'd put flowers everywhere and sat dreamy eyed on the terrace breathing in the fragrance.

His last thought before he knew no more was that her fragrance was even more intoxicating.

Annabelle left the farmhouse before Lucca awakened and took off for her next destination. If he'd been up to say good-morning, she might have had difficulty leaving at all. Something was happening inside of her she didn't have the power to stop. Like a color enhancer on a movie cam, the world suddenly had a new brilliance.

She rounded the hairpin turn and fell instantly in love with the Amalfi convertible parked below the steeply terraced vineyards of Furore. The only way to describe the paint's color was to compare it to a semiprecious sea-green jade stone, light and lustrous. Combined with the creamy leather interior, it took her breath.

The crew hailed her. Basilio guided her to park behind the van as close to the wall of the road as possible. At this dizzying height, it was the only thing keeping all of them from falling into the sparkling blue depths below.

Being that it was a Saturday, everyone was anxious to get finished early and enjoy the rest of the weekend. The hairdresser quickly caught Annabelle's hair back in a loose chignon. Once her makeup was done, Marcella helped her into an eggshell-toned blouson of pin-tucked thin crepe.

The tucks ran vertically down the front, but were horizontal on the three-quarter sleeves. There was some chain-stitching detail Annabelle loved. The waist pulled it into shape over matching colored wide-legged pants.

After she'd put on sandals with bands of blue and green, Marcella produced a scarf the same color as the car's exterior and put it around her neck, knotting it loosely at the side. For an added touch, she put her in jade earrings.

The result brought a smile from Basilio, who proclaimed the whole effect perfection. Secretly Annabelle wished she could wear this outfit back to the farmhouse. She wanted to look beautiful for Lucca, but the price tag would be astronomical.

"What we want you to do is lean against the side of the car and reach for the bunch of purple grapes here. You saw these and you couldn't resist stopping for a taste. Giovanni will film you at various angles to capture the car as well as the view behind you."

"Be careful you don't drip juice if you bite into one," Marcella cautioned her.

Annabelle turned to Giovanni. "Do I have to eat them?"

"I don't know yet."

In the end he was satisfied with the shoot without her tasting the fruit. Both Annabelle and Marcella breathed a sigh of relief that the clothes weren't stained.

Basilio clapped his hands. "Everyone? We meet Monday morning in Sorrento. Eight o'clock sharp."

For a day and a half she was free. She went back to the van to change into her jeans and T-shirt. After removing all her makeup, she slipped into her car to go home and saw that it wasn't even one o'clock yet. She felt like a schoolgirl playing hooky for the rest of the day.

Lucca would be surprised to hear her drive in. He wouldn't be expecting her until evening. Would it be too much to ask that he'd already gotten in touch with his father to let him know he was back in Italy?

Until Guilio knew the truth, there was nothing to

work out with Lucca. Once Annabelle reached the farm-house to freshen up, she would try to get her mind off her worries and take off on a long drive. She would fill her eyes with the mind-blowing scenery found only in this part of the world. But when she pulled up in the drive a little while later, thoughts of her day trip left her mind when she saw another car parked there.

At first she thought it might be Guilio's. Or maybe it was one of Lucca's stepbrothers on an errand of some kind for their stepfather. But the car wasn't an Amalfi, nor was it luxurious. Of course the visitor could be any-one, but it meant Lucca wasn't alone.

CHAPTER FIVE

ANNABELLE got out of the car and entered the kitchen, not knowing what to expect. Voices drifted in from the living room. One belonged to a female. In between pauses, both were speaking Italian in hushed tones.

If Annabelle stayed in the kitchen, Lucca wouldn't know she was here. Since she didn't want him to discover her and think she'd been eavesdropping, she had no choice but to hurry down the hallway past the living room. That way he would see her on the way to her bedroom.

Out of the corner of her eye she glimpsed a dark-haired woman in his arms. She was probably Annabelle's age. Sobs punctuated her words. An old girlfriend perhaps? She had to be someone important to Lucca, a person he trusted implicitly, otherwise he wouldn't have told her she could come over.

The moment she closed her bedroom door, he rapped on it. "Annabelle?"

She wheeled around in surprise, cross with herself for having any feelings one way or the other about Lucca's personal life. "Yes?"

"When you're ready, I'd like you to come out and meet Stefana. She's the wife of my pilot friend Leo who was killed."

Annabelle's eyes closed tightly. "I—I'll be right there," she stammered as she tried to gather her wits.

How awful for the other woman. It hadn't occurred to her that this Stefana was here for any other reason than the seemingly obvious one. Annabelle had jumped to the wrong conclusion. Probably because she'd listened to the film crew make the odd remark here and there about Guilio's son being somewhat of a Casanova.

She imagined most attractive bachelors carried that same label. It went with the territory. But after their conversation last night, she had the feeling that if Lucca were ever to marry, he wouldn't be one of those rootless men who was easily distracted. Or was she only trying to convince herself.

Once she'd freshened up, she walked the rest of the way to the living room, which was decorated in authentic country Italian, if there was such a thing. Annabelle had only peeked in before now.

Lucca sat on a chair opposite Stefana, who was perched on a rose settee. He'd prepared them an elaborate lunch. It appeared they'd been together for quite a while. The moment he saw Annabelle standing in the doorway, he got to his feet.

"Come in, *Signorina* Marsh. I want you to meet Stefana Beraldi. I told her you're employed by my father."

When the other woman stood up, Annabelle could see she was pregnant. Probably six months. Her heart lurched because the baby would grow up without its father.

"How do you do, *signorina*," Stefana said in English with a heavy Italian accent.

"It's nice to meet you, *Signora* Beraldi. I'm so sorry

to hear about your husband. There really aren't any words, are there."

"No." Her brown eyes filled with liquid. "It's still hard to believe he's gone. I came to see Lucca. We've had a long talk. I asked him if he would be godfather when our little girl is born."

Being a godfather signified a great responsibility. Lucca's eyes traveled from her to Annabelle. "I told Stefana I'd be honored. She made this special trip from Naples to ask me in person."

She sniffed. "My husband and I talked about it the last time he was on leave. He loved Lucca."

"I understand Lucca loved your husband, too." Annabelle would never forget his sobs as he relived the horrific moment in the sky when Stefana's husband was shot down. She would be lucky to have Lucca for a lifetime friend.

The other woman smiled at him through the tears. "Don't forget. I'm planning on you coming for dinner after you're settled."

"I'll look forward to it."

"Good. Now I have to go."

"Let me see you out to your car."

Annabelle put her hand on the woman's arm, squeezing gently. "I'm glad you don't have too far to drive in your condition. Take care of yourself and your baby."

She nodded. "I will. She's all I have left of him." With tears streaming down her cheeks, she hurried off with Lucca. Annabelle watched from the kitchen doorway.

For a long time she'd wished she had Ryan's baby, even if their marriage hadn't worked out. But now she wasn't so sure. Stefana would have to raise her daughter on her own. How hard that would be.

It wasn't just the physical side of earning the living and seeing to the baby's every need. There was the financial and emotional drain of not having the father an intimate part of everything. Stefana would have to go through labor alone, shoulder the heavy responsibility alone. Unless she married again. But that could be a long way off.

Deep in thought, she watched the two of them converse a little longer before Stefana drove away. By the time Lucca came back in the house, lines had marred his face. The loss of Leo had taken its own toll.

"How long were you friends with him?"

"For the last five years."

"You two really had to be close for her to want you for the godfather of their child."

She saw the sadness in his eyes. "Being pilots together causes you to build a special bond. We were like brothers and talked about going into business together when we retired from the air force. But destiny had a different idea," he whispered.

Annabelle put a hand on his arm, desolate for him because the loss was a blow to his vision for the future. "Does his wife have family to help her?"

He nodded. "Lots of relatives. She phoned me yesterday and left a message. When I called her back and told her I was home from the Middle East, she begged to come over and see me."

"She's lovely. I have no doubts you'll make a wonderful godfather."

His eyes probed Annabelle's. "What would make you say that?"

"Do you really need me to tell you? How could you be anything else when you were her husband's best friend? I heard the love for him in your voice during your flashback. I'm sure he's up in heaven thrilled you're going to do the honors."

When she didn't think it was possible, a glimmer of light ignited those somber depths. "You're just what the doctor ordered today. How come you're home this early?"

"Our film crew worked fast this morning. Everyone wanted to get away to enjoy a long weekend." The word everyone included Annabelle, who couldn't wait to return to the farmhouse.

"Since my father flew to Milan this morning, does it mean you have no more calls on your time?"

"He did?" She wheeled around. "How do you know that?" she cried.

"I called him last night and told him everything."

She let out a happy gasp and wanted to throw her arms around him, but of course she couldn't. "Everything? Literally?"

"*Sì.*"

Her eyes misted over. "Thank heaven." The news that Lucca was home meant the timing for Guilio's surprise would have to be moved up. No wonder he'd gone to Milan today. He had to make new arrangements. His staff would have to work miracles.

"That sounded so heartfelt, I realize you really have been carrying a heavy burden. I admire your loyalty to my father. Very much in fact."

"He's a terrific man to work for."

Lucca's chuckle told her he had his own opinion on the subject. "We had quite a conversation about the beautiful *Signorina* Marsh. I told him I liked your company and want you to stay on."

She wanted that more than anything. It was a thrill to wake up in the morning and know Lucca was in the house, that they'd talk and fix food and just be together.

"Take your time to decide while you're enjoying your day off. What were you planning to do?"

A certain inflection in his voice convinced her he had to be at a loose end. "I thought I'd take a long drive and do exactly what I want to do."

She thought her response might have deflated him a little. Now that *Signora* Beraldi had gone, maybe Annabelle's company was better than none. Ironic that he'd craved his solitude, yet this week of being cooped up by himself was probably making him claustrophobic.

"Want to do it with me? You're welcome to come."

"I'm afraid I can't go swimming yet."

Even so, it sounded as if he would like to take her up on her offer.

"That's not on my agenda."

"I'm surprised." He gave her a speculative glance. "Most foreigners can't wait to ruin their complexions by tanning themselves on every beach they come to."

"Well, I'm not your typical tourist. Today I'd rather give my eyes a workout. Giovanni, the photographer, warned me not to get a sunburn or anything close to it." She flashed him a smile. "If you're interested, get what you need and meet me at the car."

When she went outside a few minutes later, she discovered him in the front passenger seat. With everything out in the open, she felt like she was walking on air.

Until now her dilemma had tortured her. Whose secret could be revealed first that would cause the least amount of damage? She knew enough of both men's past history to realize they were equally vulnerable. But now she didn't have to worry about it. Guilio's plan to surprise his son was still safe. The relief was exquisite.

Lucca turned to her, but she couldn't see his eyes for his sunglasses. "What's the verdict? Is my nurse going to leave me high and dry, or can I count on you to be around when I need to talk? Normally night is the time when I get my restless attacks. To know you're just down the hall gives me more comfort than you can imagine."

She sucked in her breath. "I'm still deciding." That was because the alarm bells inside her head were going off, warning her to proceed at her own risk. This was a man who already meant too much to her. Any more time spent with him, and he would become her whole world. But if he didn't reciprocate her feelings, then she was in for a letdown she might never get over.

He slanted her a glance. "I'm assuming there are times when you've had ragged moments since your divorce and need to unload on someone you can trust. I can be a pretty good listener if you'll let me."

There'd been times when she would have loved a confidant besides her parents. Lucca sensed it because he was a very intuitive man. It was also true that he'd needed help and their unplanned housing arrangement made it easy for her to provide it.

Annabelle didn't know when it had happened, but she did feel secure around him. For so long she hadn't believed she could depend on a man again, let alone want to. She'd thought Ryan's betrayal had caused a part of her soul to die, but Lucca's effect on her made her realize it had only gone into hibernation. Otherwise she wouldn't be taking this drive with him.

"You're like your father, hard to turn down."

"I like being compared to him, but it makes for fireworks when he and I are on opposite sides of an issue."

With a laugh she started the car and they were off. Lucca made a fabulous navigator and told her which roads to take for the most superb views. She chauffeured them through mountaintops and rows of grapevines blanketing the hillsides.

Hours later when darkness had fallen, they stopped for seafood at a charming fishing village outside Solerno, with its beach of black sand. The restaurant looked out over the water. People were dancing. Everything was perfect. Too perfect?

Afraid she was getting ahead of herself where Lucca was concerned, she didn't want to make a mistake that could be fatal in the end. Already she sensed he meant far too much to her.

"Isn't the fish to your liking?" He'd long since removed his sunglasses. His eyes traveled over her, taking their time.

"You know it is."

"Then why do you look...anxious? Surely you've been out to dinner with other men since your divorce."

"Only on business."

"Is that the reason you can't commit to staying on with me? Why do I get the feeling you're concerned my father's opinion of you will be altered in some way if you do?"

Annabelle stared at him over the flickering candle. Taking her courage in her hands she said, "Not just your father's. Yours, too. You see, I've come to revere both of you."

Revere was an interesting word, throwing Lucca for a loop. It went deeper than *like* or *admire*. Love didn't come into it.

Her eyes had flecks of violet among the blue. Right now they stood out. Lucca had noticed they did that when she was in a highly emotional state.

He was damned if he could figure her out. While they were eating, he'd been tempted to dance with her, but the doctor had told him not to do that kind of activity yet. To his consternation, the face and body that had lain next to his for that short time the other night had taken hold of his mind and wouldn't let go. After the time he'd been spending with her, he needed to feel her soft curves in his arms.

She smelled as good as the flowers surrounding the house. Better even, because she was a woman with her own feminine scent.

That time in the backseat of the car with her, the evening they did dishes together, the night when she'd arranged the pillows for his leg, he'd breathed in her essence. It filled him with longings more profound than those he'd felt with other women. He had the disturbing impression that one night's possession of her body wouldn't be enough for him.

The fact that he could admit it made him realize he was swimming in deep water himself. Never in his life had he been jealous of another man, but he suspected her ex-husband still had hold of some part of her heart. Otherwise she'd probably be married again by now or at least in a serious relationship.

She had that vulnerability about her that had brought

out his father's and Mel Jardine's protective instincts. She brought out more emotions in Lucca than he'd felt in the whole of his life where another woman was concerned. Before she bewitched him completely, he pushed himself away from the table and got to his feet.

His gesture startled her. She jumped up, too. "Are you in pain?" she whispered softly.

Yes. But not the kind she was referring to. He put some bills on the table. "A little. It seems I was so eager to spend the day with you, I left the house without bringing my pills with me."

A rose tint sprang to her cheeks. "Then we'll hurry back."

She turned and walked through the restaurant ahead of him, drawing the eye of every male in the place. Besides her long legs and other stunning attributes, her hair gleamed silvery-gold in the candle light, as if each strand gave off inner properties like the elements themselves.

When they reached the car, she opened the front door for him. The nurse in her proved to be ever attentive. Once he'd eased his sore leg in, she went around and started the motor. Was that all he represented to her? A patient?

The drive home didn't take long. Neither of them spoke. He waited until they were back in the house and he'd taken another pill. She was on her way to the bedroom by the time he called to her from the hallway. She turned around, eyeing him with what he thought was mild trepidation.

"I enjoyed today, Annabelle."

"So did I."

"Knowing how you feel about my father, you need

to hear that he ordered me to treat you like the princess you are. In other words, he gave his blessing because he has the highest regard for you and wants to trust me. With my reputation, which has had its moments of truth, I'm afraid I'm the one who has yet to prove myself worthy."

That brought a smile. "So far I can vouch for you."

His jaw hardened. "Don't count on that lasting too long. Would it shock you if I told you I'm a little frightened by the way you make me feel? *Buona notte.*"

Annabelle braced herself against the closed door, burying her face in her hands. *Lucca, Lucca.* Today he'd set her on fire with one look. Tonight at the restaurant when he'd helped her to the table, his touch had electrified her.

Given enough time she'd probably make an utter fool of herself with him. Intuition told her that once involved, she'd never want to get uninvolved. But she had to admit it was hard to walk away from him knowing he was still fragile.

Tomorrow morning she would move her stuff to the hotel before she left for the photo shoot. The pills always knocked him out. When he woke up, he'd see it was for the best.

Annabelle slept poorly for the rest of the night. Around seven she awoke after hearing a noise. She sat up in bed and listened for it again. Maybe Lucca hadn't been able to sleep and had gotten up to fix himself some lemon tea he favored.

There it went again, that mournful sound. An animal outside maybe? She threw on her robe. The minute she opened the door, she realized it was coming from Lucca's room. After listening again she realized he was in the middle of another nightmare. It didn't surprise her. Stefana's visit would have triggered memories from his subconscious. Unfortunately they'd found expression once he'd fallen asleep.

She tiptoed into his room. His covers were strewn on the floor. He lay on his stomach wearing nothing but the bottom of his sweats. Her heart ached to watch gut-wrenching sobs shake his body while his face was buried in the pillow. His hard-muscled physique was as stiff as an iron poker.

Without conscious thought she sat down on the mattress and curved one of her hands around his shoulder. The other went to his hip. "Lucca," she called softly to him. "Wake up. You're dreaming. Come on." Using a gentle rolling motion, she managed to get him on his back. More unintelligible words flew out of his mouth.

His tear-washed face was her undoing. She bent over him and started kissing his eyelids and cheeks. "Lucca?" she whispered. "You're no longer in the air force. You're home and safe." She ran her lips over every rugged line and angle of the face haunting *her* dreams. Her hands massaged his shoulders, willing him to relax and let go of the powerful flashback.

"Hush now," she murmured against his lips, both of theirs salty from his tears. "You're not alone. I'm here."

Just when she thought she wasn't getting through to him he muttered, "Annabelle?"

"Yes," she cried, so relieved he'd come back to reality, she didn't care what he thought of her unorthodox methods. Her sorrow for what he'd suffered went too deep for tears. He'd been injured and had lost his best friend. She rocked him in her arms. With a swift strength she could scarcely credit, he pulled her body all the way on to the bed.

"Your leg—"

"I'm being careful," he assured her. "Take off that nurse's hat and give me the kiss of life again so I know I'm not dreaming." In the next second his mouth covered hers and she found herself opening up to him. She couldn't hold back, not when she wanted him with such a hunger she was shocked by it.

Lucca had come awake, drawing long, deeply passionate kisses from her mouth until she couldn't breathe. They moved as one flesh, giving and taking their pleasure. She'd entered a realm of rapture she'd never known before and time ceased to exist.

Under his spell she was so far gone, she didn't hear the knocking on the kitchen door until Lucca relinquished her mouth with a groan and sat up to listen. He was more beautiful to her than any Roman god.

The knocking persisted even louder than before. "Someone wants to see you."

"Maybe its Basilio from work with a message from your father. It must be important, but I don't know why he didn't phone me. He has my cell number."

Embarrassed to be caught like this, Annabelle scrambled out of Lucca's warm arms and got off the bed, totally disoriented and disheveled. She could tell his morning whiskers had given her a slight rash.

"You stay here, Lucca. I'll see who it is."

His eyes were still slumberous from their passion. "Hurry back."

The huskiness of his tone set her body trembling. She shut the door to the bedroom and raced through the house to the kitchen, cinching the belt to her robe tighter around the waist.

"Who is it?" she called from behind the door.

"*Signorina* Marsh? It's Fortunato Colombari!"

Guilio's grandson. She'd never met him, but she'd heard about him. Taking a second breath she opened the door. A dark blond Italian teen, maybe sixteen or seventeen, stood there rocking back on his heels with a surprised look of undeniable male interest in his brown eyes. He stared at her for what seemed a full minute. Had he noticed her swollen lips, which Lucca had nearly devoured because they couldn't seem to get enough of each other?

"My *mama* sent me down to see if you require anything," he explained in very good English. "Guilio, my grandfather, is in Milan, so she agreed to watch out for you."

"How nice of her. It's a pleasure to meet you, Fortunato."

"Same here. *Mama* sent you some fresh melons. I will put them on the counter for you." Without waiting for permission, he walked inside carrying a basket of them. When she shut the door and turned around, her eyes saw what he could see.

Lucca must have been so tired last night, he'd pulled off his clothes and had thrown them over one of the kitchen chairs. His socks and shoes lay on the floor, one shoe on its side. Though he'd brought the dishes in from the living room, he hadn't cleaned up the kitchen after the big lunch he'd made for him and Stefana yesterday.

After almost staggering out of Lucca's bed and room, Annabelle had been so enthralled with him, she hadn't noticed anything else. But there was no doubt Fortunato was looking at everything and coming to the conclusion that she wasn't living here alone. And she was a messy guest, too.

"That was so kind of you to bring me fruit, Fortunato. Please thank your mother for me."

His eyes slid to the white cargo pants and blue sport shirt. He gave her a devilish grin. "I will tell her you are enjoying Italy very much."

She felt heat swarm to her face. *Guilty as charged.*

On his way out the door, he paused. "I will also tell her you are more *squisita* than Grandfather Guilio says you are. When the women in our family meet you, they will all be jealous and the men will wish they had met you first." He blew her a kiss. "*Ciao, signorina.*"

"*Ciao.*" She watched him drive away in a fabulous champagne-colored Amalfi four-door voyager.

"Sounds like you made a conquest of Ruggero's son." Lucca had come up behind her. His warmth enveloped her as his hands slid around her waist from behind. She felt his lips kiss the nape of her neck. It sent rivulets of desire through her body, causing her to gasp softly. But much as she wanted to go back to the bedroom with him and pick up where they'd left off, she couldn't.

"Lucca, he knows—"

"He knows a man is in the house," he said against the side of her neck and kissed her skin again. The mere contact made her feel light-headed. "He just doesn't know who. Once he tells his *mama* about the *squisita signorina* staying in my house, she'll be down to investigate.

"Does it matter? *Papa* knows I'm home." Lucca spun her around, wrapping his arms around her neck. "Now

I have to have this." He planted a hot kiss to her mouth, melting her bones in the process.

Annabelle could have stayed crushed against him indefinitely, but not wanting to get caught by Fortunato's mother, she tore her lips from Lucca's so she could ease away.

He studied her upturned features for a moment. "Don't be concerned. Fortunato is harmless."

"But he'll tell everyone what he saw and it will get out that *Signorina* Marsh has a lover."

"That frightens you, doesn't it?"

"Yes."

His black brows knit together. He grasped her upper arms. "Something tells me this has a lot to do with your ex-husband."

"What?"

A tiny nerve throbbed at the corner of his compelling mouth. "Some women feel guilty about enjoying another man even after they've been divorced. It usually means she still imagines herself in love with her ex-spouse and is waiting for him to come back to her."

"You may have known a woman like that, but that's an absolutely crazy theory and doesn't apply to me!" she cried.

"Doesn't it?" Lucca wouldn't let this go until he got the answer he wanted. "Ryan won't last long with the woman he's married to, even if they have a baby. You can count on it."

"Well you can count on this—examine my heart and you'll discover no trace of him there because he became extinct the day I learned he betrayed me."

He gave her a speculative stare until she wanted to

scream. In this mood, the passion they'd shared earlier might never have happened.

"Do you honestly think I would have switched hospitals, let alone have gone to work for Mel, if I'd still had the slightest hope Ryan would regret what he'd done and ask for a second chance? He destroyed every particle of affection I ever had for him."

Lucca gave an elegant shrug. "You've convinced me. I won't bring him up to you again."

"Thank you." Her voice shook.

"So what else is going on with you?" One brow had dipped dangerously.

"I don't know what you mean." Except she did because he always seemed to know when she was keeping something from him.

"I gave Papa my word where you're concerned. It seems to me you're more worried about your image with him."

She lowered her head.

Lucca heaved a frustrated sigh. "Let me tell you something about my father, Annabelle. If you were that kind of woman, he'd have seen right through you and he would never have asked you to model for him. You're someone very important to him. You must know that."

"I do. I just want those warm feelings to continue."

Everything Lucca said and did was making chaos of her emotions, but no one was as important to Guilio as his own son. One day soon he'd see what his father had done in his honor.

He brushed his lips against hers. "Let's get dressed and go down to the beach. I'll find one of my mother's sun hats for you to wear. We'll rent a cruiser and spend the day on the water."

She averted her eyes. "That sounds wonderful." Away from the farmhouse she wouldn't feel like they were sitting ducks.

The whole time she rushed to get ready, she feared there'd be another knock on the door. But when she walked through to the kitchen minutes later, he was there alone waiting for her with a covered basket.

Their gazes fused. "I made us a picnic."

"You're amazing. Have you got your pills?"

"Yes, nurse."

She ignored him and hurried out to the car to pop the trunk. He trailed her and put their things inside. When they were settled in the car, he smiled at her before putting on his sunglasses. "There's nothing like having my own driver and medic in one. I could grow to like this arrangement."

"Until the doctor tells a certain fighter pilot he has recovered enough to get behind the wheel of a car again."

When he laughed, Annabelle gave him a covert glance. "With rest and good food, you're walking so well, you're hardly recognizable from that first night." She drove out to join the road leading down to the major highway.

"You sound happy."

"I am." *I am.*

"Even though you had to supply comfort to a vet this morning?"

"Let's not pretend I didn't enjoy it after you woke up." *Enjoy* didn't cover it. "You proved to me there's life after death."

"That's nice to hear."

"Mel has been worried for me, but if he'd seen us together, those fears would have dissolved. That's your contribution, Lucca. Would you hate me if I told you I'm grateful to you for making me feel like a woman again?"

"I only kissed you a few times."

"It was enough for this relic to feel the heat."

She heard a harsh sound come out of him. He jerked his head toward her. "Is that how you really feel about yourself? How old are you? Twenty-five?"

"Almost twenty-seven."

"Don't you know what a beautiful girl you are?"

Oh, Lucca.

"I'm no girl." Yet his father had called her the Amalfi Girl.

"You're the stuff men's dreams are made of. Don't let what your ex did distort the truth. This morning I found out what a loving, giving woman you are. Don't tell me I don't know what I'm talking about because I was there with you."

She smiled. "I know. That means there's hope for you, too. For two survivors, we're not doing so badly after all. We've got a bit of a drive ahead of us to reach the marina. Tell me about your stepbrothers. What are their names again?"

"Ruggero and Tomaso."

"Do you like them?"

"Not in the beginning. We all had to live together in a villa farther up the mountain."

After losing his mother, Annabelle couldn't imagine how hard that would have been. "I didn't realize they had children as old as Fortunato."

"They were a couple of years older. I'm surprised my father hasn't told you all this."

She put on her sunglasses. "I think you're under the

impression I've spent loads of time with him, Lucca. But you'd be wrong. Guilio was only in Los Angeles two days. During that time we were in meetings with Mel. When I flew to Rome last week, he met my plane and it's been work ever since."

He rested his head against the window. "Have you met Maria?"

"Not yet."

"Aren't you going to ask me if I like my stepmother?"

"No."

"Why not?"

"Because I know how much you loved your mother."

"I adored her, but I've come to care a great deal for Maria."

"I'm glad." Wanting to know anything and everything about him she asked, "What's Fortunato's mother like?"

"Besides other girls, I dated Cellina before I joined the air force."

Out of the frying pan, Annabelle.

She swallowed hard. "Is she another reason you didn't want anyone to know you were home yet?"

"No." was his blunt answer. "You know my reasons. I didn't want my father to hear I was home before I could tell him myself. But to satisfy your feminine curiosity, if I'd been in love with her, I wouldn't have left Ravello."

Her fascination with him was so great, she couldn't stop asking questions. "Has it made things difficult for you and Ruggero?"

"Not anymore. But in the beginning I think my stepbrother was glad I had a career that kept me away for long periods of time."

"I thought it strange she sent those melons."

"It's not strange at all." She felt his eyes impale her. "The whole family has to be intrigued by my father's sudden affection for the American woman he met in California."

The chemistry between them was palpable. "How about a little music?" She turned on the radio and grazed the channels until she found some soft Italian rock. After their conversation just now, she needed anything to help contain the feelings he'd aroused in her.

When she saw the sign for the marina, her heart leaped because they would be spending the afternoon alone on a boat. She pulled around past a string of launches and stopped near the office.

"I'll be right back." Before she knew what was happening, he cupped the back of her head and kissed her hard on the mouth. Annabelle was moaning by the time he finally relinquished her lips and got out of the car.

CHAPTER SIX

O<small>N</small> Monday morning, Lucca heard his father's car in the drive and walked out of the house to greet him. They hugged.

"You're really home for good. I can't believe it." They hugged again.

When Lucca had arrived at two in the morning last week, he'd been in such a terrible place emotionally, he couldn't have imagined feeling this good today.

"Come in the house, *Papa*. I've made *Mama*'s lemon tea for you."

"I haven't tasted that in years."

No. Lucca didn't imagine he had. "Everything's waiting for us out on the terrace." He'd prepared their favorite eggs, fruit, yogurt and pastry.

His father followed him. "You have a slight limp, nothing more. I thank God for that."

"I do, too. Once all the pain is gone, you won't even notice that. Come and sit."

Guilio looked around. Lucca watched his eyes glaze over. "Daisies on the table, just like your mother used to do. As if there aren't enough daisies surrounding the place."

Lucca fought his own tears. "How is your work going lately?"

His father rubbed his eyes before digging into his breakfast. "Your uncles and I can't complain. The good news is, we have a much larger market than we used to and need more help, but I know the family business has never been your interest."

"I'm glad it's growing, *Papa*."

His father chuckled. "You sounded like my little boy just then. I am, too. So...you're really decided on this farming business."

"Yes. That's why I want those two properties. Along with this one I plan to make a good profit. I intend for Cavezzali to sell the premier *frutta deliziosa* in all Ravello."

"This is your grandfather's doing."

"Only indirectly. I was born with some of *Mama*'s genes. She helped with the farming as a girl. I took to it pure and simply. But I also inherited some of your genes. You loved car design. I loved jet planes. It's all mixed around inside me."

His father eyed him for a long time, but for once Lucca couldn't discern what was on his mind. "You hated me for marrying Maria so soon after your mother died," he began without preamble. "I don't blame you. If I'd been in your shoes, I would have felt the same way."

Lucca was stunned by his father's unexpected remarks. "We went over all this years ago. There's no need to talk about it ever again."

"Perhaps not for you as much as for me. As you know, Donata and I were childhood sweethearts. I loved your mother so much that when she passed away, I couldn't bear it for myself or you. Not many people loved the way we did. We had an idyllic marriage. When you came along after many tries, your mother looked at me and said, 'Our cup has run over, Guilio'."

"I didn't know she suffered a miscarriage."

"Four of them."

Four?

"We wanted a big family. I have to tell you she was the sweetest mother." *She was.* "You were our one and only. She doted on you. I think I was a little jealous." He wiped his eyes.

The revelations coming out of his father knocked Lucca back on his heels.

"I'd grown up knowing Maria at school and liked her. Her husband's sudden death from a heart attack was a shock to her, too. We saw each other at church. In our grief, we gravitated to each other for comfort to stave off the pain. We were two brokenhearted people with three brokenhearted sons and realized that if we got married, we could provide something solid for our children."

Lucca's eyes closed tightly.

"In the beginning our union truly was for the children." Lucca believed him. "We had friendship and respect going for us. Over time I grew to love her in a different way that I loved your mother. She's a good woman who has supported me in the business and has been a fine companion."

"Don't you think I know that? I care for her very much."

"But not at first. When you left for Bari, I got so angry because I didn't want to lose you, too. Your mother's death almost killed me. I wanted to keep you close

to me, but the harder I tried, the more you pulled away."
He got up from the table and walked over to him. "Can
you forgive me, Lucca?"

Too choked up from emotion to talk, Lucca hugged
his father. "If anything, I'm the one begging for it."

Guilio hugged him harder. "Maria and I have been
planning a get-together on Saturday. Besides family,
there'll be some friends and business people. Now that
you're back, we'd like to turn it into a real 'welcome
home party' for you. How does that sound?"

"I'm already looking forward to it, *Papa*."

His father wept. Lucca hadn't seen that happen since
the doctor had summoned them into the hospital room
where his mother was taking her last breath. But this
time they were happy tears.

"Come on," his father finally said, wiping his eyes
again. "Let's go take a drive and look at those properties. I'm glad you're going to do something about them
and want to hear all your ideas. They're already an eye-
sore. That's why I wanted to sell them. Thank goodness
you stopped me in time."

Thank goodness.

"The light is perfect. Annabelle? You will sit in the
passenger seat with one foot on the ground as if you've
fallen in love with this field of sunflowers and are ready
to get out and run through it. Can you give me the look
I'm after this early in the morning?"

That part was easy. The memory of Saturday on the
water with Lucca was a day out of time with a real man
who was starting to share his feelings. While they'd
boated in and out of sandy coves and enjoyed their picnic, he'd given her a history of the area.

Against a backdrop of medieval towers and terraced orchards, he'd talked about his plans to become a farmer. With his love of the land, it really didn't surprise her. Slowly the conversation drifted to her. He got her talking about her own future. She knew that one day she'd go back to nursing. His words touched her deeply when he told her she ought to specialize in helping veterans because she had the two necessary gifts of empathy and compassion.

After he took his medicine, he eventually grew sleepy. She suggested they go back to the farmhouse so he could get to bed. After a day like they'd enjoyed, he'd seemed so peaceful, she had a feeling he wouldn't be tortured by nightmares.

Sunday had been a repeat of Saturday. Lucca was unwinding even more now. They ate a leisurely breakfast, then took another boat out in a different direction so she could see more sights and islands. Lucca lay on the padded seats, comfortable enough to enjoy being gone all day. They snoozed, ate, read and took in the scenery. She thought of them as healing days. For a little while they had no cares.

"Annabelle needs more apricot in her cheeks. I want her hair cascading over her left shoulder," Giovanni ordered, firing directions to the staff until he was pleased with the results. "See how the sun brings out the metallic gleam of those strands, Basilio?" The other man nodded. "With the bay of Naples sparkling in the background, that's the shot I want! Don't move!"

Annabelle marveled at the color coordination. A bright yellow Amalfi sports car convertible with creamy leather seats formed the centerpiece. Marcella had dressed her in a three-piece, short-sleeved crisp white suit and creased slacks. The jacket had four pockets trimmed with yellow braid.

The same trim ran up the openings and around the lapels. An enamel sunflower in each earlobe brought the color to her face. White sandals with elaborate criss-crossing straps completed the look.

"*Perfetto! Perfetto!*" Giovanni cried. "Now I want you to get out and lean against the car with the door still open, your left foot just so. You're holding this basket of sunflowers while lifting one to admire it. This time your smile holds a secret."

His directions unknowingly caused her body to break out in goose flesh. Earlier this morning Lucca was supposed to have made breakfast for his father. Right now she was holding her breath, dying to know how it had gone for both men. That was the problem with being a bystander. She was caught up in the lives of another family, yet could do nothing but hope it was a joyous one.

"That's not the smile I want, *signorina*. Where did the other one go?"

She fixed it for Giovanni. "I was thinking how hard it's going to be to leave Italy."

"Then don't! I'm sure Basilio will put in a good word for you with *Signore* Cavezzali if you want to stay. Now give me what I want!"

Annabelle tried her best. When he declared they were through shooting for the day, she was glad to get back to the van to change out of her clothes and remove her makeup. Once she was dressed in a blouse and skirt, she said goodbye to everyone.

Basilio reminded her they were doing the shoot in Ravello tomorrow. Relieved she wouldn't have to face another long drive in the morning, she got in the car. Before she drove away, she checked to see if there were any messages. Her body quickened when she saw that Lucca had called. She clicked on.

"Papa and I have spent the day together and are out looking at the properties I was telling you about. I'm not sure how soon I'll be home. Ciao, bellissima."

It sounded so much better than she'd hoped for.

She started up the engine and pulled out to the main road. Sorrento was sprawled across limestone cliffs where the houses looked like colorful children's blocks stacked on top of each other. Everything was beautiful along the Sorrentine Peninsula, but the drive was hot, even with the air conditioning on, and seemed to take forever.

As soon as she reached the farmhouse, she dove into work for something to take her mind off of Lucca and put in a wash. No sooner had she done that than she heard a knock on the kitchen door. Maybe it was Fortunato again. She hurried to open it.

"Buon giorno, signorina. I am Cellina Colombari. You met my son the other day."

Annabelle couldn't believe the timing. If she'd arrived a half hour later, she could have avoided this meeting. "Yes, of course." She smiled. "I ate one of the melons he brought. It was delicious and very kind of you."

Lucca's former girlfriend was probably in her midthirties. A real Italian beauty with dark blond hair and dark eyes. She must have gotten pregnant with Fortunato at nineteen or twenty.

"Can you stay and visit?"

"If it is all right."

"I'm through working for the day. Please. Come in." She went into the living room and Cellina followed. "Won't you be seated?"

"Thank you." She chose the rose settee. "When Guilio said you were staying here by yourself, I thought it might get a little lonely. I know I would be if I were living by myself."

"Since my divorce, I'm used to living alone."

"That must be very hard for you. It's so sad. Basilio lost his wife last year," Cellina informed her.

"So I understand."

"Do you find him good-looking?"

Annabelle knew where this was leading. Fortunato hadn't wasted any time. "I think every male in Italy is too attractive for his own good. Don't you?" She winked at her.

The other woman looked surprised before she unbent and gave a soft laugh. "Yes."

Cellina might be too curious for her own good, but she didn't take herself too seriously. Lucca would have liked that about her.

"So tell me about you and your family. I'd like to know a few things about you before I meet everyone at the party Guilio has planned for Saturday."

They chatted for another twenty minutes, then Cellina said she had to go and start dinner for her family. Annabelle liked her. She was glad the other woman wouldn't be a stranger to her at the family party.

Lucca still hadn't called or returned. Unable to stand her own company any longer, she left the house and went for a walk. She almost forgot the floppy hat she wore to keep the sun off her face and had to go back for it.

When evening rolled around, she bought herself a cola, then geared up for the steep climb back to Lucca's house. On the way, her cell phone rang. It was Guilio calling!

She moved to the side of the road and braced herself against a palm tree, not knowing what to expect when she clicked on. "Hello?"

"Annabelle? You're a dark horse but I forgive you with all my heart for helping my son make the transition back to civilian life."

Her throat swelled. "You should have seen us the night he fell in the hallway."

"He told me about that."

"You must be so thrilled to have him back for good." Annabelle was overjoyed, not bothering to tamp down her excitement.

"You'll never know."

"Where is he now? Where are you?"

"One question at a time." He chuckled. "I dropped him off at the farmhouse. Now I'm home at the villa."

She gripped the phone tighter. "Is everything all right?"

"It couldn't be better."

"That's music to my ears."

"A lot of the reason for that has to do with you. Thank you for keeping my secret."

"I about died when he appeared out of the blue. I was so afraid he'd find out."

"Thanks to you, he didn't!"

"So what are you going to do?"

"I've got everything under control for the big surprise. I can't change the date of the grand opening in August. However, we can honor him at the party. When

I was in Milan, I moved up the date to Wednesday night and have informed Mel to change his flight arrangements. Your photo shoots will be over by then. We'll have a mini grand opening where my son will meet the Amalfi Girl in person when he's honored."

Only two days away... Though she'd been in Italy just a short while, she felt like she'd lived here much longer. The images filling her mind were suffocating her. His farmhouse felt like home. She and Lucca had lived in every part of it. Each room—the hallway...the terrace...the kitchen—had their own memories.

"I'll keep in touch with you about the details, but before we hang up, I just want to say thank you."

"For what?"

"Lucca's told me how you've nursed him. There's no one tougher than my son, but after what he's been through, he's more grateful than you know for what you've done. I have it on good authority he'd like to keep you until you leave. He says you're better than any nurse who has taken care of him since he was shot down."

Annabelle groaned inwardly. She'd hoped Lucca wouldn't want her to leave at all, but if he only thought of her as a nurse, and didn't care for her for her real self, she couldn't bear it. "I'm very flattered," she said in a wooden voice.

"He tells me that after you go home, you're thinking of taking up your nursing career at some point to work with war veterans like himself. My son has great admiration for you. Is that true?"

She stared blindly into space. "Yes, but I haven't said anything to Mel yet. That's something we'll have to discuss after I get back."

"Mel's not going to like it, but be assured my lips are sealed. I'll be checking in with you over the next few days. *Ciao,* Annabelle."

"*Ciao.*"

Feeling the happiness drained out of her, she clicked off, hugging the phone to her chest.

It was déjà vu when Lucca heard a firm knock on the kitchen door. If it were Annabelle, she had a key and could let herself in. She'd left her car in the drive and had obviously gone somewhere. A walk maybe?

She was constantly on his mind. Disappointed that she wasn't back yet, he walked through the house to the kitchen. The knocking persisted. "*Signorina* Marsh?" a familiar voice called out.

Fortunato again. He was a good kid. A little mischievous, but fun. So he'd come to see Annabelle again. The boy had good taste and eyes to see.

Out of his five nieces and nephews, Lucca had to admit he enjoyed him the most. Fortunato had this idea he would go into the military, too. None of the family was happy about it, and Lucca had never encouraged it. But at seventeen, a boy had his dreams. No one understood that better than Lucca.

He unlocked the door, surprising the life out of Fortunato. "Hey—when did you come home?" If Lucca didn't miss his guess, the teen sounded a trifle disappointed.

"I got in the other night."

"You did?"

"*Sì.*" He smiled. "Want to come in?"

"Yeah." After the door closed they high-fived each other.

"How's life treating you?" Lucca tossed him a plum from the fridge and took one for himself.

"It's okay." He squinted up at Lucca. "How long are you home for this time?"

"For good."

In a matter of seconds he'd surprised his nephew again. Fortunato looked perplexed. "I thought you were going to stay in the military until you retired."

"So did I, but my plans changed."

"How come?"

He gave his nephew the same answer he'd given his father. "Because I got injured and my priorities changed. I decided I wanted to do something different with the rest of my life."

"Yeah? Like what?"

"I'm going to be a farmer."

"You're kidding! You? A fighter pilot?"

"That's right. I've spent enough time in the air. Now I want to stay on the ground and get my hands dirty."

Laughter burst out of his nephew. "That's cool." Lucca finished off his plum while Fortunato looked around. "I saw *Signorina* Marsh's car in the drive. Is she here?"

"You mean the American who's working for your grandfather. She's probably still out with some of her coworkers."

"Oh." His face fell. "I met her the other day."

"Papa told me he'd hired her to do modeling for some of his ads."

"That's what I heard, too. She's one babe."

"But a little old for you, right?"

A ruddy color stained Fortunato's cheeks. "I bet she's no more than twenty-five. There's no harm looking."

"No. There's no harm in that." Lucca had done it himself, but not nearly long enough. In fact he planned to tell Annabelle what his nephew had said. She needed to realize she wasn't all washed up after what her ex had done to her.

Fortunato's blond brows lifted. When they did that, he reminded Lucca of Ruggero. "She's already got some guy hanging around."

"How do you know that?"

"I saw his clothes in here. You know…like they'd been partying and got carried away. She's only been in Italy a little while. He's one lucky stud. If I were just a little older…"

"But you're not." He reached out and tousled his hair.

"*Mama* thinks maybe it was Basilio."

"Basilio is a little too old for her, don't you think?"

"Not if she's after his money."

"I guess anything's possible."

"*Papa* says Basilio is gaga over her. It's all the talk at work."

"What's all the talk?"

"How gorgeous she is. You ought to see her, Uncle Lucca. Even you would have a coronary."

Lucca had already come close to having a heart attack and quite a few other things as well at the sight of the silvery-gold tigress ready to attack him with the cane that first night. He grinned at his nephew. "Even me, huh?"

"Yeah, well, *Mama* says you can get any woman you want."

Lucca hoped so, because he wanted Annabelle. "Aren't you working in the shop this summer?"

"Yeah. I have to be there at noon every day. Guess I better get going. Mama will have dinner ready."

"Do you want another plum on your way out?"

"Sure. Thanks."

"You're welcome." Fortunato was growing up in more ways than one. Little did Annabelle know she was his nephew's new fantasy, not to mention Lucca's. He watched the boy walk out to his car. "By the way..." he called to him.

Fortunato turned to him. "Yeah?"

Before shutting the door he said, "I'm the lucky stud whose clothes you saw lying around."

Annabelle let herself in the house and was clasped in a strong pair of arms. "At last," Lucca whispered, burying his face in her hair. "I've been watching for you. Where have you been?"

"Walking."

"I thought so." He pressed kisses all the way to her mouth. She couldn't deny that his hunger was as great as her own. Since his arrival in Ravello, they'd been thrown into an intimate situation. Lucca had never married and wouldn't be a man if he didn't want to enjoy his nurse until she'd gone. Annabelle didn't blame him at all.

Thank you, Guilio, for the heads-up. After their conversation, she was afraid she was in a different place than Lucca emotionally. Guilio had indicated Lucca valued her medical assistance. If that was all, then the trick was to be her wisest self until the party was over and she went back to California.

She eased herself away enough to talk to him and

cupped his face. "I have to know. How did it go with your father? He loves you so much."

His gaze wandered over her features in the semi-darkness. "Can't I tell you later? To be honest, all I've been able to think about is getting you alone." He began kissing the daylights out of her. Annabelle had never felt this alive before. Being with Lucca was like being reborn.

He started to maneuver her into the other room, but the fear that she would go on reading too much into his lovemaking prevented her from indulging herself for long. If he wasn't starting to love her as intensely as she did him, then she was playing with fire. Slowly she eased out of his arms.

"Why are you pulling away from me?"

"I didn't eat much today. Do you think we could go to dinner first? Then you can tell me everything."

Lucca's gaze swept over her. "I should have realized, but when I saw you come in the door, I only had one desire. Is there anything you need to do before we leave?"

"I'll just freshen up. Be sure to bring your pills."

He nodded. "I'm looking forward to the day I don't need them anymore."

"I want that for you, too."

After he'd held her back for another kiss, she hurried through the house to change clothes and run a brush through her hair. She put on the same sleeveless orange shirtwaist she'd worn the other day. On a warm night like this, the linen breathed.

When next she saw Lucca, he'd just come out of his room, walking toward her with barely a sign of a limp. He wore a pair of beige trousers and a silky white sport shirt, where she glimpsed the dusting of hair on his chest at the opening.

His sudden white smile sent her heartbeat skyrocketing. He was so Italian and attractive, she had to look down for a minute to get a grip. They left the house together and went out to the car. In the next instant he'd climbed in the passenger seat next to her.

"Hi." He leaned over and kissed her neck. The contact of his mouth against her skin radiated through her in waves. "Remember me?" The exact words she'd said to him last week.

"Yes." Her voice sounded all breathy. That was the way he affected her. She thought he was going to kiss her again, but to her surprise he squeezed her hand instead. "I don't dare do what I want to you right now or we'll never leave the farm."

"Maybe you should get in the back," she teased.

He drew in a harsh breath. "I prefer to be right where I am, up close and personal." So did she. Annabelle wished she could be more like Lucca and go with her feelings without dissecting it and imagining it taking on major significance. "What kind of food are you in the mood for?"

"Anything you choose. Surprise me." She put the key in the ignition and started the car, afraid to look at him directly. If she did, she'd beg to stay here and crawl into his arms.

"You're in a different mood this evening."

His radar never failed. "I think I got a little too warm during my walk."

"Then we need to hydrate you. I know a place not far from here." He gave her directions. After that, the pregnant silence on the drive to the restaurant passed in a blur because she was too conscious of his nearness and her susceptibility to him.

Every eating establishment on the coast was a scene of enchantment facing the sea. Lucca led them to a divinely romantic spot overlooking the water. He plied her with juice from the bar. Afterward they were shown to an individual terrace with a table for two, separated from the others by flowering trees for the diners' privacy. The blossoms gave off their own perfume. In the background a live band was playing Italian love songs for those who wanted to dance or simply listen.

After they'd been eating mouthwatering hors d'oeuvres automatically brought to every table, she found herself gazing into those gray-green eyes staring back at her between black lashes as silky as his shirt.

"I know the reason why you went away and joined the air force, Lucca. But if I'd been born in this particular spot on earth, I don't think I could have left it."

He finished the last of the olives the waiter had told them were freshly harvested from a nearby grove. "You have places in Southern California that rival our coast."

She shook her head. "No. Like these hors d'oeuvres I've been enjoying, places like Laguna Beach and La Jolla are merely appetizers compared to Ravello."

His eyes smiled at her. "That's a fascinating analogy."

"But true," she insisted. "On my walk, I stopped by the Villa Rufolo today. The place is an arabesque fantasy within a fantasy. With those enchanting gardens, it's no wonder Wagner was inspired for his *Parsifal*." She sipped her coffee. "I understand the Wagner festival will be on next month. You lucky people who live here."

"I prefer listening to Wagner when the town isn't overrun with tourists."

"I hear you." She smiled. "Southern California is like a wall-to-wall carpet woven of tourists. That's why I've loved staying in your home so much."

"You prefer it over the large villas?"

"They're lovely, but too big. There's a cozy warm feeling to your little farmhouse. The fruit trees and flowers surrounding it are like tufts of clouds, hiding it away from everyone. I'm crazy about it. If I were an artist, I'd paint it at various hours of the day."

"You mean like Monet, who kept turning out his poplar trees?"

She winked at him. "Exactly like that."

The waiter arrived with their fish entrée.

"I believe you're an artist in your soul," Lucca observed after they were alone again.

"I'm afraid I fixate on a subject rather than create from it." She'd fixated on Lucca from those very first moments and there was no antidote except to remove herself. "How did your day go today? Honestly."

"Honestly, my father and I are at peace. He told me he's behind my farming idea a hundred percent. And it seems he's decided to turn his business party into a homecoming party for me. But it's going to be on Wednesday instead of Saturday. I'm very touched."

"He's incredibly proud of you." Annabelle didn't know how she was going to wait that long for the big night to unfold.

As she looked at him, a mysterious gleam entered his eyes. "After Papa dropped me off, I had a visitor who looked shocked when I answered my own door. Care to make a guess?"

"Fortunato?" She'd almost said Cellina, but caught herself in time. Naturally the whole Cavezzali family had to be curious why Guilio had let Annabelle stay in his son's house.

He nodded. "I hate to have to tell you this, but the latest gossip has put you and the widower Basilio as an item."

She burst into laughter. "If your nephew had looked closely, he could have seen that your shirt and cargo pants would hardly have fit Basilio."

"He was too focused on you to notice details like that. I'm afraid he's smitten. That's when I informed him *I* was the other man in the house the other night. I could care less what conclusions he's drawn. According to him you couldn't be more than twenty-five."

"I don't believe it." She laughed.

"That's nice when you do that. For your information he's wishing he could make the stretch that would put the two of you into the category that you might treat him as a romantic equal."

"I'm afraid we've all been there before."

He leaned forward. "Who was Ms. Marsh's fantasy?"

"My art teacher in high school. He was probably forty, but I thought that was the perfect age for a man. He was so mature and self-assured. He made all the boys look pathetic in comparison. I used to think up reasons to hang around his class after school."

"You mean he let you?"

"Yes. Now that I think about it, it was pretty naughty of him."

Lucca's shoulders shook with laughter.

"Now it's your turn."

CHAPTER SEVEN

LUCCA gave her an unconsciously seductive smile. "Which fantasy would you like to hear about first? One of my father's secretaries, or the mother of one of my high-school friends?"

"Oh, brother." Annabelle shook her head.

"No fantasy ever looked better than the one sitting across from me." There was a tone in Lucca's voice and a look in his eyes that raised her temperature.

She took another drink of her coffee. "After Fortunato left, what did you do?"

He sat back in the chair. "Looked at the list of notations I've made of all the things that need fixing around the house."

"That's good you're staying busy."

His jaw hardened slightly. "You mean so I won't brood?" He'd jumped on her remark so fast, her head spun.

"No, Lucca. No…" she placated softly. "I didn't say that. You know I only meant until your pain was a little better."

"But you were thinking it. With good reason I might add. There are a lot of things I'd like to tackle, but for my leg."

"It's getting better every day." She knew that after a certain amount of work he got tired. That's when it started to hurt and made him edgy. "I've a hunch patience was never thy name, but you'll make it through this."

"I'd ask you to dance, but that's *verboten* for a time. So is driving."

"Lucca…haven't you listened to anything I've said? It's early days yet." Annabelle put the empty coffee cup back in the saucer.

A faraway look entered Lucca's eyes. "I've been dreaming too much about my plans for the farm. I want it too much."

"That's your pain talking. Remember you have a plate in your leg. That's making all the difference in your recovery."

"Why?" he snapped at her. Finally he was listening.

"You live with a constant ache and are probably dealing with some arthritis. The plate the doctor put along the side of your thighbone is helping bear your weight and has made early movement possible. However, the plate is shielding your bone from stress, which is not necessarily a good thing."

He sat forward. "Are you saying the doctor didn't know what he was doing?"

"No, Lucca…" She shook her head. "After your crash, you needed the surgery immediately to safeguard against further nerve damage. But because some stress on the bone is necessary to strengthen it as it heals, this stress-shielding has had some consequences, like your pain, for example."

His features broke into a grimace. "The news gets better and better."

"Actually it does," she assured him. "Considering that you experience pain when you're fatigued, I'd advise you to consult an orthopedic surgeon here and see if you're a candidate to have the plate removed at some point down the road."

She saw his hands close into fists. "If I thought I could get that thing out of there…"

"I know it's possible, but I'm not a doctor. Only he can determine if it's a procedure for you and how soon it could be done. If so, you could probably do most everything you used to do and be free of pain. If nothing else, it will improve the quality of the life you're living now."

He stared at her through new eyes. "You've given me hope I thought was gone."

"Hope is everything, isn't it? But if the doctor advises against it in your particular case because it could leave your bone with a residual weakness, I know you'll handle it. You're not an ace pilot for nothing."

She didn't have to look at him to feel his energy. Something earthshaking was going on inside him. "Do you want dessert?"

"After that fabulous meal, I couldn't eat another thing."

"Then let's go home, unless you've decided you'd rather stay at the Casa Claudia."

She wouldn't desert Lucca now. The possibility that something could be done for his leg meant he would want to talk about it. Since she'd brought it up, she needed to see it through.

"No. Much as I think it would look better to those on the outside, I'm afraid I've fallen in love with your house." *With you.*

"Good, because I already canceled your reservation and paid your bill."

While Annabelle sat there astounded, he got to his feet. She followed suit. There was a new gleam in his eyes.

"Papa had something delivered to the farmhouse earlier today. I'd like you to help me christen it."

Her heart thumped. "Subtlety isn't your strong suit."

One side of his seductive mouth lifted. "It's not a mattress, although that item is going to be next on my shopping list." He left money for the bill and ushered her out of the restaurant.

She walked out to the car with him. "The word *christen* has a definite connotation. I'm intrigued."

He squeezed her around the hip. "It signals that something new has been launched."

Lucca's choice of words reminded her of Guilio's plans for his fabulous new sports car. But she could hardly concentrate because Lucca was touching her and now her legs felt like mush.

"Sort of like your new life when you thought the other one was over after you landed in that war zone?" It was a miracle she could start up the engine and pull out on to the main road without having an accident.

His arm rested across the back of both their seats, creating havoc with her body. She felt him finger the ends of her hair. Electric currents shot through her. "That, and other things," he murmured, sounding the slightest bit cryptic.

"Shall we drive to Solerno for some more *torta*?" She couldn't take much more of his attention. It was driving her mad with desire. They needed to stay busy.

He angled his striking face toward her. "Are you

afraid to go home with me? The nerve at the base of your throat started throbbing before we got up from the table."

His eagle eye didn't miss anything. *You idiot, Annabelle.* He had to have eagle eyes to be a pilot, so it shouldn't have surprised her. "Maybe. Having agreed to stay with you, this is all new to me."

"Your honesty is refreshing." He tugged on a strand. "I promise not to do anything you don't want me to do."

"*Signore* Cavezzali—" Her mouth had gone dry. "We can't sleep together."

She heard him suck in his breath. "If you're telling me you don't want me, you'd be lying."

"I want you very much," she confessed with total candor. "But I'm sure your doctor told you it's too soon after your surgery."

"If he did—" Lucca's words came out like a growl "—I was probably too drugged to hear him."

"Then all the more reason to consult a doctor here. If this plate can be removed, then you don't want to injure what has been repaired to this point. It's not worth the risk. We can thank Fortunato for showing up before any harm was done the other morning."

She pulled into the drive and shut off the motor. Before he touched her, she sprang from the front seat, eager to see what he wanted christened.

Lucca moved ahead of her and opened the French doors to the terrace. "It's out here."

She followed him and looked to the left. "A swing!" It was long and roomy, just his size, with padded arms and extra cushions. The floral pattern matched the colors of the farmhouse's exterior. "How perfect for you!"

"For *us*," he corrected. "If you'll sit at this end, I can put my head in your lap and stretch my legs."

He had her royally caught, but it was where she wanted to be. As soon as she'd seated herself, he sat next to her, then lay down, extending his hard-muscled length where he could prop his feet on the cushion.

Lucca caught her hands and kissed the palms. "Since this is our favorite place in the house, I decided I wanted us to be comfortable. Our family used to have another one, but it got old and died."

The reality of Lucca made this her favorite place on earth. She looked down into his eyes and got lost in them.

"Come closer, Annabelle."

She needed no urging, but the awkward position made it difficult. "I have a better idea," she whispered against his lips. "Sit up for a moment." When he did, she slid off the swing. "Lie down so I can kiss you the way I want." She would indulge herself for a little while longer without hurting his leg.

Annabelle got on her knees and wrapped her arms around his neck. Their mouths fused at the same moment in an erotic explosion of need. No experience in life could have prepared her for this kind of ardor. The giving and taking transported her. His exploration of her features and mouth sent her into another realm of pleasure too exquisite to describe. She gasped softly because her emotions were brimming over.

He plunged his hands in her hair. "I could eat you alive, Annabelle."

She buried her face in his neck. "I thought that was what I was doing to you. It's a good thing I'll be going back to California soon. Otherwise you won't be safe from me," she joked, but was hoping with all her heart he might tell her he wanted her to stay with him permanently.

Instead he said, "Back to *what*?" He sounded upset. His free hand still cupped the back of her head.

"My job with Mel, at least for the foreseeable future. I'll have to ease him into the idea that I'm returning to nursing."

Still no hint from Lucca that he wanted her to be in his future.

She pressed a tender kiss to his lips. "Lie there and relax. This swing is perfect for you to lounge on. While you do that, I need to get ready for bed."

He frowned. "It's not that late."

Lucca needed company. She needed more than that. "It is for me. Tomorrow I have to be in Capri early. On my return I'll pick up some groceries and fix us dinner. How does *that* sound?"

By the expression on his arresting face, he needed appeasing. "You'll cook me something American?"

She kissed his jaw. "The kind of food my family loves."

That seemed to cheer him up to an extent. "When do you think you'll be back?"

"I'm not sure. Capri is only twenty miles from here, but with the traffic, it could be several hours." She kissed his lips. "I promise to hurry."

"If I'm not here, just let yourself in with your key."

Naturally he had his own life to lead. Now that he didn't need to worry about being seen, he could call on his family to get him around, or take a taxi. "Do you need anything before I go to my room?"

"Only you." He gave her one last ravenous kiss until she could hardly breathe.

It would be so easy to forget everything and climb on that swing with him. But she resisted the impulse and eventually pulled away. When she stood up, she had to rub her knees after being in that position for so long.

"You look comfortable lying there. Stay put and enjoy the beautiful night." She turned to leave, but he caught her hand.

"Please don't touch me anymore tonight," she begged.

"Just one more kiss to help me get through it. I don't mind being alone through the nightmares if you're there to bring me awake."

"Oh, Lucca." She had no will when he told her things like that. She leaned down and clung to him while her heart steamed into his. He'd become her whole world.

When she finally stood up, her desire for him was so strong that if he'd called her back, she would have stayed in spite of all her good intentions. But he didn't say anything… Was it because he was being the Italian male who still reserved a part of independence for himself?

She gave the swing a little push to rock him. "Good night, Lucca," she whispered.

"Sleep well, *bellissima.*"

Capri metallic blue described the Amalfi sports car gleaming in the sun. The white sailboat on the water formed the perfect backdrop. Even Annabelle could see that and she was no photographer.

The car had been parked at the Marina Piccolo. Annabelle found the little harbor enchanting and she loved the outfit Marcella had chosen for her. It was a white silk cheongsam with an all-over medium-sized print of flowers in various shades of blue. Heavenly.

Her hair had been put up in a loose knot, caught with real blue flowers. On her feet she wore a pair of high-heeled sandals in metallic white. Her wrist was encircled with three rows of light blue sapphires. The same sapphires adorned her ears.

"*Mama mia*—" Giovanni exclaimed when she stepped out of the van ready for the shoot. "You have never looked this beautiful before. I wonder why."

Lucca had everything to do with it. Her heart was bouncing all over the place.

Basilio nodded with a wide smile. "*Bellissima, signorina.* Bravo, Marcella! The Chinese style is *bella bella.* Annabella? Today you will stand at the front of the car with one hand on the bonnet, the one with the jewels. Look out toward the boat. You are waiting for your lover."

Annabelle got into position. She would give anything if Lucca were at the helm of that boat. When this shoot was over, she would swim out to him and kiss them both into oblivion.

"That's the look!" Giovanni cried a minute later. "Don't move!"

This morning she was definitely a woman in love. If that was the look Giovanni wanted to capture, he shouldn't have any trouble no matter which angle he wanted to take.

"With these photographs, Guilio won't be able to keep his calendars in stock." He moved around her snapping one picture after another.

She smiled. "Are you trying to butter me up, Giovanni? If so, you're doing a good job."

"You are the easiest model I ever worked with and you're not even a model."

"Nope, and I don't want to be one. I'm only doing this for Guilio."

"When his son sees this picture, he will fall instantly in love."

How about permanently? The words hadn't passed Lucca's lips. They might never.

"Hey, Annabelle—where did the Amalfi Girl just go? I want a few more shots."

"I'm doing my best." For the rest of the shoot, she focused on the meal she planned to make for Lucca.

"All right. That's it. Tomorrow we meet in Vietri at nine before the shops open and we're overrun with tourists. It will be our last day of shooting."

Annabelle was of two minds. Part of her couldn't bear for it to be over because it meant she had to go home to Los Angeles and leave Lucca. The other part was glad that the modeling would be over. She wasn't meant for this business. But she'd worry about that later as she raced back to the van to change and remove her makeup. She couldn't wait to get to the grocery store and do her shopping. When she stepped outside again in jeans and a pink T-shirt, Giovanni made a face.

"A woman who looks like you shouldn't run around dressed like any tourist."

"But I *am* a tourist. In a few days I'll be back in California doing my old job."

"Do you know how many would-be models would sell their souls to do what you're doing here?"

"Yes. Though it has been a wonderful experience for me, they are welcome to it. By the way, do any of you know if there is a supermarket around here? There isn't one in Ravello."

"*Sì*," Basilio said. "On the Via Matermania." He gave her directions.

She pecked his cheek. "Marvelous! Thank you, Basilio. A *domani*, everyone!"

Lucca saw the caller ID and clicked on. "*Prego?*"

"This is Dr. Cozza's office calling. The doctor is on the line."

"*Grazie.*"

"*Signore* Cavezzali?"

"*Sì*. Your nurse said you would phone me back when you weren't busy. I appreciate it."

"Sorry it's so late in the day. She told me about your surgery and the pain you've been having. That could be the irritation of the tissue from the plate causing tendonitis for example. Then again it could be caused by something else. There's no way I can make a judgment until I've seen you and taken X-rays. I have an opening next Monday."

"That's fine." Another week. Lucca would have to live with it. "But it *is* possible to have it removed?"

"Yes. In patients who have pain that is clearly coming from irritation caused by the metal, the chance of pain reduction is much more likely. However, you must keep in mind that if the pain is more generalized, and not clearly an irritation, the chance of pain resolution with the metal removed is more difficult to predict."

"I understand." Lucca gripped the phone tighter. "What are the risks?

"Obviously there are potential complications with this type of surgery. The most common problem is that metal removal can lead to a weakening of the bone where the implant is removed. Sometimes fractures form through the holes where the screws were implanted. But that may not have happened in your case and a certain amount of normal stress is necessary to keep the bone strong."

Annabelle had said the same thing.

"The point is we want to cut down on your pain and hopefully alleviate it all together. I'll put my nurse back on to give you a time for your appointment and I'll see you then."

"Thank you, Doctor."

He hung up, excited to tell Annabelle the news. For most of the day he'd been making phone calls to various contractors for bids. The house had sat empty for fifteen years and called for a lot of repair work to be done. The bathroom needed a total remodel into a master bath. He made a list of items he wanted replaced or installed, like a dishwa—

The phone rang before he'd finished the thought. He grabbed for it. When he saw who it was, his pulse accelerated to a feverish pitch. He clicked on. "Annabelle?"

"Hi! How are you?"

"I'm waiting for you. That's how I am. When can I expect you?" He didn't want to hear that there was a problem and she wouldn't be able to make it.

"I've finished the shopping and am on my way home."

"How long do you think that will be?"

"About forty-five minutes?"

He would have to live with that. "Make it a half hour."

"Hmm. You really are feeling closed in. I'll hurry."

"Not too fast. I want you to arrive in one piece. You're an excellent driver, but you're in Italy now."

"I've driven the freeways of California all my life and so far have lived to tell about it," she informed him with a laugh.

"That's not funny."

"I'm sorry. See you soon."

He clicked off, but it couldn't be soon enough.

Thirty-five minutes later, Annabelle pulled into the drive. He got off the swing and hurried into the house. Once he'd opened the kitchen door, he helped Annabelle with the groceries she was carrying. "It's about time you got here."

He put the bags on the counter, then reached for her. He must have taken her by surprise because she let out a cry. Her gorgeous violet eyes searched his. "I know I'm a little late. What's gotten into you? That's quite a welcome after the way you greeted me the first night we met."

"Forget that man. He no longer exists." Needing her like he needed air to breathe, Lucca crushed her against him and started kissing her in earnest. They were both trembling when he lifted his head.

Lucca couldn't take his eyes off her. She was the most beautiful sight he'd ever beheld. "What took you so long?"

"It's because the only corn you sell here is for the pigs and you can't buy it in a grocery store. I had to stop at a farm along the way. The woman said it was for the animals, but I talked her into letting me buy half a dozen ears. I heard her mutter something about Americans that I'm positive wasn't flattering."

Lucca burst into laughter. "You're fixing me corn on the stick?"

She laughed out loud. "Not exactly. It's called corn on the cob. Have you ever eaten it?"

"No, but there were some Americans guys I flew with who dreamed about eating it."

"Then you're in for a special treat."

"How can I help?"

"I need a big pot. Fill it a third of the way with water. I also need a saucepan filled halfway with water. Then I need a frying pan and masher for potatoes. Could you put some flour in a bowl for me and hand me the olive oil, pepper and salt?"

Lucca couldn't remember the last time he'd had so much fun. Maybe never. He got busy helping her. Within minutes she'd started frying chicken and peeling potatoes. Once everything was cooking, she drew out the corn.

"I'll cook four of these because I can't stop with just one corn on the cob. I'll want at least two, maybe more. This is called shucking."

He watched in fascination as she denuded the corn and dropped it in the boiling water.

"I bought butter for everything and some cream to mix in with the potatoes. We'll be ready to eat in a minute, then I want to hear about your day."

Before long, they sat at the table on the terrace. She watched with avid interest as he took his first bite of chicken and mashed potatoes. "Now butter and salt your corn and just start munching away."

When he'd eaten half the cob she said, "You've now had your christening of American food Annabelle-style. What do you think?"

"I'd tell you it was delicious, even if I didn't think it. But the truth is, it's delicious. All of it. You're a terrific cook."

Her full smile lit up his universe. "Thank you. Coming from the famous Chef Cavezzalli himself, that's a real compliment." She looked at him over her second piece of corn. "Judging from your mood, I take it this was a productive day."

He nodded. "Very."

"That's wonderful."

"So is your food." Not able to get enough of her mashed potatoes and chicken, he reached for the last of everything, including a fourth piece of corn. "Before you drove in, I was on the phone with an orthopedic man from the hospital in Naples. He's going to fit me in on Monday."

She went still for a moment. "For him to accommodate you this fast is the best news I've heard to date."

"If he can operate, I want you stay on and be my nurse. I realize Mel Jardine wants you back, but I need you more and will pay you whatever you ask."

That was twice she'd heard that Lucca needed her for medical assistance. She was afraid that what she needed from him wasn't in her stars, but it was a little too soon to tell him yes or no. The doctor might decide not to operate. It was possible Lucca wouldn't make a good candidate for the removal of the plate.

"Why don't we talk about that after you've had your initial visit with the doctor? In the meantime I want you to lie down on the swing and rest your leg while I do the dishes."

"I'll help."

"No, no. Have you forgotten the rule? Whoever cooks in this house does the cleanup."

Annabelle could understand why Vietri was called the pearl of the Amalfi Coast. The seaside village was dominated by St. John's 17th Century church. On the top was an elegant dome in majolica that stood out and provided the background for the shooting.

The rich jewel colors on an opaque white base forming the dome were symbolic of the art form developed by the artisans of Vietri. Their ceramics were sought by collectors from all over the world.

Guilio was supervising this last shoot. She had to admit she coveted the huge vase he'd chosen from one of the studios to place in the passenger seat of the sports car. It was worth thousands of dollars, decorated in colors of greens, oranges and browns on white.

The rich lagoon-green of the vase matched the painted green exterior of the Amalfi convertible. This model had been upholstered in a light tan to pick up the other colors.

Annabelle wore a sleeveless Etruscan print dress. A cape, denoting royalty, was fastened at the back of the shoulders and fell to the hem of the pencil-slim skirt. The outfit had been coordinated to match the design on the vase. Her light brown high-heeled sandals had straps wrapped to the ankle.

The hairdresser had taken a long time to form Annabelle's hair into braids, like the Etruscan women wore. The braids were caught at the back of her neck with a gold clasp. It matched the bracelets on her arms. These pieces represented some of the most fabulous jewelry she'd ever seen.

Marcella explained they were reproductions of Etruscan jewelry. Gold had been soldered to wide metal bands in hundreds of little dots. They glittered like gold dust in the sun.

For this shoot, her makeup had been applied in more dramatic fashion. They'd given her elongated eyes in darker eyeliner and she wore a dark bronze lipstick. The whole crew let out a collective cry of astonishment when she emerged from the van ready to pose.

"My dear—" Guilio walked toward her "—your hair rivals the jewelry. I knew you were the one to help me launch my new car, but not even I guessed how far you would surpass what I had in mind when I approached you."

Annabelle couldn't swallow for the emotion. "Don't tell me that now or I'll smear my makeup."

She noticed he had to clear his throat. "Today you're here on a buying spree and have stopped to pick up this treasure."

"Please don't ask me to hold it. I'd die if anything happened to it."

He chuckled. "Nothing so potentially dangerous. Pretend you've just bought it and are putting it in the car."

"All right."

The shoot began. Giovanni tried it from several angles and kept snapping away. Marcella rearranged the cape several times for the best effect.

Tourists had gathered round at a distance. They always did, but even with the security Guilio provided, they came closer than usual. When Giovanni announced he'd gotten the pictures he needed, the crowd broke into spontaneous applause. A lot of them wanted an autograph, but Guilio, along with the security people, waved them off with a smile.

She hurried back inside the van and began removing clothes and jewelry. Once that was accomplished, she got rid of the makeup, then checked her cell phone. She'd been hoping Lucca might have called, but he was probably busy with workmen who were supposed to be coming to the house today.

Heartsick because her days with Lucca were numbered if she went home, she emerged from the van sober-faced. Guilio had been waiting for her and picked up on it.

"Come with me. We have much to discuss and we'll do it over a late lunch. The seafood here is excellent. See that little restaurant farther along the sea wall? We'll just walk over there."

They both said goodbye to the crew. Within a few minutes he'd ordered scampi for them with scallops for hors d'oeuvres. He eyed her with affection. "Did you hear that applause today, and at the hotel in Amalfi?" She nodded. "We're going to be taking orders for so many cars, we won't be able to keep up with the supply."

"I hope so."

"I know so." He poured them a little wine. "Now let's get down to business. Tomorrow Marcella will come to the villa with her team to get you ready. You'll be wearing the outfit you wore during the shoot in front of the jet. We're going to do two launches. The big one in August is going ahead as planned with the media people from the television studios.

"Tomorrow night before dinner will be a sneak preview in front of the dealers and the family. It will be for Lucca, of course. I'll give my speech to honor him. We'll do it in the screening room with a slide show of all your shoots including today's.

"Giovanni is going to have to do a rush on this last shoot so it will be included. I'll explain that these slides will represent the pictures in the calendar we'll be sending out in August.

"When it's over, I'll ask you to come into the room and introduce you as the Amalfi Girl who will help launch the full-scale blitz in August. Be prepared to be besieged. The picture of you in front of the jet has been made up into three-by-five posters for them to take back to their places of business and display as a teaser. I'm afraid you'll be signing a bundle of them as the Amalfi Girl. Will that be a problem?"

"Of course not." He'd thought of everything and sounded in complete control. But Annabelle was pretty sure she had a fever. After worrying for so long about both men's feelings, the day was almost here. She didn't want anything to go wrong now.

"Maria phoned me while you were getting changed. She told me Mel is already at the villa. I'm sure you two have a lot of catching up to do."

Mel was already here? That was good. She needed to stay occupied until tomorrow was over. Surely when Lucca found himself the center of attention and realized what Guilio had been planning all this time, there'd be nothing but an Amalfi sun shining on his horizon.

"Since you refuse to relocate here and work for me in my office, you'll probably want to fly back with him when he leaves. It's entirely up to you, my dear. If I had my way, you wouldn't go, but you're too much like Lucca. No matter how much I might want it, I can't talk either of you into anything you don't want to do. You're your own people and I have to respect that."

He gave the waiter his credit card. When the other man returned, Guilio said, "Shall we go? I have a dozen details to attend to."

Guilio was so excited. She was, too, but when it was over, joy would go out of her life.

By the time Lucca had got up on Wednesday morning, Annabelle had already left for his father's villa. Lucca knew the homecoming party was a mixture of business and pleasure. He supposed Guilio had involved her in some way, but he was disappointed she hadn't told him her plans for today. He'd wanted her to go shopping with him, but it was evident he wouldn't be seeing her until the party.

Over the last few days she'd been preoccupied, even elusive at times. Much as he appreciated what his father was planning for him, he would be glad when it was over. With her no longer doing photo shoots for his father's ad campaign, Lucca was excited to spend whole days with her. Among many things, he wanted her opinion of where would be the best place to add another room on to the house.

At noon Fortunato came by to pick him up so he could buy a new suit. Since his nephew had recently got his driver's license, he jumped at the chance. After lunch at a teenage hangout, they did some shopping.

Lucca hadn't had a new suit in ages. He didn't like to wear them unless he had to. Guilio despaired of his son's preference for casual clothes. Tonight Lucca decided to surprise him and show up wearing something his father would approve of. Annabelle had never seen him in a suit, either.

Fortunato told him to go the whole route—new shoes, tie, shirt. The works. By the time they got back to his house, Lucca was tired. He hid the pain from his nephew. But when Fortunato drove off with the assurance that he'd be back later to pick him up, Lucca took some painkillers to ensure he got through the evening without anyone suspecting something was wrong.

Annabelle would know, of course. She noticed everything. He'd missed her so much he was half out of his mind.

"Hey, you look all right," Lucca teased his nephew when he came by for him at six.

"Yeah? You look spiffy yourself."

"Thanks. Your parents don't mind my borrowing you once in a while?"

"Of course, not. I heard *Mama* tell *Papa* maybe I'd stay out of trouble now. When are you going to go looking for a car?"

"I don't know. I'm trying to figure out what kind I want."

"Can I go with you?"

"Sure."

Fortunato grinned. "I want a sports car some day and race it along the Corniche. I love driving."

"And girls."

"Yeah. That, too."

Lucca chuckled and pushed him gently on the shoulder. "You're all right, Fortunato."

"She's going to be there tonight. I can't wait."

Neither could Lucca.

When they reached the villa, it turned out Annabelle

was nowhere to be found. After a while her no-show made Lucca feel as if he'd been punched in the stomach.

The family welcomed him en masse, as did the staff from the plant his father had invited. He gave Maria an extralong hug. Guilio worked his way through the crowd and embraced him. His eyes reflected pure pleasure when he took in Lucca's new suit.

"Now that you're here, we can get started. We're going to begin in the screening room before we have dinner out in the garden."

Lucca sensed something big was about to happen. His father was actually acting nervous, which wasn't like him at all. He followed him through the villa to the room his father had added on many years ago. He needed his own place to work and view his designs on a theater screen. This evening the room was packed with at least sixty chairs. Enough to accommodate everyone.

"You sit here, Lucca." Front row center.

As the others filed in, Lucca felt the hairs lift on the back of his neck. What in the devil was going on?

His father stepped back. "Tonight is really a twofold celebration. It represents two dreams of mine that have come to pass. The first is that my son Lucca would survive the war and come home for good one day."

Hushed cries of surprise and happiness broke out from the family seated around Lucca.

"The second has to do with the first. You see, I thought he wouldn't be coming for a visit until August. But he surprised me, forcing me to move up my timetable two months for the surprise I've been planning in his honor for over a year."

What?

CHAPTER EIGHT

"Years ago I saw the design for a sports car in my dreams. Amalfi has never made a sports car. Except for my wives, Donata and Maria, no one else knew about it. Once it was perfected, I shared it with the engineers and a prototype was made."

His father's eyes found Lucca's. "I've called it the Amalfi MB-Viper after the fighter jet Lucca has been flying in combat. I want my decorated son to know how deeply proud I am of him for serving his country so well and nobly. It is a great honor to be your father, Lucca. If your mother could be here tonight…"

The room broke into clapping. Everyone stood up and cheered. It went on and on. Lucca sat there in disbelief, absolutely stunned by his father's tribute.

"*Grazie, Papa.* I'm overwhelmed," he said in a husky voice.

"Welcome home, *figlio mio.*"

Lucca stood up and approached him. Deep inside of him he felt gratitude that he could walk up to him on both legs. After kissing his father on both cheeks, he put his arm around his shoulders and faced the audience. "Every son should have a father like Guilio Cavezzali."

"Hear, hear," everyone shouted.

"I wouldn't be surprised if *Mama* can see what you've achieved, *Papa*, but she couldn't be more proud of you than this son. I'm thankful you're my father, and I'm thrilled to be home with you and Maria." He gave his father's shoulders a squeeze before going back to his seat.

After a few minutes of thunderous clapping, the din finally subsided and people sat down. Guilio had to clear his throat several times.

"Tonight you're going to see the Viper's unveiling through a slide show. These photographs will go into calendars you will receive in August when the cars go out on the market. Every client who buys one will be given a calendar. Believe me, the calendar will do the word-of-mouth advertising for you.

"The launch will take place in Milan with total media coverage. Those of you dealers here tonight are getting a sneak preview. I'll send posters back with you. They're made up from the cover of the calendar. Basilio? If you will turn off the lights and start the show please."

Lucca had to blink back the moisture glazing his eyes several times while he tried to focus on the theater-sized screen. Suddenly there was a larger-than-life photograph in living color of a fabulous, gleaming white sports car convertible parked in front of an actual fighter jet. The lines were fantastic. His father had created a true masterpiece.

But dominating everything for Lucca was the jaw-droppingly gorgeous woman draped across the pearly-looking upholstery, twisting her delectable body just enough as if waiting for the pilot to come and join her.

Annabelle!

The blood pounded in his ears.

He could tell the picture had been taken at twilight at the air base outside Rome. His thoughts flew back to that first night in the hallway of the farmhouse when he'd vetted her rather cruelly and she'd said she'd just come from there.

Her skin gave off that magical glow. She was wearing a deep purple cocktail dress with spaghetti straps and a diamond necklace around her throat. A matching diamond bracelet was wrapped around her wrist. Her semicurly hair gleamed a silvery-gold over one shoulder. Her eyes shone pure violet.

She was so bewitching, he was dumbstruck. So was everyone else. A hush had fallen over the room. At first there was total quiet. After a moment he heard cries of "bravo" followed by heavy clapping and more cheers. Everyone got to their feet in tribute. They went crazy, as much for Annabelle as for the car.

In his gut he knew a poster of this photograph would be sold by the hundreds of thousands throughout the world. His father had known what he was doing. It filled Lucca with a deep sense of pride at Guilio's colossal achievement. The knowledge that he'd named the sports car to honor Lucca's choice of career was so humbling, he couldn't find the words.

Several of the dealers called out to Guilio in excitement. Soon the questions were flying at him. They wanted to know where he'd been hiding this breathtaking model. Who was she? Would she be visiting the different dealerships? Would she pose for pictures with them to put on their own websites?

The agreement was unanimous. Sales would skyrocket and they all wanted to meet the woman who'd made the launch of this magnificent car a transcendent moment. Guilio simply answered with a mysterious smile.

While Lucca was still trying to recover from the emotions bombarding him, another photo appeared on the screen. There she was, exactly like she'd been that first morning on the terrace, wearing that broad-rimmed hat and white eyelet sun top. The shot had been taken at Positano.

She sat in the black sports car with its black leather upholstery while she gauged the steepness of the terrain. Her appeal reached out to the audience like a living entity. A completely spontaneous, ear-splitting ovation broke from the crowd.

While Lucca was clapping with them, a third photo filled the screen. It showed her reaching for a cluster of grapes growing in a vineyard at the side of the road in Furore, Italy's own version of the hanging gardens of Babylon.

She was more luscious than the purple fruit that matched her eyes. She wore a cream-colored outfit and leaned against a light jade version of the sports car. Lucca sensed every male in the room wanted to catch hold of her jade scarf and pull her out of the screen into his lap.

He studied the photograph, marveling at the amalgamation of his father's creative engineering genius and nature's flawless design of womanhood in all her springtime glory. Everyone sat there mesmerized. A man could be forgiven for buying the car in order to own the photograph that came with it. Lucca could guarantee the calendar would become a collector's item.

As the next picture lit up the screen, all the oxygen seemed to be sucked out of his lungs. At the side of the gleaming yellow sports car, Annabelle held a basket of sunflowers picked from a whole field of them reflected behind her. They'd shot this in Sorrento. In the three-piece white suit with yellow trim, she looked good enough to eat.

It reminded him of the morning she'd picked the daisies pushing through the grillwork of the terrace. Like his mother, she responded to his world of growing things. He felt his whole body and soul respond to this woman who in a very short time had become a living part of him. The idea of not being able to wake up to her every morning for the rest of his life was unthinkable.

The photo taken in Vietri nailed him to his seat. She looked like some exotic Etruscan princess come to life who was so damn beautiful in those braids, he was hypnotized. You could believe the rich green sports car was her personal chariot. The sight brought another chorus of bravos from the crowd.

His father's exceptional vision had found Annabelle clear across the ocean.

What exactly do you do for my father, Signorina Marsh?

I'm helping him with his ad campaign.

Guilio had brought her to Italy and now his finished product had been translated into something wondrous to behold. Not until this evening did Lucca fully appreciate his father's expertise that would blow every other car off the road once it hit the market. With Annabelle's help, he would succeed in triple spades.

Still staggering from the impact of so much beauty, his eyes fastened on the shot of her dressed in a cheongsam, looking out over the waters of Capri from the

side of the metallic-blue sports car. He'd been to China
many times, but he'd never seen beauty like hers.

With each photograph, the energy in the room had
become electric. The talk had grown louder as they reacted to what they were seeing.

"I saved December's photo for last," Guilio finally
said.

Oohs and ahs came out unsolicited as every eye was
riveted to the bride at the footsteps of the church in
Amalfi with the flame-red sports car parked below her.
The sudden explosion of excitement in the room went
over the top. Everyone was on their feet shouting con-
gratulations to Guilio.

But Lucca couldn't move from the chair. His lungs
were frozen at the exquisite sight of Annabelle in that
gown and mantilla. He couldn't make a sound. He'd had
a complete physical before coming home from the hospital, but wondered if his heart could withstand this.

"Basilio?" his father called out. "If you'll turn on
the lights, I'd now like to introduce you to the woman
in the photos."

As the lights went on, Lucca turned in time to see
her make her entrance from the back of the room. She
was wearing the purple cocktail dress and diamonds.
The whole room burst into stunning applause and stood
to clap as she walked up to a smiling Guilio.

Lucca's gaze took in her tremulous eyes, then the
other parts of her, bit by gorgeous bit, until it fell to
those fabulous legs where the frothy purple fabric
danced and teased him.

He watched his father put his arm around her
shoulders. "Annabelle Marsh is from Los Angeles,
California. She works for Mel Jardine, my best dealer

in the States, who's here tonight. Annabelle is my not-so-secret weapon anymore." Everyone laughed. "She's going to put the Amalfi MB-Viper on the map. Ladies and gentlemen? May I present, the Amalfi Girl!"

When the applause finally died down, Guilio quickly led Annabelle out through a side door to escape the crowd. As soon as it closed, she gave him a hug. "I know this night meant everything in the world to him."

His eyes watered. "I know it did, too. For both of us. Thank you again for not giving my surprise away."

"As if I would have!"

He wiped his eyes. "It would have been understandable. My son had to have been dying of curiosity since he arrived at the farmhouse. It's just a miracle you could keep it from him."

"It was brilliant of you to move up the date of the party. He had to know something unusual was going on. As for your car, it's sensational, Guilio. I listened in the back during the slide show. Every dealer was bowled over with excitement to start selling them."

"Let's hope the sales reflect my belief that we have a winner here."

"You're too modest. You already know it is."

"And you're too kind." He walked her over to a table. "We've put you out here so you can sign the posters. People are coming through now. I'll be back in a little while."

Annabelle sat down, looking out on the garden. The lights had been turned on, transforming it into a fairyland. Guilio's new sports car sat on a raised platform. It was the one in flame-red. The dealers could examine it, climb in it, check out the engine and take home a brochure with all the specs printed.

While she was looking for Lucca, one of the dealers came up and asked for a signature of the Amalfi Girl. At that point a line started to form. For the next while she was besieged just as Guilio had predicted. While she answered dozens of questions, she wrote on each poster as fast as she could, losing track of time.

"Sign mine 'from Annabellissima,'" instructed a deep, beloved voice.

She threw her head back and discovered Lucca's grey-green eyes staring down at her, liquefying her bones with his intimate gaze. He'd dressed in a formal light grey suit and tie. She didn't know a man could be that handsome. His eyes swept over her in a restless motion, missing no curve or detail about her. Blood swarmed into her face, making her go hot.

"Lucca…" she whispered in an aching voice.

"I can't find words, either," came his husky admission.

She knew what he meant because the sight of him robbed her of breath. Her fingers curled around the marking pen. "Maybe now you won't be as upset with me."

He cocked his dark head, gazing at her through shuttered eyes. "Upset?"

"You know—for begging you to let your father know you'd come home early."

"With a divine surprise like this, how could I be?"

"I'm so glad this night finally came. He wanted everything to be perfect for you."

"It *was* perfect. *You* made it perfect. Now I want my own autograph from you."

The way he said it in that deep tone sent a thrill through her sensitized body. She unraveled one of the posters and signed it in the bottom right corner. When she'd finished, he rolled it up and tucked it beneath his arm. The look in his eyes set her trembling.

"You have no idea how hard it was not to tell you what your father was planning. Please don't take this wrong, but under the circumstances, it was a good thing you couldn't drive a car yet. Otherwise—"

"Otherwise I would have followed you because I couldn't have helped myself and curiosity would have killed the proverbial cat."

"Yes." She laughed softly.

"My father knew what he was doing when he stole you away from Mel. More than the fact that you're incredibly beautiful, you didn't let him down. After watching the slide show tonight, I'm convinced you could have a career as a top model."

"Those are heady words, *signore*, but for now I like being Mel Jardine's assistant at the showroom in L.A. when I'm not nursing." She'd leave Italy with a smile on her face if it killed her. Looking at the Italian soldier she loved to the depth of her soul, it already was killing her.

"Signorina Marsh?"

She jerked her around. Since Lucca had come to the table, she hadn't been aware of anyone else. "Hi, Fortunato!"

He broke into a broad smile. "Those pictures were fantastic. You look fantastic! Would you autograph the rest of these posters for me? I'm going to give them to my friends. They're going to eat their hearts out when they find out I know you."

Annabelle chuckled. "You know how to make an old lady feel good."

"Old lady—are you crazy?"

"Thanks, Fortunato. You've made my night. I'd be happy to sign these." She felt Lucca's hot gaze on her while she autographed the last six for his nephew.

"Thanks." He gathered them up and turned to Lucca. "Do you want me to drive you home now?"

She held her breath while she waited for Lucca's answer. "That's very nice of you to offer, but Annabelle's going to drive us back to the farmhouse. Here." He pulled some bills out of his pocket and put them in Fortunato's hand. "I owe you for today."

He stared at the money. "What's this for?"

"For chauffeuring your old uncle around town and showing me the hottest clothes to buy. See you later."

"*Ciao.*" Fortunato's eyes lingered on both of them before he disappeared.

"He's darling," she remarked.

"Ruggero says he's incorrigible, but I couldn't ask for a nicer nephew." He shifted his weight. It made her wonder if his leg had started to ache. "Do you have to stay around here much longer?"

"No. I'm through. Your father will be talking business half the night. I'll go inside the villa to change and meet you at the car in the courtyard. Give me ten minutes."

"Make it five."

"I don't think that's possible."

"Try." He sounded out of breath. "While you're gone,

I'll gather up some food for us from the party and we'll eat when we get back to the farmhouse."

His male virility was so potent, she'd forgotten all about food.

The blood surged through her veins as she left the table and rushed inside the villa. Marcella was there to relieve her of her clothes and jewels. She hugged Annabelle.

"Because of you, my shop in Rome will be besieged by women wanting to look just like you. Of course that's impossible, but it's the thought that counts."

Annabelle burst into laughter. "Thank you for everything you've done. I know Guilio is very grateful."

"You were a delight to work with."

"I'll never forget you, Marcella."

After she left, Annabelle removed her makeup and tied her hair in a ponytail. Once she'd slipped into pleated khaki pants and a light blue cotton knit top, she hurried back outside.

Lucca stood by the car, holding the door open for her. There weren't words to describe his looks adequately. She felt like a frump in comparison, but kept a smile pasted on.

"The Amalfi Girl is gone."

"No." His eyes traveled over her before coming back to her face. "The real Amalfi Girl is standing in front of me, the one my father saw when he went to California."

"Incredible, isn't it?" She got in the car and waited for him to go around and get in the other side. "He said he saw my bones and knew I was the one he wanted."

"My father has a visionary side to him. The other side is the persuasive businessman."

She started the motor and drove down the gravel drive to the road. "I found that out."

Lucca's hand slid to her thigh and gave it a gentle squeeze. "I'm not going to apologize for touching you like this. After the way I saw all the dealers devouring you with their eyes, I'm feeling possessive of you. Since I came home, we've lived in our own private world and I've grown to crave it."

What he'd just said had silenced her. In the palpable quiet that followed, his cell phone rang. Annabelle bet it was Guilio wanting to talk to his son. It was only ten o'clock, but she knew Lucca's leg was hurting. He'd been at the party long enough to start feeling uncomfortable.

He gave her leg another squeeze before removing his hand to answer it. She expected to hear him talk in affectionate tones to his father, but there was silence. She glanced sideways at Lucca and her spirits fell. There were long periods where he listened, then spoke in low tones. Annabelle couldn't make anything out except that his body had tensed and that wasn't a good sign.

After he hung up, her anxiety increased while she waited for him to tell her what was wrong. By now they'd reached the farmhouse.

"That was Stefana Beraldi's mother calling from the hospital in Naples."

Uh-oh.

"Stefana started bleeding earlier in the day. She was rushed to emergency hoping the baby could be saved, but it wasn't possible. It seems she's in the operating room right now having some kind of procedure done."

"A *D* and *C*," Annabelle said quietly.

"What is that?"

"An abbreviation for a dilation and curettage. Sometimes tissue remains in the uterus and it has to be removed."

Lucca grimaced. "Her mother said she'd be in the hospital for another twenty-four hours. I've got to go to her."

"I'll drive you now, but before we leave here, I'll run inside for your pills. Don't move. By morning you're going to be exhausted and will start hurting without them."

When she came back to the car a minute later with his pills and a couple of colas, Lucca had pulled some ham-and-cheese rolls from a sack. He handed her one with a napkin. "After the day you've been through, you need to eat first or you'll be too tired to drive."

She finished hers fast and drank half her cola before starting up the car once more. Lucca devoured five in a row and swallowed all his drink before settling back against the seat with a heavy sigh.

"Why did this have to happen to her?" The bleakness in his tone caused her to groan inwardly. To hear this awful news after the wonderfully unforgettable night...

Annabelle drew in a shaky breath. "One obstetrician I worked with told me a miscarriage can mean something was wrong with the baby and it wasn't meant to be, but I realize that won't be of any comfort to Stefana."

He turned toward her. "Do you know my mother had four miscarriages before I was born? I only found that out the other day."

"Your poor parents. How hard that had to have been on them, but especially your mother. With every conception, all the hopes and dreams start up. Thank heaven she was able to carry you to term."

A harsh sound escaped Lucca's throat. "Now Stefana's hopes are dashed."

"She'll mourn the loss for a long time because it has followed on the heels of losing Leo, but it won't last forever."

"I won't know what to say to her."

"There isn't anything to say. Platitudes don't help at a time like this. What she needs is for people to be there for her, Lucca. Seeing you, drawing from your strength—that will do her the most good. She'll probably want to talk about her husband because you were with him at the end. It'll do you good to mourn with her too. There's comfort in doing that together. One day she'll get better."

Lucca moved his arm to the back of the seat. She felt his fingers massage the nape of her neck. "Are *you* better, Annabelle?" he whispered. "Some people say divorce is worse than death for a spouse."

Not since I came to Ravello. Annabelle wanted to say those words aloud, but then Lucca could be in no doubt how she felt about him. Until he spoke the words she needed to hear, they'd remain unsaid.

"It's true my divorce left a void because my husband took up space. But I feel fine. Who would want a rootless man who isn't capable of love? You taught me that."

He reached for her hand and grasped it. "Did you want a baby from him so badly?" He was terrified for Stefana.

"I thought I did, but with hindsight I can see I wouldn't want to raise a child alone. In time Stefana will meet another man and have babies with him. Wait and see."

Annabelle didn't tell him that to a girl growing up,

the idea that one day she'd become a woman and carry the child of the man she loved was part of what a woman believed was her rite of passage. To see him in her child, to see his smile or his eyes, or the way he walks or laughs—that was a woman's dream.

To have Lucca's babies, to watch for his traits in them—for Annabelle *that* would be one of the ultimate joys of marriage to him. But she feared it wasn't going to happen.

It was seven in the morning when Annabelle pulled into the drive of the farmhouse. The visit with Stefana had drained Lucca. Upon leaving the hospital, he'd taken three pain pills because the pain was worse. Ten minutes ago he'd fallen asleep. She'd almost gone to sleep at the wheel herself.

Somehow she managed to wake him long enough to get him to his bedroom. She undressed him down to his suit trousers, then made him lie down so she could pull off his shoes and socks. After adjusting the pillows between his legs, she started to draw the lightweight cover over him and felt him tug on her arm.

"Don't go away," he begged, sounding drugged. "I need you next to me."

To appease him, and herself, she curled up next to him. His arm automatically went around her and pulled her closer, as if they'd been doing this for years. She was in love with this man, the heart-wrenching kind you never got over. To lie in his arms all night was her dream, but he was in a deep sleep and most likely wouldn't waken until afternoon.

When next she had cognizance of her surroundings, she heard her cell phone ringing. It came from her purse, which she'd put on the dresser when they'd come in. Carefully she slid off the bed and made a grab for it, afraid it would waken Lucca.

She hurried out in the hall to a kitchen filled with daylight. One glance at the caller ID showed it was her boss. She'd assumed it was her parents, whom she'd neglected for the last few days during the rush to get ready for the party.

"Mel?" Her mind was so blank, she had trouble gathering her wits. "Hi! How are you?"

"More to the point, how's the Amalfi Girl this afternoon?" She looked at her watch. It was one o'clock. She'd slept close to six hours. Lucca was still out for the count and probably wouldn't stir till later in the day.

"I'm back to being Ms. Marsh."

He laughed. "Lovely as she is, that's good to hear. I miss my assistant. Guilio and I had a long talk at breakfast with his staff. He said he was through with you until August. He said he felt guilty to have kept you away from me this long. But not too guilty obviously." Mel chuckled. "Since I'm flying out of Naples at five this evening, do you want to fly home with me?"

No. No. No. No.

"Annabelle? Are you still there?"

"Yes."

"For a minute it went so quiet, I thought our call had been dropped."

"I thought the same thing," she said.

"If you're going with me, it means we'll have to be at the airport by three at the latest. Because of traffic, Guilio said we'll need to get going within the hour. He's going to drive us to the airport. On the way he'll tell you all the wonderful things everyone said about you."

She'd just come from Naples. She'd spent all night with Lucca. How could she just leave?

How can you not, *Annabelle!*

Her work was done here a few days earlier than originally planned.

Lucca and his father had enjoyed the long-awaited reunion. They needed time to cement their new relationship. He was starting on his remodeling plans for the farmhouse. He had a doctor's appointment on Monday to see about his leg. The man had a new life to put together, plans to make.

Except for him to want her as his nurse, at no time had he talked to Annabelle about a future with her. If he'd ever told her he was in love... If he'd ever said he couldn't live without her... He'd had opportunity after opportunity. Though they'd discussed her future, he hadn't indicated he wanted to be a part of it, or her to be part of his.

She left a note on the terrace table for him.

Dearest Lucca. I've enjoyed this unexpected interlude with you more than you can possibly imagine, but interludes by their definition always come to an end. Ours is over, but I'll never forget. The Amalfi Girl is gone until August, when I'll be resurrected for the media blitz. I hope to see you then. Annabelle.

Steeling herself not to peek in on Lucca and kiss his mouth one more time, she stole out of the farmhouse with a heart heavier than the bags she'd packed. After closing the door behind her, she took off in the car with her purse. With a whole family ready to wait on him, Lucca would be perfectly taken care of.

Before she reached the villa, she phoned her parents, who were still up watching television before going to bed. They were overjoyed to hear she was coming home and told her they would pick her up at the airport. Her mom wanted her to stay with them for a few days, but Annabelle told her she had to get right back to work Monday morning.

She adored her family, but right now she was in too much pain to be leaving Lucca to think about anything else. Once she'd gotten off the phone, she had to pull over to the side of the road because she was sobbing so hard. Emotions she'd been holding back began to pour out of her. She didn't know if she could stop.

In truth she felt more married to Lucca than she'd ever felt with Ryan and they'd only been together a week. When the worst of her paroxysms had passed, she wiped the tears off her face and lifted her head.

She needed to get going, not daring to hold up the men. For the first time since she'd been in Italy, she wished her makeup woman were here to give her a fresh face, but all that was over and Annabelle would have to make the repairs herself from now on.

Just like Stefana, you're going to have to find a way to go on, Annabelle.

CHAPTER NINE

DR. COZZA motioned Lucca over to the screen to see his X-rays. "I've been through your file. The doctor who operated on you did an excellent job. I see no fractures. It appears the pain you're having is local."

He turned off the light and looked at Lucca. "I can take your plate and screws out right away." The news elated him. "I believe it's the right decision to prevent deterioration and stop the stinging. Some people don't realize this procedure can be done and they wait years. Your doctor didn't tell you?"

"He probably did, but I wasn't listening at the time. Actually it was a friend of mine who's a trained nurse. She said it was possible."

"You're lucky she was so on the ball."

Dr. Cozza didn't know the half of it. "This isn't too soon?"

"No. You were operated on close to four months ago. You're good to go. Let me talk to my nurse." He stepped out of the examining room while Lucca paced the floor. Before long he came back. "I have an opening on Friday morning. You'll have to be here by five-thirty to get prepped."

"You can fit me in that fast?"

The doctor smiled. "I make room when my patient is a returning war vet hero."

"*Grazie*," Lucca murmured with heartfelt gratitude. That was only four days away. Lucca's mind reeled. "If all goes well, how soon can I get back to regular activity?"

"Two weeks on crutches, more to give the incision time to heal than anything else. You'll need someone to help you. Then you can throw the crutches away."

"Does that mean I'll be able to drive and swim?"

He nodded. "And have sexual intercourse. That's the greatest concern of all my patients with your kind of injury."

After they shook hands, Lucca left the hospital and climbed in the limo he'd hired. He instructed the chauffeur to drive him back to Ravello. He called ahead to the villa and was relieved when Maria told him his father was busy in his office off the screening room, working out the details of the media blitz he was planning. After telling her to expect him, Lucca stared at the view, not seeing it because Annabelle's image got in the way.

After waking up at four on Thursday afternoon and not finding her there, he'd called the villa, assuming she was having a conference with his father. When Maria told him she'd left for the airport with Mr. Jardine to fly home to Los Angeles, he almost did go into cardiac arrest. Then he saw her message on the patio table that left him shocked and then hurt to the quick.

At that point it had been too late to reach her by phone. She'd already boarded the plane. By the time he figured she'd touched down in California, he'd decided it was best to leave her alone until he'd been to the doctor. When he knew anything about his condition and prognosis, then he'd know what to say to her.

"Lucca, come on in," his father exclaimed when he saw him in the doorway. He got up to give him a hug and kiss him on both cheeks. "Do you have any idea how happy it makes me to know you're just down the hill and can drop in on your old dad when you feel like it? Sit down. Tell me what's on your mind."

He explained about the new surgery planned for Friday, delighting his father that this operation could take away his pain altogether.

"Do you want to recuperate at the villa, or would you like me to find someone to care for you? Whatever suits you best."

Lucca's heart thudded. "I want Annabelle back."

"*Grazie a Dio!*"

They stared at each other with a perfect understanding.

"Would you lean on Mel Jardine before I phone her?"

"You know I'd do anything for you."

"Right now?"

His father broke down in laughter. "I've been waiting for the day when my bachelor son finally went running the right way."

Annabelle waved to the salesman who'd been popping in and out the last few days to tell her they were glad to see her. But it was surreal to be back at the dealership. The receptionist out in front was doing her job. It was business as usual around the dealership.

"Line three for Colin.

"Line seven for Rick. Your party's been holding for five minutes."

"Line two for Annabellissima."

The receptionist pronounced Lucca's name for her like Annabellisthmus. She almost fell out of her chair from shock.

Trembling in every atom of her body, she picked up the phone. "H-hello, Lucca?" she stammered.

"I've needed to hear your voice. It's felt like months."

Years. She'd been praying for this. Her eyelids squeezed shut. "How are you?" She could hardly talk.

"Nervous."

Her hand tightened on the receiver. "Why?"

"I saw the doctor today. He's going to perform surgery on my leg Friday morning. He says I'm going to need help for two weeks. I don't want anyone else but you around because you're the only one who understands about all my problems. Do you think your boss would let you come for a medical emergency? I'll prepay your airline ticket."

Annabelle didn't have to think. After talking to her mom the last few days, she wondered if she hadn't made a mistake leaving Ravello so fast. What if Lucca had been waiting to have a serious talk with her? If so, Annabelle hadn't given him a chance.

"Hold the line for a minute and I'll ask him." She lay the receiver down and raced into the adjoining office. Mel was on the phone. He gestured her to come all the way in and sit down until he was through.

She was too emotional to sit. He finally hung up from his call. "What's going on? I've never seen you pace before."

"Mel? Lucca just phoned me. He's still on the line." In the next breath it all came out in a gush.

He smiled. "I can hardly deprive him of a good nurse

when I once had the best. Will you at least wait to fly back until Wednesday? I need your help with some matters backed up around here. You're the only one who can sort them out."

"Thank you!" She hugged him around the neck and hurried back to her office. "Lucca?"

"*Si*? You sound out of breath."

"I had to run to his office." But that wasn't why she was close to hyperventilating. "He says I can come. I probably won't be there until Thursday. It all depends on my flight schedule."

"Let me know the time and I'll send a limo for you."

"Thank you." After a pause she continued, "Lucca...?"

"I can't wait to see you. All that's important now is that you're coming back to me. *Ciao*."

The doctor told Lucca the third day after surgery would be the worst. Maybe it was, but with Annabelle waiting on him, he didn't notice it as much. It certainly couldn't compare to the pain he'd suffered the night he'd come home and had fallen in the hallway.

"Uncle Lucca? Annabelle wants to know if you're hungry for dinner."

Fortunato had been a constant visitor in the evenings after he'd got off of work. He'd let him lean on him in and out of the shower. Lucca welcomed his nephew's help.

When the two-week recuperation period was over, Lucca would be helping Annabelle into the shower, only one of the many things he planned to do with her. Tonight he planned to open up to her, but he was nervous. That, more than anything, had put him off his food.

"Maybe some grapes and a roll."

"I'll tell Annabelle, then I've got to go. Carlo and I are going to a soccer match."

"That sounds fun."

"Not really. Our team's going to lose."

"Maybe you'll meet a cute girl there."

"You mean one who looks like Annabelle?"

Since there was no chance of that, Lucca didn't say anything

"Did I hear my name taken in vain?" She breezed into the bedroom carrying another vase of freshly picked daisies and put them on his dresser.

Fortunato grinned. He wasn't the only one who enjoyed looking at her dressed this evening in jeans and a jade-green blouse with cropped sleeves. Lucca could feast his eyes on her indefinitely.

"Uncle Lucca wants some grapes and a roll. Now I'd better leave or Carlo will have a fit. See you tomorrow. Thanks for dinner, Annabelle. You're not a bad cook."

"You mean for an American."

"I was just teasing. Those fajitas were awesome! You'll have to teach *Mama* how to make them."

"Fajitas?" Lucca questioned.

"Mexican food," she explained. "You take strips of steak, peppers and onions stir-fried in a special sauce. Then you roll it all up in a flour tortilla. I brought a couple of cans of them in my suitcase to fix a different kind of meal for you."

"Yeah, Uncle Lucca. Too bad you don't feel good enough to try one."

"Maybe tomorrow," Annabelle said. "For such a lovely compliment, you can come over anytime, Fortunato."

"Thanks for helping me," Lucca called after his nephew.

Soon they were alone. Annabelle's smile faded as she stared at him. "You're not hungry, are you."

"Not particularly. Why the concern?"

"Maybe it's the new painkiller you're on. I'll call the doctor in the morning and see if he'll prescribe your other one. You need to eat."

"It's not the medicine."

"So you admit there's something wrong."

He heard the alarm in her voice. "Yes. There's been something wrong for a long time, but I couldn't speak about it until now."

She stood by the bed looking nervous. "What is it?"

"I've never asked a woman to marry me before. If I can't have you, I plan to remain a bachelor for the rest of my life because you've spoiled me for anyone else. I'm not going to give you any time to think about your answer. Do you love me?"

A cry escaped her lips. "How can you even ask me that? I'm desperately in love with you. It's why I came back." The love-light in her eyes almost blinded him.

"Don't come any closer. My heart can't take it when I'm lying here incapacitated right now. I love you, Annabelle Marsh," he said, his voice throbbing. "I want to put my roots down with you so thick and deep, you'll know this is for real and forever."

She nodded.

"First we have to get married. Just as soon as the doctor gives me a clean bill of health. How about at the church we pass between my farmhouse and the villa?"

Her beautiful blond head nodded again. "Is that the one you went to with your parents?"

"Yes. I'll fly your parents and family over. You don't know how eager I am to the meet the people who raised such an angelic daughter."

She crept over to him and sat down, burying her face against his shoulder. "My parents will adore you. They won't believe the beauty of this place."

"Have you told them much about me?"

"I guess I'd better admit to the truth now, because you'll hear it from Mom when you meet her." She leaned over to kiss him.

After kissing her back he said, "What truth?"

"She's been worried about me for a long time. But after you and I clashed in your hallway, I phoned her and told her I'd met a man who'd already changed my life. And if I was lucky enough, maybe I would change his. I kind of told her you looked like a god with black hair and gray-green eyes. I also said Dad would be jealous because when my mom first met you, she would go weak in the knees and might faint, just like me."

Lucca laughed quietly before rewarding her with more kisses.

"You're my beloved, Lucca. I'm so madly in love with you, if I lost you now, I'd want to die!"

Lucca couldn't take it in. "You're my life, *adorata*. After your confession, I guess I can tell you mine. The night you came at me with the cane, I knew somewhere deep inside you were the woman I'd been waiting for all my life. But I was terrified because I wanted to be ready to give you all the things you deserve. I feared that after what you'd been through with your first husband, you wouldn't be able to trust me."

"Darling…" She traced his profile with her finger.

"You have a lot to learn about a woman in love the way I am with you."

"I'm finding that out," he said in husky voice. "Now I've got another question."

She read the anxiety in his eyes. "You mean about being a farmer's wife? I can't wait! Do you know something? I guessed that about you right from the beginning."

He looked surprised. "How?"

"I actually pictured it in my mind that first morning sitting on the terrace. You'd just crept back to this farmhouse in the dead of it because you're a home boy at heart. Your mother and her family had a love for the earth and all the beautiful things that grow here. Though you have a lot of Guilio in you, you're an extension of her and your grandfather."

She nestled closer. "When I got into bed that first night, before you fell in the hall, I felt that the family who'd once lived here had been supremely happy. Through all your pain and suffering, I saw how much peace the farm gave you. Your eyes would go soft when you looked around. The sight of the daisies I picked seemed to speak to you."

He nodded. "My mother used to pick them in the morning and bring them in house, just like you did."

"What a wonderful memory you have of her. When you made tea from the lemons growing outside, I learned something profound about you and could imagine you out pruning the trees. I could see myself watching you, coveting your body from a distance while I thought up ways to lure you back in the house."

"Annabelle," he whispered, his voice raw with

emotion. "Keep saying things like that and never let me go."

"As if I could," she cried, covering his mouth with her own.

"This is Canale Eight, with the six o'clock news, broadcasting live from Milan. Tonight ladies and gentlemen, we're at the Amalfi main showroom in Milan where Guilio Cavezzali, CEO of the one of the most prestigious lines of cars in Italy, is about to unveil their latest creation."

Annabelle sat in the driver's seat of the black-on-black sports car, knowing the television camera would be on her the second the curtain was drawn. All she had to do was drive the car into the center of the showroom and follow Guilio's lead.

Her hair had been swept to one side and cascaded over one shoulder to reveal diamond earrings and a diamond choker. Marcella had decked her out in a stunning flame-orange cocktail dress in a chiffonlike fabric. The straps went from the center of the bodice and fastened at the back of her neck. Her high-heeled sandals were covered in diamondlike brilliance.

Lucca was out on the floor with Maria and Basilio, watching Annabelle from a distance. He'd dressed in a silky black shirt and tan trousers. Her gorgeous husband ought to be the one in the spotlight. She happened to know the black model sports car with the million-dollar price tag was his favorite.

As soon as she got the cue from one of the guys, she started the car and drove to the spot where she'd practiced several times to get it right. Guilio stood front and center with a microphone.

"Here comes the Amalfi Girl now. You'll see her picture in all our showrooms around the world. Tonight we are happy to announce the launch of the first convertible sports car our company has ever designed. I've named it the Amalfi MB-Viper in honor of my son, who served our country flying one of the Viper fighter jets.

"She'll get out and open the hood so you can zoom in for a closer look."

Guilio gave a rundown of the impressive stats as Annabelle stepped from the car with as much as grace as she could and did the honors. So far so good as she moved from spot to spot, demonstrating the car's features.

Even from a distance she noticed Lucca's eyes smolder as he watched her walk around and open the passenger door to point out the luxurious upholstery and dashboard.

Finally her father-in-law smiled into the camera. "From zero to sixty miles per hour in three seconds. Take a drive in the MB-Viper and slide silently into the future."

With those words spoken as the new slogan, the filming came to an end. After a year or more of planning, the night Guilio had dreamed about was over. Much as Annabelle had been willing to do this favor for him, she was glad she wouldn't have to do it again. But thank heaven he'd approached her that day in California. Otherwise she would never have met the love of her life.

After the film crew cleared up their equipment and left, Lucca walked over and put his arm around her. "You were a vision up there," he whispered against the side of her neck.

"Thank you, darling."

"You were superb, Annabelle." Guilio had never looked happier. "To show my appreciation, I'm giving Lucca the car and you the diamonds for your wedding presents. Marcella wants you to keep the dress you're wearing as a memento of this night."

"I'll never be able to thank you enough for having faith in me. But most of all—" her voice caught "—I thank you for bringing your wonderful son into the world."

Lucca's eyes gleamed as she kissed his father and Maria on either cheek. Later she would thank the designer. "Basilio? No one could have been easier to work with. Thank you for your patience."

"It was a pleasure, my dear. The whole staff, Giovanni especially, sing your praises."

"Thank you."

Lucca was right behind her to embrace his father and stepmother. Then he stunned her when she heard him say, "Would you two mind making sure our bags go back on the plane with you? I've got plans for my bride and me."

Before she knew what was happening, he'd ushered her back to the car and helped her in the passenger side. "Enzo?" he called from behind the wheel to one of the staff. "Would you be good enough to open the bay door for us? I've a need to show off my unique driving skills to my gorgeous wife."

Everyone laughed before he backed them out of the showroom onto the outside lot. He shot Annabelle a mysterious smile before revving the smooth quiet engine. Suddenly they wound around to the main arterial and were whizzing through the streets of Milan.

Annabelle's heart steamed into her chest. Her gaze

fixed on Lucca, who drove with an expertise befitting a fighter pilot. "Where are we going?"

"Home."

"You mean all the way to Ravello? In this car?"

His smile melted her bones. "That's what it's for."

"I know, but we didn't bring anything with us. I'm still dressed like the Amalfi Girl!" Her silvery-gold hair radiated out in the warm August night air.

"Since she'll never be seen in public after tonight, I like the idea of driving around with every man's fantasy. Don't look now but you've already stopped traffic."

She blushed. "Lucca…"

"It's true. The guy in the other lane was staring at you so hard, he just rammed into the back of a truck."

"You made that up."

"If you don't believe me, turn around." His hand reached out and clasped her thigh. He liked to do that a lot. Every time he did it, the contact made her gasp in pleasure.

"I think you'd better keep both hands on the wheel, darling."

"Don't ruin things now and tell me you're going to be a backseat driver."

Her eyes filled as she looked at him. "I'm so happy, I'm in pain."

"So am I, but it's the best kind."

"*Lucca*—"

"There's a charming palazzo not far from the city. We'll stop there for the night where I plan to ravish you and hopefully get you pregnant."

Her heart thudded. "Promise?"

A half hour later they pulled into the grounds and

parked the car in a private garage that led to their own luxurious apartment. She hurried inside, sick with excitement. They'd been married several weeks, but every day with him was like the first day. Making love with him had become necessary to her existence.

After he closed the door, he pulled her back against him and slowly removed her earrings and choker, kissing every spot his lips could find. She moaned deliriously as he undid the back of her dress and turned in his arms, sensing his urgency. He crushed her against him until their bodies pulsated as one entity.

Annabelle didn't remember being carried to the bed. They no longer had to worry about his leg. This was her husband loving her with the kind of hunger she couldn't have imagined before meeting him.

"I love you," he cried. "I can't get enough of you, *bellissima*."

"Now you know how I feel." Her heart surged as their mouths and bodies began giving and taking, whipping up their passion until they spiraled out of control. He brought her joy beyond comprehension.

Later, when they were sated for the time being, Lucca reached for the remote and turned on the television. "The ten o'clock news will be on in five minutes. I want you to see what you look like from the audience's viewpoint."

She rested her head against his shoulder. "You'll have to translate most of what the TV announcer says." She'd been working on her Italian, but it was going to take a lot longer to master his beautiful language. When the film segment came on, Annabelle couldn't relate to the woman in the black sports car.

"It was terrifying to be live on camera. I was praying I wouldn't make a mistake, or fall on my face."

He pulled her closer. "You were sensational. My father looks good there, too."

"You both have intrinsic class. Not every man is so blessed. It's a quality you have to be born with. My mom remarked on it the day of the wedding." She hugged him tighter. "Didn't you love our wedding?"

"Yes," he whispered. "The only thing missing was my mother. She would have loved you."

Annabelle kissed the tears that moistened his eyelashes. "I'd like to think she was there to help your father give you away to me for safekeeping. I made vows then, and I'll say them again now. I, Annabelle Marsh Cavezzali, promise to take care of you and love you all of our life and beyond, my dearest, darling husband, Lucca Cavezzali."

* * * * *

A DEVILISHLY
DARK DEAL

MAGGIE COX

Maggie Cox is passionate about stories that can uplift and transport people out of their daily worries to a more magical place, be they romance novels or fairytales. What people want most, she believes, is true connection. She feels blessed to be married to a lovely man who never fails to make her laugh, and has two beautiful sons and two much loved grandchildren.

CHAPTER ONE

Tipping up the brim of her wide straw hat, Grace Faulkner settled back in her deckchair, glanced through her over-large sunglasses at the glinting aquamarine ocean and sighed. She should be making the most of the tranquil scene and just relaxing, but it wasn't easy when her insides were deluged with querulous butterflies.

She was so besieged because very shortly she planned to confront one of this elite area's most revered and wealthy entrepreneurs and petition him to become a patron of the children's charity in Africa that was dearest to her heart. And not just to become a patron—but also to make a much needed generous donation so that essential building could commence on a new orphanage. The present one was all but being held up by hope and prayer alone.

What had fuelled her aim was hearing the owner of the café she'd been sitting in the day she'd heard the buzz that Marco Aguilar was visiting the area telling an American tourist that he'd known him as a young boy—that he'd grown up in a local orphanage and hadn't he done incredibly well for himself when you considered his start in life?

That overheard snippet had seemed more and more like divine providence to Grace as she'd mulled it over, and she didn't intend to let it go to waste. She knew she would probably only get the smallest window of opportunity to catch the businessman's eye before she'd be hauled off the premises by one of his security guards, and she should be prepared for that. But when it might mean the difference between helping to improve the lives of the children who had moved her so unbearably and returning to Africa with the news that she'd failed to secure them the funds they were so desperately in need of, a security guard trying to eject her seemed a small price to pay. Having recently seen for herself the squalor in which those orphans lived daily—a squalor that only the chance of a good education and caring patrons could help them out of—Grace had vowed to her charity worker friends before she left that she would do everything she could to help make that chance a reality. *But first they had to rebuild the children's home.*

The drowning noise of a helicopter coming in to land alerted her. *It had to be him.* Because she'd been so troubled and exhausted after her return from Africa, her parents had persuaded her to stay at their holiday home in the Algarve to take a much-needed break. For once she hadn't resisted their steering of her movements, and she was glad she had not—because on only her second day there she had heard the local buzz that Marco Aguilar was due to make a visit to one of his myriad exclusive hotels for a meeting. That particular hotel was situated in the resort complex right across the road from where she was staying, and if the rumours were at all to be relied upon *today* was the day. The arrival of the helicopter— the first she'd heard in three days at the resort—surely confirmed it?

With her heart pounding, she got up from the canvas chair positioned on the baking hot patio and quickly returned inside to the villa's pleasantly cool interior. Flying into the kitchen to grab a bottle of water from the refrigerator, she dropped it into her straw bag, repositioned her sunglasses on her nose, then pulled off her hat and threw it onto a nearby chair. Checking that she had her keys, she hurriedly left the building…

The helicopter had landed on a discreet pad somewhere amid the lush pine trees, and now there was a bank of sleek cars—mostly black—parked in front of the hotel. The impressive modern façade was edged by a pristine emerald lawn, and already there was a bevy of reporters and photographers running across it—a few that were ahead were moving swiftly through the revolving glass doors into the lobby. By the time the *mêlée* had disappeared into the hotel, and just as Grace was stealing a few apprehensive moments to decide what to do next, a gleaming black jaguar drew up at the front of the lawn. A burly cropped-haired bodyguard exited the car first then smartly stood holding the door wide as the man who was clearly his boss climbed out of the vehicle.

Due to his phenomenal success in business, and the purported enigmatic nature that was so indisputably appealing to admirers everywhere, photographs of Marco Aguilar were a regular feature in newspapers and magazines round the world, including the UK. There was no doubt that it was him.

Grace's first impression of the businessman that had made his fortune in the field of sports and leisure—in particular exclusive golfing resorts like this one—was that his physical presence was as commanding as his much-admired reputation. The impeccably stylish linen suit he wore was a perfect foil for his hard-muscled physique, and the moneyed air that radiated from the top of his shining black hair down to the tan-coloured Italian loafers he wore on his feet definitely suggested that the man had an unerring eye for the very best of everything. As he leaned over to speak to his bodyguard she saw even his eyes had the luxurious sheen of the finest dark chocolate. The sweltering Mediterranean sun was all but baking everything in sight, but in contrast he appeared ice-cool.

Narrowing her gaze to view him more clearly, she saw with trepidation that his hard jaw was undeniably clenched and the set of his well-cut lips formidably serious...perhaps even angry? Panicking slightly because if he was already ticked off about something then it was highly unlikely that he would even acknowledge her, she thought dismayed. Worse still, if he thought she was making a nuisance of herself he might call the police to arrest her.

Swallowing down her nerves, she tucked the leather strap of her straw bag neatly down by her side, then endeavoured to stroll casually towards the hotel entrance just as if she was a guest there—for surely this must be the window of opportunity she'd prayed for? It occurred to Grace that the reporters had made the mistake of assuming the VIP they so eagerly sought was already inside the hotel—perhaps smuggled in through a side entrance somewhere? Wishing that her heart wasn't beating so fast that she could scarcely hear herself think above the throbbing sound of it in her ears, she endeavoured to slow and deepen her breath to calm herself. *She had to do this.* The businessman's reputation and aura might be intimidating, but she couldn't let that stop her. Come what may, there was no backing out now.

'Mr Aguilar!' When she was about five feet away from him on the baking walkway she called out his name. The bodyguard immediately moved his intimidating bulk

Grace's way, to prevent her from getting any nearer. 'Mr Aguilar…please can I have just a moment of your time before you go inside to your meeting? I promise I won't keep you very long.'

'Mr Aguilar does not talk to anyone from the press unless it is prearranged.'

The bodyguard's heavily accented voice was a growl as he reached out to physically waylay her. She flinched as the man's huge hands encircled her bare arms in her sleeveless cotton dress, and at the same time saw a bead of sweat roll down his ample cheek.

His manhandling of her lit a furious spark of indignation inside her. 'Let me go! How dare you grab me like that? For your information, I'm not a reporter.'

'You have no business trying to talk to Mr Aguilar.'

'For goodness' sake—do I *look* like I pose any kind of threat to your boss?' Grace couldn't bite back her frustration. To get so close to the man she desperately needed to talk to and then be denied access to speak to him at the very last moment was *beyond* frustrating.

'Let her go, José.'

The man behind them snapped out a clear-voiced command and her heart hammered even harder beneath her ribs. The bodyguard immediately released his hold and she stepped to the side of him, at last coming face to face with her hard-jawed quarry.

'If you do not belong to that mercenary rabble from the press, who are primed to try and get me to answer questions about my private life and then embellish them for their undiscerning readership, what exactly *do* you want from me, Miss…?'

Indisputably his accent was Portuguese, but his English was close to perfect. The intensity of Marco Aguilar's examining gaze threw her for a second. The rich caramel eyes with their fathomless depths seemed to bewitch her. 'Faulkner...' she answered, her voice not quite as steady as she would have liked. 'Grace Faulkner. And, just to reassure you, I'm not remotely interested in your private life, Mr Aguilar.'

'How refreshing' His remark was like a sardonic whip-lash. He folded his arms.

Grace made herself press on regardless. 'I'm here be-cause I'd like to tell you about an orphanage in Africa that badly needs help...specifically *financial* help...to rebuild the falling-down shack that houses it and to provide a school and a teacher. I've recently come back from there, and it's quite unbelievable how these poor children are living—not even living... just existing. There's an open sewer right outside where they're sleeping, and several of them have already died from drinking contaminated water. This is the twenty-first century for goodness' sake! We're so rich in the west... Why are we allowing this to go on without doing something more about it—without every one of us feeling outraged on a daily basis?'

'I admire the passion and dedication you exhibit in the name of your cause, Miss Faulkner, but I already give fi-nancial aid to several charities worldwide. Do you think it fair to corner me like this when I'm about to go into what is to me a very important meeting?'

Grace blinked. The rumour ran that he was there to oversee the takeover bid of a less prosperous resort. It was what he was known for excelling at...buying ailing resorts and making them thrive, thereby reaping the ben-efits. If the newspapers and magazines were to be be-lieved, the benefits aided his playboy lifestyle. *But how much more money and power did the man need before he decided enough was enough?*

Her indignation and temper got the better of her.

Pushing her fingers through the fall of blonde hair that glanced against her perspiring brow, she levelled her gaze with the billionaire's and didn't flinch even once. *'Fair?'* she echoed angrily. 'Do you think it's *fair* that these children are dying for want of even the most basic sanitation—and more importantly for want of love and care from the rest of humanity? Surely your "very important meeting" can't possibly be more important than that?'

In less than a heartbeat Marco Aguilar had positioned himself in front of her. The brief contraction in the side of his smooth cheekbone warned her that she'd struck a nerve. At the same time the sweltering heat that beat down on them from the dazzling sun up above seemed to magnify the hypnotic effect of his spicy cologne. Feeling a little bit more than slightly giddy beneath the twin onslaught of burning sun and aggrieved male, Grace wondered where she'd found the audacity—some might say *stupidity*—to imagine for even a moment that this was the way to get someone as wealthy and influential as him on her side. Clearly it *wasn't*.

'Let me give you a word of advice, Miss Faulkner... Please don't ever seek a career in a field that requires great diplomacy. I fear you would not get past the first round of interviews. You are very fortunate that I do not get my bodyguard to physically eject you from the complex. Forgive me...' the dark eyes swept mockingly down over her figure and up again to her face '...my guess is that you are *not* a guest here, are you? In which case you are already on dangerous ground, accosting me like this. Now, if you'll excuse me, I have a meeting to go to. My fellow attendees may not be as needy as your orphans, but I assure you they will be baying for my blood if I do not put in an appearance soon.'

'Look, I'm very sorry if I was rude to you, Mr

Aguilar… Honestly, I meant no offence.' Grace clamped even white teeth down on her lip for a second, in a bid to keep her passionate emotions under control, but it still didn't stop her from bursting out, 'All the same, you shouldn't sneer at my clothes and make me feel small in order to make yourself feel superior, should you? Besides, I'm not here to try to impress you. I'm here for one reason and one reason only: the orphaned children that I told you about. Yes, I *am* passionate about this cause, but I defy anyone *not* to be if they'd experienced what I experienced over the past few weeks. I really hoped you might help us…especially when I heard that you'd been raised in an orphanage yourself.'

The businessman stood stock-still and the bronze pigment in his skin seemed to bleed out and turn pale. 'Where did you hear that?' he asked, low voiced.

Her mouth dried. 'I heard it…just the other day.' Feeling almost faint with unease, and not wanting to incriminate the café-owner, she made herself lift her chin and not flinch from the steely-eyed glare in front of her, 'Is it true? *Are* you an orphan, Mr Aguilar?'

He exhaled a long sigh, as though to steady himself, then bemusedly shook his head. 'You say you are not a reporter, Miss Faulkner, but you attack your prey just like one. You must want what you want very badly to be so impertinent.'

'I do,' she admitted turning red. 'But only for the children…not for any gain for myself, I swear. And I didn't mean to be impertinent.'

Just when Grace thought she'd absolutely blown any chance of getting his help, and had started to regret being so bold, astoundingly, the businessman appeared to reconsider.

'Now is clearly not a convenient time for me to discuss

this matter further, Miss Faulkner, but you have sufficiently got my attention to make me consider a meeting with you at a later date.' Reaching into his inside jacket pocket, which she glimpsed was lined with light coffee-coloured silk, he withdrew a small black and gold card, extricated a pen as well, and scribbled something down on the blank space on the back of it. 'Give me a ring tomorrow at around midday and we will talk some more. But I warn you… If you tell anyone that we even had this conversation—and I mean *anyone*—then you can forget that you ever saw me, let alone hope to receive my assistance for your cause. By the way, what is the name of this charity that you so passionately support?'

Grace told him.

'Well… I will speak to you again soon, Miss Faulkner. Like I said, I will expect your call around midday tomorrow.'

Marco Aguilar turned and walked away, his faithful bodyguard hurrying after him and mopping his brow with his handkerchief as he endeavoured to keep up with his boss's long-legged stride. Gripping the card he'd given her as if it was the key to unlocking the secrets of the universe, Grace let her captive gaze ensure she followed the pair until they went through the hotel's entrance and disappeared inside…

Grateful for the almost too efficient air-conditioning in the luxuriously appointed boardroom, after the unforgiving midday heat outside, Marco restlessly flipped his gold pen several times between his fingers as he tried to focus on his company's earnest director, seated at the far end of the long mahogany table.

The loyal Joseph Simonson was being as meticulous and articulate as usual with his information about the takeover bid—the man's presentation couldn't be faulted—yet Marco found it difficult to pay proper attention to his opening speech because he couldn't get the memory of a pair of flashing brilliant blue eyes and a face that was as close to his imagined depiction of the mythical Aphrodite out of his mind.

Grace Faulkner.

But it wasn't just her beauty that had disturbed him. Marco wondered how she had learned that he had grown up in an orphanage when it wasn't something that he had ever willingly broadcast. A further conversation with her was imperative if he was to impress upon her the folly of repeating that information to the media—even though he knew there were local people who had always known it to be true. Perhaps he had been uncharacteristically foolish in hoping for their loyalty and believing they wouldn't talk about his past with outsiders? He'd already been through a torrid time with the press… The last thing he needed was some new revelation to hit the headlines. And this one would perhaps be the most difficult for him to face out of all of them.

His thoughts returned to the image of Grace Faulkner that seemed to be imprinted on his mind. She'd declared that she wasn't trying to impress him, but inexplicably she *had*. He'd already telephoned his secretary Martine and asked her to undertake some research on the woman and the charity she supported before he took her phone call tomorrow. *Unfortunately, it wouldn't be the first time that a female had behaved dishonourably to win herself the chance of getting close to him…accepted a fee from a newspaper for passing on some invented salacious anecdote about his life for them to print.*

Marco found himself wishing that the girl *was* unquestionably who she said she was, and that the only reason she had waylaid him *was* because she wanted his aid for the cause that was apparently so close to her heart. When he'd stood in front of her, so close that gazing into her eyes had been like being dazzled by a sunlit blue lake, she hadn't flinched or glanced guiltily away. No, she'd stared right back at him as if she had absolutely nothing to hide…as if she was telling him nothing but the truth. *What would she think if she knew how seductive and appealing that was?* He had dated and bedded some very beautiful women over the years, but their mostly self-seeking natures had *not* been beautiful.

Take his ex-girlfriend Jasmine, for example. The fashion model had made the mistake of trying to sue him for breach of his alleged promise to support her when the famous fashion house she'd modelled for hadn't renewed her contract because she'd preferred to party and get high rather than turn up for work. Marco had made no such promise to her…in fact he had already told her that he was ending their relationship *before* her illustrious employers had dropped her. The woman had been a liability, but thanks to his lawyers the case had been more or less thrown out of court for a laughable lack of evidence. Shortly after that sorry episode she had sold her lurid little tale to a tabloid for some ludicrous sum, inventing stories of 'ill treatment' and making him look like some despicable misogynist.

That whole sorry debacle had happened over six months ago now, and ever since then Marco had become even more wary and cynical of women's motives for seeing him. Despite his understandable caution, the fact that Grace Faulkner seemed far more interested in helping others instead of herself definitely made him want to find out more about the angelic-faced beauty, with a soft heart for needy children and the daring to just walk right up to him and present her case as if she had every right in the world to do just that...

'Marco?'

Joseph was looking decidedly ill at ease, because his boss hadn't replied to a question he'd asked, and Marco had the vague notion that he'd already addressed him twice. The rest of the board members shifted their gazes uncomfortably. Clearly they weren't accustomed to their illustrious leader being so distracted.

Folding his arms across the hand-tailored jacket of his cream linen suit, he allowed an apologetic smile to hijack his usually austere lips. 'Could you go over that again for me, Joseph? I think I must be a little jet-lagged after flying in from Sydney late last night and I didn't quite take it all in.' He shrugged.

'Of course.' At this amenable explanation, the British director's shoulders visibly relaxed. 'I'm sure that all of us here will endeavour to keep the meeting as short as possible in light of the fact that you must be understandably tired after your travels.'

With a little dip of his head Marco indicated his thanks, making sure to include every one of the well-dressed ensemble in his amicable gaze.

'By the way,' the other man added, his smile a little awkward, as if he were much happier dealing with matters appertaining to the business rather than making polite conversation with his boss, 'how does it feel to be back home? It must be at least a couple of years since you were here for any length of time?'

'That's right...it is.' His usual guard slammed down into place and Marco deliberately ignored the first part of the question. *Home was a concept that even his immense wealth had never been able to make a reality for him.* When a man had grown up an orphan, as he had, 'home' was just a tantalising dream that was always mockingly out of reach…a fantasy that just wasn't on the agenda, no matter how much his heart might ache for it to be possible…

A palatial house or mansion didn't equal a home in the true sense of the word, although he had several of those round the globe. Lately he'd been working particularly hard, and his plan had been to stay in the Algarve for a few weeks at least, to kick back and take a long overdue rest, but the instant he had recalled his humble beginnings growing up Portugal, the idea suddenly lost most of its appeal. The prospect of spending time alone didn't sit well with him either. Marco had plenty of acquaintances, but no real friends he could truly be himself around… *Even as a child he had never made friends easily.* One of the carers at the orphanage had once told him he was a 'complicated' little boy. With his child's logic, he had judged that to mean that he was difficult to love…

Once more he flipped his pen, hating the sudden prickling of anxiety at the back of his neck and inside his chest—a sign that he was feeling hemmed in, almost *trapped.* Because for him there was neither solace nor reassurance in revisiting scenes from his past.

'Let's continue, shall we? I'm sure we are all very busy people with much to accomplish before the day is out, and time is not standing still,' he announced abruptly.

Grimacing in embarrassment at his boss's terse-voiced remarks, Joseph Simonson shuffled the sheaf of papers in front of him and cleared his throat before proceeding…

Grace's insides were churning. It was a minute or two away from midday, and three times now she had snatched her shaking hand away from the telephone. Right then the fact that she might be just a conversation away from get-

ting the financial assistance the charity needed to rebuild
the children's home, set up a school and employ a teacher,
didn't seem to help overcome her nerves. Yesterday she'd
been fired up…*brave*…as if neither man nor mountain
could stop her from fulfilling her aim of getting what
she wanted. Today, after a more or less sleepless night
when memories of Marco Aguilar's piercing dark eyes
had frequently disturbed her, she didn't feel capable of
much…let alone feel brave.

'Oh, for goodness' sake!'

Exasperated, she grabbed the receiver from its rest
on the kitchen wall and punched out the number she had
determinedly memorized, in case by some cruel twist of
fate she lost the card.

On arriving back at the villa yesterday afternoon,
Grace had been seriously taken aback when she'd realised the number Marco had given her belonged to his
personal mobile. It wasn't the same as any of the numbers printed in gold on the front of his business card.
Now, briefly shutting her eyes, she recalled the shining
hopeful faces of the children she had left behind in that
feebly constructed orphanage back in Africa and felt a
resurgence of passion for helping make things right for
them. *Marco Aguilar was only a man.* He was made of
flesh and blood and bone, just as she was, she told herself. It didn't matter that he wore hand-tailored suits that
probably cost the earth, or that he might regularly make
it onto the world's rich lists. *That didn't make him any
better than Grace.* In this instance they were just two
humane people, discussing what needed to be done to
help those less fortunate than they were, and she would
hold onto that thought when they spoke.

The softly purring ringtone in her ear ceased, indicating someone had picked up at the other end.

'*Olá?*'

'*Olá.*'

'Mr Aguilar?'

'Ah…is that you, Grace?'

She hadn't expected him to address her by her first name, and the sound of it spoken in his highly arresting, accented voice made her insides execute a disorientating cartwheel. Staring out of the opened windows at the sun-baked patio, and the usually inviting deckchair that she'd had to vacate when the heat grew too intense to bear comfortably, Grace nervously smoothed her palm down over the hip of her white linen trousers.

'Yes, it's me. I presume I'm talking to Marco Aguilar?'

'Just Marco is fine.'

'I wouldn't presume to—'

'I am inviting you to address me by my first name, Grace, so you are not being presumptuous. How are you today? I trust you are enjoying this glorious weather?'

'I'm…I'm fine, and, yes I am enjoying the weather.' Threading her fingers through her wheat-coloured hair, Grace grimaced, taken aback that he should address her so amicably and not quite sure about how to proceed. 'How are you?' she asked cautiously.

'I wasn't planning on making this conversation *that* long,' he commented wryly.

Colouring hotly, she was glad that he couldn't see her face right then…just in case he imagined that she was one of those starstruck women who didn't have the wits to separate fantasy from reality…

'Well, I know you must be a very busy man, so you needn't worry that I'll talk your ears off.' She made a face, thinking that she sounded like some immature schoolgirl with that infantile remark. 'I promise,' she added quickly, as if to emphasise the point.

'Talk my ears off?' Marco echoed, chuckling, 'I hope you won't, Grace, because they are extremely useful at times…especially when I'm listening to Mozart or Beethoven.'

'I shouldn't have said that. It was a stupid comment.'

'Why? Because you think I might lack a sense of humour? I hope I may have the chance to prove you wrong about that.'

Taken aback once more by such a surprising remark, Grace hardly knew what to say.

'It may surprise you,' the man on the other end of the line continued, 'but I have unexpectedly found myself with an entirely free afternoon today. Instead of us talking on the phone, I could send my driver round to where you are staying and get him to bring you back to my house. That would be a much more agreeable way of conducting our conversation don't you think?'

She must be dreaming. Confronting him outside the exclusive resort was one thing, and talking to him on the phone was another…but never in her wildest dreams had she envisaged a man like Marco Aguilar inviting her to his house to discuss the charity she was so determined to help—just like that. If she didn't know better she'd think she was suffering from heatstroke!

'If you—if you really do have the time then, yes… I'm sure that would be a much better way to discuss the charity.'

'So you agree to allow my driver to pick you up and bring you back here?'

'I do. Thank you, Mr Aguilar.'

'Didn't I already tell you to call me Marco?' he answered, with a smile in his voice.

All Grace knew right then was that her parents would have a fit if they knew she was even considering going to a strange man's house in a foreign country in the middle of the day—even if that stranger *was* an internationally known entrepreneur. But then they were always so over-protective. She'd literally had to *steal* her freedom to leave home. Even when she'd made the decision to go to Africa to visit the children's charity she worked for in London she'd had to stand her ground with them...

'You can't keep me wrapped up in cotton-wool for ever, you know,' she'd argued. 'I'm twenty-five years old and I want to see some of the world for myself. I want to take risks and learn by my mistakes.'

'Grace?'

Frowning, and with her heart beating a rapid tattoo inside her chest, she realised that Marco Aguilar was waiting for her reply. 'I'm still here... I suppose I ought to give you my address if you're sending a car for me?'

'That would definitely be a good start,' he agreed.

CHAPTER TWO

THEY called them *casas antigas* in Portugal…manor-houses and stately homes. Grace's eyes widened more and more the further Marco's chauffeur Miguel drove them up the long sweeping drive that had met them the moment he'd pressed the remote device in the car to open the ornate electronic gates at the entrance. As they drove past the colonnade of tall trees lining the way she caught sight of the palatial colonial-style house they were heading towards, with its marble pillars glistening in the afternoon sunshine. She stared in near disbelief, murmuring, 'My God…' beneath her breath.

Inevitably she thought of the ramshackle building that housed the orphanage back in Africa, and was struck dumb by the heartbreaking comparison to the dazzling vision of nineteenth-century architecture she was gazing at now. Did Marco Aguilar live here all by himself? she wondered. Just the thought seemed preposterous.

The smiling chauffeur in his smartly pressed black trousers and pristine white shirt opened the Jaguar door at her side to let her out, and as Grace stepped down onto the gravel drive the scent of heady bougainvillaea mingled with the heat of the day to saturate her senses. Lifting her sunglasses up onto her head, she glanced back at the house and with a jolt of surprise saw Marco, standing on one of the wide curving upper steps, waiting. *'Olá!'* He raised a hand, acknowledging her with a brief wave.

He wore khaki-coloured chinos and a white T-shirt that highlighted his athletic, muscular torso, and his stance was much more at ease than when she'd seen him yesterday. Her trepidation at speaking with him again eased slightly...but only *slightly.*

When she reached the level just below where he stood, he held out his hand to warmly enfold her palm in his. He smiled. 'We meet again.'

His touch submerged Grace in a shockwave of heated sensation that rendered her unable to reply immediately.

This is terrible, she thought, panicking. *How am I supposed to sound at all competent and professional and say what I want to say if I'm completely thrown off-balance by a simple handshake?*

'Thanks for sending the car for me,' she managed. 'This is such a beautiful house.' Quickly retrieving her hand, she tried hard to make her smile relaxed to disguise her unexpectedly strong reaction to his touch.

'I agree. It is. Why don't you come inside and see it properly?' he invited.

If Grace had felt overwhelmed at the imposing façade of Marco's house, then she was rendered almost speechless by the opulence and beauty of the interior. A sea of marble floor and high intricate ceilings greeted her over and over again as her host led her through various reception rooms to what appeared to be a much less ostentatious and intimate drawing room. Elegant couches and armchairs encircled a large hand-knotted Persian rug in various exquisite shades of red, ochre and gold, whilst open French doors revealed a wide balcony overlooking landscaped gardens stretching right down to the sea.

This time it was the bewitching fragrance of honeysuckle drifting into the room that fell like soft summer rain onto Grace's already captivated senses. She was utterly enchanted.

'Do you want to sit outside on the balcony? I trust you are wearing suncream on that delicate pale skin of yours?'

'I'm well protected—and, yes…I would very much like to sit outside.'

Settling herself beneath a generously sized green and gold parasol in a comfortable rattan chair, Grace glanced out over the lush landscaped gardens in front of her and sighed. 'What an amazing view…your own private paradise on earth. I hope you regularly get to share it with your friends. It would be a crime not to. I bet you must really love living here?'

As he dropped down into a chair opposite her at the mosaic tiled table a myriad of differing emotions seemed to register on her host's handsome face and she didn't see *one* that reflected pleasure.

'Unfortunately I probably don't appreciate it as much as I should, seeing as I am not here very often,' he said.

'But you do originally come from here don't you…? From the Algarve I mean?' The impetuous question was out before she could check it, and straight away she saw that Marco was irked by it.

'Now you are sounding like one of those too-inquisitive reporters again. By the way…where did you hear that I'd grown up in an orphanage?'

Swallowing hard, Grace sensed hot colour suffuse her. 'I didn't hear it directly… I mean…the person who said it wasn't talking to me. I just happened to overhear a conversation he was having with someone else in a café I was sitting in.'

'So it was a local man?'

'Yes. He sounded very admiring about what you'd achieved…he wasn't being disrespectful in any way.'

'And when you heard that I was due to visit the Algarve, and that I was an orphan, you thought you would take the opportunity to petition my help for your orphans in Africa?'

'Yes…I'm sure you'd have done the same in my position.'

'Are you?'

Folding his arms, Marco looked to be pondering the assumption—not without a hint of sardonic humour, Grace noted.

'Perhaps I would and perhaps I wouldn't. Anyway, I think we should talk a little more in depth about what you came here for…get down to the details, hmm?'

'Of course.' Relieved that her admission about hearing a chance remark hadn't prejudiced him against talking to her some more, she lifted her gaze and forced herself to look straight back into the compelling hooded dark eyes. 'But I just want you to know that this isn't the sort of thing I do every day…spontaneously railroading someone like you into giving their help, I mean. When I'm working at the charity's office in London I have to be completely professional and adhere to strict rules. We either do a blanket mailshot of people likely to make donations, or once in a while I might get the chance to ring somebody who's known for being charitable and talk to them personally.'

'If you're being honest, then that makes a very welcome change.'

Marco considered her so intently for a moment that Grace all but forgot to breathe.

'Honesty I can deal with. Subterfuge is apt to make me angry.'

'I'm not a liar, Mr Aguilar, and neither am I trying to fool you in any way.'

'I believe you, Grace. I believe you are exactly who you say you are, and also the reason why you accosted me yesterday. Did you not think that I would check? So… That aside, tell me some more about this cause that makes you risk being apprehended to get to me—I would very much like to hear how you got involved in the first place. Why don't you start by telling me about that?'

She shouldn't have been surprised that he'd checked up on her, but all the same she *was*.

Immensely relieved that she had nothing to hide, Grace told him about finishing her studies at university and still being unsure about what career she wanted to take up. Then she told him about a conversation she'd had with a friend of her parents whose son had been giving up his post at a children's charity in London to travel a bit and see the world. That family friend had suggested she apply for the post. As luck had had it, she'd done well at the interview and got the job. Grace had been there for a couple of years when the opportunity had arisen for her to go out to Africa and visit one of the many orphanages the charity was endeavouring to assist. She had visited several times since, but that first visit had changed her life, she told Marco, feeling a renewed rush of the zeal that gripped her to personally try and do something about the heartrending plight of the children she'd witnessed.

As she finished speaking, with hope travelling to the highest peaks one minute as she believed she might elicit Marco's help, then plummeting down the slopes of anxiety the next in fear that he might refuse her, Grace heard nothing but the sound of her own quickened breath as she waited for his response.

The sun's burning heat seemed to intensify just then—even beneath the wide umbrella that provided shade for them. A slippery trickle of sweat ran down between her breasts inside the silky white camisole she wore, and unthinkingly she touched her fingertips to the spot to wipe it away. When she glanced up again she saw an expression in Marco's eyes that was so akin to naked desire that she froze, her heartbeat slowing to a deep, heavy thud inside her chest and a carnal longing so acute invading her that the power of it made her feel quite faint...

Her soft voice had died away to silence, but more than a little transfixed Marco found himself helplessly staring at the sight of Grace's slender fingers moving to the neckline of her camisole. Diverted from her explanation about how she'd become involved with the charity, he'd already tracked the little bead of sweat that had slithered down from the base of her throat, and when he saw her dip her fingers inside the plain white silk underneath the small embroidered buttons to deal with it he was gripped by an all-consuming lust so blazing that it turned him instantly hard. His desire was fuelled even further by his conviction that her action had been totally innocent and unconscious.

Grace Faulkner was already making his heart race faster than it had done with any other woman whose company he'd shared in a long, long time, and he realised that he wasn't in a hurry for her to leave him any time soon.

'Would you like something to drink?' he asked, getting abruptly to his feet. At his guest's hesitant nod, he started to move back towards the open French doors. 'What will it be? A glass of wine? Lemonade or some fruit juice, perhaps?'

'A glass of lemonade would be perfect…thank you.'

'I will go and find my housekeeper.'

When he returned from the kitchen, where he'd arranged for their drinks to be brought out to them by Inês—a local woman he had hired as housekeeper and cook—Marco returned to the balcony, feeling a little more in control of the fierce attraction his pretty guest had unwittingly provoked. Yet his pulse still raced at the sight of her sitting quietly beneath the parasol. With her pale blonde hair lying softly against her shoulders, even her profile was angelic. He privately confessed he would do almost *anything* to get her to stay with him for the rest of the afternoon.

Her smile was shy and a little reticent as he sat down again. He had the sense that when she wasn't championing a cause she was the quiet, reflective sort. *He liked that*. It would be a refreshing change from the women he usually dated…all spiky demands and too-high expectations of where a relationship with him might lead.

'Our drinks will be along shortly,' he told her.

'Mr Aguilar…' she began.

He raised an eyebrow. 'Marco,' he corrected gently.

Her incandescent summer-blue gaze slid away for a moment. He saw her take down a deeper breath, as if to centre herself.

'I was wondering if you'd made a decision about whether you might be able to help the children or not?'

He took a few moments to marshal his thoughts. He hadn't embellished the truth when he'd told Grace at their first meeting that there were many charities he supported, and there were quite a few children's charities amongst them. Yet none of them was directly helping orphaned children. The subject was apt to bring back memories of a childhood that he had striven hard not just to forget but to *hide* from the world at large. Perhaps he had subconsciously aimed to dissociate himself from that quarter entirely in case it brought forth more intrusive and uncomfortable questions from the media about his past?

'I have no doubt that your children's cause is one that a wealthy man like me ought to readily support, Grace, and while I am definitely not averse to making a donation, having listened and talked to you, I would like a bit more time to reflect on what level of help I can give. If you leave the details with me I will look over them at my leisure and get back to you. Is that all right with you?'

'Of course…and it's fantastic that you've decided to help us. It's just that…'

She leaned forward and he saw conflict in her eyes—maybe at trying to press him to take action sooner rather than later, which warred with her innate impulse to be polite. Even so, he wasn't above using whatever weapon he could from his personal armoury to get what *he* wanted. His success in business hadn't come about without a propensity to be single-mindedly ruthless from time to time. Pretty little Grace wanted something from him, and likewise he wanted something from *her*, he realised. He didn't doubt there had to be a way of gratifying *both* needs.

'It's just that I don't want to take up any more of your time than necessary,' she said in a rush. 'I know you must be an extremely busy man.'

'Are you in a hurry to leave?'

'Not at all, but…'

'Yes?'

'I really don't want to offend you, or perhaps bring back hurtful memories of your past, but I just want to paint a picture for you if I may? Can you imagine what it must be like not only to have to contend with being be an orphan, with no mother or father to love you and take care of you, but also to live in a dirty shack without even the most basic amenities that most of us take for granted? I don't mean to be pushy, I really don't, but the sooner we can alleviate their dreadful living conditions and put up a new more sanitary building, the better. For that we desperately need financial help. So when you say you'll look over the details at your leisure…do you have any idea how long that might take?'

Inside his chest, Marco's heart was thundering. No, he didn't have to imagine what it was like to grow up without a mother or father to take care of him…not when he'd personally experienced it, growing up in a children's home where there had been about five or six children to every carer. The sense of emotional deprivation it had left him with would be with him for ever, and no amount of money, career success or comfortable living would alleviate his underlying feelings of being isolated from the rest of the world and certainly not as deserving of love as other people.

But at least the building he had lived in had been safe and hygienic. He abhorred the idea of innocent children having to contend with the dreadful conditions Grace had emphatically outlined to him, so he *would* be writing her a cheque so that they could have their new building. But he wouldn't be hurried.

'Whilst I am a compassionate man, Grace, I am first and foremost a businessman, who is meticulous about looking over the details of every transaction I make. I'm afraid you are going to have to be a little more patient if you want my help.'

'It's hard to be patient when you personally know the children who are suffering,' she murmured, her cheeks turning a delicate rose. 'You've checked out that I am who I say I am, and that the charity I represent is absolutely legitimate, so why delay? I can assure you every penny of the money you give us will be accounted for, and you'll get a receipt for everything.'

'I am pleased to hear it, but if you knew how many worthy charities petition me for financial aid you would perhaps understand why I must take the appropriate time to discern who receives it and when.' He paused to bestow upon her a more concentrated glance. 'You're studying me as if you cannot understand my caution in writing you a cheque straight away? Maybe you think that because I clearly have the money I shouldn't hesitate to give it to your charity? Perhaps you believe that I should feel guilty about having so much? If that is so, then you should know that I worked hard from a very young age to have the success I have now. One thing is for sure… I did not grow up with a silver spoon in my mouth, and neither was good fortune handed to me on a plate.'

The woman sitting opposite him at the table bit down heavily on her plump lower lip and her glance suddenly became fixated on the mosaic-tiled tabletop. When she next looked up her lovely blue eyes were glistening, Marco saw.

'I'm so sorry. I had no right to rant at you about the situation. I get too passionate, that's the trouble. You've been nothing but hospitable and gracious, giving up your time to talk to me like this, offering your help, and now I've been unforgivably rude and presumptuous.'

'I don't believe for one moment that you meant to be discourteous. However, I am beginning to realise that underneath that angelic exterior I see before me there is a veritable *wildcat*.'

'Only when I see injustice and pain.'

'Ah… God knows there is enough of that in the world

to keep you busy for the rest of your life, no? But, tell me, was that the only reason you came to the Algarve, Grace? To see if you could petition my help for your charity?'

Tucking a strand of drifting fair hair behind her ear, she released a long, slow breath. 'No, it wasn't. I truly only thought of asking your help when I overheard that conversation in the café. I'm here because I'm having a bit of a break from work, since you ask. I'm afraid I returned from Africa feeling rather exhausted and a little low after my last visit there. The sights I've seen haunt me. Anyway, my parents have a holiday home here and they suggested I come out for a rest.'

'So you are, in effect, on holiday?'

Her big blue eyes visibly widened, as if she was taken aback by the mere idea. 'I suppose I am. Although the truth is I'm not very good at relaxing. After being in Africa and seeing the children at the orphanage I can't stop thinking about them and constantly wondering what else I can do to help.'

'So when you learned that I would be in the area for a meeting you were determined to try and talk to me?'

'Yes…I was.'

Helplessly, perhaps *inevitably*, Marco found himself warming to his refreshingly candid guest even more. 'Clearly your desire to assist those less fortunate than yourself drove you to risk something you perhaps would not ordinarily do. You must be possessed of an exceptionally kind heart, Grace.'

'You make it sound like it's something unusual. There are some wonderful people who work for the charity who are equally committed and devoted.'

Inês appeared through the elegant French doors with a tray of drinks. The plump Portuguese woman's smile was positively beatific when Grace warmly thanked her for the tall glass of lemonade, and right then Marco thought it would take a stone-hearted soul indeed *not* to respond similarly to this young woman's generous warm nature.

When the housekeeper had left them alone again, he took a long cool sip of his drink then leant back in his chair. 'I told you that I unexpectedly find myself with a free afternoon today? I think I would very much like you to spend the rest of it with me. We will start by going out to lunch.'

Grace was sure that most women finding themselves in her position right now with the arresting Marco Aguilar sitting opposite and declaring they would go out to lunch, would silently jump for joy at having such good fortune. But Grace *didn't* jump for joy. The situation was just too unreal to be believable, and she didn't feel anywhere near equipped to go out to lunch with such a man. *Especially when she'd probably just offended him with her passionate outburst and more or less telling him he should help the charity.*

He was a successful and wealthy man, yes. But she'd learned that he knew personally what it was like to be deprived and go without—*emotionally* at least—having been brought up an orphan himself. Why he wanted to be with her for even a minute longer bewildered her. And if she *did* agree to go to lunch with him, what could she talk about? Save helping the orphans and maybe complimenting him again on his beautiful house?

Before leaving home she'd led a more or less uneventful life. In fact, Grace hadn't felt as if she'd really experienced life at all until she'd stolen her freedom and permanently left home after returning from university. God knew she loved her parents…was grateful for all that they'd done for her…but in truth there were times when their protectiveness all but suffocated her. They were always so afraid she'd make the wrong choices, always wanting to protect her from the possibility of making mistakes.

That was why she'd never felt able to tell them that she'd once briefly dated a man who had hit her in a drunken rage and tried to rape her. He'd never got the chance to hurt her a second time, but the psychological wounds he'd left her with had not easily nor quickly abated. Though she would never regret her decision to break free, that experience had made her wary of getting involved with anyone again. Even a so-called simple date seemed fraught with danger now.

'It's very kind of you to offer to take me to lunch, but… don't you have someone else you'd rather go with?'

Looking honestly bewildered, her companion shook his head—as if not quite believing what he'd just heard. 'In answer to that strange question I will only say that I would rather go to lunch with *you,* Grace. I wouldn't have suggested it otherwise.'

'But you hardly know me—and I hardly know you.' Tearing her glance free from Marco's disturbingly frank examination, she stared out at the sublime vista of shimmering verdant green that stretched out like an infinite plateau in front of them. It might as well have been a vast ocean and she a small rudderless boat lost in the middle of it, she thought. That was how vulnerable and afraid she suddenly felt.

'And how will we *get* to know each other if we don't spend some time together?'

As if to prompt her into making a decision, pangs of genuine hunger registered inside Grace. She'd been so keyed up about meeting with Marco again that she hadn't been able even to contemplate eating breakfast. *What harm could it do simply to have lunch with him?* In fact it would seem ill-mannered *not* to in light of him agreeing to help the charity.

She proffered an uncertain smile. 'All right, then. I accept your offer…thank you.'

Already extracting his mobile phone from a back pocket, her host flashed a disarming grin. A grin that could melt a girl's insides at fifty paces… 'I know the perfect restaurant,' he said.

Another worrying thought seized her—one that she was nervous of drawing attention to. 'Is it the kind of place where you have to dress up?' she asked.

Marco's glance made a leisurely reconnaissance of her face, neck and shoulders. Her blood started to heat the second she drew his gaze. 'You don't have to worry about that when you're with me, *meu querida*. Besides… your beauty would grace *any* establishment. It matters not what you are wearing.' His smile became even more seductive. 'However…what you have on is extremely becoming.'

'Even if I'm not up to the standard of your usual guests?' she quipped daringly.

'I am sorry I said what I said to you yesterday about your clothes. It was not the behaviour of a gentleman.'

'But now that you've apologised I promise I won't hold it against you.'

Even as he frowned thoughtfully at this response, Grace's lips were forming an unrepentantly teasing grin…

Marco's chauffeur drove them to a three-storeyed restaurant that overlooked the ocean. As they walked up the winding path to the entrance a small group of staff were waiting to greet them—just as if the handsome businessman was someone whose presence lit up their day.

They apologised profusely that the manager was away attending his daughter's wedding and couldn't be there to welcome Marco and his guest personally.

Her companion had a friendly word with all of them, Grace noticed, acting as if he had all the time in the world to spare. As she watched him effortlessly interact, she reflected on how different he seemed from the way the press depicted him. She hadn't read a great deal about him, but what she'd read definitely painted him as some kind of playboy, intent on enjoying the fruits his wealth and status had brought him to the maximum. But now, with the palm of his hand pressed lightly against her back, a more immediate realisation troubled her. The thin top she wore ensured that her spine was sizzling beneath his touch, just as though his fingertips had stroked over her naked skin.

A strange sense of *How on earth is this happening to me* assailed her as two of the attentive young waiters led them up the stairs onto the roof terrace.

The ambience was surprisingly intimate for what was quite a large space. As they were escorted to what was clearly the best table in the house, with a prime view of the matchless sunlit ocean, an equal fuss was made of both of them. Already in her mind Grace was calling it *the Marco effect*. Even if he hadn't been as well-known as he was, she didn't doubt he would draw attention—just like a sudden flash of dazzlingly bright light in a darkened room.

Having ordered their drinks, they were now on their own again—apart from the inquisitive glances of nearby diners, sneaking a look at her impossibly handsome companion every now and then that was...

Lowering the leather-bound menu he'd been given, Marco frowned. 'The emphasis is on seafood here. I should have asked if you were okay with that… If not, I am sure the chef can prepare something you would like more.'

Having glanced at the extensive menu herself, Grace realised again how ravenous she was. 'I love fish…in fact, I prefer it to meat. This restaurant was a good choice,' she reassured him.

'I bask in the light of your approval.'

'I wasn't being condescending. I'm just grateful that you brought me here. Look at the view—it's absolutely fantastic!'

'You don't need to feel grateful or deserving, Grace. The fact is I wanted your company. I want to get to know you better. Tell me…is there a boyfriend at home?'

She thought he was teasing her, and half expected to see his sculpted lips shape a gently mocking smile, but when she glanced back at him Marco's expression was quite deadly serious. 'I've been too busy to have a boy-friend,' she told him. Even though she tried not to let it, inevitably some defensiveness crept into her tone. Her fingers restlessly unfolded the starched linen napkin in front of her on the table, then folded it back again into its perfectly formed square.

'So there is no man to take you out to dinner or to the movies?'

It wasn't just this man's looks that were compelling—his deep, rich voice had its fair share of magic in it too. So much so that Grace was all but mesmerised by the sound of it. 'I have some good friends. If I want to go out to dinner or to a movie I go with them.'

She heard his quiet intake of breath and was transfixed by the indisputably intimate tenor of his beautiful dark eyes. 'And what about those other needs that a woman might want a man for?' he asked softly.

CHAPTER THREE

THOSE *needs* Marco referred to had been deliberately and carefully suppressed ever since that horrible evening when her then boyfriend, Chris, had flown into a dangerous rage because Grace had refused to give in to his demands to have sex. After accusing her of flirting with another man at the party they'd attended, he'd pushed her up against a wall and slapped her hard across the face. Just as she'd been reeling with the shocking ending to what had been a pleasant evening at a mutual friend's birthday party, he'd pinioned her to the floor, as if he would force her to give him what he wanted.

She had been beyond terrified. It was only when she'd made herself not give in to her fear and spoken in a quiet, reasonable tone, urging him to think about what he was doing and telling him he would bitterly regret it in the morning, when he was sober again, that he had seemed to come to his senses and let her go. She'd left him sleeping and never returned.

'The kind of needs you're referring to aren't that important to me,' she said now with a feeling that was a mixture of despair and dread settling in the pit of her stomach. 'They're certainly not as important as other things in my life.'

Leaning towards her across the table, Marco drove

every single thought out of her head when he gently caught hold of a blonde tendril of her hair and slowly entwined it round his finger.

'You mean like saving the orphans?' he suggested huskily.

Even as her blood heated, and the resultant intoxicating warmth drove away all traces of despair, out of the corner of her eye Grace registered the brief flash of a digital camera going off.

Her companion had registered it too. Unravelling her hair from round his finger, he rose smoothly from his seat and strode across the polished wooden floor to the smartly dressed male perpetrator, sitting across from them with his female companion. Without saying a word he removed the camera from the surprised man's hands, pressed what Grace was certain was the 'delete' button on the back, then calmly returned it.

Having obviously identified the couple as British, he declared, 'If you ever try and do that again I will sue you,' and only a fool would ignore the underlying fury in his tone. 'I see that your meal hasn't arrived yet. Take my advice: make your apologies to the *maître d'* and go and dine somewhere else.'

His point made, and frighteningly succinct, he returned to sit down again opposite Grace, not sparing the man he had warned so much as a single glance to see if he and his companion had taken his advice. Only seconds after he sat down again the couple had collected their things and swiftly exited the terrace.

'Does that sort of thing happen often?' Grace frowned.

The broad shoulders that his white T-shirt fitted so mouthwateringly snugly and that accentuated his strong toned musculature, lifted in a shrug. 'Often enough to be tedious,' he replied, a thread of weariness in his tone, 'but it will not spoil our lunch together because I will not let it.'

Even so, the intimacy that had hovered so tantalisingly between them before the man had foolishly snapped the picture had definitely disappeared. Grace told herself she should be pleased, but strangely…she *wasn't*. Now Marco's dark gaze was clouded with unease, and his shoulders looked tense despite his assertion that he wouldn't let the incident spoil their lunch. Suddenly she had a glimpse of how the downside of fame and celebrity must so heavily encroach upon the recipient's understandable desire for privacy. It made her partially regret her impulsive 'accosting' of him yesterday…

'Marco?' The distinct wariness in his returning glance upset her. 'If you would rather leave we can perhaps meet up again tomorrow instead? I know I pressed you about making the donation, and as far as the children are concerned it's definitely urgent, but I'm here for at least another week and a half.'

For the first time in longer than he could remember Marco had laid aside the demands and concerns of running a hugely successful enterprise for a while in order to give his full attention to something purely enjoyable for himself. This afternoon he had willingly surrendered his corporate persona to fully embrace the experience of being young and less careworn in Grace's refreshingly innocent company. But that thoughtless diner had tainted his pleasure, making him only too aware that he *wasn't* as carefree as he wanted to be. He'd had plans to enjoy a long, lazy lunch that could possibly extend into the evening. Now Grace had asked him if he would like to forego that and meet up tomorrow, or at a later date instead.

It wasn't an option he wanted to entertain even briefly.

The truth was he really liked the way this woman made him feel, and he craved more...*much* more of the feeling.

'I don't wish to leave, and nor do I want to postpone our lunch for another day.' As to if to highlight his intention, he snapped his fingers to attract the waiter hovering nearby, who had clearly been assigned to their table, 'I believe we are ready to order,' he announced, deliberately catching Grace's eye and smiling. 'Do you mind if I order for us both? If you like fish then I know the perfect dish. You will love it, I am sure.'

'Be my guest,' she replied quietly, her blue eyes flickering in surprise that he wished to stay after all. 'Go ahead and order.'

To accompany their meal he ordered a bottle of the very good light red wine the region was known for. Perhaps a glass or two would relax his pretty companion, he mused, thankfully sensing his previously less tense mood return. 'I am sorry if you were disturbed by that thoughtless idiot trying to take our picture,' he remarked. 'These people never seem to consider that I might need a private life as much as they do.'

'Having transgressed your privacy myself yesterday—albeit for the charity—I must admit I don't envy you, having to put up with that. It makes me realise that it's a great gift to be anonymous—to come and go wherever and whenever you please and to know that the public at large don't have a clue who you are and nor do they care.'

'You are fortunate indeed if you never crave the recognition of others to make you feel valued.'

The pale smooth brow in front of him creased concernedly. 'Do *you*?' she asked him bluntly.

Though no one would ever know it, Marco privately owned that sometimes he *did*. But he wasn't about to admit that to a woman he'd only just met. In fact, he wasn't going to admit it to *anyone*. It was a painful aspect of his ego that frustrated and irked him. But also perhaps inevitable that a man whose father had abandoned him to an orphanage as a baby because he couldn't take care of him on his own after Marco's mother died was fated to crave the recognition of others in a bid to help him feel worthwhile…

'Do I strike you as a man who courts the approval of others?' he answered, his tone a little more clipped than he'd meant it to be.

'I don't know. I've only just met you.'

Once again, Grace's luminous sky-blue gaze unsettled him, suggesting as it did that she intuited far more than was comfortable for him.

'But I imagine it's not easy to be in business in this world…especially if you have a high profile. It must be a lot like being an actor—you're always playing a role, and you can't really be yourself, can you? Especially when people believe that it's your success and reputation that defines you as a person. It must make it difficult to foster good relationships at work, and even in your private life.'

'So what have you personally heard about my reputation? I'm interested to know.'

The smooth space between her slim elegant brows crumpled a little, almost as though it grieved her that he should ask such a question. 'I don't read the newspapers very often, and when do I'm apt not to believe what they write about the lives of people in the public eye.'

'But nevertheless you *have* heard things about me somewhere along the line yes?'

'I've heard it said that nobody can be as successful as you are unless they're a little ruthless… But then they say that about a lot of successful businessmen, don't they?'

'Do you believe it? That I am ruthless I mean?'

'I trust that I'm intelligent enough to make up my own mind about a person. I certainly don't go blindly along with what the papers or the media says. And as far as thinking that you might be ruthless sometimes goes, I hardly know you well enough to form an opinion. But I do believe that the press has its own agenda, and I don't think it's got a lot to do with telling the truth. See what I mean? Everyone is playing a role...even journalists. Why isn't it enough to simply just be who you naturally are in this world? People are too afraid to let down their guard, that's the trouble. If they did, then they *would* be communicating authentically...but it's not something that's promoted in our culture.'

The waiter brought their wine and offered Marco a taste first. He took an experimental sip, pronounced it 'perfect' and waited for the man to pour some for Grace then leave again before commenting on her statement—a statement that had both shocked and surprised him with its insight.

'In business, to let down one's guard in front of the competition would be deemed corporate *suicide*,' he declared, at the same time wondering what she would have to say about that.

Lifting her hair briefly off the back of her neck, unwittingly drawing his attention to the graceful and seductive shape of her long, slim arms, she gifted him with a smile so charming that it made his stomach flip.

'Not if someone has faith in their own ability to make things work, no matter what the competition is doing. It seems to me that if you're not towed round by the nose by what your competitors think of you, then you're onto a winner...you're free to do whatever you like.'

The burst of laughter that left Marco's throat was

genuinely joyous—so much so that the other diners on the terrace couldn't stop themselves from smiling at the sound.

'I don't think I meant that remark to be funny.'

His lunch guest's pretty lips pursed a little, and she looked so adorable just then that Marco wanted to kiss her...wanted to obliterate every bit of her softly shaded pink lipstick and explore her mouth until time stood still. And even then he guessed that wouldn't be enough to satisfy his craving.

'I'm not mocking you, *namorado*...the exact opposite, to tell you the truth. You have no idea how refreshing it is to have someone genuinely tell you what they think. Sometimes it is hard to know who to trust because of the lack of that kind of honesty in my working life...even amongst my closest colleagues. Perhaps you ought to go into business yourself, Grace? You could spearhead a new trend for fostering good relationships and authenticity in the corporate world.'

'Now you *are* mocking me.' But even as she uttered the words the corners of her mouth were wrestling with a smile. 'I'm afraid I'm the last person in the world who should go into business. I'm neither clever nor ambitious. All I've ever wanted to do was to help people.'

'I don't believe you are not clever. You went to university and presumably got a degree, didn't you?'

'What if I did? Anyone can learn a bunch of facts and explain them in the way the system wants you to. That might be regarded as "clever" by some, but it doesn't mean that you're intelligent...at least not in the way that I understand the word.'

The waiters arrived with their meal right then, and Marco reflected that their arrival was most opportune—because the break in his and Grace's conversation allowed him some time to assess his feelings. The fact was, the more time he spent in this unusual and refreshing woman's company, the more her unsophisticated beauty and intelligence enthralled him, and his desire to take her to bed, to get to know her even *better*, intensified.

As the waiters once more left them alone, he raised his glass in a toast. *'Saúde.'* He smiled. 'Which means, to your health.'

'Cheers,' she answered shyly, touching her wine glass carefully to his…

He'd left her in the drawing room to go and talk to Inês about preparing dinner for them later on that evening. The feeling that she'd somehow stumbled into somebody else's dream continued to dog Grace. She'd eaten the most sublime lunch, been wined and dined at a beautiful restaurant overlooking the sea by a man whose photograph had probably appeared in every newspaper and style magazine worldwide, and even if she pinched herself she'd hardly believe it. Marco Aguilar was so charismatic and good-looking that she guessed a lot of women would even *pay* for the privilege to sit and admire him, just listen to him talk, simply because he was so mesmerising.

Less than halfway through their meal, the wine she'd imbibed heightened a worrying revelation: she was becoming more than a little attracted to him. Just the *idea* was enough to terrify her. Frankly, it was absurd. When they talked about people being 'poles apart' the description could so easily apply to Grace and Marco. There probably wasn't even *one* thing that they remotely had in common.

Now, relaxing on one of the elegant couches, with the still-hot sun beaming into the room through the open French doors, she could barely fight the fatigue that swept over her, let alone resist her host's indisputable powers of persuasion to stay longer and have dinner with him. She really ought to get back to the villa, she thought sleepily. Clearly she wasn't quite recovered from the exhaustion that had hit her on returning from Africa. She had to make the most of this holiday and rest properly. That was why she should go *now*.

Making a half-hearted attempt to get up from the couch, she slumped back down almost straight away—because her legs just didn't seem to want to hold her up. A few moments later her backless sandals slipped off her feet as she dropped her head down onto the silk cushion behind her and fell fast asleep...

'It's all right, little one I'm here now... I'll stay and hold you until you fall asleep I promise...'

Her arms full of the warm weight of a baby, Grace rubbed at the surge of hot tears that welled up in her eyes. Every day when she visited the orphanage and saw the mixture of sad and hopeful faces that waited to greet her it became harder and harder for her to leave. *She'd become particularly fond of the baby boy that had been put into her arms a few days ago, after his birth mother had died of Aids.* Now on every visit she made a beeline for him. *He was so easy to love. That was the most heart-rending thing...* He deserved to have parents who adored him. Surely there must be some kind couple in the area who could adopt him and give him a home? *God, it was so hot...* If she stayed here for another year she doubted she'd ever get used to the enervating heat...

Opening her eyes, Grace shockingly registered that she wasn't in fact in Africa, at the orphanage, but was instead in the elegant high-ceilinged drawing room of Marco Aguilar's home. She swung her legs to the floor, pressed her hand to the side of her head because the sudden movement had made her head spin then stared straight up into a pair of concerned dark-lashed brown eyes.

'I'm so sorry,' she murmured, beyond embarrassed and wishing that the ground would open up and swallow her. 'I don't know what came over me…falling asleep like that…a bit too much wine, I think.'

'You were dreaming,' Marco told her low-voiced. Dropping down with ease to his haunches, he reached out a hand to brush away the lock of hair that had tumbled onto her forehead. 'It was a dream that clearly distressed you. Would you like to tell me about it?'

'I thought I was back in Africa.' She tried for a smile, but her heart was bumping so hard beneath her ribs at his closeness that it turned into a grimace.

'It sounded as though you were comforting a child?'

'A baby,' Grace answered straight away. 'His name was Azizi—the helpers who work at the orphanage named him. It means beloved or precious one.'

The tight knot of tension that gathered inside his chest at her words made Marco rise to his feet again. He couldn't deny that he was touched by how genuinely loving she'd sounded about the baby…an infant that wasn't even her *own*. If only he had had someone even *half* as loving to look out for him as a child. It would have made a world of difference to him. He might not have grown up as emotionally detached as he had become…

One thing seemed clear: when Grace became a mother herself, her natural proclivity to be tender and loving would come into its own. Marco *envied* the man who would be the father of her children.

'If his destiny proves to live up to his name, then he will be a fortunate boy indeed,' he remarked, crossing the cool marble tiles to the opened French doors. Turning

back to observe the pretty woman perched on the edge
of his couch, her golden hair sexily mussed from her nap
and one thin strap of her silk camisole sliding arrestingly
down over one perfect satin shoulder, he folded his arms
to try and contain the carnal heat that threatened to consume him. 'When I walked back in from the kitchen after
talking to Inês I thought I had stumbled upon Sleeping
Beauty,' he confessed. 'I should have pretended to be the
handsome prince and kissed you awake.'

Her big blue eyes widened to saucers, then she sighed.
'But you didn't,' she uttered softly.

The throbbing heat that had already invaded Marco
inflamed him even more, and he almost had to suppress a
groan. 'Would you have liked me to?' he asked, his voice
sounding like a hypnotised stranger's to his own ears.

Leaping suddenly to her feet, Grace hastily repositioned the silky spaghetti strap that had drifted down over
one shoulder, then slipped her prettily arched feet into
the sandals that were at the foot of the couch. 'I should
go. It's probably not a good idea for me to stay for dinner after all. You've already taken me out to lunch and
given up a lot of your valuable free time to be with me
as it is.'

'You can't go,' Marco's reply was unequivocal.
Already he knew that his house—this 'paradise on earth',
as she had called it—would feel like a suffocating if luxurious prison without her presence this evening. She was
more than just a breath of fresh air… she had him spell-
bound. And he scarce knew what to do with the torrent
of feelings that were coursing through him. Never before
had he experienced such an instantaneous and passionate attraction towards a woman practically on sight.

'What do you mean, I can't go?'

'I mean that Inês has already started to prepare the meal she is cooking for us tonight.'

'But we've only just got back from having lunch.' Running her hand over her hair, his guest lifted her wrist to examine her watch. She moved her head in stunned disbelief when she saw the time. 'It's just after seven o'clock... We left the restaurant at half past four. You don't mean to tell me that I've been asleep on your couch for nearly two hours?'

'You clearly needed to rest. In this part of the world it is not unusual to take a siesta after lunch.'

'You should have woken me...what must you think of me?'

It surprised him that she seemed so distressed. Most women would have taken the opportunity to maximise *any* chance to spend time with him...but not *Grace*. Accustomed to thinking on his feet, Marco moved towards her, circled his hands round her slim upper *arms* then smiled down into her upturned face with every ounce of the charm that newspapers and magazines regularly claimed he had. And not for an *instant* did he chastise himself for utilising that asset.

'It would have been a crime to wake you when you looked so peaceful. While I sat here and watched you I made the most of the time to reflect upon helping your charity and I'm pleased to tell you—rather than wait any longer—I've decided to write you a cheque tonight to pay for the new orphanage. To cover *all* the costs.'

'You mean to buy the land, purchase the materials *and* pay for the work to be done to build it?'

'That's what you wanted, wasn't it?'

'Yes, but I didn't expect you to— Oh, my God, that's wonderful! I could—I could *kiss* you!' Her cheeks flooded with the becoming colour of dewy pink roses even as her lips curved into the most bewitching sunny smile Marco had ever seen.

'You won't find me protesting about that,' he teased.

'But… You—you watched me sleep? Why?'

He lifted a shoulder in an unrepentant shrug. 'What do you expect a normal red-blooded male to do? Ignore the unexpected opportunity to gaze at such sublime beauty—undisturbed and at my leisure—when it was right here under my nose?' He stole a couple more seconds to look more deeply into her startled blue eyes before dropping his hands from her arms and stepping away…but not *too* far away. His palms tingled as if they'd been burned by the sun—just because he had touched her.

'Anyway…'

Unable to disguise her surprise—and also what he perceived to be her general awkwardness at what he'd just revealed—Grace linked her hands as if to steady herself.

'You really will write a cheque for the orphanage tonight?'

'I will indeed.'

'I can hardly believe it. You have no idea what this will mean to the children, and to the people who help care for them.'

'I think I do.' Helplessly remembering the long, empty days when he was growing up in the orphanage, craving love and attention and not getting it, he thought, *At least now I can do something to help another child growing up in similar circumstances to have a more comfortable and caring existence*… 'Why don't you come into my study and we will get our business over and done with before dinner?'

His smile enigmatic, Marco moved towards the door,

knowing that he had no qualms about the additional un-
conventional agreement he was going to propose as soon
as he wrote the cheque for Grace. None at all…

CHAPTER FOUR

It was about an hour away from sunset, and the fiery orb still burned high and bright in the azure sky as Grace followed Marco through stunning marble halls into his study. In fact the light that beamed through the huge plate glass windows was so dazzling upon their entry that she squinted to protect her gaze. Her companion immediately pressed a button on a wall panel to lower stylish honey-coloured blinds, then gestured for her to sit down opposite him at the large beechwood desk that dominated the room.

Still feeling stunned that Marco was going to give the charity the help it so desperately needed to rebuild the orphanage, and anxious that at any time he might change his mind, she attempted to introduce some levity into the proceedings. 'I feel like I'm about to be interviewed for a post at one of your resorts.' She smiled. 'Would I pass muster do you think?'

'I only ever employ the very best people. If you are capable of rising to the challenge of doing an exemplary job then, yes…you would definitely stand a good chance of gaining a position in my company.'

The merest shadow of a smile touched lips that suddenly appeared austere, and Grace couldn't help feeling a little defensive at the idea her host might be privately questioning her ability and finding it wanting. All desire to lighten the mood fled. Was Marco subtly reminding her just who he was, and that she was lucky he'd agreed to talk to her at all about the charity—let alone invite her into his home? As soon as the thought entered her mind she gave herself an instant pep talk that she shouldn't be daunted by someone just because he was rich and well-known—she was sitting on the other side of his desk because her priorities, her ability *and* her heart were good. There was absolutely nothing she needed to feel 'less than' about.

He reached into a desk drawer, and she saw him withdraw a chequebook. Her heart started to thud a little. She caught her breath as she watched him write the name of the charity on the top line, then scrawl in an amount. Ripping out the cheque from the book, he turned it round so that it was facing her, then pushed it across the desk. The inside of her mouth turned dry as dust as Grace inclined her head to examine it.

'This much?' she exclaimed, hardly daring to believe the eye-popping amount on the cheque. 'It's at least triple the amount that we need. Why? Why have you decided to give us so much?'

The man at the other side of the desk finally let down his guard and smiled without inhibition. For the first time she noticed the crinkled laughter lines at the corners of his deep brown eyes. Now she was agog for an entirely different reason…

'As well as rebuilding the orphanage, this money is for the charity to do whatever it sees fit to help the children… Your passion and dedication to their cause, Grace, has helped bring it home to me how I have neglected the one area of need that I can personally identify with.'

He folded his arms over his muscular chest and briefly

glanced away, as though struggling with the memories that might still haunt him. Grace sensed her insides lurch sympathetically.

His arresting gaze returned to study her. 'The cheque is yours to take with you. However, there is something I would like to add before our transaction is concluded.'

About to pick up the cheque to examine it more closely, Grace stilled apprehensively. 'Oh? What's that? Is it perhaps that you want to go out to Africa to visit the orphanage and confirm what's needed for yourself? I'm sure the charity would be delighted to arrange—'

'I do not want to visit.' There was a hint of steel in his reply. Then he drove his fingers through his hair, as though frustrated that she should jump to that conclusion. He leant back in the impressive Chesterfield-style chair and exhaled a sigh. 'What I want is to make a personal arrangement with *you,* Grace.'

Her brow puckered. 'What kind of arrangement? You had better explain.'

'You told me that you have another week and a half left of your holiday?'

'That's right…'

'For the first time in quite a long while I find myself with the desire to take a sabbatical from work, and I would like to have an attractive and pleasant companion to join me for a while. If you agree to spend the remainder of your holiday with me, Grace, I will show you some of the finest private beaches, take you to eat at some of the best restaurants, and let you partake in any leisure activity you so desire. I have, of course, access to the most exclusive golf courses, if you're interested in learning how to play, and in the evenings if there is a performance somewhere we can go to a concert or a recital, perhaps? My personal preference is for classical music, but I fully accept that you might prefer something else.' Pausing, he lightly drummed his long, tanned fingers on the desk, his glance honing in on her like a laser. 'All this will, of course, be at my expense. Each morning I will send a car to collect you and bring you back here. Once you arrive we can discuss what we would like to do that day. And there is one more thing...'

If she hadn't felt quite so numb with shock, Grace would have pricked herself with a pin to convince herself that she still inhabited her physical body and wasn't either hallucinating or dreaming. 'What's that?'

'I forgot to include shopping in the itinerary. I have never met a woman yet who would not put that at the top of her list of favourite things to do on holiday.'

'Well, you have now.' Shakily circling a small patch of the desk with the tip of her forefinger, she couldn't help but be affronted. 'It's never been top of any list for me and never *will* be.'

'Hmm...' Marco's expression was definitely amused. 'Do you really expect me to believe you do not like beautiful clothes...exquisite jewellery?'

'Why would I pretend I'm not interested if it's the truth?'

'Maybe you think you should play down such an interest? Who knows? There is no need. I am an extremely wealthy man. The women who come into my life have certain expectations. Clothes and jewellery are the very *least* they expect.'

'What a shame.' A strong wave of compassion assailed Grace as she thoughtfully digested this information and observed him.

'What do you mean?' A shadow moved across his piercing dark gaze.

'I mean it's a shame that women can't just like you for yourself...without you having to buy things for them.'

'Thankfully, I do not suffer with the same regret. I am a realist, if nothing else. And the truth is I do not indulge their love of beautiful clothes and expensive jewellery for *nothing*. I too have certain expectations—of them.'

Embarrassment at what he alluded to made Grace shift uncomfortably in her seat. But she was still genuinely sorry to learn that Marco must enter into such cold-blooded liaisons with women believing he had to pay for the privilege. She didn't doubt that it couldn't exactly make him feel very good about himself, for all his talk about being a realist. Inside, she guessed that the small boy he had once been was still searching for evidence that he was valued in some way, and maybe felt he always had to *give* something in order to get something back in return. It made her want to show him that he *was* valued and didn't need to deserve it. He was a good man. Grace was certain of that.

'That's all well and good,' she said, 'but I still think you're missing something important if a woman doesn't just want to be with you because she genuinely finds pleasure in your company and—and cares about you.'

He scowled. 'You are clearly a romantic, Grace, and not remotely a realist.'

'If realism means that people can't like me unless I give them something, then I'm glad I'm what you label a romantic. Look...please don't be offended by what I've said...' Her irked glance automatically softened. The last thing she wanted to do was alienate or wound him by expressing her perhaps *too* frank opinions. After all, she had utterly no experience of the kind of world Marco moved in, or the compromises and personal sacrifices he found himself having to make. 'It's just that the things I find most beautiful are all natural…a sunset over a green valley, a deserted sandy beach as dusk falls, a bluebell-carpeted wood or the scent of roses in an English country garden…the joy on the faces of children who are simply happy that an adult is paying them some real attention…'

Her avid listener sat up straight in his chair and a much more interested glint came into his eyes. 'If you genuinely prefer all those things then you are indeed a unique woman in our consumer-driven day and age.'

'I don't think so. If you haven't met other women like me it doesn't mean that they're not around. You just move in a very elite sphere where perhaps the women's focus is more on the material. I'm not unusual or special in any way. Besides, it's not in my nature to crave lots of new clothes and jewellery. At the end of the day whatever small pleasure they give you is only ephemeral. Too many possessions—whether clothes, jewellery or anything else—just make a person dissatisfied, because whatever they have it's never enough, and they always end up wanting more.'

Linking his long fingers together, Marco leant across the desk towards her, close enough that the scent of his arresting spicy cologne made her insides knot. 'If you agree to spend your holiday with me, what if buying you nice things makes *me* feel good?' he asked, his rich voice pitched intimately low.

She frowned. 'Marco…?'

'Yes, Grace?'

'You said you wanted a—a *companion* to join you on your break from work…'

'Specifically, a pleasant and attractive one…in *your* case a very beautiful one.'

Another woman would no doubt find such a lavish compliment coming from a man as extremely attractive and influential man as Marco a huge boost to her self-esteem…but not Grace. Ever since that frightening incident with her ex-boyfriend Chris she had deliberately steered clear of interested men. The truth was she was understandably nervous about giving them the wrong signals, and consequently about what they would expect if she inadvertently did so. There were times in the past when she might have been worryingly naive, but not any more. One of the most handsome and admired entrepreneurs in the world wouldn't ask a woman to be his companion for even a short time and not want something a bit more than her company she realised. *Hadn't he already alluded to similar arrangements with women?*

The shocking heat that suddenly suffused her at the idea made her nipples tingle and tighten beneath the flimsy silk of her camisole and she crossed her arms over her chest to prevent Marco from noting the fact. 'Is my company *all* that you want of me?' She blushed hard as she waited for his answer, in a state of tension in case he said, *No, that's not all that I want.*

Could she agree to his incredible offer to spend the rest of her holiday with him if it entailed something far more intimate and compromising than simply being a companion?

Resting his elbows on the desktop, Marco knew his hungry gaze was drinking her in like intoxicating wine—a wine that went immediately to his head. It simply wasn't possible for him to disguise the fact that he wanted her… If possible he wanted her even *more* after her assertion that she preferred the natural things in life—in particular the joy on the faces of children when an adult paid them some proper attention. Inwardly he had rejoiced with every fibre of his being when Grace had said that. Her words had acted like a salve on some of the desperate hurt he'd experienced as a child, and to be honest had knocked him sideways.

'You have asked me a straight question and I will give you a straight answer,' he replied. 'Yes I *do* want something other than your company. You are very different from most of the women I come into contact with, and that has an irresistible appeal for me. If, in the course of our time together, it should transpire that you share a similar fascination for me, then *yes*…of course I want to take you to bed.'

He shrugged a shoulder, as if it was a foregone conclusion. Her cheeks flushed as prettily as a wild rose in response, making his heart pound at even the mere idea of her slim but curvaceous body entwined with his in an embrace, let alone sharing the eroticism of lovemaking. It jolted him when Grace scraped back her chair and stood up.

'And is my receiving this cheque for the charity conditional on whether I accept your offer or not?'

Marco shook his head. Even if making his offer conditional *was* the only way to get her to sleep with him, he wouldn't do it. He might have a propensity sometimes to be a little ruthless in his business dealings, but he wouldn't be able to live with himself if he even attempted to coerce or blackmail a woman like Grace. She might be a self-confessed romantic but he didn't want to be the one to shatter that pretty illusion…

'No it isn't. The cheque is yours, come what may. You have my word on that.'

She sighed and her relief was palpable. 'Thank you. While we're talking so frankly, there's something I need to tell you. The thing is—the thing is sex isn't a simple or casual thing for me…I think you should know that.

Being a friend or companion to you while you're on a break is one thing…intimacy is entirely another.'

Saying nothing, Marco simply watched the visible interplay of emotions crossing her face, silently drawing his own conclusions about them.

'Can I give you my answer about this tomorrow?' she asked. 'Only I'd like some time to think it over. Also, in spite of my nap on your very comfortable couch, I'm still feeling rather tired. Do you mind if I don't stay for dinner? I hope your housekeeper hasn't gone to too much trouble getting the food ready…'

On his feet in a flash, Marco dropped his hands to his hips and ruefully shook his head. At least she hadn't given him a flat-out no in response to his frank admission that he wanted to take her to bed, he mused. As once again he fell under the spell of her incandescent crystal gaze he determinedly held onto that. Not that it had really surprised him when Grace told him that sex wasn't a simple or casual thing for her. Even before she'd revealed that nugget of information he'd sensed that she was a woman who would need to be seduced in the most subtle and artful of ways… If he was too demanding too soon she would quickly depart for good, never to be seen by him again, most likely. And now that he was set on making her his lover that was the very *last* scenario he wanted.

'Inês will be happy to accede to whatever arrangements I make for dinner—no matter how many times I may change them. What is much more important to me right now is that I have your promise that you *will* return tomorrow, Grace.'

'You have it. I'm a woman of my word, so I'll come back tomorrow and give you my answer then.'

'Good. If you follow me, we will go and find Miguel

to drive you home. In the morning he will return to your villa to collect you.'

'Thanks. Thanks also for taking me to lunch today. I really enjoyed the food *and* your company.' She smiled shyly, but then her glance darted helplessly to the cheque still lying on the desk.

Immediately Marco picked it up and handed it to her. 'You might want to post this to the charity.' He smiled, 'You can tell them that I will write soon, to confirm that I am in full agreement with them using it to help the children.'

'I'll also give them your address here, so that they can forward their thanks to you. Can you tell me what it is?'

He collected a sheet of personally addressed notepaper from the wooden letter-holder on his desk and gave it to her. Something told him she would put the task top of her list of priorities and the idea touching him, a warm sensation flooded into his heart.

'Well, I expect I should get home now.'

The shy smile that he was fast becoming addicted to returned.

'Let's go and find Miguel. I see now that you are indeed very tired. The sooner you get back to your villa and go to bed, the better.'

The repetitive thump on the villa's front door made Grace blearily open her eyes. Turning her head, she glanced at the clock sitting atop the neat pine cabinet and released a disbelieving groan followed by a very unladylike curse. Good God! She'd slept the evening and the night away. She hadn't stirred once, not even to go to the loo. Now it was a little after ten, and some determined caller sounded as if they were intent on breaking down her door. Her dad wouldn't be best pleased if they caused any damage…

Even as she had the thought she remembered that Marco had promised to send his car for her, to take her back to the palatial mansion that was his residence. Then she remembered the *reason* for her return. Her insides did a one-hundred-and-eighty degree roll. She muttered another ripe curse. *How could she have forgotten such a commitment for even a second?* No matter *how* tired she was?

Grabbing the short textured cotton robe at the end of the bed, she hurriedly got to her feet and pulled it on over her matching white nightdress. Barefoot, she flung open the door and moved quickly down the cool tiled corridor that led to the front of the house.

'*Olà,* Senhorita Faulkner.'

The chauffeur Miguel stood on the other side of the door. Conscious that her hair was tousled and uncombed, and that her short robe perhaps revealed too much leg for her to be comfortable displaying in front of almost a stranger, Grace pulled the sides of the garment more securely round her, then lightly knotted the belt. 'Hello, Miguel,' she answered, silently noting the faint surprise in his deep black eyes that she had addressed him by his name. 'I'm really sorry but I'm afraid I overslept. As you can see, I've just got out of bed, and I'm nowhere near ready to leave yet. Do you want to come back for me later…after lunch, maybe?'

'No, Senhorita Faulkner. Senhor Aguilar will not be happy if I do not return with you this morning, as arranged.'

She could well believe it. A man who probably just had to snap his fingers to have his every whim fulfilled would clearly *not* be happy if Grace had the audacity to be late…especially when he had been so generous with his donation to the charity. She didn't know much about the culture in Portugal, but she'd heard via her dad that to be late for an appointment with someone—especially someone high up the business world hierarchy—was considered a serious lack of respect.

'In that case you'll just have to come in and wait while I get myself ready.' She held the door wide to allow the chauffeur entrance into the hallway, but he stayed right where he was, his tanned face impassive as a rock.

'I am sorry, Senhorita Faulkner, but that would not be at all appropriate. In any case I must phone Senhor Aguilar right away and explain the reason for our delay. Then I will wait for you in the car.'

Grace watched him walk with purposeful gait back to the gleaming black Mercedes parked outside the villa's entrance, with its climbing red and pink bougainvillaea trailing up traditional white-painted walls. Then she turned on her heel and headed straight for the bathroom and the quickest shower she could manage—all the while apprehensively contemplating what her answer should be when Marco Aguilar asked her if she'd decided whether or not she would become his companion for the rest of her time in the Algarve.

Remembering the cheque he'd donated to the charity, and imagining what joy such an amount would bring to everyone concerned with the desperate and poor orphaned children it had been set up to help support, she already knew that his offer would be hard to turn down. Yesterday, when she'd sensed that Marco had very definitely *not* come to terms with his emotionally impoverished childhood it had made her want to know more about this darkly enigmatic man. And when she thought about the way he made her feel, the effect he had on her body... Maybe if she allowed herself to experience intimacy with him it might be a way to help herself overcome the pain of her ex's attempted rape and allow her to move on psychologically too, and truly put that horrific episode behind her?

On her arrival at the palatial villa, his housekeeper Inês greeted her with the invitation to wait in garden while Marco finished an important phone call. Sitting under a parasol in her host's incredibly beautiful private shaded garden, Grace made herself breathe out very slowly to help calm her nerves. Her time with Marco yesterday had taken on the surreal quality of an unbelievable dream. Finding herself yet again with the prospect of not only his arresting company but a conversation she was bound by promise to have with him about his proposition it was surely understandable that she should be seized by sudden nerves?

Reaching for the long cool glass of lemonade that Inês had thoughtfully brought her, she glanced down at the sleeveless red and white maxi-dress that she'd donned. It was one of only two dresses she had packed to come out here, and it was pretty and cool in the heat and indisputably feminine. It certainly wasn't the kind of clothing she wore every day. At work she invariably got away with the much more casual attire of T-shirt and jeans, and sometimes a trouser suit if she had to go a meeting with a potential patron. Now she was glad of the protection of the parasol, as already she sensed her exposed shoulders were frying a little beneath the hot sun.

She sipped her drink. Time ticked by. A drowsy buzzing insect flew right by her ear and startled her. She wondered how long Marco would be, then decided there was no option other than to try and relax and simply enjoy a garden that had all the seductive attributes of a floral sensual paradise. Sighing, she briefly shut her eyes to appreciate more fully the sweet bouquet of the yellow and white gardenias that wafted beneath her nose and the hypnotic sound of the splashing waterfall just a few feet from where she sat.

But suddenly impinging on her enjoyment came the contrasting images and sounds of an African city slum, where the poorly erected houses were fashioned from mud and metal and where the children played in an area teeming with heaving mounds of garbage. *The heat there was unbearable and stifling, and made even more intense by the ever-present heavy smog...*

The disturbing memory jolted her sickeningly and tears of compassion and frustration because more people didn't try and do something to alleviate the situation surged hotly into her eyes.

'My sincere apologies for keeping you waiting, Grace. Ah... I see that Inês has given you a cool drink? That's good. Today is going to be even hotter than yesterday, I believe.'

She hadn't heard his soft-footed approach across the grass, and when she opened her eyes to acknowledge the figure that instantly captivated her gaze, the nerves she'd tried hard to subdue sprang into unsettling life again. The sight of Marco wearing an immaculate white shirt, with the sleeves casually rolled up to just beneath his elbows, and fawn-coloured chinos that were clearly meant to be equally casual but on his tall, athletic frame looked effortlessly stylish and elegant too made her heartbeat hop, skip and jump, and her mouth turned as dry as though she hadn't had a drop of water to drink for days.

Before she could summon up words of greeting, he moved towards her and leaned down to plant a sizzling little kiss at the corner of her startled lips.

'I—I didn't mind waiting,' she responded at last, with

the imprint of his warm mouth lingering disturbingly, like an intimate brand. 'It's so lovely out here, and anyway…it was *me* that was late in the first place. I'm sorry about that, by the way. I overslept.'

'So Miguel explained.' His dark eyes twinkled. Then he pulled out the sunchair opposite Grace at the table and adjusted the aviator sunglasses he'd been wearing on the top of his head over his eyes.

Now it would be impossible for her to guess what he was thinking…

His unexpectedly personal greeting had set off a veritable firework display of reaction inside her, and she knew that any remaining reservations she had about accepting his offer were assuredly being demolished one by one.

She made a discreet attempt to wipe the moisture from her eyes that had arisen when she'd mentally been transported back to Africa and her handsome companion frowned. 'Is everything all right? You seem a little upset,' he commented.

'I'm fine.' She made herself respond with a reassuring smile, even though the slight quaver in her voice no doubt made a liar of her.

'I do not entirely believe you, but I hope you can put whatever troubles you to one side so that you can enjoy the day. It is far too beautiful to be sad, yes?'

Marco wondered at the cause of the distress reflected in Grace's crystal-clear blue eyes. *He prayed it wasn't bad news from home that would make her cut short her stay.* He schooled himself to relax, studying her pleasingly curvaceous form in the very becoming red and white dress, her golden hair curling prettily down over her shoulders. The arresting sigh of her intensified the drugging sensual heat that had already invaded him at the prospect of seeing her again.

Anticipating the long break that he intended, he'd informed all of this morning's telephone callers that he would only be contactable if there was an emergency— at the back of his mind had been the irresistible thought that he intended to be far too preoccupied with the lovely girl he'd found himself infatuated with to think about business. The kiss he'd planted at the corner of Grace's pretty mouth just now had been an exciting revelation. Her skin was softer than velvet and down combined. *She'd smelled irresistible too.* Recognising the alluring French scent, he made a mental note to send some to her villa as a gift.

Now he would not wait a moment longer to ask her the question that had ensured he'd more or less had a sleepless night because he hadn't been able to stop dwelling upon the outcome of it…

'So, Grace… I trust you have now had plenty of time to think over my proposition? What will be your answer, I wonder?'

CHAPTER FIVE

GRACE didn't answer him straight away, but appeared to be thinking deeply. He knew it was in his nature to be impatient, but the tension that gathered in the pit of Marco's stomach as he waited for her to speak made him feel as if he was wearing an increasingly tightening iron band round his middle. No woman had ever said no to spending time with him before…was this engaging British girl going to be the *first*?

Folding her hands in her lap, she locked her brilliant blue gaze with his at last and a tentative smile gently raised the corners of her lips. 'My answer is… Well, it's *yes*. And I'm going to be honest with you… The reason I've said yes is that I—I…' Gnawing at her lip her cheeks turned engagingly pink.

'Go on,' Marco encouraged.

'I've discovered that I *am* attracted to you. Otherwise I wouldn't consider it—no matter how lovely the inducements. And I was going to be on my own the entire time I was here, and now I have someone to share my holiday with…I'm grateful.'

He'd told her once before that her honesty was refreshing, but never had it mattered more to him than right now. She knew exactly what he was asking and had accepted the offer he'd made because she was attracted to him.

She hadn't run away or taken refuge behind being coy. She had admitted that she liked him outright. Now there was no need for any tedious mind games or manipulation. All they had to do was let nature take its course. *Marco had not the slightest doubt that it would...*

'I'm very pleased you've accepted my offer, Grace. Now all we have to do is get to know each other a little and enjoy ourselves.' Rising to his feet, he took her by the hands and gently urged her up from her chair. 'Fortunately you are perfectly dressed for what I have in mind today. Some time ago I received an invitation from a business acquaintance of mine to attend a garden party she is having. At the time I told her I wasn't sure whether I would even be in the country, but now that I am and you have agreed to be my companion...I think we will go.'

'A garden party, you say?'

Still holding onto her hands, and noticing the brief flare of doubt in her eyes, Marco smiled. 'You know...? Champagne, exquisite food, music played soothingly in the background by a specially hired professional ensemble and some amicable conversation with our host and the other guests in a setting just as beautiful as this... It's the perfect way to start our holiday together, don't you agree?'

'It all sounds rather grand. The garden parties I've personally experienced have been on a much more modest scale...usually thrown by my mum and dad. My mum spends the entire week before frantically cleaning the house and planning what food to buy, while my dad is relegated to the garden to cut the grass and make sure the barbecue is clean and ready for use. The guests are generally extended family and friends—some of whom have young children. There's no soothing music playing, but generally there's plenty of hilarity and laughter amongst the children playing on my dad's pristine newly cut lawn.' Grimacing, she gently tugged her captive hands free to smooth them down over her dress, 'I'm sorry... I'm babbling again. That's because I'm nervous.'

'Am I so intimidating that you have to be nervous of me?' Marco frowned, quite charmed by her sharing of the experience of garden parties with her parents and their friends. Silently he attested to feeling rather envious of Grace's very normal-sounding and happy family life. In contrast to growing up without parents or any other family at all how could he *not*? 'Now that you have accepted my invitation, I'd like to think you can relax and just be yourself around me. If you are wary of me for any reason then you will put up a guard, and that is the very last thing I want.'

'I've never met anyone like you before, Marco.' He heard the quiet intake of breath she softly released. 'And I've certainly never been around great wealth or fame before. I'll try not to be intimidated by you, or the company you keep, but I can't pretend it won't be a challenge. I'm a girl from a very ordinary background, and I've never mixed with the kind of people who inhabit your world. I still can't understand why you'd even ask someone like me to spend time with you. Surely you must...you must know plenty of much more suitable women?'

'If you knew these so-called "more suitable" women, you would not even ask me that question, Grace.'

Folding his arms across his chest, Marco realised he was feeling quite bereft because she'd withdrawn her hands from his clasp. He yearned to grab them back and hold them again. Already he was addicted to the touch of her peerlessly soft skin.

'Now I have to go and locate my bodyguard José. I

regret we have to attend this function with a third party accompanying us, I really do. But I know for a fact that the paparazzi will be very much in evidence this afternoon, and they can be intimidating—even to those of us who are quite familiar with the lengths they will go to in order to get a picture. Sit down, relax and enjoy the sunshine. I will be back soon.'

There...she'd done it. She'd said yes to Marco Aguilar's astonishing invitation to spend the remainder of her holiday with him in the full knowledge that she was also agreeing to a short affair.

Just the thought made her feel weak. But it wasn't the kind of weakness that emanated from being frightened, she realized. Quite the *opposite*, in fact. A frisson of shivering excitement ran through her. She was twenty-five and had not yet experienced having a lover. Because of her highly upsetting and demoralising experience she had kept men at a distance—but the truth was she had often yearned to know what it would be like to have someone make love to her that really liked and regarded her. Ultimately she yearned for a man to love her with all his heart, but if she refused to give in to her fears of being hurt again being with Marco might turn out to be an important step on the road to healing the shadows that dogged her. Fervently, Grace hoped so.

Sighing, she mentally shook her head in wonder at the extraordinary situation she found herself in. Now that she'd committed herself to going through with Marco's request to be his companion she was determined to try and be more confident and face everything. That included every potentially intimidating situation she might encounter during the next few days—situations that would no doubt occur simply because she was in this man's revered company.

To help her deal with whatever challenges might arise she would simply remind herself that when her totally unexpected sojourn with him was at an end she would return home to London, to her normal everyday routine and her work with the children's charity. The upside of that was that she would be returning with the knowledge that—thanks to Marco—the charity now had the necessary funds to rebuild the orphanage. It would make a monumental difference to the orphaned and abandoned children she'd so come to love, and that made everything else pale into insignificance.

She dropped back down into the comfortable sunchair, and into her mind stole the memory of Marco's voice saying, 'If, in the course of our time together, it should transpire that you share a similar fascination for me, then, yes…of course I want to take you to bed.' *Well, she she'd admitted that she was attracted to him. Now all she had to do was just let things unfold and see what happened.* It sounded so easy, but Grace knew it was anything *but…*

Arranging her sunglasses back in front of her eyes, she found her avid glance cleaving to the arresting sight of his tall, athletic figure strolling nonchalantly back across the verdant grass to the house…

As he pointed out various interesting landmarks on the hour long drive to his friend's residence, Marco's level tone definitely conveyed pride. Yet Grace detected a strange *ambivalence* too. As if he was somehow conflicted about his right to take pleasure in his beautiful country. She couldn't help but be intrigued by the thought. But then, the more time she spent in his striking presence, the more she became intrigued by everything about him. Sometimes when he leaned nearer to her, to point out something of interest through the passenger window, she breathed in the subtly arousing warmth of his body that mingled with his expensive spicy cologne and everything in her tightened and contracted, in case she completely yielded to the disturbingly powerful urge to touch him that so worryingly kept enveloping her.

'We are here.'

Miguel, with the much bigger-built José in the passenger seat next to him, drove the sleek Mercedes up to the tall iron gates that had appeared at the end of a narrow road shaded with tall pines. Just before they reached those imposing barriers Grace saw several cars haphazardly parked in front of them, and their waiting owners hurriedly exiting their vehicles with high-tech cameras in tow. She sucked in a breath. At the same time she sensed Marco's cool hand firmly slide over hers.

'There is nothing to worry about, *meu querida*. They will get their pictures and then hopefully leave us alone. If not, José will help them to do just that.'

There was a distinct twinkle in his deep brown eyes as his glance met hers, and her stomach plummeted again—but this time with pleasure.

As soon as the car manoeuvred to a stop in front of the gates the photographers literally swarmed over it, their fast-flashing cameras and camcorders all trained on Marco and Grace seated in the back. José had climbed out as the vehicle had glided to a halt, and Grace heard him shout commandingly at the voracious throng to clear a space so that they could drive through the gates. She heard plenty of curses and yelps of protest too, as he physically removed bodies from climbing across the car's bonnet, with intrusive cameras pointing at the windscreen in a bid to get pictures of Marco and his guest.

With her heart pounding, Grace turned to glance out through the tinted window beside her at the exact same moment as a camera flash blinded her from seeing anything other than that disorientating bright light.

José jumped back into the front seat and shouted, 'Go!' as a uniformed man standing behind the gates spoke urgently into a mobile, nodded towards the car in recognition of its VIP passenger, and stood aside as the now opening electronic gates allowed the vehicle entry.

As the gates rapidly closed again behind them, Marco tapped on the small front window separating him and Grace from the two men in the front. When the window immediately opened, he leaned forward to speak to his bodyguard. Although she didn't understand what he said, because he spoke in his native Portuguese, Grace intuited by the concern in his voice that he was asking his employee if he was okay. The intrepid José must have taken quite a few knocks dealing with the unruly mob that had accosted their car, she realised.

The window closed again and Marco leaned back in the luxuriously upholstered leather seat, cursing softly beneath his breath.

'Is José all right?' she ventured.

'He's fine. He has dealt with much worse than that before, I assure you. Now, let us forget about that rabble at the gates and try to enjoy ourselves…okay?'

After driving for a while through stunningly landscaped gardens, with orange, lemon and tall palm trees lining the straight drive that led to the dazzling white villa that was their destination, Marco's chauffeur steered the car onto a sickle-shaped gravelled area that was already filled with impressively gleaming vehicles. Grace's stomach plunged at the prospect of meeting and mingling with other no doubt extremely wealthy and important people like Marco. In a moment of doubt and uncertainty her fingers curled anxiously into the crisp cotton of her dress. She sent up a silent heartfelt plea for help.

Miguel politely helped her out of the car. As she straightened she briefly met his eyes and saw that they had a reassuring twinkle in them, as if he'd intuited how overwhelmed she must be feeling and wanted to lend his support. José was already standing outside, conversing quietly with Marco. As she tentatively moved towards the man who was his boss, Marco caught hold of her hand and smiled.

'Grace…this is the home of—'

'Marco!'

The loud male shout made them both turn round abruptly. Hurrying towards them was a well-built middle-aged man in a smart petrol-blue suit and an open-necked white silk shirt, with the kind of craggy good-looks that suggested the legacy of a life well lived and perhaps a little *too* over-indulgent?

A ripple of surprised recognition went through Grace. *Lincoln Roberts*…The man was a seriously famous movie-star, whose visit to rehab in California a couple of years ago had been splashed all over the tabloid newspapers…as had his previous affair with another star's very young wife. Was that why Marco had known for a fact that the paparazzi would be very much in evidence this afternoon? An A-list celebrity like Lincoln was bound to attract major interest.

'So glad you could make it, my friend. Francesca and I were afraid you wouldn't. God knows, you're a hard man to pin down!' The well-known actor gave the businessman a brief hug and then, before releasing him, slapped him affectionately on the back.

'I was pleased to be invited. You're looking well, Lincoln. Very well.'

Marco sounded somewhat reserved, despite his words, and the edges of his well-cut lips lifted in a smile that was quite some way short of being as open as his friend's. When he stepped back and automatically reached for Grace's hand, to enfold it almost possessively inside his palm, a distinct wave of warmth and pleasure quivered through her.

'Thanks. I've been taking much better care of myself since I've been with Francesca. The woman has transformed me! By the way, she'll be along any moment now. She's powdering her nose…you know what women are like! And who's *this* lovely lady that you've brought with you?' Lincoln asked, his interested, almost *greedy* blue eyed glance moving from Grace's face down to the modest cleavage of her dress in one disturbing swoop.

She found herself moving a little closer to Marco's side, as if subconsciously seeking his protection. Lincoln Roberts might be one of the most famous movie stars on the planet, but she knew almost instantly that she didn't like him…didn't like him *one bit*.

'This is Grace Faulkner.'

Marco had provided the other man with her name almost reluctantly, Grace thought.

'A beautiful name for an undoubtedly beautiful lady… I'm delighted to make your acquaintance, Grace. I really am.'

In a blink he had separated her hand from Marco's and clasped it firmly between his own bigger, slightly *sweaty* palms. It was hard not to cringe. 'It's nice to meet you too, Mr Roberts,' she murmured politely, at the same time quickly disengaging her hand.

'Call me Lincoln, sweetheart. We don't stand on ceremony here. Francesca wants all her guests to feel relaxed and to make themselves at home. These little gatherings she has are always very informal…aren't they, Marco?'

'They are indeed.'

'Talk of the devil—here she is now. Doesn't she look ravishing?'

'*Ciao*, Marco…I'm so glad that you were able to come. I doubted that you would, you know…'

Both men turned to greet the vision in figure-hugging white that had joined them. The dark-eyed brunette with her perfectly arched eyebrows and scarlet-painted lips had straight away made a beeline for Marco and was regarding him with undisguised pleasure, Grace noticed, watching apprehensively as the woman kissed him resoundingly on both cheeks, then dropped slender hands with myriad glinting diamond rings lightly yet almost *possessively* onto his arms.

'Handsome as ever, I see. Broken any poor woman's heart lately—like you broke mine?'

Grace's stomach flipped as she waited to hear his answer.

'No. And I doubt very much that *any* man could break *your* heart, Francesca.'

Their eyes locked for a scant second, and Grace didn't think she imagined the regret in the Italian woman's beautiful dark gaze. *Did Marco feel the same?* She was about to distance herself from him a little when he turned towards her, smiled, then once again enfolded her hand in his.

'Grace, this is Francesca Bellini, our charming hostess. She is becoming a force to be reckoned with in the world of high fashion. Francesca, I'd like to introduce Grace Faulkner.'

'Grace…delighted to meet you.' The woman shook her hand limply and almost instantly let it go. She was anything *but* delighted, Grace thought wryly. Clearly she and Marco had once been an item, and it was obvious that the Italian wished that they still *were*. The realisation didn't exactly bode well for a relaxed afternoon...

Lincoln stepped in just then, to loop his arm round his girlfriend's tiny waist, cinched in with a broad patent leather white belt with a huge gold buckle. Could she even *breathe* in such a tight outfit? Grace wondered. She was suddenly very glad of her own more comfortable and practical summer dress.

'Darling, I was just telling Grace that our parties here are always very relaxed, informal affairs.' The American smiled.

Informal and *relaxed* weren't the two descriptions that naturally sprang to mind, Grace wryly reflected as she scanned the perfectly manicured grass that ran down to a shimmering blue lake with two pairs of regal swans gliding across it, then looked back again to the sight of small clusters of guests dressed glamorously enough for a garden party at Buckingham Palace.

To add to the indisputable impression of the kind of wealth that went far beyond most ordinary people's dreams, on the air floated the sound of a well-known Vivaldi composition played by a sublime string quartet. Grace immediately had the strongest urge to move closer to where the musicians were performing, so that she could simply stand in the sunshine and listen to them play at close quarters. It would be such a privilege, she thought.

She glanced up at the dark-eyed man by her side, and something told her that *he* too would infinitely prefer to do just that, rather than spend too much time with their hostess and her infamous boyfriend.

The knowledge made her suddenly bold, and briefly

buried her disquiet that Marco should bring her to a garden party at the house of an ex-girlfriend. 'Is that lovely music being played nearby?' she asked, proffering what she hoped was an eager and appreciative but not too *presumptuous* smile to the party's glamorous hosts.

'Yes, honey—they're sitting right over there by the fountain,' Lincoln answered.

'It sounds so wonderful. Marco? Shall we go over and see them?'

'Go ahead,' Francesca urged helpfully, but not before Grace had witnessed the undisguised flash of jealousy in her glance. 'I'm sure we'll hook up again later. By the way, there are a lot of people you know here already, plus a few that you *don't* who are anxious to meet you. In the meantime, go and enjoy the music with the beautiful Grace.'

When they were less than halfway across the shimmering lawn that led to a spectacular fountain with an audacious sculpted mermaid, Grace murmured, 'I hope you didn't mind that I suggested going to listen to the quartet?'

Touching his hand to her bare arm, Marco came to a standstill. Staring back at him in surprise, she saw the frown that creased his tanned brow as his dark eyes thoughtfully roved her face. 'Francesca and I dated for a short while about five years ago. These days she is no more than a business acquaintance I occasionally bump into at corporate functions. Did you think that she meant something more to me than that? As far as I know she is quite happy to have her name linked with a movie star like Lincoln. She's always been very ambitious, and their romantic partnership certainly hasn't hurt her career.'

'She's seriously stunning.'

'So?'

'I just wondered why you would bring me to a party thrown by an ex-girlfriend. I know we're not serious or anything, but—'

'I told you…we were over a long time ago and there's nothing for you to worry about. Can't we simply enjoy the party?'

Grace shrugged, feeling slightly miserable that she might be spoiling things between them before they'd really even begun. 'Okay.'

'Come here.'

'What?'

'I said come here.'

Catching hold of her by her slim upper arms, Marco impelled her against him so that she was suddenly on dizzyingly intimate terms with the hard, lean physique she'd been secretly admiring since setting eyes on him again that morning. The heat from his body all but burned her through the elegant cotton of his shirt.

Tipping up her face, he gazed down at her, saying, 'You know…I have a sudden profound urge to make you stop talking.'

The unexpected confession was accompanied by the most enigmatic of heart-stopping smiles. His seductive warm lips covered hers. She didn't even have time to gasp her surprise.

It was a kiss that sent a molten river of irresistible longing pumping right through her body, and Grace's lips parted almost the instant he touched his lips to hers. Less than a moment later her knees all but threatened to fold at the hotly melting exploration of his erotically silken tongue. Her hands automatically moved either side of his straight lean hips to anchor herself.

Just when the incredible assault on her senses felt as if it might grow even stronger—turn into a veritable wildfire that would burn them both to cinders with its power—Marco cupped the side of her face with a warm palm and gently and regretfully separated his mouth from hers. 'I desired to stop you talking so that I could sample the sweetness of your lips…but now I am almost rendered speechless myself due to the fire you have stoked in me, Grace.'

He meant every word.

Inside his chest, Marco's heart was thundering in an amalgam of desire, urgent longing and deep, deep shock at the depth of feeling that kissing this woman had aroused in him. All he could think right then was that he wished he hadn't been so hasty in making the decision to come to Francesca Bellini's garden party—if he were at home now with Grace he would be making it his mission to get her into bed…

Carefully moving her to his side, Marco slipped a deceptively casual arm round her waist, just so that he could maintain the contact that was becoming the most essential factor of all for determining his happiness that day—especially after that explosive little kiss they'd just shared. He was still walking on air from the sheer pleasure of it.

'Let's go and listen to the music together, shall we? I've heard this particular string quartet perform before at La Scala in Milan…'

After some companionable time had passed, during which Grace and Marco sat side by side sipping champagne on the edge of the sculpted fountain, listening to the sublime soaring notes of Vivaldi's *Four Seasons*, Marco was invited to join the well-dressed group of businessmen and women who had been eyeing him ever since he'd walked across the perfect emerald lawn to sit by the water fountain with Grace.

Assuring him that she was quite happy to sit there by herself for a while as he conversed with them, Grace shut her eyes to simply let the stirring music envelop her. It had the same delicious effect as cooling summer rain after a hot, dry spell. In truth, she was glad of the opportunity not just to listen to the music but to mull silently over the soul-stirring kiss that Marco had initiated and she had eagerly complied with.

It had been a revelation just how much she'd enjoyed it. Since that dreadful incident with her ex-boyfriend she'd secretly feared another man kissing her, in case she was immediately repelled by the contact. But the *opposite* had happened. Even now the memory of Marco's lips against hers made her tingle fiercely and long for more... *much* more of the same. She briefly held her breath at the thought, then batted away a buzzing insect that brushed against her cheek. The day was once again incredibly hot, and the soporific intensity of it was making her drowsy. She wished that she'd remembered to bring the straw hat she'd left lying on a chair in her villa's hallway.

Just then there was a break in the music, and when Grace opened her eyes she was taken aback to find a small auburn-haired girl standing in front her. The child's skin was as fair as her own, but she was sensibly wearing a sunhat, its brim decorated with very becoming pink and white daisies.

'What's *your* name?' the girl demanded, head tipped to one side and jade-green eyes squinting in the sunshine.

Grace smiled. 'My name is Grace,' she answered. 'What's yours?'

'I'm Cindy Mae Roberts and I'm here with my daddy. He's a movie star.'

Glancing round the various little knots of men and women gathered together on the rolling lawn, Grace saw this little girl appeared to be the only child there. Instantly Grace's heart went out to her, perhaps doubly so because she had the onerous legacy of Lincoln Roberts' world-wide fame to contend with growing up. 'Well, Cindy, I'm very pleased to meet you.'

She held out her hand but the child ignored it, demanding instead, 'Are you in the movies? If you are I've never heard of you.'

'That's because I'm not…in the movies, I mean.'

'Then what *do* you do?'

'I work in London for a charity that helps children who are orphaned and abandoned.'

'That must be *so* boring!'

Grace's lips curved in a gently understanding smile. 'It's not boring at all…it's quite the opposite, in fact. It's wonderful to help make children happy—especially children who don't have any parents or anyone else to love them and look after them. It's very satisfying.'

An expression crossed Cindy's freckled face that was surprisingly thoughtful. 'Do you really like children, then?'

'Of course. I like them very much.'

'My daddy doesn't. He just thinks they're a nuisance… At least, he thinks *I* am. I'm glad I only stay with him now and again, because sometimes he's not very nice. The other times I live with my mom in New York…she's *very* nice.'

Now Grace's heart really *did* go out to the girl. What a horrible thing for any child to believe…that her father thought her a nuisance. She noticed that Cindy held a lime-green tennis ball down by her side. 'Didn't any other children come to the garden party for you to play with?' she asked.

'No. My daddy said one little nuisance was enough, without inviting any more, and Francesca agreed. She doesn't like children either.'

Grimacing at that, Grace immediately got to her feet. 'How about a game of catch?' she suggested, smoothing her hands down over her dress and at the same time kicking off her backless sandals, then bending down to pick them up and carry them.

The child's vivid green eyes lit up like a light bulb. 'Really? I'd love that!'

'Good. Then let's go and find a big patch of grass where we won't get in the way of people with their drinks.'

'Sure.' The child unhesitatingly slipped her hand trustingly in Grace's and beamed up at her with a look of unconstrained anticipation and delight.

CHAPTER SIX

MARCO was looking for Grace, but she'd somehow disappeared. He'd met and conversed with a few people from the corporate world with genuinely interesting ideas and a couple of business propositions they'd asked him to think about, but none of them—neither the people nor the ideas—held his attention like *she* did. Now he experienced a sense of irritation mingled with discomfiting panic that he couldn't find her. *Where had she got to, for goodness' sake?* Had it been too much to ask for her to wait for him by the fountain where he'd left her?

After asking a couple of guests nearby if they'd seen a very attractive blonde wearing a long red and white dress, and having them regretfully shake their heads, a frustrated Marco headed across the grass to where his two loyal employees were deep in conversation by the parked cars.

'Have either of you seen Miss Faulkner?' he demanded.

'She's over there by the pine trees.' Miguel pointed helpfully, with what appeared to be an almost indulgent and knowing smile crossing his face. 'She's playing catch with Senhor Roberts' young daughter. There are no other children here, and she said that the child was looking for somebody to play with her.'

'So naturally Miss Faulkner volunteered?' Feeling somewhat bemused, Marco thought wryly that he shouldn't be surprised. It seemed that whenever children's needs were on the radar Grace would somehow be involved. He'd had no idea that Lincoln even *had* a daughter, because the man had never so much as mentioned her in his hearing. Clearly that didn't bode well for her. *Poor kid...*

He found himself reflecting that there wasn't one other single woman he knew who would put a child's enjoyment before her own, or potentially give up the chance to make an impression—especially at a gathering like this, where celebrities and influential guests could literally be picked off like cherries from a tree...

'She has a very kind heart,' his chauffeur observed— *unnecessarily*, Marco thought.

'Her conduct so far definitely seems to bear that out,' he commented. 'In any case, I think I will go and join her. The pair of you should go and get yourselves a drink. It is a particularly hot day, no?'

'Yes, boss.'

'And stop grinning like I'm the butt of some kind of joke I don't know about!'

'Yes, boss.'

Shrugging irritably, Marco turned away to stride down towards the bank of pine trees, where he'd already caught a glimpse of Grace's very fetching red and white dress and the bright banner of a child's auburn hair.

His elusive lady had missed her catch and dropped down onto one knee, laughing out loud as the small girl standing a few feet away from her clapped her hands together and squealed in delight, 'I caught you out again! I thought you'd get better but you're really not very good at this at all, are you?' she taunted.

'That's why they called me butter-fingers at school,' Grace replied good-humouredly. And then in the next instant her cornflower-blue eyes widened when she saw that Marco stood watching them. Now *he* was the lucky recipient of her bright, engaging smile. 'Hi, there,' she called out, 'did you have a good time chatting with your friends?'

He had the same incredulous reaction he probably would have had if he'd been singled out for special attention by the Queen of England herself. Warring with a great desire to grin back at her like some infatuated schoolboy, instead he shaped his lips into a sardonically tinged smile. 'I was not "chatting with my friends" as you so ingenuously put it, Grace. You do not "chat" with a prominent executive of the Banco de Portugal as if he were a long-lost buddy you last saw in the school playground!'

'Obviously not, if he takes himself as seriously as *you* do.'

Dumbstruck by her audacity, Marco nonetheless saw the funny side of Grace's lightning-quick irreverent reply. Before the idea had even formed in his mind he was striding across the perfectly mown grass to take hold of her by the waist and haul her to her feet. 'You deserve to be severely punished for that,' he told her, a husky catch in his voice.

The laughter in her eyes immediately died. It was replaced by the kind of fearful look that shocked Marco to his boots. She was genuinely terrified, he saw. He instantly released her. Inside his chest his heart was thumping as hard as a blacksmith's hammer striking an anvil.

'I was only joking,' he stared back into her apprehensive glance ruefully shaking his head. 'Are you okay? Do you always react like this when a man makes a harmless jest?'

'No.' She forced a smile, but distinct wariness had replaced the joyful laughter of only a few moments ago.

Marco felt as if he'd just lost something precious.

'You took me by surprise, that's all,' she finished.

Her soft golden hair had been tousled by her energetic game with the girl and lay across her pale satin shoulders in inviting buttery curls. God help him, but he ached to drive his fingers through those silken strands and then lift them away from her beautiful face so that he could kiss her passionately —just as he'd dared to do earlier, when they'd been heading towards the fountain to listen to the music. Only this time he would not be in any hurry to relinquish those petal-soft lips for anyone or *anything.*

'I apologise if I frightened you. That was definitely *not* my intention. I came to find you to tell you that the buffet is ready and I think we should go and eat. Will you come with me?'

He despised the uncertainty he heard in his voice— uncertainty that Grace would agree to go *anywhere* with him after that look of dread on her face when he had hauled her to her feet to chastise her playfully. For a woman to have such a hold over him that she made him doubt his powers of persuasion, the fact that he could have anything he wanted and not be refused, was *dangerous*, he reflected. *A genuine first for him...*

To Marco's intense relief she nodded, shrugging the slender shoulders exposed by her sleeveless dress. 'Of course. I *am* feeling rather hungry come to think of it. Cindy can come with us. By the way, Cindy is Lincoln Roberts' daughter—perhaps you two have met before?'

'No. I have not had the privilege.' He turned to smile at the auburn-haired girl with the bright green eyes that she must have inherited from her mother. None of her dainty features remotely resembled her father's. She was moving warily towards them. When she was level he lightly shook her hand. 'I'm very pleased to meet you Cindy. My name is Marco.'

'Marco Aguilar?'

He frowned in amusement. The child had sounded much older than her years when she'd asked that. 'That's right.'

'My daddy told me to mind my manners if I spoke to you. He said that you're a very important man…very *rich* too.'

Forming a nonchalant smile, nonetheless Marco was irritated. The child's innocent remark had once again brought home the sobering fact that he only seemed to be of interest to people because of his wealth and success—*not* because they enjoyed his company. For years now he'd been okay with that. He was a realist like he'd told Grace. But lately, for some reason, his wealth and success didn't seem to be enough to fill the sense of emptiness inside him.

'Grace and I are going to get some lunch. Would you like to join us?' Deciding that it was probably best to ignore the child's comments—after all, she wasn't responsible for her father's mercenary attitude—he chose to press on with his own plans.

'No, thanks. I'm going back to my room for a while. Thanks for playing catch with me, Grace…even though you can't catch! Will you be okay with Mr Aguilar?' The green eyes flashed suspiciously as they turned back to Marco.

He shrugged ironically as he glanced from her over to Grace. 'Think you'll be okay with me?' he asked lightly, praying he would never see that haunted look of fear in her eyes ever again.

'Of course I'll be okay,' she settled her gaze confidently on Cindy. 'Mr Aguilar is a friend...a friend that I *trust*,' she told her.

Warmth cascaded into his insides at her unhesitating reply.

'Bye, then.' With a brief wave, the small girl danced away.

'She acts a bit like a prickly pear, but underneath she's a sweet little thing,' Grace murmured, colouring a little as she bent down to the grass to slip her sandals back on. 'She just needs her father to show her a bit more love and affection—that's my guess.'

The observation made Marco feel a little hollow inside, because he knew that it was most likely true. 'You certainly looked as though you were enjoying yourselves.'

'It's always good to remind yourself what fun it can be to behave like a child again. It helps us grown-ups not to be so serious, don't you think?'

'I'm sure that's true—if you were lucky enough to experience having fun as a child. Not everyone is so fortunate.' The words were out before Marco had the chance to check them. Feeling awkward, and annoyed that he'd inadvertently revealed something about his past that he normally took pains to conceal, he felt hot, embarrassed colour sear his cheeks.

'Marco? I'm sorry if I—'

'Let's go and get some food, shall we? And you ought to get out of this heat for a while. You look hot and flushed after your exertions, Grace. We'll go and find some shade.'

Grace couldn't honestly have recounted what she'd eaten that day if anybody had asked. The food that had been laid out so abundantly and extravagantly onto the white linen cloths at the buffet tables had been a colourful and sumptuous banquet. Yet it hadn't tempted her at all. She'd merely picked at the few items that a waitresses had put on her plate.

After the comment Marco had made suggesting that not everyone was lucky enough to remember having fun as a child, she'd lapsed into a quiet reverie about him, her mind tumbling with questions that she ached to have answers to. He was a man that to the acquisitive outside world seemed to have everything anyone could ever want—certainly in terms of a successful career and the material wealth that it had brought him. But behind the soulful dark eyes that she now knew had the indisputable power to make her melt whenever he trained them on her, Grace had glimpsed a man who had had his fair share of heartache too, and she longed to discover the truth about that and perhaps to somehow ease some of his pain.

But she hadn't forgotten the river of icy shock that had cascaded through her bloodstream when he'd hauled her to her feet and said, 'You deserve to be severely punished for that.' *Her drunken ex-boyfriend Chris had said something similar that horrible evening.*

Of course Marco had only been teasing, but somehow his innocent action had unleashed the frightening memory of that devastating incident, and now it made her wonder again if she would ever be able to enjoy intimacy with a man without being afraid. She prayed that she would... More than that, she was *determined* that she would.

When Marco suggested that they should leave, Grace was honestly relieved. Not for want of trying, she had endeavoured to converse with the other guests at their table, but it had quickly become apparent that the social and material gulf between them was *vast*—too vast to be bridged even at a so-called 'relaxed' social function like this. How could she relate to a vacuous conversation that centred primarily round yachts, private planes and the latest Paris fashion trends? *It was a joke.* To be honest, she was genuinely sorry that they had such empty lives, with nothing other than the fruits of their material wealth and the desire for more of the same to occupy their minds.

Heading back to Marco's villa in the luxurious confines of his car, after a second flurry of paparazzi interest at the gates as they drove out, they both fell quiet. Had the desire he'd expressed to have her spend the rest of her holiday with him dissipated in light of the now obvious fact that Grace clearly didn't gel in any way with the elite social set that he moved in? If he now wanted her to leave then it would make it hard for her to accept the cheque he'd made out to the charity—not because she didn't greatly desire them to have it, but simply because she would feel that she'd let him down in some way.

'Marco…?'

Their gazes met and locked at the same time. A knowing smile raised the corners of her companion's sculpted lips. 'Please don't tell me that you now have reservations about our arrangement. I know the garden party must have been extremely tedious for you, and it was wrong of me to imagine that you might enjoy it, but for the rest of the day I will let *you* decide what we will do. Just name it and I will endeavour to make it happen. Any ideas?'

Stunned that he wanted her to stay, Grace stared. 'I thought—I thought that you'd had enough of me,' she lifted her shoulders in a painfully self-conscious shrug. 'You must have seen that I was like a fish out of water at lunch? I didn't have anything remotely in common with any of those people.'

'And I thank God that you didn't, Grace. But if you believe that you have nothing they might admire or want then I have to tell you that you're *wrong*. Why do you think that they were practically falling over themselves to tell you about their expensive toys and hobbies? I will tell you why: it was because they wanted to impress you. When they didn't get the reaction they wanted it probably made them feel quite insecure and jealous.'

'I can't believe that… Jealous of what?'

Marco sighed and combed his fingers through his hair. 'Your ability to simply be yourself…your *innocence*… You radiate the kind of goodness and beauty that money can't buy, and that's unsettling to people who believe they have it all.' His gaze intensified a little as he observed her, as though a slow fire simmered behind it. 'And I have definitely *not* had enough of you, *meu anjo*. Nowhere *near* enough.'

The water was deliciously and delightfully cool after the heat of the day. As Grace swam lap after lap of the azure marble-edged pool in the opulent villa she sensed the tension that she'd been holding in her body fall away and some measure of peace return. Marco had readily concurred when she'd told him she'd really like to go for a swim, and her pleasure at his agreement had soared when he'd shown her the beautiful outdoor pool in a secluded section of the landscaped gardens that she hadn't visited yet.

It was lucky that she'd had the presence of mind to bring her swimsuit, she thought, even though Marco had informed her that there was a large selection of swimming costumes in one of the guest rooms upstairs—just in case any visitors were bereft of one. But Grace was very glad of her one-piece suit. She'd bought in it in last year's spring sale, from a local department store that was part of a popular UK chain. The colour was a deep royal blue, and it had a bodice that wasn't cut too low and a high back. In truth, she felt *safe* in it. She certainly hadn't bought it because it was fashionable or might attract attention to her figure. Just the thought was anathema to her.

When Inês had briefly appeared at the poolside to tell Marco that he had an important phone call, Grace had been relieved, because it had meant she'd been able to get changed in private behind the poolside screen and quickly slip into the water before he got back.

After a while she stopped swimming, preferring to float on her back, her hands lightly paddling the azure water to keep her buoyant.

'You look like a mythical mermaid that's floated up from under the sea to grace the world with her beauty and remind us that magic still exists.'

The captivating male voice not only startled Grace, but made her turn upright in a hurry. She spluttered a little, because the sudden uncoordinated movement had sent a wave of water splashing into her face and she'd accidentally swallowed some.

Marco dropped to his haunches by the side of the pool, with his elbows resting on the knees of his elegant chinos and his long fingers loosely entwined. His dark hair gleamed bronze in the late-afternoon sunshine, and the strongly defined contours of his handsome face looked relaxed...*amused,* even. All of a sudden Grace was terribly self-conscious. How could she *not* be, in comparison to that vision of perfectly sculpted masculine beauty gazing back at her?

'I'm sure I look more like a drowned rat after that,' she quipped, as some sopping wet strands of hair strayed into her eyes and her long bedraggled ponytail plastered itself heavily against her shoulder.

'Don't put yourself down. You look nothing of the sort.'

'Well, you always look so effortlessly turned out and perfect. It's bound to make even the most confident girl feel a little insecure!'

'So I look perfect, do I?'

Before Grace even had an inkling of what he was going to do, Marco stood up, kicked off his shoes, then jumped fully clothed into the pool. Even as she stared at him in abject disbelief he started swimming towards her in an easy front crawl. Stopping in front of her, he smoothed back his seal-wet dark hair and disarmed her even more with the sexiest smile she'd ever seen.

'You're crazy…' she husked.

'If I am it's because that's how you make me feel when I'm with you.'

By the time his hands had settled round her hips under the water Grace's blood was already on fire with the need to have him touch her. When his beautiful mouth hungrily and a little roughly claimed hers *she* became a little bit crazy too…

CHAPTER SEVEN

As Marco's hands followed the slim yet curvaceous lines of Grace's body in the clinging wet swimsuit he didn't care that a moment of sheer uncharacteristic madness had prompted him to jump into the pool like that. All he knew was that expecting him to be further away from this woman than touching distance was akin to expecting him to comply with the near *impossible*.

Kissing her was the greatest sensual delight he had ever experienced, he'd discovered. She had a mouth that was made for long, drugging kisses that suspended time…could even make him forget his own name if he'd let it. Being with her, knowing that she had such a pure and giving heart, honestly made Marco feel like a better man. Instead of making him tread water in a pool of sharks, as he'd done for so long to make it in business and elevate himself far above his humble beginnings, fate had unexpectedly gifted him with the most beautiful golden-haired mermaid to remind him of other very important human needs. Needs such as the company of a woman whose presence and beauty he genuinely enjoyed and appreciated. And those qualities had become even sweeter now Marco knew he desired her too.

Twisting his mouth away from hers, he tugged down the soaking wet straps of Grace's swimsuit to expose her pert, duskily tipped breasts. The river of flame that was already flowing straight to his loins ensured that he didn't have a prayer of resisting the erotic temptation they presented. His mouth captured one, drawing the rigid velvet nipple deep inside, whilst his hand cupped and stroked the other. His heart leapt when, with a soft moan, Grace slid her fingers through the damp strands of his hair to keep him there.

Several mindless seconds later, when Marco honestly thought he might explode with the longing to be inside her, to join his painfully aroused body to hers in the most uninhibited and feral way, he lifted his head to capture her lips in another ravenously hungry kiss. His heart started to gallop in alarm when he sensed her stiffen, just as if she wanted to draw away, and gazing down into her shimmering blue eyes he saw a reticence he hadn't expected. The panicked look of dread that he'd witnessed earlier at the garden party, when he'd grabbed her up from the grass to tease her playfully, had not resurfaced—thank God—yet neither was she totally at ease.

He hadn't guessed wrongly about her intentions. She was already pulling her costume's straps back over her shoulders and tugging up the front of her suit to cover herself.

'What's wrong?' His fingers fastened round her chin to lift it higher and make her look at him.

'I just—I just need us to take things more slowly.'

Marco swore. He couldn't help it. It was his own damn fault, but he was in a near *agony* of lustful need.

Then he saw the glitter of moisture in Grace's eyes—saw one lone teardrop hug the side of her cheek as it tracked slowly down her face. He took in a deep, steadying breath. *She was afraid*, he thought incredulously. His chest welling with compassion—because it dawned on him that a man must have treated her badly, perhaps even hurt her *physically* somewhere along the line—he followed the trail of moisture with the pad of his thumb. *What he wouldn't give to meet the bastard that had hurt her and teach him a lesson that he'd never forget!*

'It's all right, my angel,' he soothed. 'I wouldn't dream of forcing you to do anything you don't want to do or aren't ready to do. That's a promise. I guess that something happened before with a guy? Will you tell me about it?'

Her hand resting lightly against the hip of his sodden chinos under the water, Grace stared back into Marco's arresting and compassionate dark gaze, knowing without a doubt that—aroused as he undoubtedly was—he wasn't the kind of man who would dream of taking cruel advantage of a woman…not like her drunken ex had tried to do.

It was only fair that she gave him an explanation. She hadn't exactly tried to stop him from becoming amorous—not when she had been equally turned on. It had only been when she'd realised where his passionate kisses and inflammatory touches were leading that Grace had suddenly felt overwhelmed. She wasn't afraid of Marco mistreating her, but after Chris's brutal assault it had become increasingly hard to trust a man to be tender with her feelings and wishes where her body was concerned… *any* man. Even a man she found she desperately wanted.

She sucked in a breath, smoothing back her hair with a tremulous hand. 'My ex-boyfriend tried to rape me.'

Marco's eyes glowered with fury as he bit out a curse in Portuguese. 'Did you call the police? Was he punished for such an assault?'

'He was drunk at the time, much more drunk than I realised, and—no…I didn't call the police. I was just so relieved that I was able to stop him.'

'How long ago was the attack?'

'About two years ago now.'

'And you have not been with a man since?'

Her cheeks flushed pink. 'No...I haven't.'

Marco reached out and tenderly stroked her cheek. 'You are young and beautiful, Grace. Please don't let the actions of one insensitive and unintelligent animal like him spoil your right to intimacy...nor your *enjoyment* of it.'

Entranced by his desire to console her, she nodded. Instead of being angry—perhaps believing that she'd led him on—Marco had reacted to the halting of their lovemaking with understanding and kindness. Deep inside she sensed the spell he'd already cast on her senses and on her heart becoming even more compelling, like a silken web it was hard to disentangle herself from.

'I'm doing my best to forget what happened—I really am... But it's not easy.'

For a long moment he stayed quiet, his hands lightly firming on her arms. 'I understand that,' he began, 'and I want you to know that whilst it is hard for me to be patient...when I find myself so passionately attracted to you...I will *learn* to be, because I believe that you are worth the wait.'

'Maybe—maybe we could try again later?' she suggested softly. The deeply carnal ache inside her was flaring more strongly now he was being so chivalrous and understanding of her hesitancy.

He nodded slowly, lowered his head towards her, then took possession of her surprised open mouth with a teasing erotic kiss, his tongue dancing with hers. As he started to withdraw, his teeth trapped her plump lower lip and nipped it slightly.

'Maybe we could,' he agreed, with a husky catch in

his voice that sounded like smoke and whisky. 'But right now I should get out of these wet clothes and dry myself. I am expecting a visit from my secretary very soon, to drop off some mail and give me an update on things. It shouldn't take long, as I've told everyone I'm taking a break, but we will have to confer in private for a while. There is a pile of towels over there on the lounger, and a robe. Behind those trees—can you see that low white roof?—is a changing facility for guests. You should be able to find everything you need in there, including a shower and hairdryer. When you're ready go and sit out on the patio outside the drawing room and Inês will get you a drink. Whatever happens we will have an enjoyable evening together, I promise.'

Turning away and swimming back to the edge of the pool, he hauled himself out, padded across to the lounger in his sopping wet clothes and, without so much as a backward glance at Grace, still treading water, stripped off in front of her without a care. He dried himself roughly with one of the towels, wound it round his lean, hard middle, then strolled back across the grass to the archway that led outside the garden to the back of the house.

Knowing the arresting sight of his bronzed and toned naked body was likely going to be imprinted on her memory *for ever,* and remembering the hotly carnal sensation of his mouth suckling at her breast, Grace released a long, stunned breath and then swam slowly across to the other end of the pool.

Dressed once again in the red and white maxi, she dried her hair and re-did her light make-up. By the time she started to walk barefoot back across the white marble flagstones surrounding the pool the sun was setting. I was a given that she had to stop to view one of the world' most breathtaking displays of natural beauty—especially when the dazzling globe so dramatically dominated the horizon, its siena rays bleeding hauntingly into the darkening blue sky. She felt a near-overwhelming desire for Marco to be standing beside her, so that they might enjoy the sight together, and there was a strange emptiness inside Grace because he wasn't.

After a time she walked on, idly wondering what his secretary was like and hoping that she wouldn't deprive Grace of his company for long.

She was heading down the long marbled corridor to the drawing room when she heard Inês open the front doors to invite Marco's visitor inside. It surprised her to hear an English accent. The woman who spoke to the housekeeper greeted her with affection and pleasure in her tone. Her voice sounded cultured and kind, and the little knot of anxiety at the pit of Grace's stomach blessedly unravelled. After sitting amongst the snobbish guests at Francesca Bellini's garden party it was nice to know that Marco's secretary was not cut from the same superior and condescending cloth.

Curious to put a face to the lovely voice, she slowly retraced her steps to the other end of the corridor and, rounding it, stole a peek at the attractive middle-aged woman with dark blonde wavy hair cut flatteringly just above her shoulders. Dressed in a smart but understated dove-grey linen suit, she carried a slim dark brown briefcase down by her side, and although she was clearly having a meeting with Marco she might have just as easily been meeting friends for coffee or dinner, such was her relaxed and amiable yet undoubtedly elegant stance.

She was still smiling and talking to Inês when she registered Grace's presence. Her initial look of surprise turned to another pleased smile as she skirted round the housekeeper to walk towards her. She held out her hand. 'You must be Grace. I've been so looking forward to meeting you. I'm Martine—Marco's secretary.'

Her warm clasp was just as friendly as her manner, and Grace gave her an unreserved smile back. 'It's nice to meet you, Martine. Have you had to travel very far to get here?'

She laughed, 'Good heavens, no! I'm staying at one of my boss's hotels just up the road. Wherever he is in the world Marco likes to have me nearby. The man is constantly working, and invariably so am I. But now that he's told me he's actually taking a short holiday, after our meeting I'll have a few days off to take a break myself. I'm going to pop back to London, to my little house I very rarely get to see, and I can't tell you how much I'm looking forward to it!'

'I'm from London too,' Grace volunteered.

'I know. Marco told me. He also tells me that you've been out to Africa to help take care of orphaned children?'

'That's right. I work for a charity that's dedicated specifically to that cause.'

'I'm in admiration of you doing that, Grace. There's not many beautiful young women like you who would choose such a worthy but distinctly unglamorous career… which is a great shame, in my opinion.'

'It wasn't a hard choice, believe me. The unconditional love that those children radiate—even in the worst of circumstances—makes it easy.'

'Well, now that I've met you I can see why Marco has decided to take a holiday at last. I owe you a big thank you for that. You know he almost *never* takes a break?'

Grace was still smiling at the other woman when the pair of twin doors to the side of the vast reception area opened and Marco appeared. She didn't miss the quiz-zical little frown that creased his brow when he saw that she was chatting with his secretary.

'Martine. I didn't know that you'd arrived. How are you? Do you have everything that you need at the hotel? They're looking after you?'

'Hello, Marco. I'm fine, thank you. And although they shouldn't the staff at the hotel are waiting on me hand, foot and finger. I couldn't want for anything. I've just been introducing myself to your lovely friend.'

He only spared her the briefest glance in acknowledge-ment, but for Grace it was like being touched by living electricity and she tingled all the way down to the edges of her toes.

'Good,' he replied perfunctorily, pushing one of the twin doors opened a little wider. 'Why don't you come into my study and make yourself comfortable? Inês, can you please bring us some coffee?'

'Of course, *senhor.*'

As the housekeeper turned to go about her duties, and Martine bade goodbye to Grace and went through to the study, Marco immediately came over to join her. It hit Grace just then that he looked much more like the quint-essential movie star than Lincoln Roberts could ever as-pire to look. With his bronzed skin, sexy dark eyes and fitted black shirt and jeans, he exuded an effortless and brooding sexuality that made Grace's stomach clench and her legs go weak.

'You found everything that you needed poolside?' he asked, his cool fingers gently tilting her chin towards him.

'The changing room couldn't have been better fitted out than a suite at the Ritz! Not that I've ever *been* to the Ritz,' she added quickly.

Marco chuckled. 'One day I will take you to stay there, if you like?'

'I wasn't suggesting that I wanted to—'

'I know you weren't. But just indulge the fantasy that I might take you there one day, hmm?'

'I'd better let you get to your meeting with Martine. She seems like a very nice woman, by the way.'

'She is. She's also very efficient and intuitive when it comes to what I need at work. I told you—I only ever employ the very best people.' He deliberately let his gaze fall into Grace's eyes.

Transfixed, she stared back at him, more than a little excited that soon they would be alone together, with no one to think of or to please but themselves.

Marco lowered his voice. 'Wait for me out on the patio. This shouldn't take very long.'

As Grace returned to the elegant drawing room and walked out onto the patio she couldn't help praying and hoping that it really *wouldn't* be too long before Marco was able to join her. She was more at ease now that she had met the very warm and down-to-earth Martine, and she had been quietly gratified when she'd told her that her boss rarely took a break from work—her observation definitely suggesting that he was taking one now because of Grace's influence.

She breathed in the sultry evening air and breathed out again, jettisoning any further worries and concerns that might prey on her peace of mind to concentrate instead on enjoying the last few minutes of the spectacular sunset...

Soft lighting dotted at various strategic points round the patio automatically illuminated the area as the sun went down, and at the same time made the quarter-moon that hung in the sky seem magically brighter. The slightly chill caress of a passing breeze made her shiver. The air was no longer quite so sultry. Grace wished that she'd brought a wrap or a stole to drape round her shoulders. But that morning—along with the straw hat that she'd left behind—it had been the furthest thing from her mind.

Rising from her chair, she glanced over at the still open French doors leading back into the drawing room. A sudden doubt seized her. *What was she doing?* She really ought to be thinking about going home. Marco might be ages yet. What if after his meeting with Martine *work* dominated his mind? Maybe so much so that he wouldn't want to spend the evening relaxing with Grace?

Recalling the look in his eyes when he'd told her that his meeting wouldn't take long, and realising that she was probably being ridiculous, she breathed out a slightly more reassured breath and resolved to think about something else. But her mind seemed intent on revisiting the subject of Marco working too hard and rarely taking a break.

She was acutely aware that she was feeling unusually protective of a man whom the world undoubtedly viewed as incredibly fortunate and privileged, who surely didn't have the same ordinary wants and needs of most humans—such as the need to slow down sometimes and take stock, or the desire for a loving relationship, supportive family and friends and children of his own? From time to time, when he'd unwittingly let down his guard a little and referred to his orphaned upbringing, Grace had glimpsed both hurt and loneliness in Marco's eyes and it had made her insides knot in sympathy...

'*Senhorita?*'

Inês stood in the doorway between the drawing room and the patio, a polite but warm smile on her broad open face. 'Senhor Aguilar asked me to tell you that he will not be much longer now. He also asked me to prepare you some refreshments while you are waiting for him. I have served them in the courtyard garden. Can you come with me, please?'

With little notion of the delights awaiting her, Grace was happy to follow the friendly housekeeper down the long marbled corridor then through an airy vestibule that lead out onto a stunning sunken courtyard filled with lemon trees. In a private corner of the enchanting area a small wrought-iron table was laid with an array of appetising snacks, plus a beautiful crystal decanter of red wine accompanied by two matching glasses. The gently atmospheric lighting was provided by several pretty lanterns with candles flickering inside them. There was no evidence of a breeze here at all. Instead the air was sultry and still again, and the only sound to break the silence was the repetitive shrill of cicadas that Grace was becoming more and more accustomed to.

She turned to regard Inês smilingly. 'This is wonderful. *Obrigado*… Thank you…thank you so much.'

The other woman beamed. 'Enjoy,' she said, then left her alone.

It wasn't the same eating alone…it wasn't the same at all. Although she'd made a valiant attempt at eating some of the delicious food, Grace realised it was almost impossible for her to enjoy it when her insides were seized with nervous tension because Marco was taking so long. Time seemed to pass agonisingly slowly, and when he still didn't appear the tension inside her turned into full-blown anxiety that something must be wrong.

Had Martine perhaps brought bad news?

She had just decided she could no longer sit still and wait—she would go in search of her host herself to make sure nothing was amiss—when he appeared in the arche doorway. Its elegant stucco designs were just about visible beneath the heavy fall of red bougainvillaea that draped over it.

In the instant that she registered his arrival Grace detected a certain weariness and strain in his demeanour that made her heart race with concern. Before she knew it, she'd rushed towards him to clasp his hand. The hooded dark eyes that were so incredibly compelling flashed in surprise. When surprise turned to indisputable pleasure her heart raced not with concern but for a very different reason indeed.

He didn't loosen her hand, or berate her for being so presumptuous, as had been her fear. In fact, he used it as leverage to impel her towards him. The sheer unadulterated joy of being near him again, of scenting his provocative cologne and feeling the heat that radiated from his body, went way *beyond* simple pleasure. The contact that she'd been longing for far exceeded all her imaginative secret hopes.

'Is everything okay? I was worried,' she admitted softly.

'Worried…about me?' Marco's deep rich voice bordered on being amazed. 'Why?'

'I was worried in case Martine had brought you some bad news, or—or that you had to get back to work for some reason and I wouldn't see you tonight after all. I'd have been seriously upset about that, because it's becoming more and more obvious that you work too hard and clearly need some time off.'

Disconcertingly, he chuckled. 'I've had no bad news, and neither do I need to get back to work. Is that why you've suddenly appeared in my life, Grace? To make sure that I don't overdo things and work too hard?'

'I'm sorry if I sometimes speak my mind a bit too much.'

'Never apologise for being honest—trust me, it is far better than being lied to. Now, you can tell me the truth about something else… You told me that you were exhausted when you came back from Africa, and this morning you overslept. Are you feeling any better now? If you need to see a doctor I can arrange it…even tonight, if need be?'

'I'm honestly fine. I definitely don't need to see a doctor. But thanks for being so kind and asking.'

'Well, seeing as we are both absolutely fine, I think we can now relax and enjoy our evening together, no?' He lifted a dark eyebrow. 'Do you know, I can't remember the last time anyone worried about me?'

The shrug of his broad shoulders when he said that was almost matter-of-fact…but the expression Grace saw in his eyes was anything *but*. That was the moment when she knew she couldn't—*wouldn't*—deny him anything.

'Well, then.' Gently tugging her hand free, hardly knowing what possessed her, she boldly traced the outline of his fascinating lips with her fingertips. 'If that's the case, then your friends can't know what a special man they have in their lives.'

'If you persist in saying such things to me…and touching me like that…then my promise to you to be patient will make a liar of me—because I won't be able to keep it,' he confessed, gravel-voiced.

'Then don't.' She knew her transfixed stare devoured him, because her need to have him hold her right then *to make love to her*, was so intense that Grace couldn't begin to curtail it. It was akin to a swollen river about to burst its banks.

'What?'

'Don't keep your promise. I no longer want you to. Be patient, I mean. Remember I asked you in the pool if we could try again later?' she breathed in a velvet-voiced whisper.

He muttered something that sounded like the kind of curse a man might make when he'd been tested to the extremes of his endurance, and the ensuing kiss that claimed her lips was so hot, hard and hungry that Grace knew she didn't have a hope of holding onto her balance. But at that moment she didn't even *care*. Neither did she mind that the passionate caress was completely devoid of tenderness or finesse, because she knew it was driven by an elemental power strong enough and raw enough to knock her right off of her feet.

As a woman who had never experienced being desired with such hungry intent before, and who had never wanted a man more, in the most carnal way, she found Marco's attentions more welcome than stunning cool rain on a baking hot desert that hadn't seen the like for months. With no guilt whatsoever, she allowed herself to luxuriate freely in them, feeling nothing but gratitude…

The rough scrape of the chiselled jaw that was already displaying a five o'clock shadow and the scalding sensual demand of his lips and tongue stoked such a fire in her that in the future, when this incredible hiatus with him came to an end, she knew she would be deaf, dumb and blind to the attractions of any other man.

Breathing hard as he tore his mouth away from hers, Marco lifted his head so that he could study her. At the same time, his hands tightened possessively round her hips. 'Are you telling me that you will let me take you to bed?'

'You mean…right now?' Grace knew her question inflamed him, because she saw the molten heat that was already in his eyes flare passionately, like a fire that had just been doused in petrol.

'*Querido Deus!* Yes, *now*…before this constant craving for you drives me completely out of my mind.'

Firming his arm possessively round her waist, he urgently guided her out of the arched courtyard like a man indisputably on a mission…

CHAPTER EIGHT

WITH his heart beating a throbbing tattoo inside his chest, Marco held onto Grace's small slender hand and led her into his vast bedroom. The twin glass doors onto the wrought-iron balcony were open and a scented breeze blew in from the gardens below, making the cream-coloured voile drapes dance.

The heat that his body was gripped by hadn't cooled in any way, but Marco couldn't help remembering his vow to seduce Grace 'subtly and artfully' and not rush her. Especially when she had confided in him that her despicable ex-boyfriend had assaulted her. But the moment she turned her big blue eyes on him, and he saw her pretty, full upper lip quiver gently, every thought in his head disappeared except the one that urged him to love her long into the night…

'Won't Inês wonder where we've gone?' she asked. 'We just abandoned all the lovely food she'd prepared and came up here.'

'My housekeeper has four children…she's a woman of the world. I don't think she will wonder for very long about where we've gone, Grace.'

'Oh.'

'All I care about is that we are alone at last. We can

forget about the rest of the world for a while and just concentrate on ourselves…agreed?'

'Yes…all right.'

She visibly shivered as Marco calmly started to undo
the buttons on her red and white bodice. But if he gave
the impression of being calm and in control then he definitely *wasn't*. It took every ounce of will he possessed to
control the trembling in his fingers as he finished unfas-
tening the buttons on her dress and helped her to step out
of it. The prim swimsuit she'd worn in the pool had done
its best to disguise the allure of her shapely form—and
he had to say it had failed—but the lacy pink strapless
bra that she wore now, along with matching cotton panties, *didn't*. The word *exquisite*, used to describe a beautiful woman, was sometimes overused in his book…but
he had no argument with the description in the present
case. Grace's body was slender and supple, but her figure
also curved in and out like an hourglass, and her beautiful skin was flawlessly pale and smooth and instantly
invited his touch.

Skimming his fingertips below her breastbone and
down to her sexy little bellybutton, he held her wide-eyed
gaze with a slow, teasing smile. 'I was right,' he said.

'Right about what, exactly?'

'That underneath that not-so-effective disguise of an
"ordinary" girl that you frequently like to insist you are
there resides the bewitching body of a very hot temptress indeed.'

Blushing helplessly, she knew her glance was ador-
ably shy as she observed him. 'I don't think so.'

'Yes, I think so,' he insisted, chuckling softly. 'But
as alluring as your pretty underwear undoubtedly is, I'm
afraid I'm going to have to divest you of it if I want to
accomplish what I have in mind right now.'

'And that is…?'

'To make love to you all through the night.'

The edges of her straight white teeth clamped nervously down onto her vulnerable lower lip. Glancing over at the emperor-sized bed with its oyster silk bedlinen and luxurious pillows and cushions, her soft cheeks bloomed again with the delicate pink of a summer rose. 'That bed seems an awfully long way away,' she commented, a distinct catch in her voice.

'Not if I carry you there.'

There was something deliciously wicked and decadent about being transported across such a palatial room to an equally opulent bed covered in the finest silk by her handsome would-be lover. Indeed, Grace could have been forgiven for thinking she was dreaming the whole thing—except that the experience was light years away from any seduction her imagination could have contrived, even in the throes of the most erotic dream.

By the time Marco had lain her carefully down on the bed, kicked off his shoes and stripped down to his black silk boxers, she was shivering so hard with longing, anticipation and not a little apprehension that all she could do was stare mutely up at him. In her mind she silently paid homage to his beauty—the strong, clean lines of his hard-muscled shoulders and torso, the slim masculine hips and silkily hirsute powerful thighs—then automatically returned her gaze to his compelling, strong-boned visage to linger on his mouth…a mouth that could so easily have been sculpted by an Italian Renaissance artist it was so sublime. Lifting her glance higher, she fell into the seductive beam of depthless dark eyes that she already knew could make her dissolve with barely any effort at all.

'I want you to sit up and kiss me,' he told her, the usually resonant voice pitched a little lower because it was infused with desire.

Mesmerised, caught up in a hypnotic spell she knew she would never forget after this night, Grace did as he asked. Marco immediately circled her chest to unhook the fastening at the back of her flimsy lace bra. As soon as her breasts were freed, and she experienced the gossamer caress of warm air glancing against her skin, he claimed her lips in another long, melting kiss. After the initial urgent clash of teeth and tongues, the sensual quality of their mutual exploration of each other was akin to being bathed in moonlight and honey. As she lay down against the luxurious covers of the bed Grace knew it was a tantalising gateway to what was to follow.

When Marco planted his strong thighs either side of her, then bent his head once more to kiss and suckle her breasts, her body was seized by another bout of irresistible shivering.

'This is not your first time...is it?' Immediately he raised his head to examine her, his glance both searching and concerned.

Moistening her lips with her tongue, Grace nervously held his gaze. 'No. But I've only been with a man once before...when I lost my virginity.'

The unhappy memory of the occasion made her tense briefly. It had only happened because her university boyfriend had pressured her and the following day he told her he regretted it because there was another girl he liked more, and their fledgling relationship had come to an abrupt and *humiliating* end. So far, her experience of intimacy had not been great. But until now no other man she'd ever met had stirred the kind of powerful feelings inside her that Marco did. Instinctively she knew that making love with him would be wonderful... *more* than wonderful.

Making no comment, but with a provocative half-smile playing about his lips, he moved his hands down to her hips to remove the rest of her lacy underwear. Sucking in her breath, Grace held onto his toned bronzed biceps as he went about the sensuous task, her body trembling even more. He touched his mouth to the flat plane of her stomach, and her hands automatically fell away as he planted light but explosive little kisses all over its surface. When his lips moved lower down, and he began to kiss the delicate sensitive skin covering her slender inner thighs, she turned her head to the silk pillow behind her, closed her eyes, and willingly allowed the tide of heat that was building unstoppably inside to hold sway, fervently wishing that it might go on for ever...

As if intuiting her need, Marco let his hot silken tongue explore her more intimately, and suddenly the ability to think at all was replaced by a profound willingness to surrender, to allow this intoxicating pleasure to take her wherever it would. Grace no longer tried to still the trembling that grew more and more prevalent with every seductive volcanic touch that Marco delivered. It was a natural reaction, she realised, simply part of the erotic interplay between them. And suddenly the building storm of sensation inside her became molten lightning, an electrical conflagration bar none that had her totally at its mercy. Once again, all she could do was surrender. At the peak of the waves that flowed through her she cried out, then lay dazed and shivering as the torrid heat slowly started to ebb.

Marco's hypnotic voice murmured something that she didn't quite hear, and her eyes flew opened as she sensed his body moving over hers. She saw that he too was naked now. Her heart began to thump hard. His eyes crinkled at the corners as he bestowed a sexy smile down upon her.

She reached out to touch her palm to his beard-roughened jaw and he turned his mouth towards it and kissed her there. 'That was amazing,' she told him softly.

'It was amazing for me too. I fear I am becoming addicted to you, Grace… To your scent and to your touch. No matter how much you give me…I'm afraid I just want more.'

Sensing the tension in his body as he held himself above her, Grace instinctively raised her legs so that they clasped his slim, arrow-straight hips in a sensual vice. As she registered the uninhibited look of gratification on his face another ecstatic moan was punched from her lungs, and he plunged himself deep inside her. He stilled for a long moment, so that they both received the maximum enjoyment from the contact, their gazes meeting and locking in mutual wonderment as they did so. When Marco started to rock back and forth inside her she hungrily sought his lips, kissing him with the kind of passion and ardour that she'd never even guessed she might be capable of. Her own eager responses were a revelation to her.

And now, as her lover moved with even more ardour and intent inside her, the place the hard, scalding pleasure of his possession was taking her to started to imitate the electrical storm she'd succumbed to earlier, and she found herself tumbling into it without restraint, the ecstatic sensations that gripped her growing more and more wildly urgent. She buried her face in the warm sanctuary between Marco's neck and shoulder as she flew free. At the same time tears flowed into her eyes and spilled over down her cheeks. Just before he thrust even deeper he wound his fingers through her hair, pulled back her head and kissed her hard. Then, with a helpless guttural groan, he too flew free...

The pounding wasn't just inside his heart but in his head too, Marco acknowledged in alarm as he rolled onto his side, breathing hard. The shocking realisation of what he'd just done hit him like a hammer-blow. *Had he somehow lost his mind?* Dear God! He'd just made love to Grace without even the merest thought of protecting her. He'd been so caught up in the maelstrom of need and desire that had deluged him he'd simply lost the ability to think straight. It just hadn't been possible.

'Marco? Are you all right?'

He turned to regard the matchless blue eyes that were considering him so concernedly. A rueful smile hijacked his lips as he cupped her small delicately made jaw. 'Yes, I'm all right—although after what I've just experienced that may well be the understatement of the year. But I also have to confess to being somewhat stunned by my recklessness. I should have used protection, but I got so swept away by you...by what was happening between us...that I didn't. I hardly know what to say, Grace, except to tell you that I'm genuinely sorry.'

'I'm equally to blame. I got just as carried away as you, Marco. If anything happens as a result of this I want to reassure you that I won't take you to court to get your money...well...at least not *all* of your money.'

This was said in such a matter-of-fact tone that it took Marco a couple of seconds to realise that she was shamelessly teasing him. For a sickening moment the soul-destroying belief that had hounded most of his existence—that people only befriended him for what they could get out of him—had disturbingly revisited him. It didn't help his case right then to remember his ex-girlfriend's misguided and heartless attempt to try and fleece him to help fund her expensive drug habit.

'Don't even *joke* about that,' he growled. 'In all seriousness…if you *were* to fall pregnant with my child then of course you could rely on me to help you in any way that I can. You certainly wouldn't have to resort to taking me to court for child support! But from now on I will definitely be more careful when we make love.'

Grace was silent, propping herself up on her elbows to study him. Any sign of humour had utterly vanished, he saw. In fact, her expression was almost grave.

'I'm not taking the possibility of falling pregnant, lightly Marco. I'm well aware that it's a life-changing thing, as well as a huge responsibility…to raise a child, I mean. It impacts on a woman's life like nothing else. But we've done what we've done and now we'll just have to wait and see. Can't we just enjoy what we have right now, or is that too selfish? We both work hard…we're both responsible people—don't you think we deserve to relax and not worry? We've agreed that we'll share this one holiday together then return to our own lives. From your reaction to my little joke I'm guessing that you've probably been deceived by women before, but you've nothing like that to fear from me. I'm a very up-front kind of girl, Marco. What you see is what you get. Whilst I'll always be more than grateful that you've agreed to help the children's charity, I don't want anything for myself other than your company…at least until the end of this holiday. After that I'll go back to London, return to my work and carry on as normal. I mean it. You won't even have to hear from me again if you don't want to.'

Icy fear hurtled through his veins. He caught hold of her slender-boned wrist with a sense of hard-to-suppress fury at the idea she would so easily turn her back on him and not have a single regret. 'And what if you *do* become pregnant?' he demanded. 'What then? Will you still insist on maintaining your distance from me?'

Pulling away from him, Grace rubbed her wrist with a wounded look in her eyes. Then she sighed and lay down on her side, resting her head against the silken pillows behind her. In the soft glow of the lamplight her fair hair tumbled like skeins of spun gold down over her bare shoulders. It was the only eye-catching adornment to her lovely nakedness, Marco reflected. He didn't doubt that he was a lucky man to see her like this...to be able to reach out his hand and touch that matchless skin whenever he chose...to hear her soft moans and cries when he made love to her again—which he fully intended to do, and *soon*.

'If it did turn out that I was pregnant, then of *course* I would let you know. But let me ask you something... Do you want to be a father, Marco?'

It was the hardest question he had ever been asked. His reaction to it sent a multitude of fears and hopes crashing through him. It was the hope that disturbed him the most. 'I have no experience of what it entails to be a father...no good example,' he admitted gravel-voiced. The weight of sorrow that suddenly lay on his chest was close to unbearable. Because he was so ill at ease and uncomfortable he batted the question back to Grace. 'What about you? Do you maybe harbour a secret desire to become a mother?'

Shrugging, she reached for a section of the silk eiderdown to pull up over her chest. 'One day, perhaps. But not yet...not while I'm still young and have the time and energy to help children who desperately need a home and a school to go to. Anyway...we're hypothesising about something that probably won't even happen.' As if she'd just thought of something more pressing, she turned her glance back to Marco. 'I know you were raised in an orphanage, but did you never see your father at all?'

Manoeuvring himself up into a sitting position, Marco deliberately averted his gaze from Grace's—even when she sat up next to him, dragging the silk covers with her. 'No. My father wasn't around and neither was my mother. She died giving birth to me, and my father couldn't handle taking care of me by himself, so he gave me away to an orphanage. Are you satisfied now that you've heard the whole sad and sorry story?'

'Oh, Marco.'

The compassion in her voice burst the dam of emotion he was intent on holding back...*had* been holding back for years. He turned his head to regard her furiously. 'Don't you *dare* feel sorry for me. If you do then I'll get Miguel to take you back to your villa right now and you will never see me again, I mean it! Do you understand?'

Mutely, she nodded.

Marco could hardly hear himself think beneath the drowning wave of rage and fear that crashed over him. He didn't want his past *or* his emotions put under the microscope by anybody...especially not Grace. The kindness in her eyes would likely tempt him to reveal things that would only end up making him feel bad. He might not have made peace with the events that had shaped him, but at least he'd kept their memory far enough at bay to get on with his life and become a success of sorts. *At least he wasn't dependent on anyone else to build his self-esteem.*

Just when he believed his emotions were returning to a more even keel, with her inimitable ability to speak her mind Grace stirred them up again.

'It's not that I feel sorry for you, you know. It just

grieves me that you might believe you're not deserving of sympathy or care. At least…that's the impression I get. You're such a good man, Marco. I can't believe—'

'I warned you, but you clearly didn't listen. Now you will have to go.'

He pushed his fingers furiously through his hair, his heart thumping. At the same time he wondered why he was being so reckless and self-destructive, depriving himself of the one good thing that had really started to matter to him. He'd done the same throughout his growing up in the orphanage. If anyone had tried to get close he'd pushed them away, fearing either that they didn't mean it or that he couldn't live up to any expectations they might have of him.

'What?'

'I said you will have to go. I warned you that I neither wanted nor welcomed your sympathy, but you had to persist, didn't you?'

'All right, then.'

Although her lovely blue eyes were silently assessing him, and no doubt reaching more unwanted conclusions about his vehement reaction, Grace was already throwing back the silk covers and moving towards the side of the bed. Dry-mouthed, Marco at last came to his senses and reached for her. Enfolding her from behind, he moved his hands over her bared breasts, kneading them, playing with the rigid velvet tips and pulling her urgently back against his chest. A river of volcanic heat stormed through his bloodstream and went straight to his loins. He had no recollection of ever being this hungry and mindlessly desirous for a woman before…he only knew that he needed her almost as much as he needed his next breath.

'I've changed my mind,' he breathed against the side

of her neck under the soft fall of her hair. 'I don't want you to go. It was stupid of me to say I did.'

She carefully disengaged his hands from her breasts and turned round to study him. Her smile was tender. 'I wouldn't have gone you know. I wouldn't have left you because I know you didn't really mean it. I would have just gone to look for Inês, asked her where the kitchen was, made a cup of tea and then sat out on the patio until you were ready to talk to me again.'

'Is that so?' He stared back at her in astonishment. Then he shook his head, leaned forward, and ravished her with a hotly exploring open-mouthed kiss. When her arms feverishly encircled his waist and she pressed herself so close to him that she felt like a part of him he'd never even known he'd lost he broke off the caress to gaze searchingly into her eyes. 'You are either very stubborn, Grace, or unbelievably daring that you would risk my fury in that way. Do you know I've heard that even some of my board members quake in their boots at the thought I might lose my temper if they displease me in some way?'

'You can't believe it's a *good* thing to intimidate people like that...surely?'

'*You* were not intimidated.'

'Yes, but I'm as stubborn as a mule...so my dad often tells me. Even if I'm terrified of something I somehow can't let it get the better of me. Except when my boyfriend attacked me,' she added thoughtfully. 'Afterwards, I let my fear of it happening again stop me from getting close to anyone...I regret that. But I'll never let fear have such a hold on me again.'

In all his years of doing business Marco had never met her equal, he mused in wonder. It was rare indeed that anyone stood up to him or was so frank in confessing their reflections. Grace wasn't just brave, she was inspirational too.

Quickly, his musings turned to much more urgent and seductive reflections as he saw the sexy evidence of his passionate exploration on her moist slightly swollen lips. 'I think we have done enough talking for now, don't you? We can resume this very interesting conversation later.'

'If you say so.'

She gave him the kind of cheekily provocative grin that came close to making him vocalise his need for her in the most basic and unequivocal terms available to him in language. Instead, he tipped her back onto the bed and demonstrated his need in a much more physical and satisfying way for them both...

It was rare that he stayed in bed all through the night with a woman and didn't get up early, to work or distance himself in some way. Telling himself that it was because he was on vacation, but knowing it was more, *much* more than that, Marco turned onto his side to view his still-sleeping lover. The oyster silk cover had slipped from her body and he silently studied the naked, very feminine curves of hip and supple thigh. Immediately the waves of strong desire that seemed to be a permanent occurrence whenever he was near Grace flowed forcefully through him again.

Drawing the cover up gently over her bared satin shoulder, he realised he couldn't seem to get enough of both her company *and* her body. When once again the thought struck him that he might have made her pregnant, he sensed a shockingly uncharacteristic surge of hope sweep into his heart. He had no family. *In his will he had left most of his considerable fortune to charity.* Not once in his romantic history had he ever considered marrying and starting a family of his own. But then he had never really been in love or cared for a woman enough to contemplate it.

Examining the face that was just as lovely in repose as when she was awake, Marco felt a definite quickening inside his chest. If he and Grace *did* make a child together, what would the infant be like? he wondered. He was suddenly fascinated by the idea. He was so dark—and she, being fair and blue-eyed, was his polar opposite. Smiling to himself, he lifted the silk coverlet again to contemplate her smooth flat abdomen. Mesmerised, he grazed his fingertips over the area just below her belly-button. Grace stirred and opened her eyes. It was like looking into the most sublime sunlit blue lake.

'What are you doing?' Her soft voice was sleepily husky.

Marco let the cover drop back down over her body. 'I was simply looking at you and marvelling at how beautiful you are.'

'Flattery will get you everywhere.'

'That's exactly what I hoped you say.'

'Except that I have a sudden urge to go for a swim... may I?'

Marco tugged down the covers he had just let fall back into place and employed the most seductive smile he could muster. 'After we have made love,' he told her.

Colouring a little, nonetheless Grace made no attempt to cover herself again. 'It's a good job that you're so fit, because you really are insatiable,' she murmured, even as her slender arms wound firmly round his neck.

CHAPTER NINE

WITH unashamed charm, Marco had persuaded Grace to allow him to take her shopping. Her agreement had only come about when she'd realised that all she had to wear was the dress she'd worn yesterday because she hadn't expected to be spending the night with him.

Just the thought of how ardently they had made love made her heart race anew, and all the places on her body where he had visited his amorous attentions throbbed and tingled at the memory. The deliciously disturbing sensations were heightened by the realisation that her feelings for this man went far beyond merely enjoying his company. At every turn he mesmerised and seduced her... just by virtue of being himself. Grace loved the sound of his accented voice...the extravagant way he gestured with his hands when explaining something...the flash of an unguarded smile that was more potent even than bright sunlight illuminating a cloudy day...

When she'd suggested that she return to her own villa for some fresh clothing, Marco had caught her by the waist and silenced her reasoning with a long, lingering kiss that had made any inclination to do anything else but be with him inexorably vanish. After that he'd directed her to a luxurious wet room, so that she could take a shower, while he made some arrangements for their shopping trip. Grace had quickly learned that there were always arrangements to be made whenever he ventured out—simply because he was so well known. She'd also intuited that public interest in his activities gave him little pleasure. It was simply a have-to-deal-with by-product of his phenomenal success.

Shortly after his own shower, Marco changed into fresh military-style chinos and another loose white shirt and appeared on the patio, where she was waiting for him.

With his dark hair gleaming, he was looking fresh-faced, unbelievably handsome and somehow endearingly boyish too. Whenever she recalled him angrily asking her if she was satisfied now that he'd told her the full 'sad and sorry' story of his upbringing, she sensed the shame he clearly still felt. She wanted to tell him that it was hardly *his* fault that his grieving father had left him there—that he deserved nothing but admiration for being able to transcend his challenging and tragic start in life to become the incredible success he was now. There should be no hint of shame whatsoever…he was an *inspiration*, Grace wanted to say.

The only problem was that their relationship wasn't yet on the kind of footing where she could demonstrate her understanding and compassion towards him without risking being angrily rebuffed. Having already experienced how swiftly Marco's defences had slammed into place when she'd been about to express her concern for what he'd endured, she knew she had to rein in her natural instinct to try and get him to talk about it more…at least until he was sure she wasn't going to betray him in any way.

'I see Inês has made you coffee?' he observed, smiling

'Your housekeeper is a godsend. You're very lucky to have her.'

'You think I don't know that?'

'I don't doubt that you know it. You're probably extremely appreciative of every person who works for you, if the truth be known. Likewise, they must be very appreciative of you,' she added brightly.

Frowning thoughtfully, Marco pulled out the chair opposite her at the table. For a long moment he silently surveyed the stunning vista spread out before them. Already a shimmering haze of heat hung over it. 'Don't be in such a hurry to elevate me to Employer of the Year,' he advised, helping himself to some coffee. 'I am not always so popular...particularly when it falls to me to make some of the tougher decisions. For instance when I have to let people go.'

'I expect that comes with the territory. In your position you're always looking at the bigger picture, aren't you? What's cost-effective and what's not etc. Did you always want to be a businessman?' Relaxing back into her chair, Grace offered Marco the little dish of sugar crystals, but with a slight shake of his head he declined it. She stirred another couple of crystals into her own beverage, grinning unrepentantly when he lifted an eyebrow.

'I see that you have a sweet tooth, Grace?'

'It's only a small vice. Anyway...you haven't answered my question.'

'My answer is no...I didn't always want to be a businessman. I started out just wanting to play golf and to become good at it. There was a course not far from the orphanage...'

He winced—*but at least he wasn't avoiding mentioning it*, Grace thought. She almost held her breath at what she couldn't help but see as a breakthrough.

'When I turned fifteen,' he continued, 'I got a job here, collecting all the stray golf balls. One of the members befriended me. He asked me to be his caddy. He also started to teach me how to play. After a while, I did indeed become good at the game.'

'But you didn't want to take it up as a career?'

His dark eyes silently assessed her before he replied, as if he was not quite sure she was being serious. 'You have never looked up my name on the internet and read my bio?'

Slightly bewildered, Grace swallowed hard. 'No, I haven't. Should I have?'

'I was what they call a scratch golfer...good enough to turn professional. I did indeed have a very successful career in the game for a few years, and won several trophies. But then I started to see that the men and women who owned the prestigious courses we played on made even more money than the professional players. That was when I decided on a change of career, and became the businessman and property developer that I am today.'

'And there are no regrets about leaving your golfing career behind? I mean, do you equally enjoy what you do now?'

He smiled. 'I do. Especially when it brings me into unexpected contact with a smart, stubborn, pretty woman like you, Grace...a woman who will risk everything— even being detained by my security guards—to help further a cause she believes in.'

She was still reeling from his admiring words when Marco strode round the table and urged her to her feet.

'Mmm, you smell nice,' she told him, even as her heart leapt at his nearness.

'You always say what you're thinking, don't you?' he remarked, looking amused.

'Do you think that's a bad trait?'

'I'm not saying that at all. But I can see how it could get you into trouble.'

Grace frowned. 'I know… But I never say anything horrible or harsh to offend anyone.'

'I believe you. You are far too well-meaning and kind for that.' He tweaked her earlobe, then brushed her lips with a brief kiss. 'But what if I were to adopt the same approach? What if I told you exactly what *I* was thinking right now, hmm?'

Her legs turned as weak as a kitten's at the lascivious look in his eyes. As much as it thrilled her to have him want her so, Grace definitely sensed a need to put a little breathing space before the answering leap of desire that he inevitably ignited. Right now events seemed to be gathering speed with dizzying effect, and it would surely be wise to take some time out to reflect upon where they might be leading her. *She had a powerful notion that they were going to lead to the breaking of her heart.*

The thought of not seeing Marco again when the time came for them to part was frighteningly distressing—but he was a rich and influential man who had brief flings like this with women all the time. Now Grace's stomach really *did* plummet. She hated the idea of him making love to any other woman but *her*. When she'd seen the stylish and picture-perfect Francesca Bellini it had been hard not to feel a little insecure. She might have fooled herself that she would take a 'wait and see' approach to the possibility that Marco might have made her pregnant, but in truth her feelings were not remotely so *laissez-faire*.

What would she do if she *was* carrying his baby? An answering frisson of excitement arrowed through her but, telling herself to get a grip, she quickly poured cold water on the feeling. Yes, she loved children, but she hadn't planned on becoming a mother herself until she was in a stable and loving relationship. Besides…men like Marco Aguilar didn't fall in love with girls like Grace, so the sooner she disabused herself of *that* ridiculous little notion, the better.

Anyway…her thoughts ran on…there was still so much she wanted to accomplish in her work with the charity. She definitely wanted to return to the African village to visit the wonderful children she'd befriended and see the new orphanage finally standing proud…maybe even a school too? The next time she visited she might even extend her stay and help teach some basic reading and writing skills herself.

Touching her palm to the side of Marco's clean-shaven face, she made her smile as nonchalant as she could. 'I trust what you're thinking is *We really should go shopping now, or else Grace will look slightly the worse for wear in the crumpled dress she's wearing for the second day running?*' she quipped.

Gathering her hand, Marco pressed his lips warmly into the centre of her palm. 'I confess my thoughts are more along the lines of *I really want to strip off that pretty dress of hers and take her back to bed.* Are you surprised?'

'Flattered, maybe…but not surprised, no.' With an apologetic shrug, she quickly stepped out of the circle of his arms. 'But I really would like to get some fresh clothes on soon. We don't have to go shopping. In fact it would be much easier if Miguel just drops me back at the villa and I choose something from my own wardrobe.'

'Uh-uh. You don't get out of it that easily. I want to show you Vilamoura Marina. There are plenty of very nice clothes shops there for you to browse in, as well as a good selection of restaurants and bars we can choose from when we're ready to have lunch. So come…we'll go and find Miguel and enjoy a leisurely drive there.'

Marco had never known a woman so reluctant to shop. Grace had already told him that shopping was never going to be on her list of priorities, but he'd hoped that when she learned money was no object and he would gladly buy her anything she wanted she would change her mind. That wasn't the case. She made some polite comments here and there regarding the clothes or jewellery that he steered her towards, in the hope of getting an interested response, but on the whole seemed singularly unimpressed. His frustration grew—would she allow him to buy her anything at all?

Then, half an hour into their tour of the stunning marina, with its plethora of expensive yachts lining the harbour and exclusive boutiques, he noticed that they'd acquired the inevitable entourage—consisting of inquisitive sightseers plus a good few of the locals who had recognised him. His sense of protectiveness towards Grace strengthened even more. When she too realised they were being followed he sensed her uneasiness, and Marco knew her mind was far away from the meant-to-be enjoyable task of choosing a new dress.

Feeling increasingly irritated, he firmly held onto his companion's small hand as they stopped in front of one of the most reputable and expensive boutiques on the marina. Glancing round to face the small knot of locals and holidaymakers that trailed them, he sighed and said, 'Come on, guys. I'm trying to enjoy a rare day off, here. Don't you enjoy doing the same with your families and friends? Leave us in peace and go about your business. I promise you there are far more interesting sights to see on the marina than me trying to impress my beautiful companion.'

An agreeable cheer went up, followed by a couple of risqué comments made by two young men at the back.

'Is she your new girlfriend, Marco? We all thought your preference was for brunettes.' This even bolder remark emanated from a lanky Australian in Hawaiian-style shorts and a baggy yellow T-shirt, who had positioned himself at the front of the onlookers. As he spoke, he was busily snapping shot after shot of Marco and Grace with a professional-looking camera.

Recognising the man as a regular member of the paparazzi that showed up at various functions and events he attended, Marco drew in a deep breath. 'I think you've taken enough pictures, and I'd like you to stop. As far as my preference about anything goes, the truth is that you don't know me well enough to have an opinion.'

He'd stupidly kidded himself that he could get away with just strolling round the marina with Grace and nothing untoward would bother them. He'd even given his bodyguard José strict instructions to wait by the car and not follow them. Today he'd just wanted to be like any other man holidaying with his wife or girlfriend. It seemed the perhaps *foolish* hope he'd secretly nurtured was to be denied.

Glancing at Grace, he pulled her firmly into his side.

'We don't have to do this today,' she murmured, her cornflower-blue eyes utterly bewitching as she glanced up at him from beneath sweeping fair lashes. 'We can shop another day.'

'No!' he snapped. 'That is *not* what I want. What I want is to buy you a dress, and I want to do it today. Come with me.'

He herded her ahead of him through the shop's glitzy

glass and gold entrance and when the pencil-slim brunette with silver flashes in her hair standing behind the marble kidney-shaped counter, came over straight away to attend them Marco didn't waste time with preliminaries. The woman had immediately recognised him, he saw, and that was all to the good.

'Close the shop,' he briskly instructed her in Portuguese, nodding towards the small knot of onlookers with their cameras that stood outside—still determinedly taking pictures despite his plea. 'As you can see, *senhora*, I have an unwanted entourage. Don't worry—if you close the shop I will compensate you for any loss of custom.'

'It will be my pleasure to do as you ask, Senhor Aguilar.' Briefly turning away, the woman called out for assistance.

Within seconds, a thickset young man with cropped brown hair, dressed in a security guard's uniform appeared. Judging by the nicks and scars on both his face and his hands, it looked as if his chosen sport was bare-knuckle fighting, Marco observed wryly. Following a very brief exchange with the woman—presumably his boss—he immediately stepped outside and shut the heavy glass door behind him. Marco felt a little more able to relax when he saw the man firmly plant his feet and fold his arms across his ample chest—his intimidating stance alone transmitted a warning to anyone that dared to try and get passed him.

'When you are ready to leave we have an exit at the back.' The woman whose silver-grey badge on her lapel proclaimed her name as Natalie gave him an unreserved broad smile.

'That's good to know. Thank you.' He turned his glance back to Grace. Some of the rosiness in her cheeks had definitely faded, he saw. He had a feeling that she was really hating what he'd hoped would turn out to be a nice experience. 'Are you okay?' he asked, and it was hard to keep the strain from his voice.

'I'm fine. I'm more concerned about you. You must really get fed up with all this intrusive attention.'

'Some days it definitely bothers me more than others, but I refuse to let anyone spoil our time together. We've come to one of the most exclusive boutiques on the marina, so we ought to buy you a dress, no? I am sure that Natalie here will give you all the assistance you need to help you choose.'

Grace spun round on her heel to observe warily the very select display of women's clothing that hung on wafer-thin mannequins. 'There probably isn't anything here above a size zero. Don't you think that's an insane concept? Are all the women in the world trying to disappear?'

'Go and have a proper look,' Marco urged, his hand lightly touching her back.

Silently he agreed with her. The attentive and perfectly made-up Natalie transmitted a sympathetic look to him that immediately rubbed him up the wrong way. Having already seen her arrow a glance straight in on Grace's slightly rumpled red and white dress, and fail to hide her distaste, he abhorred the idea that the woman believed for even a second that she was somehow *better* than his lovely, unaffected companion.

'Why don't you show her what you have?' he said tersely. 'Presumably that's what you are being paid for, Natalie?'

'Of course, Senhor Aguilar... May I ask what the young lady's name is?'

'I'm sure you can manage just fine without it.'

'Of course.' The uneasy smile she gave him was visibly nervous.

'And when my friend finds something that she likes, I would like to see her wearing it.'

'Yes, *senhor.*'

Natalie dipped her head in a short, respectful bow, and when she moved across the room to join Grace he registered with relief that her tone was far more helpful. His tension easing a little, Marco strolled across the marble floor to one of several white couches dotted round. Dropping down into one, he reached for the neatly folded newspaper that lay on the table in front of him.

Feeling uncomfortably pressured to choose a dress that she hadn't even wanted in the first place, but at the same time wanting to please Marco and not add to the palpable tension she sensed in him, Grace took the strapless smocked dress she'd finally selected, which they thankfully had in her size, and went into the scented and luxurious changing room to try it on. When Natalie offered to come in and help her she straight away called out that she could manage just fine by herself. She'd bet her last penny that the older woman was busy wondering what a man like Marco must see in a very average sort of girl like her.

Especially when he preferred brunettes...

Unhappily she recalled the Australian photographer's tactless jibe, and consequently derived no pleasure in trying on the pretty and feminine maxi-dress whose attached labels were festooned with a French designer's name all over them. She was more than discomfited to discover there was no price-tag in evidence. And even though the changing room was more than adequately air-conditioned, Grace was suddenly too hot, not to mention feeling a little claustrophobic after being stalked by that intrusive little crowd waiting for them outside.

How did Marco bear it? From what she knew of him he didn't seem like a man who craved the constant attention of admirers *or* the press. He was essentially a very private man. She had a real yearning to be alone with him again, to ascertain if he really *was* doing all right, and to tell him that she would much prefer to spend the rest of her time with him talking and relaxing rather than going out, with him misguidedly feeling as if he needed to buy her things to keep her happy. Hadn't he learned enough of her nature to know that that would *never* be the case where she was concerned?

Her fingers fumbling with the lavender-coloured ribbon on the ruched bodice of the dress, she almost jumped out of her skin when her mobile phone's salsa beat ringtone broke into her reverie. Dropping down to the carpeted floor to delve inside her straw bag, she located the phone, fully expecting the call to be from her parents. She hadn't spoken to them in over three days now, and no doubt they were getting anxious about her.

But the number that was flashing didn't belong to her mum or dad. It belonged to Sarah, the manager of the children's charity in London. Grace frowned, her heart bumping in alarm.

By the time the conversation came to an end she was sitting on the floor, leaning against the changing room wall, with her knees drawn up to her chest and scalding tears of grief and aching regret streaking down her face. Someone knocked on the door. When she didn't respond, it was immediately pushed open. *It was Marco.*

'The manager told me that she heard you crying. What has happened? Are you hurt?' Suddenly his handsome face was right in front of hers as he dropped down to the same level as Grace, his fingers concernedly squeezing her shoulder.

'I've had some bad news.' She sniffed, hastily wiping her eyes. At the same time she registered that she was probably creasing a very expensive designer dress that Marco would have to pay for. The panicked thought added to the drowning sensation of sorrow and distress that was already washing over her, breaking her heart.

'Somebody rang you from home?' Lifting her hand, Marco examined the slim silver mobile she was still gripping. 'Tell me what's wrong, I beg you. I cannot bear seeing you so upset and not knowing the reason.'

Grace lifted her sorrowful gaze to meet his, striving with all her might to gain better control over her emotions and utterly failing. 'Remember the baby I told you about back in Africa?'

'Azizi you said his name was?'

She was startled that he should recall that.

'Yes. I remember. You told me that it meant beloved or precious one.' The hooded dark eyes in front of her had deepened to almost black.

'Well…my manager just phoned to tell me that he— that he *died*. A couple of days ago he developed a fever, and although one of the charity workers managed to get him to a hospital in the city he had a bad fit during the night and—and he didn't make it. He was just a few weeks old…' Pausing to wipe away another tear, Grace had tremendous difficulty in swallowing across the aching lump inside her throat. 'It doesn't seem fair does it? I mean…to have had such a tragic start in life and then to die just as tragically before you'd even had the chance to live. You said that Azizi would be fortunate if he lived up to his name…now he *won't*…'

'*Não chorar, a meu amor, que o bebê e seguro com*

Deus agora.' The words were out before Marco had realised he would say them out loud. It literally made his
heart ache to see Grace like this and the need to console
her took precedence over everything else…even the risk
of his words being overheard by the woman who ran the
boutique and reported back to the press for a no doubt
ludicrous sum…

The shimmering blue eyes in front of him widened
as his hand tenderly stroked back her hair, then cupped
her cheek. 'What does that mean?' she asked, her voice
lowered to a mesmerised whisper.

'I said, do not cry any more. The baby is safe with God
now.' *He didn't even know if he believed in God.* Perhaps
his early programming of being raised as a Catholic in
the orphanage had made him err towards believing rather
than not—even though some people might regard his own
start in life as tragic and not understand it. He omitted to
tell Grace that he'd actually said, 'Do not cry any more,
my love'. Never in his life had Marco addressed a woman
in such a tender way. It jolted him to realise what a different man he was around her.

'That's beautiful. Thank you.'

'I will do everything I can to help you come to terms
with this loss, Grace…I promise. Would you prefer to go
home and have lunch rather than eat here at the marina?'

She looked relieved. 'Can we? I'm really sorry… I
didn't mean to spoil your plans for the day.'

His throat a little tight, Marco forced a smile. 'You
have spoiled nothing, my angel.'

Helping her to her feet, he felt his senses suddenly besieged by her—by the exquisite softness of the hands he
held onto—almost as if she were a lifeline, helping him
out of the sea of loneliness and pain that had dogged his
footsteps ever since he was a child. No matter how much

worldly success he'd achieved. Knowing he was staring, he was staggered by the natural beauty and grace that seemed to define her so effortlessly... *Grace* was the perfect name for her. *How had her parents known that their daughter would grow up to embody it?*

'Marco? Don't you like the dress?'

He gazed at her, unable to look away. The beautiful garment she wore with its riot of spring colours was lovely. But more than the dress itself, it was the bewitching girl who wore it that elevated it to something special. Caught up in the spell of her, the ability to respond with mere words deserted him.

'Marco? What's wrong? You're worrying me.'

Gathering her urgently into his arms, he crushed her to him and kissed her as if he might *die* if he didn't.

Neither he nor Grace heard the changing room door open and Natalie murmur, '*Desculpe me*...excuse me...' then quietly and discreetly leave.

CHAPTER TEN

True to her word, Natalie had shown them out the back way, and thankfully they'd escaped the notice of the predatory crowd waiting for them to emerge outside the front of the boutique. They'd run all the way back to the car, and had both been breathless when they arrived. Miguel had given them a bemused glance, then gunned the engine, and they'd left the glamorous marina behind to travel back to the villa.

Marco held her hand throughout the entire journey. Grace fought hard to contain her grief—lodged like a burning stone inside her chest as she recalled gazing down into Azizi's big brown eyes and seeing the absolute trust there that she would take care of him. She had had a special bond with the baby boy since the night a co-worker had put him into her arms. At every opportunity she had held him, bathed him, sung to him if he was fractious and it cut like a knife that she would never take care of him again...

Stealing into the midst of her grief came the thought that she might have a baby of her own if Marco had made her pregnant. Instead of making her feel apprehensive, as it had done before, the idea actually started to console her. She even began to pray that it would come true. Even though he'd said that he didn't have any good example of what it meant to be a father, Grace didn't doubt that Marco would make a good one. She'd had too many examples of his kindness and concern for people *not* to believe it. If he could only endeavour not to keep his emotions locked up so tightly they might even have a future together, she mused.

The notion rocked her world off its axis.

Lifting her gaze to his as the car drew nearer to the villa, she became intimately aware of the hungrily burning intensity that glowed in her companion's hooded dark eyes. It caught her in a spell that even the most powerful magic would never free her from. It was as though every unfulfilled hope, dream and desire they'd ever had had erupted inside them the moment his lips had brushed hers in the changing room back at the boutique. It had literally been like touching flame to tinder. And now they were set on a course to fulfil those dreams and desires…

As soon as they'd reached the villa and gone in, Marco waited only until they were at the foot of the grand staircase before sweeping Grace off her feet into his arms and transporting her upstairs to the bedroom. Once there, they hungrily tore at each other's clothes, sharing each other's breath with drugging, rapturous kisses, until they fell onto the bed in a flurry of searching hands and tangled limbs, eager and impatient to stop the world and any notion of pain or sadness—to make love until they were utterly spent and exhausted.

Lying on her front in the opulent bed, the covers in a pool of oyster silk around her, Grace turned her head to examine the lazily sexy smile of the man beside her. 'Do you have any idea how much I like you, Marco Aguilar?' she whispered.

Exhaling a long, slow breath, he trailed his fingertips up and down her spine, sending a cascade of delicious shivers throughout her body. 'Why don't you tell me?' he urged.

'I like you more than any other man I've ever met... But please don't let that scare you. It doesn't mean I expect any more than you've already given me or are willing to give while we're together.'

'Why do you think it would scare me to hear you say that?' His ebony brows lifted quizzically.

'Because I get the feeling you don't want anyone to get too attached...especially a woman.'

'You think so?'

'Why don't you answer the question? *Do* you fear a woman getting too close to you, Marco?'

His fingers stopped trailing up and down her spine. His expression had a shuttered look about it, and Grace tensed apprehensively.

'What do you think?' he said slowly. 'Everyone that should have been close to me...would have been close to me...I've lost. Maybe I associate becoming too attached to someone with loss? Can you wonder why I wouldn't want it?'

Even though she knew he was reluctant to talk about personal things, Grace sensed a definite opening in his usual guard—perhaps brought about by their passionate and tender lovemaking? She hoped so. At any rate, she wouldn't let the possibility of a deeper conversation go.

'Marco...?'

'Hmm?'

Reaching out, he manoeuvred her round into his arms, smiling wickedly and making her heart race like mad. Poignantly, she saw how he hoped to deflect her questions with humour.

'What is it now, my angel? Think of me as your very own personal genie...your wish is my command.'

She sucked in a breath. 'Will you talk to me…? I mean *really* talk to me?'

If her request disturbed him, there was no immediate indication that it did.

'What is it that you want to discuss? Tell me.'

'I'd like to talk about *you*…'

'Ah.'

'You just mentioned the loss in your life. Can I ask you about your childhood?'

'What do you want to know about it?'

'You said that your father abandoned you in the orphanage when your mother died? Did you ever find out where he went afterwards? I mean, did he never get in touch with you while you were there?'

The sudden tension in his muscles was slight, but she immediately detected it and held her breath.

'The answer is no to both questions. My mother and father were sixteen and seventeen respectively. They were both orphans…no parents, no home. When my mother died giving birth to me my father was apparently so broken-hearted that all he could think of to do when he went back to the hospital to collect me was take me to the orphanage where he himself had been raised—in fact where he and my mother had met. At the time he was doing some casual labour to make money, and was renting a small inadequate room in the town. He pleaded with them to take me because he had neither the means nor the ability to raise me by himself…and no doubt that was true. After promising to keep in contact, he left. They never saw him again.'

Rubbing his hand across his eyes, Marco deliberately averted his gaze.

'It's not easy to find a seventeen-year-old youth with

no forwarding address, and no family through which he might be traced either.'

Carefully, gently, Grace flattened her palm against his chest. His heartbeat was racing slightly, and he took a long breath in, then slowly blew it out again. She waited for a few moments for him to start talking again. When he didn't, she rested her head where her hand had been. His breathing was steadier now, and his hard-muscled chest with its dusting of soft dark hair was warm and wonderful to lie against…like the safest haven she could imagine. Despite his sad upbringing he had such tenacity. She marvelled at the psychological strength it must have taken to rise above the painful start he'd had in life and—against all the odds—achieve something as remarkable as without a doubt he had.

'Your parents would have been so proud of you if they'd seen you grow up,' she murmured, tears filling her eyes not only for Marco, but for Azizi too—a boy that had also never known his parents. It was hard to understand why life had to be so hard and cruel sometimes.

'Hey.' Marco moved back so that he could study her. 'Are you crying for me? If you are, then don't. I don't want you shedding tears for what happened a long time ago…*too* long. My own policy is never to look back. I've put it all behind me now and I have no regrets.'

Grace cupped his beard-shadowed jaw. 'I'm crying for you *and* for Azizi. Childhood is so precious. Is it true, Marco? Is it true that you don't ever think about yours and wish things might have been different?'

His gaze was completely unwavering as he considered her, and the sun streamed through the huge windows, illuminating the tiny flecks of light in his dark pupils. 'Yes, it's true. I never think about the past and wish it had been different. What on earth would be the point?'

'Were you ever happy at all when you were growing up in the orphanage?'

'Not particularly, no. Are your orphans in Africa happy?'

'Sometimes they are. Their lives are challenging, of course. But they take one day at a time… Children live in the moment, don't they? They don't occupy themselves in regretting the past and fretting about the future. And if an adult is kind to them, pays them attention and gives them a hug, their smiles are unbelievable. They respond with so much love that it takes your breath away. It's the most rewarding work…helping to make them happy even for just a little while.'

'It must be for someone like *you*, Grace.'

'Like I told you before…I'm not the only one who loves those kids. You would love them too if you met them. Wasn't there *anyone* who looked after you when you were little that loved you, and you loved back?'

Scowling, he sat up, dragging the covers over his knees. 'Not that I recall. Are we finished talking about me now? I think we are, because I can tell you I've had enough of revisiting the past for one day and I'd like you to respect that.'

'I'm really sorry if it distresses you to talk about such things. but—'

'No doubt you think it's for my own good?' His ensuing sigh was heavy, and laden with irritation. 'You think it might help me release some of the hurt of rejection you imagine I feel inside and make me feel better about myself, is that it? *Deus!* You are like a dog with a bone when you want to get to the bottom of things aren't you, Grace?'

'I only want to try and help.'

'Well, don't. I'm not one of the coterie of orphans

you're intent on saving single-handedly. The only way you can help me is by being the companion I want you to be for the duration of this holiday and by sharing my bed—*not* by being a latter-day Mother Teresa! If I need to explore any angst about the past I'll go to a psychologist.'

For long moments his furious tirade crushed her. Then Grace determinedly called upon the reservoir of strength she always drew from whenever she had a challenge to face. She stowed away her embarrassment at being so brutally put in her place and somehow found a smile. Something told her that Marco's anger wasn't about her encroaching upon his painful memories of the past, but purely because he was furious with himself that those memories still haunted him.

'I hear you. Again, I'm really sorry if I've made you feel uncomfortable in any way. Let's talk about something else, shall we?'

Driving his fingers roughly through his burnished dark hair, he stared at her hard. 'Good idea. How about we talk about *you* instead, hmm? For instance, who was the guy you lost your virginity to? Let's start with that, shall we?'

She'd risked upsetting Marco and now she was paying the price. However, believing as she did that talking was good, she wouldn't flinch from telling him what he wanted to know. Perhaps her own story would help defuse his anger and frustration with himself?

Sitting up beside him, Grace turned her head to directly meet his gaze. 'He was just a guy I briefly dated at university. We only slept together that one time. It was hardly love's young dream—just the opposite, in fact. Because in the morning he told me he'd made a mistake...

that he preferred someone else but hadn't been able to bring himself to tell me.'

'So he stole your virginity just for the hell of it, then went on to some other poor, gullible woman?'

Shrugging, she folded her arms round her knees. 'We both made a mistake. I'm not proud of it. You do some stupid things when you're young—especially when you're looking for acceptance and approval.'

Sliding his hand round her jaw, Marco made her turn her head so that he could intimately examine her face. 'You're too hard on yourself. It's the guy who was stupid...stupid to think there was someone better than you.'

'Thanks,' she murmured, hoping and praying that the tenderness she heard in his voice meant he wouldn't stay mad at her for long, for daring to quiz him about his past.

'And what about the guy that assaulted you?' he asked gently. 'What was your relationship like with him?'

Her insides knotting, Grace grimaced. 'It wasn't anything special, if that's what you're asking. We just kind of fell into going out with each other because we enjoyed the same kind of movies and music... For a while he'd been part of the group of friends I hung out with, so when he asked me out I believed I knew him—I thought he'd be okay...that he'd treat me well. Everything was fine until he started pressing me to sleep with him. I kept resisting, because I didn't even know if I liked him enough to keep on dating him, let alone have an intimate relationship. We went to a party one night. He'd been drinking steadily throughout the evening so I drove us home. He didn't want to be dropped off at his place, and asked if he could go back to mine for a cup of coffee, saying he would ring a cab to take him home. I agreed. It was a stupid decision, because at the time I really believed that was all he wanted. But as soon as we got inside my flat he started accusing me of flirting with some guy at the party. It wasn't true…not *remotely*. Anyway, he started shoving me around a bit, then he pinned me to the floor and—'

She couldn't continue. The memory made Grace feel sick and wretched, scared too that she seemed to be so hopeless at choosing the right men.

'I shouldn't have made you talk about it…I'm sorry'

Easing her head down onto his chest, Marco threaded his long fingers through her tousled fair hair and tenderly massaged her scalp. It had been despicable of him to make her recall the man who had hurt her, but his own anger and pain about the past—and jealousy too, at the idea of Grace being with anyone else before him—had made him temporarily and regrettably cruel.

She shifted, and a soft sigh feathered over the surface of his skin, raining him with goose bumps. 'I don' mind you asking me about my previous relationships… if that's what you could even call them. When you're intimate with someone it's only natural that you want to know as much as you can about them.' Moving to sit u' next to him, she shook back her prettily mussed blond hair and folded her arms. 'When we first met you aske me if I had a boyfriend and I said no. You never told m if *you* had anyone on the scene. Is there? Is there som woman somewhere that you care about, Marco? Someor you maybe should have mentioned to me?'

Staring up at the ornate ceiling, he momentarily rest his forearm against his brow. Reflecting on the abhorre treatment he'd received from his ex-girlfriend Jasmin when she'd had the audacity to take him to court f breach of his so-called promise to support her when she been fired from her job, he scowled.

'No. Of course there's no one else. I wouldn't do th

to you—ask you to spend your holiday with me and share my bed if there was another woman on the scene. I know plenty of rich men that play the field...but I'm not one of them.'

'That's good to know' she replied softly, with the full force of her bewitching blue glance coming to rest unwaveringly on his face. 'Can you perhaps tell me what your last girlfriend was like? Could you at least share that with me?'

He laughed harshly, then sat up. 'If you really want to know, she was a total nightmare! I was well rid of her in the end.'

'What happened?'

'Nothing that I care to revisit or talk about.'

Grace had that look on her face that told Marco she wasn't going to let him off the hook so lightly, and inside he knew he would have to concede.

'But I just told you about *my* previous relationships... even though it was painful.'

'Okay.' He held up his hands in an exaggerated gesture of surrender, then raked his fingers through his already mussed hair. 'She was a fashion model whose looks I was briefly and foolishly enamoured with. I should have looked a lot deeper than the surface package she presented, but for some reason I didn't. Perhaps I was lonely at the time? Who knows?' He snorted disparagingly. 'It turned out that she was addicted not just to very rich and gullible men but to cocaine—and any number of other addictive drugs too. When the fashion house she worked for didn't renew her contract, because frankly she was becoming a liability, she took me to court claiming I'd promised to support her. I did no such thing. I had told her we were finished even before she lost her damn job!'

'That must have hurt…to have a woman you cared for betray you like that,' Grace murmured sympathetically.

His eyes narrowed. 'I didn't say that I cared for her.'

'It still must have hurt.'

Relenting, Marco caught hold of her hand. 'It was my pride that was hurt more than anything else. But why are we even talking about this? Can't we just forget about our pasts and concentrate on what's going on right now? I have a suggestion. Why don't you put on that pretty new dress and we'll go out?'

'Out where?'

'We'll drive to my yacht and take a cruise round the bay.'

'You have a *yacht*?'

'What self-respecting billionaire doesn't?' he joked his breathtaking smile dazzling her. 'I only have to make a call and the crew will make it ready for us. What kind of food would you like to eat? I can phone one of many restaurants and get them to deliver our order to the yacht. We can sit on the deck and eat out under the stars.'

Grace sighed. She saw how the idea of going to his yacht and arranging for their dinner to be delivered from a fine restaurant immediately put Marco back in control, returning him to the world of elite lifestyles that he'd grown comfortable with…where he knew who he was and what he wanted…where he could merely snap his fingers and have a bevy of eager retainers hurry to do his will. It also helped him temporarily hide from the hurt of his childhood, when he patently *hadn't* been control of what happened to him.

But he couldn't hide from it for ever. That would make for a very hard and unhappy existence, no matter how much money he had, Grace thought. Sooner or later everyone had to face the truth of their lives.

She'd already personally learned that repeating the same patterns—going down old familiar roads where nothing challenged you any more—didn't help ease or heal anything. It just brought more of the same silent despair that day by day ate away at your soul. *Unless you turned and faced it, that was.* That was why she'd gone out to Africa. At the time she'd been so scared of what she might encounter when she'd flown out there—the suffering she would undoubtedly see and have to find a way of dealing with—that she'd thought she would be more of a hindrance than a help. What Grace hadn't been prepared for was the joy and satisfaction she'd experienced at having the trusting sweet smile of a previously distressed or despairing child turned on *her*. The very things she'd feared had turned out to be her salvation.

Carefully disengaging her hand from Marco's, she registered the flicker of unease that crossed his glance. 'As lovely as that sounds, I'm afraid I'm going to have to say no. In fact I'm going to ask instead if I can have a little time to myself. There are a few things I need to think about.'

'You mean like the baby dying?'

'Yes.'

'I know he didn't live for long, but he was a lucky boy to have someone like you looking after him Grace…even for a little while. You asked me if I ever thought about the past…if I'd ever loved anyone that had helped to take care of me. If I had had someone like you, I would have thought myself blessed beyond measure, believe me.'

A hopeful breath shuddered through her. 'You deserved to have the very best of care and attention, Marco…*and* love. It breaks my heart to think that you didn't.'

He said nothing for a while, but his tension of earlier

had palpably eased. Then he considered her thoughtfully and said, 'You came to the Algarve for a rest and a break from work…to *enjoy* yourself. Let's go out to the yacht together. I guarantee you will not regret it.'

It hurt Grace to deny him anything…especially in light of his previous confession about his childhood. To do so made her feel as if she was another adult who had let him down. That was hard to bear, when she knew that she loved him with all her heart.

The realisation made her catch her breath. She wanted to laugh and cry at the same time. *She was in love.* She was completely and totally head over heels.

It became even more imperative that she have some time to herself—to absorb this stunning revelation, to reflect and consider what to do next.

'I'm sorry, Marco. I really just need to be by myself for a while. Please try and understand.'

'Okay. Selfishly, it's not what I want…to let you go for even an *hour* let alone an entire evening feels inde scribably hard…but I see that you need time to come to terms with the baby's death by yourself, so I won't try to stop you from going.'

Grace made herself breathe deeply. 'Thanks for that It's only for this one evening. I promise I'll come back i the morning—if you don't mind asking Miguel to pic me up?'

'Of course I don't mind. You might also bring a sui case with some of your clothes in it when you return. makes sense for you to stay here for the remainder your holiday, don't you think?'

'I suppose it does. Well, then… I'd better get dressed Moving to the edge of the bed, Grace tugged at one of t silk covers and wrapped it round her bare form, deli

erately taking her time and not hurrying, in case Marco
mistakenly believed she was eager to get away.

The words 'for the remainder of your holiday' rang
anxiously in her ears, confirming that he clearly didn't
believe they could have a future together.

On leaden legs she moved quietly round the room, bit
by bit gathering her scattered clothing as memories of the
afternoon's passionate lovemaking deluged her, making
her want to run straight back to him and beg him to love
her again…to confess that she loved him.

Having not the slightest clue as to how he might receive such a confession, she knew it made even more
sense that she have some time on her own to mull things
over.

Registering the sound of his moving behind her,
Grace glanced over her shoulder to see him pulling on
his chinos, his expression grim, absorbed in the private
landscape of his thoughts. Then he scraped his fingers
through the dark strands of hair that she loved so much
to touch and turning to face her, exhaled deeply.

'Although I've agreed to let you go, I hate the thought
of you being upset tonight and my not being there to help
comfort you.'

The confession really touched her. 'I'll think about
you saying that and just the thought will help comfort
me, Marco. It's only for this one evening, remember? The
time will soon go. What will you do? Will you go out to
your yacht as planned?'

'Probably not. I think I'll go and catch up with some
friends of mine for the evening instead. I'm not often in
the country, so I guess it would be a good opportunity.'

'I agree. That sounds like a good idea. Your friends
must miss not seeing you, Marco.'

He didn't respond. Instead he pulled his still buttoned

white shirt over his head, slipped his bare feet into tan loafers and moved across the vast expanse of marble flooring to the door.

'Help yourself to a shower before you leave,' he said over his shoulder, 'I'll go and find Miguel to tell him I want him to drive you home. When you're ready, just go and find him at the front of the house...he'll be waiting for you there. I'll also arrange for him to pick you up in the morning.'

'Thanks...' Her heart was beating double-time because he suddenly sounded so distant and businesslike. He plainly wasn't going to kiss her goodbye either. Was it a mistake to insist that she needed some time to herself this evening? Grace prayed that it wasn't...

CHAPTER ELEVEN

THE inconsequential chatter of the people sitting with him round the restaurant table washed over Marco—as though the voices came from far away...as if he was locked inside a dream. Because Grace wasn't with him, the evening was quickly taking on the quality of a nightmare. The two of them had only been apart for a few short hours, but already it felt like an eternity. There was a dull ache inside his chest, his appetite had completely disappeared, and he could hardly summon up the energy or interest to talk to his friends.

Friends... The word seemed to mock him as he glanced round at the faces of colleagues past and present. Why were all his so-called friendships work-related? he pondered. The reason he'd agreed to accept the invitation to join them tonight and had scrapped his intention to go to his yacht was because he hadn't wanted to be alone with his thoughts. He hadn't wanted to be alone, *per se*. Yet it hardly helped that the people at dinner weren't *real* friends at all.

Marco reflected that no doubt his driven desire to be a success had severed any possibility of making genuine friends from all walks of life, instead of just the elite he'd worked so hard to join. The chances had simply passed him by because his focus had been too pointed to notice them. It didn't help that most of his time was spent either *at* work, embroiled in some lengthy boardroom meeting, making deals with equally driven businessmen or women over lunch or dinner, or *thinking* about work in some way—even when he was meant to be relaxing, playing golf, or when he was at some glitzy party or casino.

Apart from working and pleasure-seeking, what else had he done with his life? Yes, he supported several different charities by donating money and being a patron, but when had he ever put himself out to get more personally involved, like Grace did? *What was he so afraid of?*

The answer came to Marco without any effort at all. Because he'd lived in what might be deemed an ivory tower for so long, he harboured a secret fear of exposing himself as hopeless when it came to everyday interactions with ordinary people. More than that, he feared he might have to face the fact that being so emotionally shut down was depriving him of some real joy and satisfaction in his life. The kind that came from really connecting with people and helping them make their lives better.

Marco's painfully analytical stream of thought didn't exactly help him feel any better about the situation—even though he knew he needed to take a good hard look at these things. The only thing that had the remotest chance of improving his mood right now was seeing Grace. *He had so easily let her go.* Why hadn't he argued more emphatically for her to stay? He hadn't even kissed her goodbye.

The arresting image of her standing in his bedroom with nothing but a silk sheet wrapped round her, to cover her shapely naked form, sent such a surge of longing pulsing through him that he briefly shut his eyes to contain

What if he never saw her again? What if she concluded in their time apart this evening that he was too shut-down for her to get close to? Too removed from the so-called 'real world' for her ever to reach?

Reaching for his wine glass, he was so deep in thought that he accidentally knocked it over with the heel of his hand, sending a wave of cranberry coloured liquid flying over the pristine white tablecloth. The two glamorous women sitting on either side of him jumped up in dismay—anxious not to get wine on their expensive outfits, but also quick to reassure him that accidents could happen to anyone.

Marco had risen to his feet at the same time, grabbing a white linen napkin to mop up the spill, uncaring that some of it splashed the sleeve of his exclusive Armani suit. Seconds later a helpful waiter attended to the mopping up much more efficiently, and with the minimum of fuss. That was the moment when Marco made the decision to quit the party. The hot, prickling sensation of feeling hemmed in and trapped had started to creep up on him again, and he desperately craved some fresh air.

Making his apologies, he accepted the generous offer from one of his colleagues to pay his share of the bill, wished everyone goodnight, and walked as if in a dream slowly down the restaurant's lantern-lit walkway to the car.

'Miguel?' When they arrived back home Marco paused as he got out of the car.

'Yes, *senhor*?'

'Join me for a drink?'

With a mute nod, Marco's loyal chauffeur followed him back inside the villa. The two men strolled out onto one of the myriad balconies that decked the building, but not before Marco had stopped by the wine cellar in the basement and collected a bottle of vintage red wine and a couple of glasses on the way. Throwing his jacket with the stained sleeve onto a nearby wrought-iron bench, he pulled out a chair from the matching table and gestured to the other man to do likewise.

Taking his time to pour the wine carefully, he gave a glass to Miguel, then made a toast. 'To truth and beauty.'

With a contemplative smile, the chauffeur touched his glass to Marco's and silently concurred. They sat companionably for a while, with just the shrill sound of the cicadas interrupting the tranquil silence that fell around them. *It was peaceful.* It made Marco realise just how much he valued the steady, thoughtful presence of the other man.

'You miss her.'

'Excuse me?'

'Senhorita Faulkner...you miss her'

Marco shook his head in wonder that his employee should intuit so much. 'We have only been apart for one evening,' he said ruefully.

'It makes no difference.' Miguel shrugged a shoulder 'When the most important woman in your life is lost to you even briefly it feels like you will never be whole again until you see her.'

'What makes you think that Senhorita Faulkner i the most important woman in my life? She is *not*. How could she be when I have only known her for the short est time?'

Even as he rushed to deny his true feelings—so soo after drinking a toast to 'truth and beauty'—Marco heart raced with longing to be with Grace, to gaze int her lovely blue eyes, bring her lush sweet body close

his and know that everything was right in his world because he was with her.

'You can meet the woman of your dreams and fall in
love with her in an instant. It does not matter that you
have only just met her.' The chauffeur's gaze was unwavering and direct.

'How did you get to be so wise about affairs of the
heart, my friend? Is that what happened to you?'

There was a distant look in Miguel's dark eyes that
told Marco he was remembering someone who had meant
a great deal to him once upon a time. Knowing that the
man was now single, he was genuinely sorry that they'd
never had a conversation personal enough for him to en-
quire about the relationships that had been meaningful
to him.

'Yes…that is what happened to me.' Pausing to curl
his hand round the stem of his wine glass, Miguel raised
it thoughtfully to his lips and took a sip of the blood-red
vintage. 'But sadly I lost the love of my life when she
fell ill and what afflicted her turned out to be terminal.
We only had the shortest time together, but it was intense
and amazing, you know?'

Marco *did* know. 'I'm so sorry that you lost her,' he
murmured consolingly.

Swallowing hard, Miguel shook off the anguish that
must have shuddered through him and smiled. 'That is
why you must make the most of the time you have with
Senhorita Faulkner. I only have to see the way the two
of you look at each other to know that you are in love.'

Even though it made him inwardly reel to hear the
other man's statement, Marco had to own privately that
for *his* part at least it was the truth. Did he dare believe
that Grace might feel the same?

'Senhorita Faulkner…*Grace*…is an incredible

woman—warm-hearted and brave. I am a poor bargain for someone like her, Miguel,' he remarked soberly.

'I do not think so.'

'She's not impressed with who I am in the world, what I've achieved or how much money I have.'

'If that is so then you are a fortunate man indeed, *senhor*, because she must clearly desire you just for yourself.'

Two of the charity workers at the African orphanage had gone down with a fever similar to that which had afflicted Azizi and were in hospital. Grace had heard the news from her dad, when she'd rung home yesterday evening. A senior member of the charity who hadn't known Grace was in the Algarve had rung her parents' number in a bid to contact her.

As soon as her dad had revealed the news to her Grace had sensed his reluctance in passing it on, because he knew that she couldn't fail to act on it—perhaps to the detriment of her own health. Now there were only two full-time volunteers remaining at the orphanage to help take care of the children—a young man hired by the charity in London, that had arrived in Africa on the same day that she'd flown out, and a local grandmother and midwife. Running over the scenario again in her mind, imagining the distress of not only the two remaining volunteers at what had happened, but the children too, Grace didn't regret agreeing to fly out there at once to help.

But even in the midst of hearing about the worrying events back in Africa she'd been consumed with an uncontainable longing to be with Marco. *She shouldn't have left him*. Their difficult temporary parting—even though she had been the instigator of it—had left her feeling as if her heart had been cleaved in two, and she had spent a mostly miserable evening on her own, mulling over the fact that she was hopelessly in love with him and wondering how she was going to say goodbye and return to living without him?

The knock on the door as she drank her breakfast coffee propelled her already anxious thoughts into overdrive. On the way out of the living room into the hallway, she glanced over at the compact powder-blue suitcase standing by the couch. She'd originally hoped to pack it and take it with her back to Marco's. Now she would take it with her to a completely *different* destination.

Just before opening the door she paused to glance down at the knee-length aubergine-coloured dress she wore. She checked the back of the chignon her blonde hair had been fashioned into to make sure that the tortoiseshell clasp held it secure. She'd deliberately made an effort with her appearance in a bid to feel more confident when it came to facing Marco and telling him about her change of plans.

But the man she had been expecting to see standing on the other side of the door was his enigmatic chauffeur Miguel...*not* Marco himself, wearing a stylish fitted black shirt and jeans, his black hair swept back by his sunglasses to reveal his strong, indomitable forehead. His dark eyes instantly devoured her, making her legs feel dangerously weak and insubstantial. He resembled some gorgeous dark angel, come to tempt her into an erotic realm she'd never want to be free of so long as he was there, and Grace could hardly think straight, let alone string words together to greet him.

In the end it was he who spoke first. '*Deus!* You are looking especially beautiful this morning, Grace...elegant and sexy. I'm very glad that I came to pick you up myself rather than send Miguel.'

'Thanks...' she murmured, her cheeks glowing scarlet. She was torn between walking straight into his arms and affecting enough distance between them so that the temptation wouldn't overwhelm her. 'It's good to see you... *really* good. Why don't you come in? There's plenty of coffee left in the cafetière...can you spare a few minutes to have a cup with me?'

'Of course.'

Stepping inside, with a knowing little smile playing round the corners of his lips because he'd sensed that she was desperate to touch him, Marco glanced towards the family photos that lined the hallway walls. They were nearly all of Grace with her parents, at various stages of her growing up. The latter ones were more recent shots of her as an adult—at her graduation, and at the twenty-first birthday party they'd thrown for her.

'I don't know why my parents want to have them all on display.' Her dismissive shrug was helplessly self-conscious, but Marco didn't immediately halt his examination of the pictures. In fact, he seemed more than a little fascinated by them. An unhappy thought occurred to Grace. Had anyone ever documented the phases of *his* growing up? She wanted to weep at the notion that they hadn't.

As the minutes ticked by, she became more and more convinced that the idea that had taken hold of her last night and wouldn't let go was a *good* one.

'They look like kind people...your parents, I mean.'

Turning round to face her, he folded his arms across his chest and smiled...a little uncertainly, Grace reflected with a pang. 'They are *very* kind. Shall we go through onto the patio and have that coffee?'

The sunshine seemed especially glorious that morning, and the sky was a perfect duck-egg-blue. There was a faint caressing breeze, and it carried the scent of bougainvillaea along with the smell of the suncream she rubbed into her skin, making her wish that she could make the deceptively simple choice merely to enjoy this holiday—to have nothing else in her mind but to spend all her time with Marco.

'You take it black with no sugar, right?' she poured him some coffee and slid the porcelain cup on its saucer across the wooden table towards him. The crockery rattled a little, as if mimicking her nervousness.

Murmuring his thanks, he lowered his aviator sunglasses down over his eyes and instantly added to the mystique he exuded so effortlessly, making Grace's stomach take a slow elevator ride right down to the tips of her toes.

'I missed you last night,' she confessed softly, not looking away when his glance intensified.

'I missed you too, Grace.'

'So…how did you spend the evening? Did you go to see your friends?'

'Yes, I did… Although in truth they aren't really friends. Simply people I once worked with or still work with.'

'Oh?'

'There was a time when I would have referred to them as friends, but not any more.'

'Why's that?'

'Since spending time with you, Grace, I have begun to see more and more who I can count as real friends and who I cannot.'

His smile at her was slow as the most luxurious honey being poured over a waffle—and a thousand times more tempting.

'I've also faced up to the fact that I've been running away from my past instead of properly dealing with my feelings about it. Hearing you talk about your own fears, seeing how you've been determined to face them and overcome them, has made me see the sense in trying to do the same—because I don't want them to impinge any more on the present. You see what you've done to me? I am a changed man because of you.'

'I haven't done anything. If you've realised these things it's because you want to see the truth, Marco… that's all.' Grace absently stirred more sugar into her coffee, because being caught in the hypnotic beam of his disturbing gaze—even behind his shades—made it hard to sit still, made it hard to *breathe*. But his admission that he was at last going to face up to his past and not let it dominate his present made her feel like cheering.

'You won't take the credit for anything, will you? I've never met a woman so generous of spirit that she would not dent a man's fragile ego by proving *she* was the one who saw things much more clearly than he did. It makes me think that I should hold onto you, Grace…yes hold onto you and never let you go.'

As well as making her heart race with joy, his sincere assertion sent her emotions into a tailspin. She yearned to tell him there and then that she loved him, but first she had to tell him about the abrupt change to her plans…

'Marco?'

'Yes, Grace?'

'I don't know how to cushion this, but I'm afraid need to go back to Africa…to the orphanage.'

'When?' He instantly removed his sunglasses, and she was sure she didn't imagine the shadow that moved across his irises. 'You're not telling me you plan on going soon? Not before our holiday is ended?'

Her tongue came out to moisten her suddenly dry lips 'I'm afraid I am. I'm going to have to go today, in fact Two of the workers at the home have contracted a fever and are being treated in hospital. That leaves only two other people to help care for the children. They're desperately short-handed, and there's nobody else that can go other than me... All the charity's field-workers are already working abroad elsewhere—plus I know the children, and they know me. As well as needing practical help, they'll need reassuring that everything's going to be all right.'

His face darkened, and she bit down on her lip. The duck-egg-blue sky suddenly didn't seem quite so blue or benign... 'It's not that I don't *want* to stay with you, Marco...it's just that this is an emergency. I have no choice but to respond to the charity's request for my help.'

He rose to his feet and strode over to the edge of the balcony, to stare out at the shimmering verdant lawns of the golfing resort in the distance. *The scene of where they had first met...*

Grace got slowly up from her chair to join him, unable to ignore the stiffening of the broad shoulders encased in his black fitted shirt that told her he was already shutting her out emotionally because of what he must no doubt see as a betrayal.

Marco turned round to face her. The shadows in his deep dark eyes made her heart sink like a boulder. 'How do you expect me to feel? I know how much you care about others, Grace, but what about yourself? You are supposed to be resting—recovering from the exhaustion you suffered after your last visit. And most of all I don't want you to put your own health at risk by going out there while a fever is raging. Didn't you already tell me that the baby Azizi died from it? How on earth could I be happy about you returning there now?'

Flushing, Grace dipped her head. 'We don't even know yet if what the workers have contracted is the same fever that killed Azizi. It could be a completely different strain altogether…a less virulent one. The hospital lab will have to run some tests. The most important thing is that those poor, defenceless children shouldn't be left without help and support. I know I was exhausted when I came back from there, but I'm strong and in good health. I'll be absolutely fine…I know I will,' she added, feeling the helpless sting of tears behind her eyes because Marco had made it abundantly clear that not only would he not consider going with her, but his tone also suggested that she was crazy for even contemplating making such a trip.

'I don't want you to go.' Scrubbing his hand round his jaw, he moved his head a little despairingly from side to side. 'I know you'll probably go anyway…after all, it's what you're all about, isn't it? Helping those less fortunate, I mean. It's commendable to be so dedicated, but being dedicated is one thing—risking life and limb is another!'

'I'm sorry, Marco…but you're right. I *am* going. Try not to think too badly of me for it.'

'I don't think badly of you…I *couldn't*. But I still wish that you'd reconsider.'

Even though she couldn't be sure that everything would be all right, Grace knew that she must still go. Her strong natural instinct to help was too compelling to ignore, so she would answer it—if only to assure herself that everything humanly possible would be done to aid the children.

Looking as though he'd wanted to say more to persuade her to stay, but had concluded that he wouldn't, Marco turned away and strode across the sunlit patio to the open French doors that led back into the living room. It hit her then that he was leaving, and that it might be long time before she saw him again. A scalding tear sli down her cheek that their relationship should take such an unhappy turn.

'Marco? Please don't let's part on bad terms. I promise I'll be okay. Can you wait just a minute?'

Flying across to the table, she picked up the notepad and pen she'd left lying there, with which she'd been making notes about her trip back to Africa. She scribbled down her mobile phone number, along with her address back in the UK. As an afterthought, she wrote down her parents' phone number and address too.

Tearing out the page from the notepad, she moved quickly across to where Marco was waiting and handed it to him. 'If you want or need to contact me, then you should have this.'

He slowly nodded his head, took the sheet of notepaper and slid it into the back pocket of his jeans. 'Have your flights been booked already?'

'Yes. The charity has arranged everything. A cab is coming soon to take me to the airport.'

'Are you okay for money?'

'Yes…I'm fine.'

'Then there is nothing more to say, is there? Nothing except take care of yourself—and don't take any more risks than you strictly need to.'

There was a husky catch in his voice that made Grace fleetingly hold her breath. Then, leaning forward to cup her face, he kissed her hard, almost bruising her lips with the passionate pressure of his mouth. Before she could gather her wits—and without so much as a backward glance—he turned and walked away. Seconds later she heard the front door slam resoundingly…

CHAPTER TWELVE

THE rain hit the concrete pavements hard, bouncing up on impact like thin, pointed daggers. Although it might be deemed refreshing, after the dry burning heat he had left behind in the Algarve, Marco felt too bleak to mind whether it rained or it didn't. As he stared out of the windows of the Mercedes at the unfamiliar suburban streets he'd never had reason to visit up until now his mouth dried, and his heart pounded at the prospect of seeing Grace again after six interminably long weeks. He felt bleak because his separation from her had been like a death sentence. It had worn him down, prevented him from concentrating at work, and made him snarl like a tiger every time something didn't go his way...

Although he'd rung her mobile several times it had been to no avail. Trying desperately hard not to let his fearful imagination run away with him, he'd followed up the futile calls with several to the charity in London, whose number he'd found out when Grace and he had first met, but the manager there had been frustratingly close-mouthed about how Grace was faring, refusing even to tell him when she might be returning home again because he wasn't family.

Marco had hated that. He'd wanted to yell at them that he fully intended to *be* her family, if she'd have him. Bu he hadn't said that. Instead he'd rung her parents' number and spoken to her father—Peter. He was the one who had told him haltingly that Grace had been taken ill at the orphanage, after practically working herself into the ground, and that after spending a week in hospital she was being flown home to London… In fact, he'd been about to fly over there to travel back with her.

That had been over a week ago now. Peter Faulkner had advised Marco to wait awhile before visiting his daughter—'at least a week'—because when she got home she would need some time to acclimatise and recover her strength before having visitors.

It had been another test of gargantuan endurance to wait for a week, not knowing if Grace's health was improving or not. Marco had been to hell and back in fear that she might not make it—that she wouldn't recover and might die before he got the chance to tell her how much she meant to him… So now, as Miguel drove the car onto the generously wide drive of a smart detached red-brick house at the end of a tree-lined avenue, Marco dropped his head into his hands and murmured a fervent prayer.

When he'd lifted his head he flexed his hands several times, because they were clammy with fear at how he might find Grace. At the back of his mind was the memory of Miguel confiding in him that the love of his life had died from a terminal disease. *Why, oh, why had he not agreed to fly out to Africa with her?* If only he had been able to get over the sense that she was abandoning him—even though he'd known what she was doing was *beyond* courageous and deserved nothing but his admiration and respect. But, in his defence, her change of plans had devastated him.

'Deus!'

'We are here, Senhor Aguilar.' Miguel opened the passenger door and held a large black umbrella over Marco's head as he stepped out onto the smartly paved drive.

The man who had become a true friend to him over the past weeks, since Grace had departed for Africa, briefly proffered a smile. Contained in that friendly gesture was a wealth of empathy and understanding at what Marco must be going through.

'I will wait in the car,' he said respectfully as Marco nervously tunnelled his fingers through his hair, then ran his hand down over the sleeve of his chocolate-coloured suede jacket.

'Thank you.' Accepting the umbrella to shield himself from the still torrential rain, he turned away to press the button that rang the doorbell on the house's scarlet-painted front door.

After briefly introducing himself to Grace's serious-faced but amiable father, he followed the silver-haired older man through a spotlessly neat living room out to a glass conservatory, where he told Marco that Grace was resting.

Marco sucked in a breath to steady himself when he saw her. She was sitting perfectly still in a rattan rocking chair that was pulled up close to the clear plate-glass windows, staring out at the sheeting rain that hammered dramatically onto the garden as though transfixed. Her pretty blonde hair had been left loose to fall softly round her shoulders and appeared to be a little longer. She was wearing a thin white sweater with denim jeans, and her small hands were clutching the wooden arms of her chair as if to anchor herself, he saw. She put him in mind of a fragile porcelain figure set on a mantelshelf—one false move would send it crashing to the ground to splinter into a thousand tiny pieces that would be near impossible to put together again.

The icy shard of fear that sliced through him made him feel almost physically sick.

'Grace?' Peter Faulkner moved up behind his daughter to lay a gentle hand on her shoulder. 'You've got a visitor, love.'

'Who is it?' At the same time that she asked the question she turned her head, and her startled cornflower-blue gaze collided with Marco's. 'Oh, my God...'

It was too quiet and too stunned to be an exclamation, but even as he registered the words Marco saw that his appearance had deeply affected her. Likewise, the sight of her staggered him.

'I tried to ring you so many times—' he started, but emotion hit him with all the force of a rogue wave he hadn't anticipated, scrambling the thoughts in his head so emphatically that he scarce knew what to say. There was so much he wanted to communicate, but where to begin?

He cleared his throat, moving a little closer to where she sat. Out of the corner of his eye he saw her father lean over and drop an affectionate kiss on the top of her head.

'I think I'll leave you two to get reacquainted. When you're ready, your mum will make us all a nice cup of tea.'

'Thanks, Dad.'

Grace waited until her father had vacated the room and shut the door behind him before she turned her face up to Marco's and gave him a smile. The gesture was no less dazzling than it had always been, even though she looked far more fragile than when he had last seen her.

'I can't believe that you're here,' she said softly.

'What have you been doing to yourself? You've lost weight, and you don't look well at all.' He bit back the despairing anger that suddenly gripped him, frustrated that he no longer seemed able to contain the great swell of emotion that washed over him at even the thought of Grace.

'I just need some rest to help me get my strength back, then I'll be fine.'

'That's what you told me the last time we were to-gether... "I'll be fine," you said. Now I see that you're not. I should *never* have let you leave.'

'Marco?'

With a tender smile that he didn't feel he deserved at all, she reached for his hand to enfold it in hers. His heart missed a beat, and when he answered his voice was a little gruff. 'What?'

'I'm so glad you came to see me. I—I was afraid you might forget me.'

'Are you crazy?'

Mindful of her weakened state, he carefully but firmly pulled her up from the chair and embraced her, clutching her to his chest as if terrified she was a mere figment of his fevered imagination that might vanish at any second. But the reality that he *was* holding her in his arms again made him feel as if he might die from the sheer pleasure and relief of it, even though at the back of his mind he registered worriedly that her bones had far less flesh covering them than they'd used to. *Had she eaten at all in six long weeks?*

Pressing his lips against her soft wheat-coloured hair he breathed in the scent of the silken skeins as if they were anointed with the most divine scent a master perfumer could devise. 'Could I forget the moon and stars.

the sun or the sky? To me, my angel, you are all those combined and *more*.'

When Grace pulled back a little and turned her face up to his Marco saw that her incomparable blue eyes were drowned in tears.

'Baby, don't cry... It near kills me to see you cry,' he soothed, cupping her face.

'I'm only crying because I'm so happy that you're here.'

Intent on stealing just a short, affectionate kiss, so as not to overwhelm her, Marco changed his mind the instant he felt her satin-soft lips quiver beneath his. He ravished her mouth with a heartfelt helpless groan. When he realised that Grace was kissing him back with equally as much ardour and passion, some of the fear that had logged him since he'd heard she had been taken ill ebbed away. As if by mutual silent agreement they slowed the tenor of the caress so that gradually it became tender rather than passionate.

Marco lifted his head to observe her with a rueful smile. 'I too am very happy to be here, Grace. I've been like a wounded bear since you left, and not fit company for anyone. But tell me...how was it that you never answered your phone? As I said before, I tried to contact you on numerous occasions while you were away.'

She emitted a soft, regretful sigh. 'I'm afraid I lost my mobile the day after I arrived in Africa, and once the orphanage I just didn't have the time or energy to source another one. That's why you couldn't reach me. But I swear I thought about you every day, Marco. Every spare moment that I had—and there weren't many—I thought of you. I shouldn't have rushed away like I did.'

She paused to brush away the tears that dampened her cheek, and her lower lip trembled.

'I mean…they needed me at the orphanage, but I was still exhausted from my last trip out there and I felt the effects almost straight away. Because we were so short-staffed the situation was almost unbearable at times. Perhaps I was arrogant, believing I could make a difference…that I could help make the situation better in some way. The three of us working together using all of our wits and know-how…every *ounce* of our energy…could only just about hold it together. You'd better not accuse me of seeing things clearly again, because it's not true. If I'd listened to my body and not my heart I wouldn't have got sick.'

Tenderly stroking back the hair that brushed the sides of her face, Marco frowned. 'Listen to me. To do what you did was the bravest and most selfless thing I've ever heard, and I had no right to try and make you change your mind about going when we last saw each other. You weren't arrogant to believe you could make a difference, and I'll wager if you asked any one of those children whether they felt safer and more secure because you were around not one of them would deny it. Talking of which—did any more children or staff go down with the fever? Apart from you, I mean?'

'One little girl of about four years old.' Grace gave a slight shake of her head, as if the memory pained her. 'But she was recovering well, thank God, by the time I was taken ill myself.'

'And what have the doctors said about your condition, hmm?' *He was almost afraid to ask in case the news was bad.* He could hardly attest to breathing as he anxiously waited for her reply.

'They've said that I'm suffering from both physical and nervous exhaustion. I didn't get the fever, thank God. But the heat out there sucked all the energy from me

It didn't help matters that the resources and help were so inadequate, and caring for the children was much harder than usual. I'm afraid I lost my appetite completely, which was an added complication, and one morning I just passed out. When I came to I didn't have the strength to get up. My co-workers said I was muttering incomprehensible things and sounding delirious. Next thing I knew I was in the hospital. Anyway…all that's behind me now. Give me just a few more days of rest and relaxation and I'll be as right as rain, I'm sure.' She glanced over her shoulder at the bucketing rain that still poured, as if to confirm it to herself.

'Hmm.' Marco wasn't nearly so sure. The faint bruising smudges beneath her eyes and the haunted look they held told a rather *different* story.

'Are you planning on staying here in Britain for very long?' she asked him, her tone a little nervous.

'Do you imagine I am going to get on the next plane back to Portugal and leave you here while you are ill?'

'I don't know. I don't know *what* you plan to do. How could I?'

'You look like you're about to cry again. Does my being here distress you so much?'

She dropped her hand to his sleeve and laid it there. Marco was so sensitive to her every touch that he swore he felt her heat burn him right through to his bones, even through the thick suede of his jacket.

'I don't want you to go. I know it probably won't do me any good, telling you that. You've no doubt had enough of my ridiculous demands. And I'm so sorry if I tried to force you in any way to confront your past, like I was some kind of expert. I'm not. Sometimes I just get carried away with my desire to make everything right for everybody. It's crazy, I know.' She gave a tired smile. 'I guess I'm more like my parents than I realised.'

'It's not crazy to want to help. And you *did* help me by getting me to look at my past and not run away from it. You certainly didn't force me. Somehow being with you, having your own bravery as an example, I *wanted* to face my demons. I only wish there were more people like you in the world, Grace.'

'I'm not unique. I told you that before. Look…I know you're a very busy and important man, and you're probably anxious to get back to your work—wherever that might take you in the world—and I know I let you down but I hope you can stay…for a little while at least.'

Marco took a deep breath in, then wiped the back of his hand across lips that were still throbbing from his and Grace's passionate kiss. 'I'm not going anywhere in a hurry…you can count on that. And you didn't let me down. You were fulfilling your dreams, that's all, and can't be upset about that when I've always tried to fulfil my own. But nothing is more important to me right now than seeing that you're all right. What I've seen so far tells me that you're a long way from being fully recovered from your trip—so, like I said, I will not be doing anything other than staying here with you until you're well again. I've booked a room in a hotel nearby, so I can be on hand whenever you need me. Plus, you and I need to have a long talk about things. But first I would like to have a word with your father, if I may?'

Grace's blue eyes widened warily. 'What for?'

'I'd like to get an update from him about what your doctors have said. I'd also like to recommend one of my own doctors to look at you. I have access to the very best medical care in the world, Grace, and I'd like you to benefit from it—if you agree?'

She turned away, folding her arms across the thin white sweater that so starkly highlighted the fact she'd lost weight. 'You don't need to talk to my dad. I've already given you an update on my health. And nor do I need to see one of your doctors. I told you…I'll be fine.'

There *was* something wrong. Marco sensed it the moment she dipped her head and turned away. His mouth went dry as a desert plain. 'You're keeping something from me…what is it?'

'It's nothing.' All of a sudden she moved back to the rocking chair. Lowering herself down into the seat, she returned her hands to its polished wooden arms and started to rock herself slowly back and forth.

Outside, the rain thundered against the conservatory's glass roof, with no sign of letting up any time soon. Staring at her, Marco curled his hands into anxious fists down by his sides. 'If you won't tell me then I'll go and find your father and ask him.'

The chair stopped rocking, and the incandescent blue eyes couldn't hide her apprehension and fear. 'You don't need to go and find my dad. It's just that…when the doctors did all the usual tests on me in the hospital…something turned up that none of us expected.'

'If you have any idea of how much agony of mind I'm going through right now, then for God's sake *please* just come out with it and tell me!' Marco implored.

Holding her hand to her middle, as if a debilitating pain had just shot through her, Grace suddenly turned as pale as new milk. He was already moving to her side when she slumped forward in the chair in a dead faint.

'Grace, wake up! *Querido Deus!*' Crouching down in front of her, he gently positioned her so that she was sitting more securely in the chair, with her head dropped onto her chest. Quickly he felt for her pulse. His own was probably just as out of kilter in fear and concern.

He was just about to leap up and call for Grace's father to ring for an ambulance when she opened her eyes and stared at him in confused distress. 'Marco,' she murmured, 'what happened?'

'You fainted that's what happened, Grace. I think you should be in bed rather than sitting in here. Your hands are freezing!' Saying so, he took her pale, slender hands in his and vigorously rubbed them, as if to invigorate her blood once again and restore her to the land of the living.

His mind was running at a mile a minute in search of solutions that might help. No matter how much Grace pleaded with him not to, Marco fully intended to speak to her father about her condition, followed by consulting his own doctors. It was unbearable to imagine that she might be taken from him through illness when he'd so recently realised that he couldn't possibly live without her...

'I'm fine.'

'Stop saying that when it is clearly not the truth!' Breathing hard, Marco couldn't—*wouldn't*—take his eyes off her, in case she fainted again. 'Just before you passed out you were holding your stomach as if you were in pain. Are you hurting, Grace? If you need medical help then you must tell me.'

A wan smile briefly touched her lips. 'I wasn't in pain I just felt a little nauseous, that's all. Can you pass me tha glass of water on the table behind you? I'd like a sip.'

He did as she asked and quickly returned. As he watched her sip the water his mind careened in all directions, imagining all the dire reasons why she woul be feeling nauseous.

Reaching forward, Grace put the glass carefully dow

on the white ledge beside the conservatory doors. 'It's perfectly natural for a woman to feel nauseous sometimes when she's pregnant,' she announced, her tone unbelievably matter-of-fact, 'especially in the first three months.'

'What did you say?'

'I'm telling you that the reason I'm feeling nauseous is that I'm pregnant.'

Even the rain that thundered so powerfully against the roof couldn't drown out the enormous sense of shock and disbelief that rolled through Marco.

If she hadn't felt quite so weak just then Grace would have quickly reassured him that he needn't worry…she wasn't about to demand he marry her or anything crazy like that. There were plenty of women all around the world who raised their children on their own, and if he didn't want to be with her then that was what she would do.

The way his arresting features had turned almost pale beneath his bronzed skin had already told her that it was hardly welcome news. Now she wished she'd kept quiet about the pregnancy—at least until she felt strong enough to deal with the emotional fall-out should Marco tell her he was sorry but he didn't want to assume the responsibility of being a father, not on the kind of regular basis that a truly loving relationship required that he be…

But now, looking a little more recovered, he clasped her hands more tightly, his hooded dark eyes roving her face as if she was indeed the moon, the stars and the sun that he'd asserted that she was earlier.

'The child—the child is…' he started to say.

'Don't you *dare* ask me if it's yours,' Grace leapt in, feeling her cheeks flush with some much needed colour.

'I wouldn't dream of it.' His lips twisted with gentle mockery, then he stared at her in wonder, laying the flat of his palm gently against her abdomen. 'I'm going to be a father.'

'Yes, you are. Do you mind?'

'Do I *mind*?'

'You told me once that you didn't know what it meant to be a father because you'd had no good example of a father yourself.'

'That's true. But I never said I was averse to learning if the right woman came along, did I?'

Grace's heart skipped. 'Am *I* the right woman, then?'

'I thought you were clever… But if you still haven't worked it out yet, then I guess I will have to enlighten you, won't I?'

Staying silent, she minutely examined every curve and facet of his extraordinarily handsome face, wondering how she had lived for so long without the sight of it yet still wary of having her longed-for treasure cruelly taken away if anything untoward should happen to either of them.

'For once you're lost for words.' Chuckling, Marco touched his fingertips to her lips and tenderly traced them. 'I love you, Grace. You have become the ground beneath my feet, the person by which I stand or fall, because I can't…I *won't* live without you. You're the most courageous, loving and loyal woman I have ever met.'

Grace's eyes had filled with tears the moment he said, 'I love you'. *Was she allowed to be this happy?* she wondered. When there was so much pain and sadness in the world, it was incredible that she should be blessed with so much joy, she thought gratefully. 'I love you too, Marco. I adore you more than you can ever know, and promise to spend the rest of my life trying to show you just how much.'

'Are you two sufficiently reacquainted to have th

cup of tea now? Only you're mum's got her best china laid out in the dining room, and she's wearing a hole in the kitchen floor waiting to get the go-ahead.'

Her dad put his head round the door just as they were about to embrace passionately. Grace met Marco's melting brown eyes and giggled helplessly.

'If we can have just five minutes more, then *yes*. A cup of tea would be most welcome,' Marco murmured in her ear.

Before Grace had the chance to convey this to her dad, Marco moved his face closer. 'Marry me,' he whispered—just before his lips ardently claimed hers...

EPILOGUE

THE VIP lounge at Heathrow was surprisingly quiet that morning. Apart from Grace, Marco and their six month old baby boy, Henry, there was a smart elderly couple and a striking lady dressed in the colourful full regalia of the African region she came from.

Their beautiful little son was already a veteran when it came to travelling. Marco wouldn't leave them at home whenever he had to travel abroad for work, and neither did Grace want him to. They'd been married for just over a year now, and she still couldn't bear to be apart from him—not even for a day.

Just a couple of months after Henry was born they'd flown back to Portugal, where her entrepreneur husband had been developing a golfing academy specifically for disadvantaged young men and women. And now, after a fortnight staying in their lovely new home in Kensington, they were at the airport again—this time to fly out to Africa and visit not only the newly erected orphanage, but also the on-site medical centre, staffed by highly trained professionals. Marco had had it set up and, they'd named it after Azizi.

She was so proud of her wonderful husband. Not only had he confronted his fears surrounding his past, he h transcended them to give his unstinting help to children raised in an orphanage just like him.

Their little son was fretting, and Grace rocked him in her arms to try and soothe him. Behind them the loud roar of a jumbo jet taking off drowned out any other sounds.

'I think his first tooth is coming through. He's been dribbling a lot, and he keeps sucking his fist,' she told her handsome husband anxiously. He was dressed as immaculately as ever, in an Italian tailored suit. Marco never failed to take her breath away with his striking appearance. But, expensive suit or not, he didn't hesitate to reach for his son.

'Give him to me. Why don't you go and sit down and relax for a while? Pour yourself some juice.'

'I wish I could have another cup of coffee. I didn't sleep much last night.'

'It's not a good idea to have too much coffee when you're breastfeeding, my angel. Remember what the paediatrician said?'

'I know. She said not to have more than three cups a day. I suppose I ought to save my quota until we board the plane, at least. No doubt it's going to be a long, tiring day.' Grace handed over the baby with a hard-to-suppress yawn.

Marco carefully nestled the infant in the crook of his arm and began to mimic the rocking motion that his wife regularly used to calm him or get him off to sleep.

Henry's still-blue eyes drifted closed immediately, and Grace shook her head in wonder. 'And you were worried about being a good father? You're a natural. You seem to have a magic touch where Henry's concerned.' She saw him flush a little beneath his tan, and he didn't need to tell her how proud of his son he was.

Wanting to take care of their newborn herself, she'd declined his offer of hiring a full-time nurse to help her. Yet when Henry woke up for his feed during the night it was Marco who leapt out of bed to fetch him and bring him to her. Then, after he'd fallen asleep again, he'd hold him for a long time—'father-and-son bonding time' he called it—before taking him back to his cot.

'Sometimes it's hard to believe how fortunate I am,' he said now. 'You and Henry have given me everything I ever dreamed of and more. For the first time when I say I'm going home I *mean* it. I love you with all my heart, my beautiful, clever girl.'

Leaning towards him, Grace stole a gently lingering kiss. The three other passengers in the lounge glanced at each other in approval. 'I love you too, my darling.' She smiled seductively. 'And I'll show you how much tonight—after we put Henry to bed,' she whispered.

His eyes gleamed with love and desire. 'If I wasn't holding our son, I wouldn't hesitate to demonstrate what I think about that, you little temptress!'

'Promises promises…' Grinning, Grace sashayed over to a luxurious leather armchair and sat down, knowing without any conceit at all that her husband's compelling dark eyes hungrily tracked her all the way…

* * * * *

'Mistress,' Nikolai slotted in cool as ice.

Shock had welded Ella's tongue to the roof of her mouth beca
he was sexually propositioning her and nothing could have prepa
her for that. She wasn't drop-dead gorgeous... *he* was! Male he
didn't swivel when Ella walked down the street because she
neither the length of leg nor the curves usually deemed neces
to attract such attention. Why on earth could he be making *her* s
an offer?

'But we don't even know each other,' she framed dazedly. 'Yc
a stranger...'

'If you live with me I won't be a stranger for long,' Nikolai pointed
ut with monumental calm. And the very sound of that inhuman
alm and cool forced her to flip round and settle distraught eyes
n his lean darkly handsome face.

'You can't be serious about this!'

'I assure you that I am deadly serious. Move in and I'll forget
ur family's debts.'

'But it's a *crazy* idea!' she gasped.

'It's not crazy to me,' Nikolai asserted. 'When I want anything, I
after it hard and fast.'

Her lashes dipped. Did he want her like that? Enough to track
r down, buy up her father's debts, and try and buy rights to her
d her body along with those debts? The very idea of that made
r dizzy and plunged her brain into even greater turmoil. 'It's
moral… it's blackmail.'

'It's definitely *not* blackmail. I'm giving you the benefit of a choice
u didn't have before I came through that door,' Nikolai Drakos
ded with a glittering cool. 'That choice is yours to make.'

'Like hell it is!' Ella fired back. 'It's a complete cheat of a supposed
er!'

Nikolai sent her a gleaming sideways glance. 'No the real cheat
s you kissing me the way you did last year and then saying no
acting as if I had grossly insulted you,' he murmured with lethal
etness.

'You *did* insult me!' Ella flung back, her cheeks hot as fire while
wondered if her refusal that night had started off his whole chain
ction. What else could possibly be driving him?

Nikolai straightened lazily as he opened the door. 'If you take
nce that easily, maybe it's just as well that the answer is no.'

MILLS & BOON®

Mills & Boon have been at the heart of romance since 1908… and while the fashions may have changed, one thing remains the same: from pulse pounding passion to the gentlest caress, we're always known how to bring romance alive.

Now, we're delighted to present you with these irresistible illustrations, inspired by the vintage glamour of our covers. So indulge your wildest dreams and unleash your imagination as we present the most iconic Mills & Boon moments of the last century.

Visit **www.millsandboon.co.uk/ArtofRomance** to order yours!

0516_AOR

MILLS & BOON®

Why shop at millsandboon.co.uk?

Each year, thousands of romance readers find their perfect read at millsandboon.co.uk. That's because we're passionate about bringing you the very best romantic fiction. Here are some of the advantages of shopping at www.millsandboon.co.uk:

Get new books first—you'll be able to buy your favourite books one month before they hit the shops

Get exclusive discounts—you'll also be able to buy our specially created monthly collections, with up to 50% off the RRP

Find your favourite authors—latest news, interviews and new releases for all your favourite authors and series on our website, plus ideas for what to try next

Join in—once you've bought your favourite books, don't forget to register with us to rate, review and join in the discussions

Visit **www.millsandboon.co.uk** for all this and more today!